Oblivion's Hymn

Divine Songs Book 1

A.J. Peterson

Dreamscape Publishing LLC

OBLIVION'S HYMN

Published by Dreamscape Publishing

First Edition: October 2025

ISBN: 979-8-9927808-0-2

Line and Copy Editor: Shay Esposito @vineandparchment

Cover Illustrator: Kim Cavrak @spiritofebullience

Interior Illustrator: Rin Varga @rinvargaillo

Content Warnings

blood and blood-letting, violence, off-page death of a parent, suicidal ideation

For the friends who help us find and raise our voices when we can't do it alone.

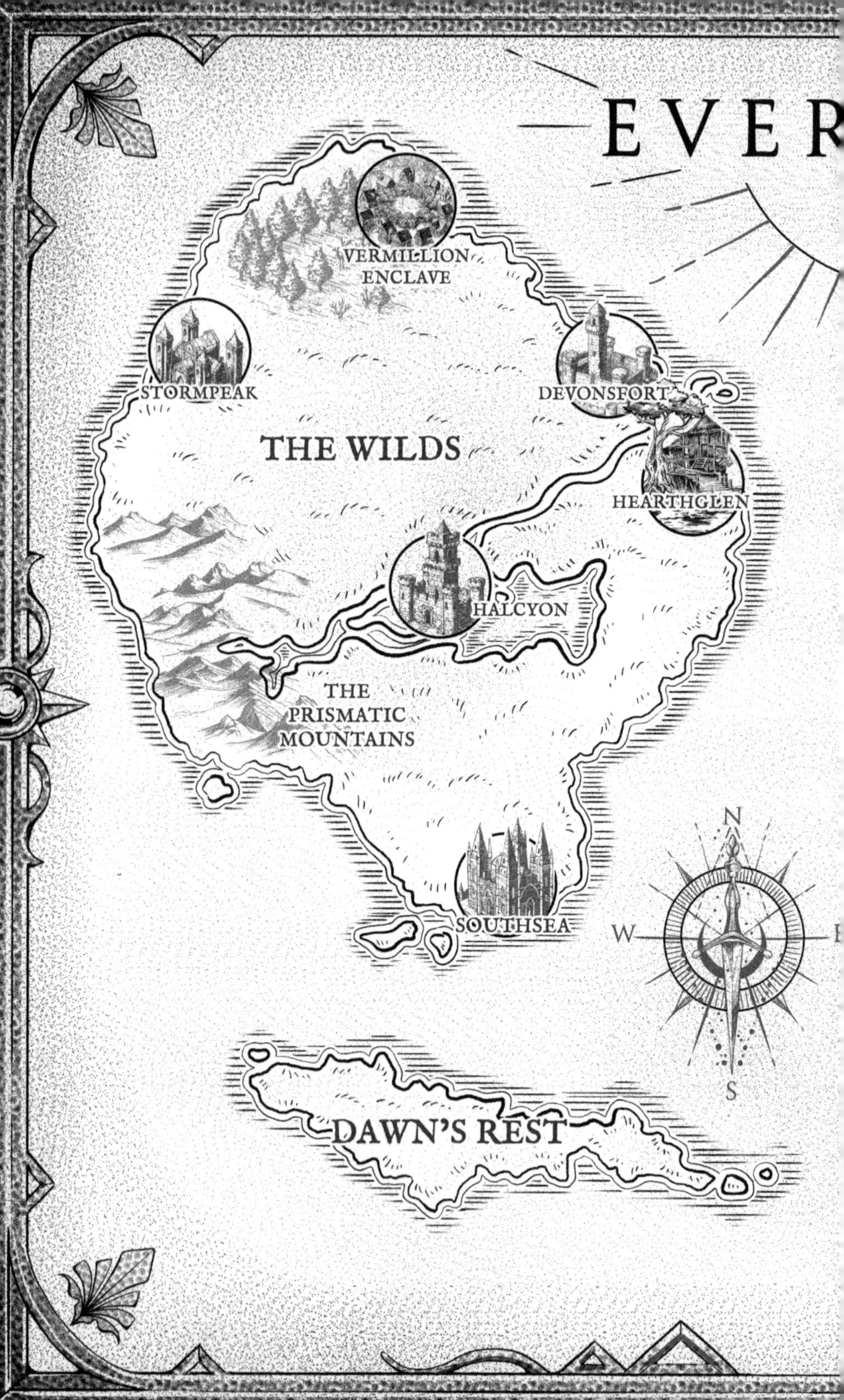

EVER
VERMILLION ENCLAVE
STORMPEAK
DEVONSFORT
HEARTHGLEN
THE WILDS
HALCYON
THE PRISMATIC MOUNTAINS
SOUTHSEA
N
W
E
S
DAWN'S REST

LAST
GRAYBARROW
FREEHOLD
UNCLAIMED TERRITORY
PORT-SAPHRAI
WILDSPIRE
THE SEVERED LANDS
KYDOREI
RAVEN'S KEEP
FALENORAN EMPIRE

People and Places of Everlast

Main Characters

Echo (Ekk-oh)
Rhienne (Ree-enn)
Mishara (Mish-ah-rah)
Irelia (Ih-rell-ee-ah)
Tash (Tah-sh)

Side Characters

Sidrin (Sid-rin)
Vala (Vah-lah)
Aderai Starfall (Add-err-eye)
Jareth (Jair-eth)
Penelope Miravin (Meer-uh-vin)
Carsha (Car-shah)
Mordach (More-dock)
Nazal (Nuh-zahl)
Silas (Sye-lis)

Gods (in order of birth)

Oblivion, The First God of Endings, Harbinger of Nothingness and Guardian of the Void
Horizon, Escort of the Sun, and Promise of the Endless Expanse (deceased)
Reckoning, The Settler of Accounts and Balancer of Scales

Exodus, The Shepherd of Wandering Souls, Warden of
Pilgrims, and Herald of Dispersion
Harvest, The Well of Growth, Bounty of Seasons, Reaper
and Sower

<u>Magical Beings</u>

mimics, descendants of Infinity
immortals, descendants of Eternity
godkin, creations of the gods (no blood relation)

<u>Places</u>

Wildspire
Graybarrow
Port Saphrai (Saff-rye)
Hearthglen
Devonsfort (Deh-vehns-fort)
The Vermillion Enclave
Falenoran Empire (Fal-enn-ore-ehn)
Kydorei (Kye-door-ay)
Dawn's Rest

<u>Planes of Existence (in descending order)</u>

The Origin
The Upper Plane (the gods' realm)
The Plane of Dreams
The Material Plane
The Plane of the Dead
The Lower Plane (hell, the realm of demons and devils)

Chapter 1

Echo

No one watching Echo's performance would suspect her greatest fear had just walked into the bar. Her fingers skimmed over her mandolin's strings and her expression remained pleasant and professional, but she allowed her gaze to linger. It was one thing to know the secret police had been sniffing around her neighborhood. Glimpsing the bones glowing through their skin was another. They'd fed on divine blood. Recently. And they were hunting for more.

But why *here*? She'd been excruciatingly careful not to change out of this body. The tavern was dingy and run-down, its patrons rough around the edges, but not nearly seedy enough for a typical mimic hideout. Three years of effort to build her identity and blend in, wasted. It wasn't fair. Then again, that had become a running theme of late.

She couldn't let them find her until the performance was done. She was *so close* to gathering enough magic to get out of this miserable hole. Just a few more songs, a stealthy escape, and all the secrets locked away in Wildspire's library would be at her fingertips.

Echo followed the melodies of the flute, horn, and vocals as her troupe finished their roaring rendition of *The Queen's Heart*. Anyone with a modicum of taste would've played the song as a ballad, but magic didn't care for the quality of the creation, only that it fulfilled the patrons' bargain for entertainment. Motes of power twinkled around the bar like fireflies, ready to be shaped into any simple spell.

And what were the tavern-goers using it for?

To get really, really drunk.

Levi, the group's lead singer, bowed to hearty applause. With a sweep of his hand and a murmured incantation, the light gathered and swirled. Keeping an eye on the two Untold—face coverings readjusted to hide their signature glow—Echo plucked a jaunty tune that turned the white motes into a glittering rainbow. The crowd oohed and aahed. Levi shot her a glare for going off-script. Her smile was the picture of innocence. He had no idea she was laying claim to some of the power. He just hated losing the spotlight.

Everyone in the bar raised their glasses, and Levi finished his spell with a flourish. A tiny firework exploded, scattering light across the room. Warmth bloomed in

Echo's chest—a spark of power that she channeled into her mandolin for safekeeping.

She must have taken a little more than she meant to, because a grumble started up. The alcohol lacked its typical enhanced kick.

Levi raised his hands. "Come now, come now. The night is young! We have plenty of time to make magic together. How about a new deal? I'll take a special request from the audience for the next round of coin." With his melodic voice and seductive smile, most of the crowd was easily placated.

Except for the Untold in the back corner. Their eyes were fixed on the stage, selecting likely targets.

Mimics' innate ability to copy a person's appearance tended to lead them down one of two paths. Most became assassins, thieves, or other criminals who thrived in a city's shadowy underbelly. More insidious were the ones with charm and guile, who could get close enough to rip out your heart and eat it.

So the stories went. Organs weren't Echo's meal of choice, and her current form was purposefully unbeguiling: middle-aged, medium height and build, mousy hair, and sun-weathered skin. The kind of person you'd forget as soon as they left the room. Levi would draw the most attention, but anyone in the troupe could be under suspicion.

"*Champion of the Black Wood* it is!" Levi said over the clamor. "Everyone ready?" The question was mostly addressed to Echo, followed by a hissed, "Follow my lead. We stick to what everyone knows. Make them happy so we get paid."

Echo ducked her head—meek, apologetic, everything expected of the body she wore.

"Good. A-one, two, three, four."

The song was a tale of adventure, where all monsters were defeated with a few sword strokes. If only life were that simple.

A toddler could've played the mandolin part, so Echo focused her attention back on the bigger problem. The two Untold were weaving through the bar now. One of them wore the deep crimson cloak of an inquisitor. Not good at all. They wouldn't send one of their ranked officers out here on a mere hunch.

She watched surreptitiously as they stopped to talk to people. They always asked the same questions: Notice anyone acting strange? Any neighbors disappear for a few days and return without explanation? Have you seen people where they shouldn't be? They loved to veil their hunger for magic under concern for the populace's safety, but she'd never seen them hunt any *human* criminals.

"Fuck off. Nothin' like that here," one of the patrons slurred.

"Your pardon, sir." Hidden beneath layers of cloth, it was impossible to make out the speaker's face. Their voice was low, that strange mix of resonance and roughness that only came from a body clinging to power it wasn't designed to hold. "But we have it on good authority that there *is* someone here worth our notice. Come with us for a moment."

Echo's heart stuttered at the confirmation. But *whose* authority had tipped them off?

Could it be Exodus? The *God of Journeys* was certainly spiteful enough. Stupid of her to have made a deal with him, but not as stupid as getting caught breaking it. He'd extracted payment once, and it had nearly crushed her. He must have decided *nearly* wasn't sufficient.

Echo's mandolin twanged so harshly, it made the whole band jump. She hunched sheepishly at the interruption—accidental, this time. They recovered well and finished the piece, and then Levi called for an early intermission.

A smattering of copper hit the stage, which Levi swept up. With both sides of the bargain fulfilled, the thread connecting the audience and the performers melted away, and a few more motes of light manifested in the air. The constriction in her chest that came with every pact—almost imperceptible, for such a small amount of magic—disappeared.

Echo stood and walked off the stage. Fenn (the flutist) and the horn player (whose name she could never remember... Veizeiros? Zereivios? Something with too many vowels) sauntered off to get drinks. The crowd shifted, some heading home and some settling in further.

"Hello? Anyone home? Natalia!" She lost sight of the Untold as Levi stepped in front of her and snapped in her face. "Have you gone deaf as well as mute?"

She shook her head, cursing silently. Not responding to her alias was a huge red flag, but couldn't this idiot leave her alone for two seconds? There were more important things at stake than his pride. *Her* pride, for starters, never mind her life. Echo gestured to excuse herself.

Levi grabbed her arm. "I said, what happened up there?"

Natalia would never slap him away. Echo gritted her teeth against the urge, instead taking out her slate and chalk to scribble a response.

"You've had your head in the clouds all night," he continued. "I did Sidrin a favor by bringing you into the group, but I don't have to put up with this. I've worked too hard to get here for someone like you to sabotage me."

Her fingers tightened around the chalk. She changed what she'd been writing and turned the board around. "*Someone like me?*"

"You could never handle the stage by yourself," Levi said with a scoff. "I know you're jealous of my talent. You don't hide it as well as you think."

Relief that she hadn't been caught washed through her, followed by a flush of heat. He thought she was *jealous?* Of a mediocre singer stuck in the Hollows, in a tavern that smelled like piss and stale liquor? She'd once lived in a palace, entertaining a *god.*

Her letters came out jagged, angry. "*Not sabotage. Didn't sleep well. Dreams about my accident.*"

The 'accident' was part of her cover story: Natalia had been jumped in the Lower Hollows, beaten to a pulp, and robbed, resulting in permanent damage to her vocal cords. Being mute was a good disguise. It was much easier than explaining that she'd broken a divine pact, and the god had taken her singing voice as retribution. She'd learned very quickly that a bard who couldn't even whisper their own lyrics was less than worthless on their own.

Levi's lips thinned, uncomfortable but not quite sorry. "Times are lean; we can't afford mistakes." He weighed the coins in his palm, then tucked them all into his pocket. "They'll come out of your pay for the night."

She gaped at him and wrote, "*It was <u>one</u> slip up.*"

"You can start fresh tomorrow," he said without reading. "Or you can try to make your own way and prove me right."

For a moment, Echo felt young again—when she'd been a solo act, in the business for the song, not the magic made through a deal to sing it. This was far from the first time someone had called her music, her *existence*, a mistake. Her initial flush grew into a fire in her belly.

She'd never been predisposed toward violence, but Levi had such a punchable face. What would it feel like for her knuckles to crunch against his perfect nose?

No sooner had the thought crossed her mind than a shiver followed in its wake—the foresight that remained from her deal with Exodus. With the Untold prowling around, acting out would be a very unwise choice indeed.

How fortuitous that Levi had given her the perfect way to divert their attention.

Echo started to cry. Big, fat crocodile tears she would've paired with hysterical sobs if she wasn't feigning muteness. Her shoulders shook, and she let her slate clatter to the floor.

"Oh. Um. Natalia—" Levi stammered as the cluster of nearby patrons turned to look at the scene. "Nothing to see here, folks. You know us creatives. So dramatic."

Fenn returned with a round of shots, her shirt rumpled and a love bite on her neck. Her merriment fell away. "Levi, did you make her cry? What the hell is wrong with you?"

The band leader's cheeks reddened. "For gods' sake, are you turning on me too?"

Echo peeked between her fingers. The Untold had moved closer, studying the commotion. Even with no logical reason to fear them, the bar patrons gave the pair a wide berth. Something was off about their aura, causing shivers that had nothing to do with the winter chill.

She bent and picked up her slate with shaking hands. Fuck this arrogant, talentless hack. The only thing Levi was good for was bait. In a script large enough for the Untold to see, she wrote, "*You know I'm behind on rent. This isn't like you to be so cruel.*"

"Cruel?" Levi squawked. "Fenn, you know I'd never hurt a fly, right?" The horn player rejoined them, and Levi added, "Ziv, come on. Back me up."

Ziv—she'd bet Levi couldn't remember the man's full name either—put his hands up. "Whoa, I just got here. What's going on?"

"I was just addressing Natalia's mistakes during our performance in a perfectly professional manner."

The man certainly knew how to put on a show.

Fenn, bless her, came to Echo's defense. "Sidrin told you how sensitive she is, didn't he? Her condition isn't her fault."

Levi drew himself up, doubtless about to say something offensive.

The temperature around them dropped as the crimson-cloaked Untold approached. "Excuse us, ma'am. Is this man bothering you?" Up close, the power-laced voice scraped across her eardrums. Echo fought not to shrink away; no one else seemed to notice it the way she did.

The second Untold stood off to the left, muttering whatever incantation was making the four of them shiver and the rest of the tavern fade to background noise.

She widened her eyes—partly for the act, partly because that was serious magic they were using—and nodded. The board was still in her hands, with the words that condemned most mimics: *This isn't like you.*

"Sir, we'd like to ask you a few questions."

"I don't think this is any of your business—" Levi choked as the inquisitor lowered his scarf, revealing the lurid yellow glow of his jawbone. The one not-panicked corner of Echo's mind noted the color. Their most recent meal had been an immortal—the other kind of people with innate power in their blood. Siphoning a mimic would've turned the Untolds' bones blue.

"Ah. I see." Levi quickly adjusted course. "Yes, yes, I'm happy to help."

Few encountered the Untold, but everyone knew the stories. They'd started as a group of fanatics who saw those with power unattached to a bargain as threats. Abominations. Thanks to a few truly terrible immortals and mimics, the Untold convinced enough of the populace they were right. Now their activities were sanctioned by governments the world over, and they acted as 'guardians of the order of society.' Failure to comply with their investigations implied guilt. So did running away. The only way out was to make them believe you were human. That enough people loved and cared for you that there was no possible way you could be a monster.

She pushed aside her pang of grief at the thought. *Charm your way out of that, asshole.*

With her magic obtained and the Untold occupied, there was no reason to linger. Echo took a minute under the pretense of calming herself, then wrote a note to Fenn that she wasn't feeling well and wanted to go home for the night.

"I'll cover for you," the flutist said, probably happy to get Echo's share of tips.

Whatever. With any luck, she'd never see these people again.

She headed for the door, watching the Untold from the corner of her eye. Everything seemed normal until the inquisitor pulled a long, black needle from his cloak and pricked Levi's finger. The Untold ignored Levi's yelp and focused on the welling blood.

This was new, and new was bad. Her steps quickened. Would Exodus have gone this far to get to her? She'd lied her way out of an Untold interview before, but that was with a lowly recruit, before she'd lost her singing voice. If they'd figured out a way to test blood for divine traces—

Something cracked against the side of her head.

"Fuck!" In her hurry, Echo couldn't stop the curse escaping her lips.

"Sorry, little lady," said the man who'd been gesticulating with his tankard. A bit of ale sloshed onto the floor.

He didn't know her, didn't know she shouldn't be able to make a sound. But Echo caught Fenn staring at her, brows knit together. The flutist's eyes flicked to the Untold.

Echo didn't wait to see what happened next. As casually as she could manage, she fled out the door.

Stepping into the cold night was like popping a bubble. The middle tier of Wildspire was carved inside the hollow trunk of a mountain-sized tree. Wind snaked in through every passage, and light was hard to come by. Echo pulled her cloak tight and hustled through the dimness. She'd been here far, far too long. Mimics didn't get to live in places this nice. They certainly didn't have music groups or landlords or favorite local cafés.

The spot between her shoulder blades prickled. Echo had to study people to take on their shapes; she knew the feeling of being watched. She kept her head down, trying not to change her pace. The Untold must have finished with Levi and followed her from the tavern. Or there were more waiting in the dark. Damn it all, she should've checked. After years of scrimping and saving from her performances, she had just enough magic to break into the library in the Boughs—the richest section of Wildspire, and the only place she had a chance of figuring out how to fix her voice. She couldn't waste any power on hiding now.

There was one other person she could go to for help.

For maybe the hundredth time since she and Rhienne had split up to pursue their own goals, Echo tugged the braided leather cord around her wrist. They'd sunk every penny they'd ever stolen into enchanting a pair of matching bracelets. One quick yank and the threads would break, calling Rhienne to her, or vice versa. They were only supposed to use them before their agreed-upon reunion in a dire emergency. So, so tempting. But her friend didn't deserve such a rude interruption. Rhienne was probably off in some exotic locale, ingratiating herself with the continent's High Exalts, politicking with one hand and picking pockets with the other.

Gods, Echo missed her.

Zig-zagging through side streets didn't ease the impression of being hunted. If she went up to the Boughs with the Untold on her tail, she'd ruin her chance of getting into the library.

She looped her finger in and out of the leather cord. By now, she was supposed to be running from hordes of adoring fans, too famous for the Untold to touch her. Did she really want Rhienne to see what a mess she'd made? A broken deal and a broken voice, no adoration to her name, resorting to playing with a *group*?

"You there, stop where you are!"

Echo pretended not to hear the Untold's ragged shout, dipped down another darkened alley, and broke into a run. A shadow moved at the other end of the road, blocking her exit.

"By order of the High Exalt of Wildspire, you will submit to questioning!"

Oh, hell. She ran for the nearest door and pushed. Locked. The next one was too. She touched the bracelet again. 'Dire emergency' was fast approaching. If the next door was locked...

Before she could try, the chord dissolved from her wrist, and Rhienne's voice filled her head. *Hey, Echo. I know it's early, but best-laid plans and all. I'm in a spot of trouble. Being held prisoner. Miiiight be executed soon. Don't suppose you're available to lend a hand?*

Echo had never been so happy to hear bad news.

Chapter 2

Rhienne

Sulking was most unbecoming of a woman her age, but Rhienne couldn't help it. Wildspire's catacombs stank of death and damp. The curve of the roots that made up the walls and floor of her cell made it impossible to sit comfortably. She hadn't had food, water, or a decent place to relieve herself in ages, and her hands were bound in frigid metal chains to prevent spellcasting. A bit overkill, in her opinion. She'd only infiltrated the Untold and tried to steal a piece of Dawnglow—one of the most powerful spell components known to the world. Not like she'd *hurt* anybody.

The real rub was how close she'd been to succeeding. She'd spent five years running the Untold's stupid errands and working her way into the good graces of one of their high inquisitors. Armed with almost every ounce of magic her deal with the god, Oblivion, had afforded her—shadows to hide in, keen vision and deft fingers to dismantle security, flight for a quick escape—it should've been simplicity itself to snatch the Dawnglow. But *something* had triggered the alarms in the vault. Rhienne couldn't figure out where it all went wrong.

The clanking as the guards snapped to attention interrupted her thoughts. Measured footsteps approached her cell. She winced at the flare of torchlight.

No one was supposed to visit. Rhienne was a traitor, and traitors to the Untold were meant to go delirious from thirst and hunger before they were hanged. Was she delirious already? She didn't think so, but maybe not being able to tell meant she'd tipped over the edge.

The figure solidified into High Inquisitor Mishara. She stopped out of reach of the bars, imperious in her crimson cloak and leathers, the ruby circlet of her rank reflecting the flickering torch. The red fabric made it impossible for Rhienne to tell if Mishara had come down here equipped with anything more powerful than her wits.

Rhienne put on a lackadaisical grin. "Has the jury been selected for my trial yet? My lawyer ought to have a period to review them, to make sure there's no bias against me."

Mishara's face remained placid. She waited just long enough to have obviously ignored the comment before saying to the guards, "I'll have a moment alone with the turncoat."

They didn't question her. Only when the echoes of their footsteps faded did Mishara drop into a crouch and lean in, her pale face ghostly in the near-dark. There was an oil-slick sheen to her green eyes that Rhienne thought was a trick of the light. But the longer she looked, the more unnatural it seemed.

No, not unnatural. Magical.

The inquisitor did not partake in the Untold's ghoulish practice that made their bones glow. She—and Rhienne—preferred their power to be self-reliant. Sacrificing your own blood was the most open-ended of deals. No second party required for siphoning *or* a bargain when you were trading a part of your life. It was dangerous, and extremely illegal, but the results spoke for themselves. Mishara had perfected the ritual for true sight.

Rhienne smothered a pang of jealousy, and the desire to ask how she'd finally cracked it. They'd been developing that spell together in stolen moments between Mishara's more unsavory work. A small consolation: it would've taken a *lot* of blood to replicate an ability usually reserved for gods.

Rhienne fluttered her lashes. "Looking for something specific?"

"In fact, I am. But I can't fathom why you would've done something as stupid as break into my vault." The tone was snide, and her shoulders were stiff with anger, but Mishara's lips twitched toward a smile—pride at figuring out the spell, and pleasure that Rhienne had noticed her accomplishment.

The inquisitor wasn't here to gloat about catching her, then. Or to wax poetic about how important *loyalty* was to the Untold, and how Rhienne had betrayed them. At least not primarily. There was, perhaps, a chance Mishara could still be her ally.

Rhienne sat up and scooted closer to the bars. "What *do* you see, then?"

"Residue from an illusion." Mishara tilted her head and squinted. "Though I can't see through it, even now. Strong magic. Stronger than any ritual we've developed." Her words became clipped, accusatory. "What have you been hiding from me?"

Ah, there it was. Not a question from a high inquisitor of the secret police, but a jilted lover. Excellent.

"I would never hide from you, Mish. It's not a disguise, only a... smoothing of roughened edges." That was true, in a way. Rhienne's illusions were small enough that she could maintain them with the thinnest thread of power. Tighten some wrinkles here, erase the dark circles there, turn the pesky gray hairs back to blonde so she still appeared young and bright with potential. "I just wanted you to think I was beautiful." Also true. Sleeping with someone at the top of a hierarchy was the easiest way to get there herself.

Some of Mishara's tension eased. "When you first came here, you said you had made a pact you regretted. Did the gods disfigure you in some way? I know Reckoning is fond of taking 'an eye for an eye' literally."

"Yes," Rhienne lied, and hung her head in shame. Her real patron, Oblivion, preferred acts of service to body parts. Not quite as nasty, but more than enough to send her after the Untold's Dawnglow instead of making another deal. "I should've told you."

"Yes, you should have. When the glamor detection spell in the vault triggered, the other high inquisitors assumed you were some mercenary, disguised to take us down from within."

"Me, a mercenary?" Rhienne forced a laugh. Inwardly, she swore. That was how they'd caught her. Half the time she forgot she even wore illusions; she'd never considered glamor detection as a security measure.

"I know." Mishara chuckled dryly. "I told them you'd never do that much work on someone else's behalf, but they didn't believe me. If you dispel your illusion and apologize, that'll be enough proof to reduce your sentence."

"The enchantment is permanent. I can't dispel it." Getting caught in a lie aside, Rhienne would rather eat gravel than apologize to a high inquisitor of the Untold. Mishara's place among the four highest ranking officers allowed her a bit of freedom to refuse siphoning divine blood, but they were *all* power-hungry, prejudiced filth thinly disguised as state security.

Doubt crept into Mishara's expression, so Rhienne put on her best apologetic voice. "I messed up. I know that. There has to be something else we can do. This place is my home. *You* are my home."

Mishara's lingering sharpness softened. Rhienne wasn't sure if it was naivety, or if Mishara was conning her right back.

"Why did you want the Dawnglow?" Mishara asked. "If there's a reasonable explanation, we might be able to get them to sympathize with you."

As if there could be any reasonable explanation why someone would want the crystallized blood of a dead goddess. Rhienne hesitated. "Will they listen to you? It's not like our relationship was a secret. They might think you're a turncoat too. I don't want to get you into more trouble."

"I can handle trouble," Mishara said. She reached through the bars and brushed her fingers over Rhienne's cheek. "Trust me."

Right. Because that always worked out so well.

Another partial truth would do the trick. Rhienne sighed and looked down at her bound hands. "My mother has been tangled up with the gods her whole life. I've tried everything to get her out of her deals. I thought if I had a powerful enough alternative to offer, I could save her."

Mishara nodded, soaking in the words with palpable relief. This was exactly the kind of reasoning she understood—the reason they'd turned to blood magic. The reality was much less sympathetic. Even mentioning her mother tied Rhienne's stomach in knots of grief and guilt.

"I wish you'd come to me first," Mishara said. "I could've tried to help. But it's too late now. I promise you, I'll do everything I can before tomorrow."

"They want to execute me *tomorrow*?" That was far too soon, and Rhienne couldn't keep the alarm from her voice.

"Yes. I came as soon as I heard. I hope I can earn us more time."

Rhienne's mouth was dry. She managed to say, "Thank you," and sound mostly sincere.

"I'll be back soon. Count your heartbeats, darling." Mishara rose, left her torch on the wall, and drifted back into the shadows.

The words sent a shiver over Rhienne's skin. Words she and Mishara had whispered to each other beneath their blankets and while crafting rituals that would have them burned at the stake if the Untold discovered them.

Rhienne had hoped their shared secret would be enough to earn Mishara's protection—out of fear for herself, if nothing else. But it seemed the three other high inquisitors held more leverage. If they wanted to expedite Rhienne's death, it would take more charm than Mishara possessed to sway them.

It was hard to think over the quickening thump in her chest (which she refused to count). Her options for escape were ruinously slim. The only drop of magic she had left was for maintaining her glamor, and letting it go wouldn't give her enough to break out of here. Asking her patron, Oblivion, for more power was out of the question. Even if she didn't loath every second she had to work for him, the potion she'd been taking to shield her mind during sleep hadn't worn off yet. She thought she'd have a few more days to plan before resorting to another bargain.

Rhienne's gaze flicked to the thin leather cord around her wrist, peeking out beneath her chains. Old and frayed as it was, no one had suspected it was enchanted.

She and Echo had been apart for a while, but not nearly as long as they'd been together. Echo would come, presuming she could untangle herself from all the glorious escapades her fame had surely brought her. Her friend would immortalize Rhienne's idiocy in song, and then, hopefully, help her disappear in that way only a mimic could.

Embarrassment was preferable to death at the end of a rope.

With her heart pounding like any beat might be its last, the wait for the changing of the guard was slow and agonizing, but she needed their movements to cover any noise she made. When they finally came, Rhienne maneuvered her chains so the bracelet was more exposed, hooked the leather around a protruding piece of metal on her ankle shackles, and jerked her wrists up. The cord snapped, and she breathed her message into the magic it released.

They hadn't been able to afford an enchantment that allowed a *response*, but they'd been young and that hadn't felt important. What could possibly keep them from each other?

Rhienne glared at the darkness and settled back against the wall to wait.

Her defiance didn't last long. Time undulated strangely in the dark. The quiet became a grating, lurking thing, broken only by the guards' occasional sniffs or shifts of weight. It was a small comfort that they had to be as miserable as she was in the cold.

Good thing Rhienne hadn't put her trust in Mishara, because she never came back.

Soon, the guards unlocked the door, unlinked her chains from the wall, and led her out into the catacombs. The Untold had maintained the headquarters of their Wildspire branch here in the twisting shadows, despite being legitimized years ago. Fitting for the vermin they were, but rather inconvenient for anyone trying to rescue her.

Low-ranking recruits trickled in to join them on the winding path. They carried no torches, hoods off and sleeves rolled up so their bones could light the way in eerie flickers of yellow and blue. Every scrape and shift made Rhienne jump, terrified one of them would rush forward and end her life before Echo could arrive.

She needed to buy her friend more time.

Patches of frost and who knew what else made the ground slick, so the going was slow. They were still in the hollowed-out roots that poked above the surface. As soon as they went underground, it would become easier to walk but even more maze-like.

Rhienne pretended to slip on the ice and fell onto her backside, letting out a very real hiss as pain spiked up her tailbone. Illusions didn't change the fact that she was getting too old for this shit.

The recruit behind her nudged her rather ungently with his boot. "Get up, scum."

Ah, a voice she recognized, with a bit of that northern lilt he could never quite escape. Orik had been her first stepping stone into the Untold. One of Mishara's trainees.

Rhienne let her head fall to one side to look up at him. "Come now, we used to have such fun together. The least you could do is give me a minute to recover."

Even in the low light, his cheeks went noticeably pink. "I have no sympathy for vow-breakers. On your feet, I said."

"But I'm ex*hausted*." She sighed and collapsed onto her back. "You haven't fed me since you arrested me. I have a physique to maintain." She grinned salaciously at Orik. "Don't you remember?"

Orik drew a foot back to kick her.

"That's enough." Mishara's voice rang from the front of the procession. Her approach was silent, her feet bare; the sashes of her ceremonial uniform were strategically wrapped to cover any power-granting wounds. The other high inquisitors were close behind, watching, their bones glowing brighter than any of their subordinates and their ruby circlets gleaming. "Let's not waste any more time on this trash."

So the ruthless leader performance was back on. Rhienne matched it with a pout. "If you didn't want someone to steal your stuff, Mish, you should've told your friends not to prance about with their power on display so often. Really, you were asking for it."

Too fast to flinch away, Mishara grabbed Rhienne's collar and slapped her, leaving a sharp, stinging mark on her cheek.

"I take it negotiations broke down," Rhienne whispered. "Starting to doubt your leadership, are they? I do hope they're not chasing down any of your other secrets."

The inquisitor was a good actress, but she couldn't hide the flash of fear in her eyes. "If you know what's good for you, you won't say another word," she hissed, and let Rhienne go.

That was a *yes*, then. Always nice to know where one fell on someone's priority list.

"You heard the traitor. She can no longer walk on her own. She must be carried like an infant. Or a sack of potatoes. Whichever feels most apt to you, recruit."

Rough hands hauled Rhienne up by the armpits. She made herself heavy and limp. She would not struggle, but damn if she'd be helpful, either. It took two of them to carry her.

The temperature warmed as they moved farther underground. She felt like she was in a dreamwalk. Any minute, Oblivion would whisper to her from the shadows, point to whatever seed of someone else's dream she was meant to unravel, and this would all disappear. She'd wake up with a full well of magic and go about her business.

Reality set in when the procession entered the cavern and illuminated the instrument of her death. She'd hoped to seem brave to the last, to stare the Untold down as they hauled her onto the wooden platform and toward the awaiting noose. The closer they got, the harder Rhienne shook. This couldn't be the end. Almost four decades of her life were gone, but she'd barely lived. There was still so much left to do.

She thought of her mother. The dreams they'd traveled through together. The freedom and joy of walking wherever they pleased. The Dawnglow *had* been for her. It was the only thing outside of a divine bargain powerful enough to raise the dead. Rhienne didn't want to have to beg her mother's forgiveness in the afterlife. She wasn't even sure what the afterlife would look like for her kind—half human, half dream spirit—or if she'd get to go there before...

Nope. Not constructive to think about right now.

"Echo, where are you?" she whispered.

Orik cuffed the back of her head. "Silence."

The platform creaked with each step under the combined weight of her restrainers. Leather squeaked. Boots scuffed. Rope circled her neck. Under the high inquisitors' watchful eyes, Mishara's lips twisted cruelly, and something in Rhienne snapped. If she was going out, she'd make sure this place fell apart behind her.

They both sucked in a breath, Mishara to give the order of execution, and Rhienne to spill the secret that would see the high inquisitor on this platform next.

A series of notes rang out from a stringed instrument, cutting them off. The gathered recruits whirled, trying to trace the source of the sound.

Another scale, as if in answer to the first, sounded from the darkness in the opposite direction. Then another, and another. Four identical women stepped out at different points around the room. They looked like Rhienne ten years ago, blonde hair decorated with provincial braids, a gleam in her eye and a tilt to her smile that said she knew your darkest secrets and had plenty of her own too. The fingers dancing on the strings were adorned with sparkling jewelry. She wore golden hoops in her ears and one eyebrow, and fine clothes edged in metallic thread. This was Rhienne as Echo had last seen her, full of vigor and possibility.

Damn, she'd looked good.

There was a brief pause in the music, during which the four Rhiennes let everyone gape in confusion and drink them in. She couldn't help but gape a little too; this was far more powerful magic than Echo had been capable of when they parted, and she'd never known her friend to use an instrument other than her voice. The copies winked, then Echo did what she did best: unleashed chaos.

Chapter 3

Rhienne

Rhienne watched with glee as the Untold floundered. The song picked up tempo. Echo's four identical figures played as one, and then sound burst around them, no longer coming from any one instrument, but from the air itself.

"Don't just stand there!" Mishara cried. Her voice was devoured by the music, but the lower-ranking Untold reacted to her enraged expression. The ones closer to Echo unsheathed their blades, while those farther away muttered incantations to channel the power stored in their bones into spells.

The copies wove and dodged through the crowd, dancing like they hadn't a care in the world. Rhienne marveled at their swiftness until she spotted one of the recruits on the outskirts of the room rush into the fray. He crossed some invisible barrier and went from sprinting full tilt to a comical, slow-motion run.

Amazing. The four women moved normally—it was the Untold who slowed down. The mischief her friend must have gotten into with a spell like this.

There'd be time to hear about it when they got out alive. She looked over her shoulder at Orik, still dumbly standing guard, and said, "You know what Mishara wants to do with that Dawnglow, don't you? I think it's curious how long she's been saving it."

"I'm not interested in what you find curious," he sneered, and made to join the fight.

"Oh, you *don't* know." Rhienne tutted. "She's working on a ritual to infuse her blood with its divine power. She'll become just like the abominations you seek to eliminate."

Orik froze. "Why would—"

"Egotism? Immortality? Does it matter why? Check her spell book if you don't believe me. She showed it to me herself." Rhienne gestured to the noose with her bound hands. "When you think about it, she's far more of a traitor to the cause than I am. It ought to be her on the gallows instead of me."

He scoffed, looked out at the battle, then moved toward the lever. "We have enough rope for both of you."

Terror tightened Rhienne's chest as Oblivion's lurking presence wrapped around her. There was one other place the god could reach her besides sleep.

"Waitwaitwait—"

The floor dropped. Rhienne fell until the rope yanked her violently to a halt, choking off her airway. The noose cut into her skin with every twitch and struggle. A small miracle her neck hadn't snapped, but she was in no mood to be thankful.

Not ready, I'm not ready, pleasepleaseplease.

She twisted unceremoniously, one moment facing the fight, the next the underside of the platform. The world narrowed to her fruitless, silent gasps and the bright spots overlaying her vision.

Was that...? She blinked hard. The glint of metal was real. There was a knife stuck in the wood. Probably meant to cut the rope—bless Echo for planning ahead—but there were much greater things Rhienne could do with a blade.

Some said blood magic was a cheat, never mind being dangerous to the wielder. They were right on both accounts. But in times like these, Rhienne didn't mind being called a swindler, and she couldn't afford to be picky.

She swung back and forth until she hooked her chains over the dagger's crossguard. She spent precious seconds maneuvering, fighting against her darkening sight. Her muscles were barely responsive as it was. Precision was key to not cutting anything vital.

I offer a piece of my life, in return for the power to save the rest. Hoping no one was paying attention to her in the chaos, she sliced her forearm open.

There was no sense of the binding or restriction that came with a regular contract; the magic was hers to shape. Crimson bubbled and darkened. Rhienne willed her spilled blood into a bolt of energy and shot it toward the noose. The rope sizzled, crackled, and broke. She hit the ground, sputtering and wheezing and wanting very much to curl up and never move again.

She allowed herself a few moments to wallow and breathe before forcing herself to her knees, working the blood oozing from her wound into the locks of her chains. With half a thought, the blood froze. She bashed the chains against the ground, and they shattered. Tears of relief pricked in her eyes. Her throat burned too much to sob.

Echo's performance carried on. Most of the recruits moved as if through syrup, but some were now shaking off the effects. The high inquisitors were sketching complex runes on the ground. A countering ritual, maybe. Too far to tell. Other officers were sealing off the exits with walls of stone under Mishara's bellowed orders.

It was time to make herself scarce. Legs shaky, Rhienne got to her feet and searched for a way through the madness.

Orik lumbered out of the battle and blocked her escape.

"Now, let's talk about this," she tried to say, but it came out as more of a dry croak. She scrambled back and hit the platform's supports.

A silver-blue sheen flashed across the man's face—the familiar indicator of Echo's mimicry. That and her quick slash of a smile were enough to clue Rhienne in. Beyond Echo's looming form, the real Orik threw himself at one of the copies of Rhienne.

"Thank the cosmos," Rhienne wheezed. "I was wondering which one was you. But they're all—"

"Illusions!" Mishara's shout dispelled one of the dancing women. Orik's fist passed through the head of another.

Echo grabbed Rhienne's arm, scooped up an instrument case hidden in the platform's shadow, and they sprinted for the nearest open tunnel.

"Do not let her escape!"

They broke line of sight around a bend, and the music stuttered to a halt, replaced by angry shouts and dozens of stomping boots. Rhienne could lose the Untold in the damp, dark maze of tunnels, if she didn't get lost herself.

"This way," Rhienne said.

They climbed and twisted and turned. Rhienne hunted for the coolness of a fresh breeze, one hand on the wall for support, breath sawing in and out of her throat. Next to her, Echo mimicked a smaller form, quieter and more like herself. The sounds of pursuit faded. Finally, far in the distance, the light of an exit appeared.

Rattling bones interrupted her triumph.

A small army of skeletons peeled away from the walls, eye sockets and rib cages laced with yellow magic. The high inquisitors' ritual hadn't been to counter a spell after all. Fucking catacombs.

Echo had no weapon, so Rhienne stepped in front of her and slashed the dagger along her calf and palm. The pain barely registered. *I offer this symbol of creation, in return for the power to destroy.* She turned her blood into more bolts of dark energy, flinging them at one skeleton after another.

Each attack blasted holes through the bones they hit, but the skeletons continued clattering toward them with their rusty weapons. Echo swung at the closest ones with her mandolin case. A few fell, and their bones scattered, but the Untolds' magic swirled and pieced them back together, unphased.

Rhienne staggered under a wave of dizziness. Blood loss on top of everything else. Not her brightest idea. Worse, she could hear their pursuers again, getting louder. She risked one more spell, calling the blood out of her veins to pool into dark, tangling tendrils on the ground, which crushed the skeletons' legs. They dragged themselves forward, relentless, their bones scraping on rock.

The Untold sounded close. If she and Echo backtracked to find a side passage, they'd be caught.

Rhienne gasped out, "Do you have anything to get us out of here?"

"You really summoned me *here* without a backup plan?" Echo hissed.

"Plans are for people who can't improvise."

Panic and anger flickered across Echo's face as she clutched her mandolin case. But after a beat, she gritted her teeth and said, voice soft and hoarse, "You owe me one."

"A lot more than one, I'd say."

Her friend took out her mandolin and started playing. Rhienne wouldn't describe the sounds she made as a song; it was a discordant series of notes that gave her goosebumps, set her teeth grinding, and made her want to flee into the daylight. Cerulean magic flashed in the center of the horde of crawling skeletons.

Just like that, they were gone.

Echo cleared her throat. "Come on. That spell only lasts a minute." She was still quiet, but some of the roughness had faded from her voice. Leaning on each other, they hurried toward the exit.

"Where did you get that thing?" Rhienne couldn't help but ask. "I've never seen an artifact that powerful."

"It's not really that powerful; all that magic was stored up over years. There's not much left now. One, maybe two spells' worth. It was... a gift."

Rhienne gaped. "A gift from who?"

"Nobody important."

An obvious lie. Echo had never kept secrets from her before. Rhienne would've pressed further, but noise from the city above crept in, and with it came light, slowly revealing the figure beside her. The forms her friend usually chose had at least one memorable quality: a face artists would paint, a fluid grace worth putting to music, or some other characteristic that entire poems could attempt to evoke and still fall short. Not this... this plain, stocky woman, so boring as to be alarming in her un-Echo-likeness.

They broke out of the tunnels and clambered over the massive roots that wove in and out of the ground on the city's outskirts, heading at an angle toward the trunk. Distantly, she heard Mishara call to fan out and search the area.

By the time Rhienne found her words again, she was struggling to breathe through her scorching throat. "Hey," she huffed. "I know the circumstances aren't ideal, but you don't seem glad to see me."

"I'm glad to see *you*," Echo said. She slid into a crevice between two roots and helped Rhienne down after. "Much less glad you dragged me into the literal *faction headquar-*

ters of the people who want to drain me to a husk. What the fuck were you thinking? I could've—" A glowing red eye streaked by overhead, and they froze.

"Locator spell," Rhienne whispered.

They ducked and waited for an agonizing minute, hardly daring to move. No inquisitors followed in the spell's wake. It hadn't seen them.

Rhienne peeked out from their hiding spot. The Untold were swarming over the roots in the opposite direction. "Coast is clear for now."

"Come on then," Echo said. "I need to stop by my house to pick up some supplies. You can explain once we're safe."

Growing up together, they'd finagled their way out of a dozen scrapes—though none quite so dramatic as this—and they'd always joked and laughed on the way home. Without Echo's constant stream of chatter and improvised lyrics about their exploits, the whole thing felt much more serious. And as that seriousness bore down, unexpected anger came with it.

How powerless she'd been. After everything she'd lost, the deals she'd made, the blood magic that was supposed to make up for it all, she could've easily died today.

Rhienne touched the burning skin on her neck. It hurt to swallow, to breathe, to speak. The cuts on her arm, hand, and leg smarted. All the sensations kept at bay by the adrenaline of escape slammed into her at once, and when they passed from the roots into the twilit city inside the trunk, the stink and bustle of the Lower Hollows was too much.

"Echo," she mumbled, "do you have anything to drink?"

There was a flask in her hand before she'd finished the question. Echo's lips twitched, a ghost of her usual smile. "When do I not?"

Rhienne took a long swig of something cool and berry-flavored that made her immediately light-headed. "Oh, that's lovely. Thanks."

Echo assessed her with a disapproving hum. Rhienne didn't need to look down at herself to know she was hardly presentable at the moment, illusions or not.

"One little detour. We need to make sure you won't fall over," her friend said, then pulled her through an alley onto another street with a crowded market.

Stalls of depressing clothes and kitschy knickknacks lined the road. Hidden among them were more utilitarian shops: potions, food, medicine. It had been a long time since Rhienne had stolen anything without the aid of magic, so she provided the distraction while Echo snatched.

They blended in with the press of shoppers, not moving too fast, stopping to ponder the wares and chat up the merchants. Echo acquired a tub of salve and a healing tincture, some bandages, a few clothing items to cover Rhienne's injuries, and a steamed bun filled with shredded meat that Rhienne would've questioned any other day but was too hungry to care about now. Mishara and her goons would be combing the city for her soon, but these things took patience and finesse. Haste was the ruin of thievery.

Once some of her strength had returned, Rhienne signaled they could leave. The old patterns of their friendship fit so comfortably. It was another shock, then, when Echo led them to the residential district of the Hollows, just one level above the Lowers, and stopped at a house. It was a bit on the run-down side, but no more than those crowded around it, with pebble-dashed walls and a tiled roof. Flower boxes decorated the glowing windows.

"This is where you live?"

"This is where I've been staying," Echo corrected. "In case it comes up, I'm disguised as someone who can't speak. You're an old friend I ran into at the market. We're just cleaning ourselves up before we go out to dinner."

"In case it comes up? Is there someone else inside?"

"More than likely." That was all the explanation Echo gave. She fussed with Rhienne's newly acquired scarf to make sure the rope marks were covered. Then, instead of a lockpick, she produced a key. The door swung open to the smell of burning wood and baking bread, garlic, and herbs. A man hummed to himself in the next room.

This was becoming more baffling by the moment. A disconcerting thought struck her, and she blurted out, "Echo, are you *married*?"

Echo swatted her and made for the room the delicious smells were coming from.

"Is that a yes or no?" Rhienne asked, rubbing her arm.

"Of course not," she whispered, knocking on the door-frame to announce herself as they entered.

"Natalia, I didn't expect you back so early." The warm humming turned into an equally warm voice. It belonged to a man whose hair had fled from the top of his head to take up residence on his chin. Crow's feet crinkled at the corners of his eyes when he smiled. "And I see you brought company. Give me a moment. I put the telepathy stone down somewhere while I was cooking."

Echo made a series of hand motions, some paired with sweeping gestures or facial expressions.

"Ah, you've been practicing! You're both welcome to have dinner here, if you like." He beamed and stuck out a hand. "Wonderful to meet you. My name is Sidrin."

"Isolde." Rhienne plucked a name from her list of aliases and shook his hand. No ring, she confirmed. Not Echo's husband. So who was he to her? Mimics never stayed anywhere long enough to make close friends. Nothing else should've rattled her after today, but this domestic bliss left her feeling very lost indeed. "And that's all right. I haven't had a girl's night out in ages. *Natalia* and I have a lot of catching up to do."

"Don't stay out too late. Word has it there was some unsavory business at the tavern last night. Did you see any of that?"

Echo shook her head, made some more hand signs, then practically shoved Rhienne away from the kitchen.

Two closed doors flanked the main room. She led Rhienne through the one on the left, which opened into a small bedroom with only the barest essentials—a bed, a small table, and a trunk.

"How long have you been living here?" Rhienne asked. "And what in the cosmos was all that?"

"Long enough," Echo whispered. She opened the trunk and started shoving things into a bag. There wasn't much. Some clothes, things Rhienne assumed were for the mandolin, and a set of more familiar instruments: thieves' tools and a forgery kit. "I came to Wildspire for information. Sidrin's husband had recently passed, and he was renting a room so the house didn't feel so empty. He took me in, tried to teach me signing, and when that didn't work, spent a small fortune on those telepathy stones. He even found me a job. The more people he introduced me to, the harder it got to change forms or leave." Once everything was packed, she paused for breath. "This was not how I imagined our reunion would go."

"Me neither. I can't believe you've been *here* this whole time. We've practically been living on top of each other." Rhienne choked on a laugh, holding back a sob. "I missed you so much." She was ready to collapse into a hug, but Echo remained wary, the weight of years stretching taut between them.

"How did you get involved with the Untold?"

Rhienne blinked, surprised. "Gods and demons, Echo, you don't think I'd ever get *involved* involved, do you?" She held up her hands to emphasize her lack of siphoned power.

"Involved enough for an execution out of the public eye. Involved enough to be using *blood magic* on top of whatever else you've been doing. I thought you and your mother went off to uncover the mysteries of Dawn's Rest."

The accusations sent a pang of guilt through her. Rhienne hadn't considered how dangerous it was to summon Echo to the catacombs; she'd only been thinking of herself. Survival at all costs. Rhienne owed her an explanation, and an apology.

Even with that logic, she had to fight to get the words past her lips. "My mother's dead."

Echo's features softened. Vala had disappeared before Echo came into Rhienne's life, and had only come back after they parted. But Echo and her mother shared a love of music and a hatred for authority that Rhienne was sure would've made them fast friends. "I'm sorry, Rhi."

"It's... it is what it is." *My own fault*, Rhienne couldn't say. Not yet. "As for the Untold, they were my plan B when plan A to bring Vala back didn't work out. Plan A was... a long story." Her breath left her in a rush. She couldn't even begin talking about Oblivion. "But I swear, I was only with them to get access to their Dawnglow. I was a lackey running supply errands. I never helped them gather information, or interrogated anyone, or siphoned."

"And the high inquisitor who seemed to have a very personal stake in your capture?" Echo raised a brow. "She shrieked like a banshee when you got away."

Rhienne ran a hand through her hair and grimaced at the grease and dirt. "Mishara. She was my way in. I picked her specifically because she doesn't siphon. She's in charge of recruitment, interfacing with the populace—the kinds of things you want to appear normal for."

Echo hefted the bag over one shoulder and shrugged with the other. "Oh, well, if she only *recruits* the ones who kill people like me, instead of actually killing them, I suppose that's fine."

"I—" Rhienne bit back a retort. "I was desperate. I'm sorry. And I'm sorry for putting you in danger."

Her friend's sigh was like the release of a pressure valve, most of the tension rushing out of her. "You saved my hide, actually. I guess the high-muckety-mucks have ramped up their paranoia, because the Untold are crawling all over the city. I don't know how they found me, but they'd backed me into a corner when you called."

"Oh, hell. Are you alright?"

"Yeah." Echo chewed her lip with a forlorn look at her mandolin. "Out of most of the magic I'd been gathering for years, but otherwise unscathed."

"I don't want to sound nosy—"

"—but you'll power through."

"But I thought you were trying to make a name for yourself at the music academy in Graybarrow." Rhienne shot her a look. It was only fair that Echo shared a *little* of her side of things, after what Rhienne had just divulged. "You said you were looking for information. Why are you here, hiding your voice? What happened?"

"Graybarrow... didn't pan out. The rest is also a long story, and I'm not even sure of all the pieces. I came here because Wildspire is supposed to have the largest library of ancient divine knowledge on the continent." She made a disgusted face. "Turns out that information is locked to everyone without a boatload of wealth and privilege. And now..."

And now she was low on magic and high on peril. Rhienne pressed her lips together in thought. Whatever Echo wanted ancient divine knowledge for, she'd find out later. The archives might contain a clue for an alternative to Dawnglow. More importantly, though, she wanted Echo's trust back. Rhienne's father had adopted Echo when they were young; they were practically sisters. They'd spent too much time apart already. Rhienne couldn't fathom any more.

Should've considered that before you slept with a high inquisitor.

Rhienne brushed the thought away. "I could help you break in. If you still want me around." Her tone was casual, but her heart thundered, waiting for the answer.

Echo surveyed her meager belongings, including Rhienne, as if taking stock of their usefulness. Time had not been as kind to Echo as Rhienne had thought. That took the sting out of her pause. Mostly.

At last, she said, "If we can get into the Boughs tonight, I know a safe place to use as our base of operations."

A hideout in the Boughs was bound to be luxurious. Not the reunion she'd hoped for, but it was a start. Rhienne mustered a smile through her exhaustion. "Lead the way."

Chapter 4

Echo

All her earthly possessions in hand, Echo looked around at the weathered floors and flaking plaster walls of the house for the last time. There wasn't much to miss. Her gaze caught on the table, bare except for Sidrin's telepathy stone. The small black rock was paired with the one around her neck, which meant he wouldn't get any use out of it anymore. She snatched it and handed it to Rhienne. It might come in handy while they were sneaking around.

Can you hear me? she thought, and Rhienne jumped. *As long as that is touching your skin, we'll be able to talk to each other.*

Whoa. Her friend's eyes lit up as she tucked the second necklace under her shirt; she'd always been enamored with anything magical. Good to know some things hadn't changed. *We're going to get into all sorts of trouble with these.*

Echo winked and headed to the door, but as soon as her hand touched the knob, a shudder ran through her brain. Her foresight always warned her if she was making a choice that would lead to her premature death. This time, it was more than the anxious prickle she'd felt in the tavern or the constant chill during Rhienne's rescue. The vision *changed*. Instead of passing peacefully in her sleep, Untold loomed over her, their skeletons glowing bright enough to light up the dark room as they inhaled the magic misting off her withered body.

She froze, and the scene evaporated from her mind.

"What's wrong?" Rhienne whispered.

Echo peeked out between the curtains. Four Untold were approaching the house, making no effort to hide themselves. For all her regrets with Exodus, the gift was never wrong. *We need to sneak out the back. Step where I step so the floorboards don't creak.*

Rhienne nodded once, all business. Her association with the Untold, whatever the reason, still sat uncomfortably in Echo's gut, but at least she could rely on Rhienne to do whatever it took to save her own skin.

When they reached the back door, the same vision returned, sharper. A shadow passed before the window. The Untold were watching all the exits.

Into my room, right now. Echo had hoped not to use up any more of her mandolin's magic—it had taken a *lot* to escape the catacombs—but there was nothing for it. They were both exhausted, and Rhienne couldn't afford to lose any more blood.

Echo closed the bedroom door behind her and took out her mandolin. She played as softly as she could.

With that decision made, the scene of her death shifted back to what she'd come to know as equilibrium: an old woman Echo barely recognized as herself, lying in bed, alone, as her last breath rattled from her chest. Not a satisfactory end, but at least it meant she had time until she reached it.

Her hands shook, but she managed the first few measures of the song she'd used to flee Exodus's realm. These were mere mortals; it would be more than enough to hide from them. Rhienne looked on the verge of protest when her skin shimmered. Another whisper of notes, like the last rays of sun disappearing behind the horizon, and patches of the wall showed through her arms and face. Then she was gone. Echo repeated the song for herself. Her body disappeared as the Untold knocked on the front door.

Sidrin answered. She could picture him exactly—the way his smile would waver, but hold—as he said, "How can I help you?" The man was too kind for his own good. Or hers.

The Untold said, "We're following a lead. Do you live alone?"

"N-no. My tenant and I are here, and a friend of hers came for dinner."

"We need to speak with all of you."

"If you believe it's necessary, then of course. Let me fetch them." A handful of intentionally heavy steps followed, then a knock. "Natalia, we have some... visitors. Can you come out?"

Silently, she edged around the room, fumbling a bit before she found Rhienne.

Sidrin chuckled, nervous. "All right, then I'm coming in." He opened the door. Took in the empty room, the curtains billowing in the breeze. "Natalia?"

She squeezed Rhienne's arm.

Behind Sidrin, the two Untold had their faces uncovered, bones glowing bright yellow with an immortal's stolen power. One wore an inquisitor's red cloak. These were the same two who'd been poking around the tavern. They glanced at the space, but their focus was on Sidrin. Each clamped a hand on his shoulder.

"What's this then? Where are these 'friends' of yours?"

"I—she must have left while I was busy in the kitchen. I have a way to contact her. Let me..." Sidrin looked to the table where he'd left the telepathy stone and found it empty. His face fell. "It's gone. They're gone."

The Untold spun him around, one pinning him to the wall while the other produced that same black needle.

Sidrin gasped. "Now hold on a minute!"

Closer this time, Echo watched them prick Sidrin's finger. His blood ran halfway up the needle before soaking into it. When it disappeared, there was a brief glimmer, like stars within the dark metal. Rhienne twitched beside her.

What? Echo asked. *Have you seen that before?*

No, but it looks... nasty.

"Not him, but it's the same as the others." The Untold frowned. "Sir, we regret to inform you that you've been in close contact with a mimic."

She'd assumed it was a test to detect divine lineage. Tracing her by proximity was a thousand times worse. It put everyone near her in danger too.

This didn't look or feel like Exodus's magic. But if not him, which god would provide such a thing?

Sidrin paled. "What do you mean? How close?"

"Quite. And consistently."

"But... why? I'm no one! I barely have anything worth stealing, never mind killing for."

The Untold released him, sympathetic now that they'd confirmed Sidrin was a victim. "You're well known in these parts; maybe it was after your connections. Maybe it needed an inconspicuous place to hide." The Untold slid the needle into an inner pocket. "The Children of Infinity have gotten creative in recent years; they know we're onto their methods. Don't worry. We'll track this one down too. The two people you were expecting in here—what did they look like? In case it takes one of those forms again."

Sidrin gave a brief, mechanical description of her and Rhienne. Height, skin tone, hair and eye color, what they'd been wearing. A description you'd give of a stranger.

"Best keep a low profile for a while," the inquisitor said. "Don't let anyone into your home, and if you see anything strange, speak to us through this. We'll be in the neighborhood." He gave Sidrin a copper Transmitter Ring.

They did a cursory search of the rest of the house before sweeping out, hoods and scarves back in place. It was a small blessing that they hadn't figured out Rhienne's savior was a mimic. Once they put those pieces together, there'd be nowhere in the city left to hide.

Sidrin hadn't moved. He was blocking the doorway, staring at the ring in his hand. "It's not true," he whispered. "It can't be true."

Echo was a maven of masks. She had to be, being what she was. For a mimic to pass in polite society, they had to immerse themselves in their role and leave no room for doubt about their identity. It was imperative, though, to remember it was an act—a disguise that could be abandoned at a moment's notice. Even after wearing it for years.

It was Natalia's heart that hurt, Echo reminded herself. It was Natalia who wanted to embrace him, apologize, and be embraced back, rather than submit to her loneliness again. Echo knew better. Nothing she could say would ever make him trust her again. Sidrin's trust might be hard for anyone to come by for a long, long time.

He closed the ring in his fist and crossed to the window.

Echo tugged on Rhienne's sleeve. *Time to go, before he locks the whole house down.*

Her friend didn't move, still primed for a fight. *You know I'd stand up for you if you asked, right?*

It's fine. He won't change his mind about me, no matter what we say. We won't see him again anyway. They'd been through this song and dance when they were younger. Once a mimic's true identity was revealed, there was no turning back. *Let's go.*

They fled from the house that had been Natalia's home for three years. An eternity for a mimic to stay in one place. She could only copy bodies as she'd seen them, frozen in her memory. People started getting suspicious when you didn't age. But leaving had always been her choice before, usually at the end of a night of drinking, song, and emptying the pockets of an airheaded merchant or three. Miserable as she'd been in this constricting life, she hated the heaviness that came with stepping out the door for the last time.

Night had taken the city. Firefly lamps illuminated the nearly empty streets. The Untold were fanned out, knocking on neighboring doors, searching houses, asking questions.

The spell will wear off in about an hour. You need a disguise before that happens, and I need somewhere to change forms. Echo clung to Rhienne's hand and made a beeline for the long path that spiraled up Wildspire's trunk.

It was a common place for couples to meet in the small hours of the morning. Romantic lighting in all the view-ports, sweeping vistas of the surrounding forest with its silver-green canopy, and plenty of shadowy alcoves carved into the trunk where people tended to forget various items of clothing. When the firefly lanterns turned from blue to green, signaling they were outside the wealthier Upper Hollows, they went hunting for a wardrobe that would let them pass into the Boughs unnoticed.

Echo found a knee-length jacket with billowing sleeves and leaf-patterned scrollwork on the hems. Rhienne fashioned a headscarf from a geometric-patterned shawl to hide her hair and the freshly applied bandages on her neck. Appalling what a halfway decent income allowed people to leave behind. Between those and the spare outfits in Echo's bag, they'd look nearly respectable, and different enough from Sidrin's description.

Spots of skin and cloth appeared in the air where Rhienne stood. As the spell wore off, Echo pulled her into the shadows. The rescue had been so chaotic, the time in Sidrin's house so brief, that this was her first real look at her friend.

Growing up, she'd likened Rhienne to a river rock, refusing to be anything other than what she was, forcing the world to bend and break around her. Echo had loved that about her (most of the time), but she also expected to see some erosion because of it, some sign of the harsh times she'd lived through. But Rhienne looked the same.

No, younger. A few scars poked out from her sleeves and collar, but otherwise, her skin was smooth and unmarred. There was no gray in her hair. There were no shadows under her eyes. She was bright, fresh, and vivid, without any record of her imprisonment, never mind the last ten years. Rhienne couldn't alter her body like Echo could. She had to be using illusions.

Echo frowned and crossed her arms.

"What?" Rhienne pouted. "You don't approve?"

"I'm just... taking it in."

"It's only a little magic."

"There's no such thing as a *little* magic." Everything came at a cost.

"Yeah, well." Rhienne—Swindler of Royalty and Queen of Changing the Subject—shrugged and pushed on. "Enough about me. Shouldn't you change? I don't think they'll let you into the Boughs as you are. Too peasant-looking."

She was right. And the further they got from Sidrin's house, the more this form started to itch. Long past time to be someone else.

Every mimicry was a little different. Bodies had signatures to them. Assumptions, expectations. A way of being that matched the appearance, even if that wasn't what was on the inside.

When Echo let Natalia go and transformed into her preferred shape, she stood taller. Prouder. It had nothing to do with the lengthening of her bones or the stretch and pull of changing skin. Her breath came easier, and so did her smile. Her hair became a cloud of snow-white curls, her body lean and toned from a career in dancing, her eyes bright with mischief. She'd met this woman on the road to Graybarrow, one marvelous night at a seaside festival. She had been captivating, confident, unforgettable. Everything Echo wanted to be. The inside still didn't quite match the outside—this body was far younger than her now, to start—but it was the closest she'd ever found to feeling *right*.

"That's better, eh?" Rhienne grinned. "I like this one. Now we look the same age too. You'll have to tell me her story some time. But first, where exactly are we going?"

It was easier, in this body, for Echo to push away her remaining discomfort. Rhienne was her friend. The sister of her soul, if not her blood. And there'd be time for proper recompense when they got out of this mess together. "You ever heard of Crystal and Evergreen?"

"The place with the private hot springs on each balcony?" Rhienne gasped. "If you're joking, I may have to hurt you."

"I've got identification papers already. Just need to make some for you." Echo busied herself with the forgery, copying the official swirling script and delicate stamps onto a new set of parchment. She checked her foresight every so often to make sure they weren't in imminent danger of death-by-Untold. "Getting into the Boughs is the easy part. The archive security is another matter."

"If we can't break in, we have to convince them we're legit," Rhienne mused.

"I haven't been able to stay up there long enough to build an identity without drawing suspicion. But with you here to corroborate my story—"

"—and my unmatched powers of persuasion—"

"—we might have a chance. A letter of recommendation from one of the rich bastards at Crystal and Evergreen should be just the thing."

Rhienne's eyes gleamed. "I've been waiting ten years to go to a place like this with you. I mean, I didn't think we'd have to lie to get in by this point, but still." She hopped from foot to foot, impatient as ever, while Echo continued her work. "How much longer before we can go?"

"Do you want me to have to start over?"

"Only if you're going slow on purpose."

Echo's gaze flicked up to Rhienne, then pointedly over to the shallow wooden bench carved into the alcove. Rhienne sat with a huff. Only a few more minutes passed before Echo blew on the ink to dry it and handed over the finished document. "That wasn't so hard, was it?"

"Every moment I'm not in that hot spring is agony." Rhienne jumped up but stopped short of taking her arm.

In the back of her mind, Echo knew the pause was to check if touching her was okay, not an expression of reluctance. But with Sidrin's devastation so fresh, she couldn't help the little spike of fear. Few things in life made Rhienne hesitate, and Echo did not want to be one of them. "I missed you too, you know," she whispered.

"Oh, good." Rhienne's voice wobbled. "For a second there, I wasn't sure."

Hot tears pricked in her eyes, and Echo stepped up and crushed Rhienne against her. Rhienne let out a half-sob and returned the embrace.

When they'd left home together, it had been the two of them against the world. Splitting up had left a crack in her heart. It was necessary, at the time, for her to pursue music and for Rhienne to travel with her mother, but difficult. So much they never could have planned for had broken them since. *Both* of them, though Rhienne tried to hide it. A small piece of that fracture healed, being together again. Rhienne's poor choice of companions aside.

Not like Echo was innocent of that, either.

After they pulled away, Echo took a moment to collect herself—Rhienne's illusions, annoyingly, masked any signs of crying—and they completed their walk up the path, arm in arm. A set of guards examined their papers at the checkpoint and waved them through. Together, they passed into the highest tier of the city.

Echo followed the wide, brightly lit avenues, which brought them to the side entrance of Wildspire's most famous and exclusive inn. "Stay put for a minute. I'm going to deliver a 'special' drink to their entertainer. Should only take a few minutes to kick in, and then we waltz in and replace them, saving the day."

"Our first mission back together, and you're putting me on watch?" Rhienne whined.

"This will be much easier if I'm alone." Echo checked their surroundings, then mimicked one of the waitstaff she'd scouted a few days ago. She opened her mandolin case and peeled back the fabric at the inside corner, withdrawing a small bag of herbs. Pity she'd never had the chance to use these on Levi. "And trust me, you don't want to see this. I'll be right back."

Chapter 5

Rhienne

Rhienne didn't have to wait long, but it gave her time to reapply salve to her wounds and start to get anxious before Echo reappeared.

"Their harp player should be making a hasty exit in the next few minutes," Echo said as she returned to the dancer's form.

This body suited her friend much better than 'Natalia' had. They'd be quite the pair striding into the hotel. Rhienne was glad to have some sense of normalcy back. She could almost pretend she hadn't barely escaped death this morning.

They circled around to the front door and into a pristine lobby of dark, polished wood, frosted glass, and pine-scented greenery. Sourceless piano music and soft lighting gave the place a relaxed, luxurious air. Power and wealth practically oozed out of the walls. The reedy man behind the front desk looked as snooty as she'd expect of someone who worked here, spectacles perched on the end of his upturned nose.

Rhienne sighed dreamily. "I'm home."

"How may I help you ladies?" asked the receptionist.

It took all her willpower not to ask if his voice was really that nasal or if it was part of the job. She didn't smile—she'd heard one didn't smile at people lower than their station—and opted for a casual, 'we do this all the time' expression. "We're headed to the lounge for a nightcap."

"Wonderful. Will you be paying the cover charge, or are you checking in for the night?"

Cover charge? Rhienne raised her eyebrow to look imperious.

"Visiting the lounge is complementary with the purchase of a room," he explained.

"Ah, of course. My apologies, we've just arrived in town and are still getting the lay of the land. How much would that run us?"

By the way his posture stiffened, she knew she'd made a mistake. She'd heard the phrase 'if you have to ask, you can't afford it' before, but it had seemed too impractical to be real.

"New in town, you say? Where is it you've traveled from?"

"Graybarrow," Echo said with a brilliant smile. "We've just finished our studies at the academy there. We're taking a tour of the continent before we settle down."

"Congratulations," he said blandly. "Be that as it may, I need to see your papers." His gaze flicked to a point over her shoulder. Rhienne hadn't thought his back could get any straighter, but it did. "Excuse me for a moment."

A figure was gliding across the lobby. Their face was all displeased angles, with narrow copper eyes and dark skin, and hair that fell artfully over one shoulder. Delicate gold jewelry decorated their ears and fingers. The impeccable burgundy suit left no doubt it was real gold, too. Rhienne would've picked them out of a crowd as *very important* from a mile away.

Adjusting his embroidered vest, the receptionist stepped out from behind the counter and bowed. "Exalt Starfall. I am at your service."

"We have a situation," Starfall said. "It appears our entertainer is ill. I need you to find a replacement immediately."

The clerk stammered, "My deepest apologies, Exalt, but the hour is so late—"

"I need solutions, not excuses, Jareth! I will not have anyone leaving my hotel with words of dissatisfaction on their lips. In this industry, reputation is everything."

Echo nudged her with an elbow, a glint in her eye. The favor of an Exalt would open any door in the Boughs. *This is going even better than I thought*, she said into Rhienne's mind. *You're up.*

"My good friends," Rhienne interrupted Jareth's stumbling apologies, "I couldn't help but overhear your conundrum. As luck would have it, my companion here is quite the accomplished singer."

"Musician," Echo corrected as she stepped forward, mandolin in hand. She ignored Rhienne's questioning look. "I'd be more than happy to assist you."

Exalt Starfall's metallic gaze raked over her and Echo in turn. "I hope you understand, I cannot let just anyone who can hold an instrument into my establishment. What are your credentials? Where have you played?"

"As I was just telling your receptionist, I'm a fresh graduate of Graybarrow's music academy. This would be my first public performance of any standing."

"Ah! They turn out some of the best artists on the continent. Nothing compared to Kydorei, of course, but... What area do you specialize in?"

Echo hesitated. She'd never had a formal education in music.

Rhienne jumped in. "Pardon my saying so, Exalt, but it seems time is of the essence. How about a brief audition? I'm sure you'll be impressed. If not, we'll leave you be. Is that a deal?"

They pursed their lips for a moment. "Yes, fine. Let's hear it then."

That had to be the flimsiest bargain Rhienne had ever struck, but a wisp of a thread wrapped around her heart all the same, tying her and Echo to the Exalt.

Starfall held their skeptical look as Echo started to play. Her eyes went far away, but not in the usual way musicians lost themselves in their song. She was looking *at* something, but when Rhienne followed her gaze, there was nothing there.

Whatever Echo saw made her frown and her fingers stumble. But she turned that into a transition, which became a song Rhienne had never heard before. It was peaceful, joyful; it reflected the awe on Echo's face as her gaze remained fixed on that distant point.

And then the owner's face lit up. With it, glowing motes appeared between the strings, sparkling along the instrument's decorative whorls. Echo used the magic to make the notes hang in the air, creating layers of harmony. The tightness in Rhienne's chest loosened, the bargain fulfilled. Starfall was impressed.

So was Rhienne, but she couldn't help feeling the breadth of the chasm created by their time apart. Where had Echo's prowess with the mandolin come from, and why wasn't she singing? If the need to impress was dire, shouldn't they use the best tools at their disposal?

Exalt Starfall applauded when Echo finished, alight with hungry opportunism. "I think you're the perfect fit for our stage. We're going to need something upbeat to breathe life back into the crowd. I trust you know all the usual favorites. But once that's sorted, you can play whatever you like. Right this way."

Rhienne raised her eyebrows at Echo. *Are you going to sing on stage?*

No way. I haven't practiced since I took Natalia's form.

Oh, come on, you don't need practice. I've missed hearing you. What was the ballad you always used to sing when we were growing up?

I said no, Rhi. Not tonight. Echo unclasped the telepathy stone and put it in her pocket, cutting off Rhienne's response.

She had no choice but to let it drop for now, but the chasm yawned wider. Her fault. If Rhienne hadn't been so colossally short-sighted, Echo might be more comfortable answering her questions.

Starfall kept up a stream of chatter, now absorbed with Echo and oblivious to Rhienne. That was fine. Easier to peel away as they all stepped into the lounge.

This was clearly the 'crystal' part of Crystal and Evergreen. The bar and all its occupants sat within a massive geode. The floor was smooth like river stone, but the walls and domed ceiling were covered in glittering spears of amethyst. Patrons reclined on leather couches, cocktails held in jewel-bedecked hands. Surely one of these high-society types knew some shady back doors of magic. Couldn't hurt to have an alternative in case their gambit with the archives failed.

The Exalt apologized to the crowd for the interruption and gestured for Echo to take the stage.

Echo bowed and said, "If you find my music pleasing, all I ask is that you sing along. We can get to more personal terms as the night goes on." She smiled slyly, earning her a few chuckles and calls of, "It's a deal!" With the fading shimmer of the bargain in the air, she launched into an instrumental rendition of *Wine and Honey*.

By the time she reached the chorus, several people were singing along. The dourness of the crowd melted away as Echo wove magic into beautifully colored illusions to match the lyrics. After *The Dragon's Hoard* and *The Desert Rose*, a few even got up to dance.

Rhienne would get her answers, from Echo and whichever of these dandies fell prey to her charms. But first, she'd enjoy the atmosphere and what were hopefully some strong drinks. It had been a very, *very* long day.

Chapter 6

Echo

After an hour of seamlessly transitioning from song to song, Echo's fingers ached, and her cheeks hurt from smiling. She called for a short break and had to stop herself from sagging into a chair. Being a solo act was marvelous. She'd forgotten it was also exhausting.

Still, Echo was riding the high of her vision. For once, her foresight actually felt like a gift. When she'd decided to play something new for Starfall—something *hers*—in this place where people actually knew what art was, the vision had changed. Instead of dying alone, there was a crowd around her bed. People who mourned her. People who sang her songs after she was gone. People who had been inspired by her presence instead of terrified. The vision hadn't appeared that way in years.

And so far, it hadn't changed back.

She scanned the room for Rhienne. Her friend hung on the arm of a gorgeous man, and if Echo knew her, her drunkenness was half-feigned in order to pick some pockets. Echo hoped that would distract Rhienne long enough to prevent further questions about her singing voice. She wasn't ready for that conversation yet.

The burgundy-suited proprietor was practically glowing as people milled about the lounge. Their eyes met hers, and they excused themselves from a group of fawning patrons, approaching with a wide smile. "Excellent work so far. I think it's time to show them what you showed me in the lobby, yes?"

An Exalt would have connections all over the continent. She couldn't stay in Wildspire long enough to build a relationship, but once she'd finished at the library, a token of Starfall's could carry her anywhere she and Rhienne wanted to go. This was her chance.

"With pleasure," Echo said.

Returning to the stage, she threw herself into her music. Half a dozen songs she'd written and failed to convince Levi to play at last got the audience they deserved. She didn't have to care about brevity, or familiarity, or the specific wording of deals. Singing would've been preferable to playing the mandolin, but she used the magic leftover from her first bargain with the crowd to tell the story her voice couldn't. Illusory images spun a tale of a woman (vaguely resembling Echo) rising up from nothing, traveling the world, outwitting the gods, and taking her rightful place in the history books. All good stories were embellishments of the truth; no one needed to know the *amount* of embellishment. Sidrin and the Untold faded to the back of her mind, and she was almost happy.

Until her foresight shimmered.

At a quick glance, it didn't seem to have changed. But looking closer, there were fewer people at her side when she died. The longer she played, the more of them drifted into mist.

Echo forced her awareness back to the lounge. It had emptied too. About half the patrons who'd been there at the start were no longer paying attention or were gone entirely. The glow of her strings faded, and the illusions winked out before she finished. Her final chord echoed off the geode ceiling to scattered applause. She took a bow, and the Exalt waved her and Rhienne over to the bar. No one approached her. No one raved of her talent. She caught snippets of conversation as she passed between couches and tables.

"Not very original, but she's got potential."

"I'd love to see what she can do in a few years."

"Her technique is good, but where's the heart?"

"She's so young. Plenty of time to grow."

What did any of that even mean? Those were her best songs! She didn't need time to *grow*. For gods' sake, she'd been doing this for decades. Bunch of pompous idiots who'd probably never picked up an instrument.

All her excitement had bled out by the time she sat down.

Starfall didn't seem to notice. They slipped behind the bar and poured three glasses of whiskey, a flush to their cheeks and a haze in their copper eyes that showed this was far from their first drink. "That was a fine performance, fine indeed. You must forgive my rudeness earlier; I was feeling rather harried. I never caught your names."

"Melinde." Rhienne stuck out her hand, and they shook.

Echo downed her whiskey in one gulp. "I'm Lyra. Nothing to forgive. It was an honor to play for you."

"Aderai Starfall," they said. "Thank you for salvaging my night. The least I can do is cover the cost of your rooms."

Echo reached into her pocket and touched the telepathy stone. *Do you think it's safe to stay the night? The Untold shouldn't expect us to be here, but I don't know how much time we have before they put Sidrin's missing tenant together with your miraculous escape.*

We're not going to not *stay the night if we get a free room,* Rhienne answered. *I can put wards down. The archives aren't going anywhere. Plus, we need to catch up.*

Echo swallowed. "How about one room and a letter of recommendation? I heard Wildspire has the best archives this side of the continent. I've been dying to get a look at any sort of" —she leaned forward— "magical enhancements they might have information about."

"I wouldn't think someone with your resources would require such enhancements." They gestured at her mandolin. "Treasures like that do not simply fall from the sky."

"One can never have too much help in the entertainment business." She waved at the space, from the crystal ceiling to the ever-lasting candle flames, all of which were either conjured or maintained by magic. "As I'm sure you know."

Aderai's chuckle sounded forced. They brushed their hair over their shoulder in a poor attempt to disguise a glance around the bar. "My dear, I can assure you I've never needed *help* to earn my success."

Right. An Exalt wouldn't stoop to making their own deals with the gods—they had people to do that for them.

Echo ducked her head in apology. "I meant no offense. We're just starting out, you understand. Even with our resources, a little knowledge can go a long way."

"And I'll never hear the end of it if we lose that bet to Penelope," Rhienne cut in. "You know how the Miravins are. Think they have the best of everything. She couldn't fathom that Wildspire would have any secrets her family didn't already know."

Aderai straightened. "You know the Miravins?"

Who? Echo asked.

A rich family in Port Saphrai. I overheard that Starfall has been trying to start up a partnership with them for ages. Aloud, Rhienne said, "Of course! We went to school with Penny. Lovely woman, and her father is a delight. Such a shame about—oh, I shouldn't gossip."

Echo hid a smile. While she had to study people and become them over time, Rhienne could improvise and ingratiate herself with anyone. Always a pleasure to watch her work.

Aderai's eagerness was palpable. "Oh, nonsense. We're all friends here, aren't we?"

"Well, you have been generous to us, but..." Rhienne bit her lip and glanced at Echo. "We really could use a reference for the archives. How about a little exchange of knowledge?"

The Exalt only mulled it over for a moment. "Deal." A thread of power snapped into place between Aderai and Rhienne. "Tell me what you know."

"As I said, Penelope is lovely." Rhienne lowered her voice. "You didn't hear this from me, but she's got a propensity for gambling, and the family is in quite a bit of debt. Her father is looking to marry her off as soon as possible. Obviously, he'd owe the partner a great boon for taking on that burden."

You got all that while I was on stage?

Just took a couple favors.

"I see." Aderai drummed their fingers on the table. "You've been frank with me, so I'll be frank with you. The Untold purged anything worth a pinch of magic when they gained their station. If you want the good stuff, the *really* good stuff, you need a godkin."

Rhienne looked at Echo. *I thought the ones on this plane had all died out.*

So did I. The gods had been created by the Mothers, Infinity and Eternity, to bring about the endings they could not. But the gods had gaps in their abilities too, and they made creatures to fill them. Godkin had no divine blood; they were more like distant cousins of the gods than their descendants. None had been spotted in decades.

"And you know where to find one?" Rhienne made a show of hiding her excitement.

"In the forest, about a day's journey east of here. Calls himself the Collector. He's an... information broker. Might be worth a visit."

"What sort of information does he collect?" Echo asked warily.

"It depends on the magnitude of what you're asking for." Aderai became very focused on their whiskey. "From what I've heard, his deals are less exacting than the gods."

That doesn't sound so bad, Rhienne thought to Echo. *Easier than combing through a library. Especially if that library doesn't have what we want anyway.*

The Exalt was being purposefully vague, but alcohol and one small deal would only make them open up so much. And Rhienne was right. As much as it pained Echo to let all her effort go to waste, a being made by the gods ought to know more about divine magic than some dusty old books. This was the best way to find out how to fix her singing voice *and* resurrect Rhienne's mother. And the sooner they were out of town, the better.

"Thank you," Echo said. "If you don't mind giving us a few more directions to find this Collector, we ought to get some rest."

With the deal satisfied, tiny motes of magic dispersed between the two of them. Echo channeled her half into the mandolin.

Aderai scribbled notes onto a napkin and said, "You could stay, you know. Some of my guests like you, and my usual performer has been looking for an understudy. I'm sure it would be a valuable experience for you. I could have Jareth put together a compensation package."

Understudy? Echo dug her nails into her thighs. The absolute nerve! "Unfortunately, we need to be on our way tomorrow. Schedule to keep. Continent to explore." She stood up. "Aren't you exhausted, Melinde?"

"Extremely." Rhienne had to steady herself against the table. Probably shouldn't have let her drink so much, considering the day's activities. Then again, all the more reason *to* drink.

They left the lounge, and Jareth gave them a key with a barely disguised expression of distaste before pointing down a hallway lined with golden-numbered doors. Echo noted the closest exits, as well as the stairs leading to the roof and basement, in case they had to make a quick getaway.

When they were alone, Rhienne growled, "Understudy? A 'fine' performance? Who do they think they are? Wouldn't recognize greatness if it bit them on the ass. You were fantastic."

An admirable attempt to smooth things over, and Echo would be lying if she said it didn't work just a bit. She loved music. She loved being on stage. But by the gods, sometimes the lack of recognition brought back a well of emptiness she did not want to examine right now. "Thanks. You sure you have enough strength to put wards up?"

"I'd summon a demon from the Lower Plane if it meant sleeping in a proper bed." Rhienne checked that the hallway was clear, then reopened one of the wounds on her arm. Echo winced on her behalf. "Protect me from intruders," Rhienne murmured, and traced a rune onto the door with her blood. It shimmered and dissolved into the wood, only detectable if you were really looking for it. "Anyone who tries to enter is in for a rude awakening. Good enough?"

"Perfect." Echo hadn't realized how exhausted she was until she stepped inside. All she saw was the bed, which she collapsed onto face-first. The lavender-scented sheets tickled her nose.

Rhienne gasped from the balcony. "There *is* a hot spring." Fabric hit the floor, and water splashed against stone. "Oh my gods, Echo, you need to get in here."

Echo wanted to melt into the mattress. This had to be the softest blanket in the cosmos. Her joints cried out in protest when she rose onto her elbows. She felt about ninety. But sleep would have to wait.

She kicked off her boots, dragged herself to the hot spring, and put her feet in the water. It was deliciously warm, and the balcony was lit with more ever-lasting candles. Rhienne's head rested against the lip of the pool, eyes closed. In just her underclothes, the sheer number of razor-thin scars visible across her body brought Echo up short. How long had she been using blood magic?

"Well, I'd say that went about as well as it could have without you using your full potential," Rhienne said. "A fancy room and a source of information we can both use."

Echo ignored the barb about her refusal to sing. "Rhi, are you okay? That was a close call today."

"*Close* being the key word."

If there was one benefit to losing her singing voice, it was that Echo had come to understand the power of a good silence. She waited for Rhienne to talk at her own pace.

"Yeah, it was." Rhienne rubbed her face, leaving droplets of water in her lashes, and sank deeper into the pool. The remains of her smile fell away. "I *almost* had that Dawnglow. You've never seen magic like it, Echo. It would've fixed everything."

"At least you're alive. That means you can try again."

Rhienne huffed a laugh. "True. And thanks for that, by the way."

"Anytime. Maybe not anytime *soon*, but—" Echo yelped as Rhienne splashed water at her.

"Don't think one daring rescue gets you off the hook forever. You know I hate it when you get all, 'Ooh, I'm a mysterious mimic, no one can know my secrets,' on me."

She pushed down a tiny bubble of resentment and kept her tone light. "Well I *am* a mysterious mimic, and it's usually bad when people know my secrets."

"I know. But I'm not people."

"Thank the gods for that." Tension squeezed her heart, but she scooted closer, and Rhienne leaned against her leg. "So. This whole 'catching up' thing was your idea."

"Was it? Damn." Rhienne moved her hands over the water, as if it were a scrying well that would show her the right words. "I guess I should start with the dangerous part. It's not just the Untold that's upset with me. I have a contract with Oblivion that I've been avoiding, and I don't think that's going to work much longer."

Echo shivered despite the warmth of the water. Oblivion was the oldest of the gods, a being of void and darkness. "What possessed you to make a pact with *him*?"

"He was the most... convenient. But restoring life isn't within his domain, apparently. Only ending it. Didn't bother to tell me that when he wrote our contract. Asshole."

"And your mom?"

One shuddering breath was all she got in response. Echo stroked Rhienne's wet hair in slow, soothing motions. The strands were perfectly golden, despite her age and time in a catacomb cell. Echo wove in little braids, like she'd done as a kid, until Rhienne collected herself.

"We did get to travel, for a bit," Rhienne said at last. "She taught me about the world, the planes, the gods. How to control the dreamwalks. Everything was going well." She swallowed. "Until I asked her about me. And Dad. I wanted to know why she left. 'It's the nature of a dream spirit,' Dad always said, but I never believed it. I should've let it go." Rhienne's expression turned stormy. "Turns out, she left because she didn't want anyone to find me. Because she'd made a deal to give up her firstborn."

Echo's blood turned to ice. She knew all too well that children were a favorite currency among the gods. All the promise and potential of a brand-new beginning. It held huge amounts of power. "For what in exchange?"

"I never found out. She said I was a workaround, since I was 'made' from her and Dad's dream rather than born, but the gods felt cheated. She left to lure them away and only came back because she needed my help finding somebody. But I got so angry that she used me like that, and I was young, and I didn't think, and I said, 'I never want to see you again,' and she... unraveled."

Understanding dawned on Echo. Contacting the gods required doing something in service to their name. Rhienne hadn't reached out to Oblivion after her mother died. "Your mother's death opened Oblivion's realm," Echo whispered. Horror washed through her, not at what Rhienne had done, but how hurt she must have been to do it.

"Her murder, you mean."

"No, Rhi—"

"That's what it was! He wouldn't have come if she'd simply died. She'd told me dreams were delicate, but I didn't understand that applied to her too, and now

I'm stuck with this stupid, useless pact." Rhienne's hands curled into fists. "I have to bring her back. It's my fault she's gone, and with everything she knows, she might be the only one who can find a loophole in my contract."

Before Echo could recover from the shock of the story, Rhienne said tightly, "So I have to ask, because you've been acting really weird: why haven't you been singing? And is there anyone else from your exploits—besides the Untold—who might have a bone to pick with us?"

"No. I don't have any outstanding bargains."

"But?" Rhienne pressed. She had an air of desperation about her—to be confided in, maybe, or to know she wasn't the only one who'd made mistakes.

"But..." Echo's thoughts were moving too fast. If only she had the excuse of writing on her slate to think, filter, edit. "I'm not singing because I *can't.*" She attempted a few bars as an example. The muscles in her throat strained. As usual, no sound came out. "I can't even hum."

"What? Why not?"

Echo tucked her knees up to her chest. Her stomach was in knots; she thought she was going to be sick. She looked out over the balcony rail at the rustling forest canopy so she didn't have to watch Rhienne's face. "I had my own run in with a god. Exodus, to be precise."

"You made a deal with him?"

"No." The lie was sour on her tongue. But Rhienne would never believe she'd willingly traded her voice, and after the story her friend had just told, how could she explain the truth? "He... got angry when I tried to leave his realm. He'd given me the mandolin, but apparently the gods don't believe in gifts. He took my singing voice as payment and threw me out."

She risked a glance at Rhienne. Her friend's expression was indignant with a trace of skepticism, but the latter quickly softened. As much as Echo's privacy annoyed Rhienne, she did understand the reason for it. Usually, Echo was thankful. This time, it only made her feel more guilty. More alone.

"So, the moral seems to be: all the gods suck." Rhienne hauled herself out of the pool and squeezed Echo in a warm, wet hug. "Are *you* okay?"

"Not really. But I'm better being not okay together. I'm glad you're here." Which, despite her misgivings and all the things she hadn't said, was true. Echo checked the vision of her future—once more an old woman passing alone in her sleep. That gave her plenty of time for the real story later. Much later.

Though, there was one thing she could disclose, if for no other reason than to move to a less precarious topic. "It's possible not *all* the gods suck."

Rhienne pulled back. "Oh?"

"Before I found Exodus, I stumbled across a different demiplane—literally, the portal just *opened*—while I was traveling. It was the strangest thing. The whole place was one giant, ancient library. Part of me thought it was a dream, but looking back, it was too similar to the way Exodus's realm appeared."

"You think this library belongs to a god?" Rhienne perked up. "Which one?"

"I thought it might be Horizon's."

"But she—"

"Died hundreds of years ago, I know. But it belongs to *someone*, and I never saw another soul while I was there. If it was the realm of a living god, why would they stay hidden?" Echo kicked at the water. This explanation could get tricky if Rhienne asked too many questions. "I don't know what I did in service to Horizon's name to cause that portal to appear. Records of how to reach her are all gone. But I thought, maybe, if I could figure out how to get back, it might hold the solution to fixing my voice."

"A realm of a dead goddess," Rhienne mused. "I'd like to see that. That'd be something to put into a song, eh? If Aderai is good for their word, the Collector should know something about it."

"You think so?"

"I hope so. It's about on par with asking for a non-contractual resurrection. If we're hiking through the forest in the dead of winter, one of us should get something out of it."

Echo snorted, but worry gnawed at her. Living without her voice wasn't something she wanted to consider, though her foresight never let her truly avoid it. Never mind having the police and a potentially angry god on their tail.

She looked over Rhienne's scars again, visible despite her glamor. It would be dangerous if anyone saw them. Why use blood magic if she'd been going after Dawnglow? Just for the sake of power? *I was desperate*, she'd said. Echo didn't want to push too far, but... "Rhienne, will you promise me something?"

"Anything. You know, within reason, obviously."

Echo brushed Rhienne's arm, near one of the fresher wounds. "Don't use it again unless there's no other choice."

Heavy silence pressed in around them. At last, Rhienne nodded. "Just for emergencies. I promise."

It was too one-sided for a bargain, so Echo could only hope Rhienne would keep her word. They sat there, watching the stars twinkle above them and candle flames flicker in the breeze, until they started to shiver.

"Come on, let's go inside," Echo said. "Don't humans need their beauty sleep?"

"Hey now. Correct, but still hurtful." Calling on some deep well of energy reserved for life-threatening crises, Rhienne leapt up and raced into the room. "I'm taking the side next to the fireplace!"

Chapter 7

Rhienne

Rhienne splayed out on the bed, too exhausted to appreciate the luxurious quilts or the warmth of the fire before sleep pulled her under. If she'd had her wits about her, she would've recognized the greediness of that pull, the tilting of the world as she slid into the Plane of Dreams. After months of taking the potion that hid her sleeping mind from Oblivion, she'd grown too comfortable letting her guard down.

She was utterly unprepared when The First God of Endings, Harbinger of Nothingness and Guardian of the Void, appeared in her room. Everything else was softened at the edges, drifting away into pastel hues, but Oblivion was a sharp black blotch against the Dream. A four-armed shadow speckled with stars, tall enough to brush the ceiling. There were two white dots where his eyes should have been and no other features on his face, but his mood hung around him like a cloud. He peered around with a detached sort of amusement as Rhienne hastily bowed.

He hadn't smote her on sight. That had to be a good sign, didn't it?

"My lord," she said. "It has been some time since you've called on me."

"Has it? So hard to keep track of time, on top of all my other endeavors." Oblivion came up to the edge of the bed, turning his gaze toward Echo. "Strange to find you with a partner fully clothed."

She wasn't going to correct him. Better he didn't know she had a more meaningful attachment. "I assume you're not here to gossip." The contract tugged on her soul, forcing the words past her lips. "Do you have a job for me?"

"I do."

Any relief she felt as Oblivion moved away from Echo disappeared when his starry silhouette grew and swallowed everything.

The colors and sounds of a hundred dreams blurred past. She caught glimpses of skin-crawling nightmares and nonsensical mash-ups of everyday moments with the fantastical. But mostly, she saw people being people, holding onto memories, anxieties, and hopes. It was the latter that Oblivion always hunted for. Caught at the right moment, ending someone's hope bred incredibly strong magic.

He brought her to a stop on the shore of a crystalline lake nestled in a caldera. It had that too-symmetrical quality that signaled it was an imagined place instead of a real one, with perfectly spaced trees and wildflowers that were all the same shade of buttery yellow. Rhienne squinted against the sun glaring off the water. An island with a smattering of cottages sat in the center of the lake. Each cottage had its own private dock. There were vague shapes of people in boats, enjoying the afternoon.

Oblivion's presence lingered, watchful. A god could move between dreams, but only a being of the realm—or a half-being, in her case—could affect them. Bargaining with her ability to dreamwalk had seemed like a good idea at the time of their deal. She missed wandering through dreams with her mother, looking closer at whatever seemed interesting. Now she could only go where Oblivion took her. The lack of freedom chafed as much as the chains in the Untold's cell. Though, compared to some of the dreams he'd dragged her into, this one was pretty innocuous.

Rhienne glided over the lake, following the sound of music and laughter coming from a large central building. Maybe it was the long time apart, maybe it was her brush with death that morning, but she was too curious to hold back the question. "What is it about this one that caught your attention?"

Oblivion's shrug rippled the edges of the dream. "He wants to leave. I need him to stay where he is."

"Since when do you care where normal people get to travel?"

"Since when do you care enough about your assignments to ask questions?"

She passed through the wall into a packed tavern. Though each face was a blur, there were so many people that there was hardly room to breathe, and in the center of it all, basking in the glow, was Jareth. The snooty receptionist. Except now he had a tag on his lapel that read, *Owner & Manager.*

Rhienne grimaced to cover the cold that twisted through her. "I don't care. You've just never made me dreamwalk with someone I've met before. It feels strange."

"Your contract stipulates—"

"I am vividly aware of what my contract stipulates, thank you." She bit her tongue and softened her tone. "My apologies for thinking out loud. It won't happen again." Rhienne took his silence for satisfaction and set to work.

The easiest way to unravel a dream was from the edges, where the fabric was less realized and the threads more distinguishable. But the most magic came from unraveling it at the center. Take out the underlying support, and the rest would fall with it.

She'd done this enough times now that her voice no longer shook at the memory of the accident with her mother. Much. Besides, she couldn't see the harm in ending such a silly little dream. With the amount of trouble following her around, she'd need the power Oblivion would give her sooner rather than later.

"The wine will taste of mud, the food of ash," Rhienne began in Jareth's voice. "No matter what you do, any establishment you manage will always fail." Patrons frowned into their glasses and plates. Jareth rushed from table to table, profusely apologizing and replacing dishes, but those were even worse.

"You'll have wasted all your measly savings on what will amount to termite food. People will laugh at you. Word will spread, and you *know* reputation is everything in this industry." Using Aderai's words whipped the dream into a frenzy. The crowd pointed and jeered. Some threw food at him before slamming the door on their way out. Others simply faded away.

Jareth stood alone in a lightless room, a pitcher of sludge in one hand. The wooden floors and ceiling beams blew away to dust.

"This was a stupid idea," Rhienne said. "It's better, safer, to stay with what you know."

Like fire burning through paper, holes appeared and ate away at the dream. Perhaps this was why Oblivion had brought her here; meeting Jareth in person had made it all the easier to destroy his hope.

"This is a stupid idea," Jareth echoed. "It's never going to work. I'll never measure up to someone like Aderai." The tavern faded. As did the island, the lake, and the caldera.

"You're better off where you are," Rhienne whispered. Then Jareth was gone, and the dream with him.

She stood once more in Oblivion's shadow, in the empty space she'd made in the dream realm. He was different now, the void that made up his form almost incandescent. She'd given him the power of an ending, and now she'd receive a fraction of it.

The nascent magic hung heavy in the air. Rhienne brushed her mind against it, estimating its size. Enough for a new midrange spell, or two smaller ones. Not enough to hide from Mishara's true sight, but that wouldn't be a problem once they left Wildspire.

"I want a renewal of my previous spellcraft," she said. "And a way to travel swiftly and stealthily."

Oblivion put two hands on her upper arms, and two more on either side of her face. He pressed his forehead to hers, and the beautiful pastels of the Plane of Dreams vanished. Void wrapped around and flooded into her. What had once felt like being knocked over by a tidal wave was now a gently flowing stream of power into her body. Revitalizing, sure, but without the thrilling surge in her blood that made her feel truly *alive*. It would suffice for now. Or at least get Oblivion off her back until she reached the Collector.

She bowed deeply. "Thank you. A pleasure to serve."

He chuckled. A sound she had never heard from him before and hoped to never hear again. It set off every alarm of self-preservation she'd earned from a lifetime of running cons. But all he said was, "Until next time, then," before allowing her to fade into true, if fitful, sleep.

All too soon, an insistent nudge forced Rhienne awake. The sun had long since risen, peeking through the winter gray as if to celebrate her continued existence. She didn't feel like celebrating. More like she'd been kicked by a horse.

"We need to get moving," Echo said.

"Hnngh." Rhienne buried her face in the pillows. Oblivion tended not to be gentle when pulling her spirit through the dream realm.

"Rhi, look at me."

Rhienne peeled herself off the bed to find Echo frowning at her. "What?"

"Are you alright? You look worse than last night."

That jolted her up. She hurried to a mirror. Her illusions were still in place, her magic replenished. It rose to her fingertips with the barest thought. But dreamwalking had taken a lot out of her—there was a glassiness to her eyes, and her limbs were heavy with fatigue.

"I saw some weird dreams. You remember how it was when we were kids." Before she'd learned to control her ability, she'd ricocheted around the plane almost every night, pulled by anyone who dreamed too loud. Working for Oblivion wasn't that bad, but it was nothing like being in control herself. She rubbed her eyes and pinched color back into her cheeks. "I'll be fine."

"If you're sure." Echo didn't look convinced, but she let it drop and stood with a spine-cracking stretch. "I'm starving."

"Me too. Let's see what fancy nonsense they have for breakfast on our way out." She dispelled the protective wards she'd put on the door and followed Echo to the lounge, her mind in a fog.

From down the hall, Aderai's voice pierced the quiet. "What are you doing here, Jareth? Yesterday was supposed to be your last day. Not that I'm upset to have more time to find a replacement."

"That won't be necessary, Exalt. I've... decided to stay."

Rhienne peered around the corner. Aderai had replaced their burgundy suit with a deep forest green ensemble. They stood behind the desk writing notes in a ledger. Jareth had just shuffled through the door, bedraggled and somber. He could not have been further from the uptight man she'd met yesterday. Nice to see she'd taken him down a few pegs.

"Ah. Well, I'm glad to hear it." Aderai snapped the book closed. "But do clean yourself up before anyone sees you."

"Of course." Jareth started to leave but paused in the center of the lobby. "Exalt?"

"Yes?"

Echo spoke into her mind, *Come on, my stomach sounds like an owlbear.* Rhienne motioned to wait. She wanted to know what would happen next.

"I—" Jareth scanned the dark wood panels, chandeliers, and frosted glass, and somehow shrank further into himself. "I look forward to working with you for a very long time."

"Likewise. Of course, now that you're staying, we'll need to schedule your performance review, and then we can speak more seriously about expansion. I finally heard back from Exalt Miravin. He has a property for sale in Port Saphrai, and we talked a bit about franchising, as long as some... other conditions are met. If all goes well, my time will be split. I'll need eyes and ears I can trust while I'm gone."

Jareth's whole demeanor changed, like he'd been lit up from the inside. "Really?"

This wasn't right. Oblivion had wanted Jareth to stay put. She normally ended dreams that were seeds of chaos—a teenager with a propensity for lighting things on fire, a spurned lover with thoughts of vengeance, even a noble with designs on the Falenoran Empire's throne, once. But a man who wanted to start his own luxury hotel? Oblivion wouldn't have asked her to dreamwalk for something so small, especially when it had immediate resolution.

Curiosity overcame wariness. She'd never talked to someone after unraveling their dream.

Rhienne hooked her arm through Echo's and pulled her into the open. "Good morning!"

"Ah, the saviors of my evening," Aderai said with a service-industry smile. They showed no signs of a hangover that Rhienne could see. Horribly unfair, the advantages of youth. "I trust you enjoyed your stay?"

"The room was absolutely divine. We forgot to ask last night: Is breakfast included?"

"For you, my dears? Of course."

"Excellent. Oh, Jareth, you poor thing. You look like you didn't sleep a wink!" Rhienne snapped her fingers, smoothing his rumpled clothes and mussed hair with a tiny spark of magic. "No nightmares of puking entertainers, I hope."

"No nightmares. No dreams either, not that it's any of your business," he said stiffly.

Fascinating. He didn't remember her interference; he didn't remember the dream at all.

Before she could pry any further, he said, "Now, if you'll excuse me, I have work to attend to." Jareth stepped around her, moving directly between her and the front windows.

Glass shattered. A fraction of a second later, an arrow punched through Jareth's throat. He gurgled, the look on his face more shock than pain, and dropped to the floor.

Rhienne registered the gleam of yellow magic on the arrowhead before it burst into flame. Her heart seized as the fire rapidly spread over Jareth's body. The Untold had tracked them down.

Chapter 8

Echo

Aderai screamed. Echo was frozen long enough for them to dash into the lounge, for horror to wash over Rhienne's face, and for figures to gather around the broken window. They wore heavy cloaks, masks, and gloves, their blades and arrows primed with lethal magic.

She grabbed Rhienne and ran for the back door. Her foresight showed the exit was clear, but it wouldn't stay that way for long.

"Wait, I have a better idea," her friend hissed as if the Untold could hear them. "We need a window. I can get us out without any chance they'll see us."

"How?"

"Just trust me!"

Echo led her back to their room, locked the door against the shouts and the scent of burning flesh, and rushed to the balcony.

Rhienne surveyed the streets below and the bare, twisting branches above. "Hold my hand and do not let go. I'm not entirely sure how this works."

The shadows on the balcony peeled off the floor and folded over them. In the dark, Echo lost her sense of gravity. There was nothing but endless black, Rhienne's fingers squeezing hers, and a creeping dread that any second the silence would start roaring in her ears, and then—

They appeared in an alley across the street from Crystal and Evergreen. Echo staggered, thankful they'd missed breakfast. Rhienne didn't look much better. Smoke was beginning to plume from the inn. Bells rang on street corners, causing servants and highborn alike to run out of buildings with buckets. Nothing to bring people together like fire in a city made of wood.

"How did they find us so quickly?" Rhienne gasped.

An excellent question, but not the first one on Echo's mind. "Where the hell was that spell yesterday?"

"It's new. I, uh, might've had a visitor last night."

"I thought you were avoiding him!"

"I was. I am. But he called on me. I had to answer. I can't say no, but I can handle him, trust me. Oblivion is..." Her last word trailed off into a whisper. "Harmless."

Echo couldn't explain that there was no *handling* the gods without getting into her own experience with Exodus, so she said, "Well, since you have it now, let's get a bit further away, shall we?"

Rhienne murmured the incantation again, but this time, when the alley's shadows swirled, they fell away without transporting the two of them.

"Did you say *Oblivion?*"

Echo recognized the voice from Rhienne's execution. The dark-haired high inquisitor appeared in the alley behind them, alone, her expression more affronted than angry. Though she had no siphoned power, sparks of a countering charm fell from her delicate fingers.

"Mishara," Rhienne said pleasantly, though her body tensed. "Fancy seeing you here."

Echo eased the mandolin off her back, cursing herself for not saving more magic from the performance last night. Best she could do was throw a distracting illusion or two and pray it was enough to interrupt the inquisitor's charm so they could teleport away.

"You made a deal. I can taste it in the air around you." Mishara's lovely face twisted in disgust. "How could you betray everything you believe in so quickly?"

"Threat of imminent death can do that to a person," Rhienne quipped.

"Imminent death?" Mishara barked a laugh. "Didn't you notice how easy it was to get away in the catacombs? The entire Untold on your tail, locator spells and all, and you slipped the net. You're not *that* clever."

Rhienne scoffed. "I'm supposed to believe you let me escape?"

Echo risked a few pianissimo notes and said through the telepathy stone, *Any time you want to leave...*

Mishara either didn't notice the music or didn't care. "Who do you think put that knife beneath the platform? I didn't want to see you die. And you repay me by spilling a secret you swore to keep—it's taking all my magic to prevent that from turning into an uproar, by the way—bargaining with a god, and running off with that *thing*? Do you know what it really is?"

"Well, that's uncalled for," Echo muttered.

"I'm well aware what *she* is, thank you," Rhienne growled. "And it's your own fault for trying to absorb the Dawnglow and make yourself divine-blooded. The inquisitors *should* be in an uproar. Talk about going against your beliefs." She reached over and touched Echo's arm. *On my mark.*

Echo strummed as quietly as she could, stopping just before magic lit up the strings.

"You know why I wanted that. You told me you'd do the same thing. All those late nights together, all the spells we made—we have a bond, Rhienne, stronger than any bargain. We understand each other like no one else does."

The sting of Rhienne's betrayal suddenly made a twisted kind of sense. That crimson cloak hid an immense amount of forbidden power. Power these two had cultivated *together.*

Anger boiled anew in Echo's chest. At Mishara for bringing Rhienne onto the destructive, horrible path of blood magic, and at Rhienne for joining in, regardless of what she'd hoped to gain from it. Anger that Echo could not displace by changing forms.

Mishara stepped forward, her voice pleading. "I haven't called the others yet. There's still a chance for you to come back and apologize. I'll even let your... infraction slide. Give it a head start on escaping." Her lips twisted as she glanced at Echo, and Echo bared her teeth. "We can forget this ever happened and return to how it used to be."

"Right. You better have some extraordinary memory modification spells at your disposal if that's going to work out." Rhienne squeezed Echo hard. *Now!*

One final chord, and a shower of blue sparks erupted from the mandolin. Echo willed them toward Mishara, stinging her eyes and face and interrupting whatever she'd been about to say. The inquisitor yelped in surprise, and her concentration broke.

Shadows swallowed them. Again and again, they leapt to the furthest visible point until they reached the edge of the city. Echo was beyond ready to leave this place, but looking back at the smoke and chaos, some lingering part of Natalia spared a thought for Sidrin. She was glad he was far from this new disaster. Silly to think about him at all, never mind worry or even *miss* him. She brushed those clinging cobwebs off once they teleported down to the forest floor.

Rhienne sagged against a tree. "All right. Should've been. More specific about... my spell request. Let's walk for a while. I don't know if I have the stomach to do that too many more times."

Agreed, Echo said telepathically. Opening her mouth right now seemed like a bad idea. Repetition hadn't made the darkness any more bearable, and she wasn't sure what other tirade might come out.

They picked their way through what ferns and needle-like bushes survived the winter until Wildspire was lost from view. Hunched against the cold, their breath clouded in front of them and soon grew heavy with exertion. Echo repeatedly checked over her shoulder for movement between the trees or hints of magic in the air. Though there were no signs of pursuit, she couldn't shake the feeling they were being watched. The forest was too quiet, everything but their footsteps muffled by the snow. Rhienne was uncharacteristically close-lipped too.

Someone had to say something, or Echo was going to burst. "That was another close call," she said when they stopped for a break. "Kind of lucky Jareth was there this morning."

"Yeah. Lucky."

"Do you... want to talk about it? Or Mishara?"

"What's there to talk about?" Rhienne took a long drink from her waterskin. "Mishara was a means to an end."

Echo leaned against a tree, grounding herself with the roughness of the bark. "It doesn't seem like she felt that way."

"Well, she's deluded. She wanted to turn herself into an immortal. Not an original idea. Dawnglow would work for a while, but her body would filter out the divinity eventually, and then she'd either end up glowing like the rest of the Untold, or age would catch up with her all at once."

She sounded like she was repeating a classroom lesson. Mishara had said Rhienne understood the desire for immortality. Surely Rhienne hadn't tried it herself. Although, considering her illusions hid her age... "How do you know that?" Echo asked.

"Oblivion told me. You're either divine or you're not, and even within divinity, there are rules. You couldn't become an immortal, for example. An immortal couldn't become a mimic. I could never be anything but a dreamwalker. Magic can't change your inherent nature." Rhienne shrugged. "I suppose he could've been lying." Despite her nonchalance, a shadow passed over her face at the idea, but she waved the conversation away. "Let me see Aderai's directions."

Echo withheld the paper. Rhienne tended to get churlish if pushed too hard, and the last thing Echo wanted was a return fire of questions, but unease sat low in her belly. The idea of people trying on divine power like an outfit when it was something she was hunted for, something the world looked at with suspicion and hatred... it opened that hollow place in her again.

Her voice came out much smaller than she liked when she asked, "Did you start it, or did Mishara?"

"You'll need to be a tad more specific." Rhienne crossed her arms.

"Playing with blood magic. Was it your idea, or were you following along?"

"Mishara started it, though I don't see why it matters. The only people we were hurting were ourselves, and all I wanted was to bring Vala back. Wouldn't you do whatever it took if it was someone you cared about?"

No. Echo did not doubt Rhienne would do anything for her. But she'd never had to wear Echo's skin, never had to prove she was more than a spy, or a thief, or a killer, or try to captivate people with her music on the off chance they could learn to love her too. There were lines

Echo could not cross, secrets she couldn't risk telling, if she wanted to live. She didn't know how to explain this to Rhienne, who mesmerized everyone she met—including crazy, blood-wielding inquisitors—and believed magic was as vital as air.

So Echo murmured, "I suppose you're right," and when Rhienne turned away, she briefly mimicked Natalia to store this newest discomfort with the rest.

The further east they went, the rockier the terrain became, slowing their pace and consuming too much focus for conversation. It was midafternoon by the time they reached the foothills, and though a dark cloud remained over Rhienne, Echo was beginning to hope. Maybe the Collector really could help her. Being able to sing again would make everything better. That must have been why her performance at Crystal and Evergreen fell flat: she wasn't using her preferred medium. Those songs were meant to be played with lyrics. Illusions weren't nearly as powerful as words.

They crested a hill to find the valley below full of wildwood trees, their black bark split by fragments of captured lightning that threw strange, flickering shadows across the ground.

"This is it," Rhienne said. "The entrance should be here somewhere."

According to Aderai's directions, the path to the Collector was hidden by a powerful illusion. That much magic always left traces, if one knew how to look. Echo followed Rhienne into the valley, scanning the trees and the scorched earth between them. The more she searched, the more she found her eyes skipping over one particular spot.

"Look over there." Echo pointed, straining to focus on one of the tree trunks. The bark was patterned like wallpaper, too uniform to be natural, and the lightning within crackled in precise time intervals. She approached and made to press her hand to the trunk. It passed straight through. "Think we found it." Echo grinned at Rhienne and stepped into the illusion.

Her foot never found the ground. She tipped forward and flailed for something solid.

Rhienne grabbed her and hauled her back from the edge, obviously trying not to laugh.

"Oh, that's funny, is it?" Echo put her hands on her hips, which only made Rhienne laugh harder. The storm-cloud had broken. Once Echo's heart was beating normally again, she cracked a smile. She never had been able to stay angry with Rhienne.

"Sorry, sorry," Rhienne wheezed. "I'm not laughing at you. That just reminded me of that stunt we pulled on the guards in Hearthglen. You remember the portable hole?"

Oh, gods. How could she forget? They'd been so pissed. They could never prove it was her and Rhienne moving it around their patrol route, though. "It took, what, three or four of them falling in before they learned to watch where they stepped?"

"And then they were paranoid for weeks! Best thing we could've filched from that carnival."

"I don't know. I seem to remember you being sweet on one of the acrobats."

"Can you blame me? I'd never seen anyone as flexible as her." Rhienne sighed and collected herself. "Simpler times. Anyway." She broke off a branch from a nearby tree and poked at the illusion-covered hole. "Some entrance. I was picturing a tower, or a museum, or... I don't know. Not a hovel in the middle of nowhere."

"There's no security either. Strange for someone who's supposed to be so powerful." Echo checked their surroundings and saw nothing unusual. "I still feel like we're not alone."

Rhienne gave a noncommittal, "Hmm," but glanced nervously at the elongating shadows. "Not much daylight left. Best get inside, eh?"

With more purpose and care this time, Echo found the edge of the hole. It led to a slanted tunnel, too steep to climb down with any sort of dignity. "Bombs away," she said, and slid down into the dark.

Chapter 9

Echo

Echo jarred her hip and elbow against the rocky sides of the tunnel before it spat her out into a large cavern. Two torches flanked another passage on the far side, illuminating the smooth stone floor and a ceiling peppered with stalactites. Wincing, she hobbled out of the way in time for Rhienne to emerge and land, graceful as anything, aided by a gentle, magical breeze.

Echo frowned. "Shouldn't you be saving that for emergencies?"

Rhienne waved her off. "It's nothing."

"It's not nothing. We don't know how the Untold tracked us so quickly, and we don't know when Oblivion will call on you again. We can't be frivolous with our resources."

"Yeah, yeah, all right. When did you get all responsible on me?"

"When being irresponsible started hurting longer." Echo walked further into the room, rubbing her aching hip for emphasis. Her footsteps were loud—too loud for the size of the space—reverberating off the walls more times than they should have.

"Wait!" Rhienne cried. Echo froze. "Don't move. Look at the floor."

It was too dim to make out details, but she trusted whatever Rhienne had seen. Echo waited while her friend dropped onto all fours, crept forward, then stuck her head into apparently illusory ground.

"It's a bridge!" she gasped and popped upright again. "Over a pit. Most likely with sharp rocks at the bottom. Fucking illusions! Aderai could've warned us about this."

"It is not their fault you came in the back door." The voice that echoed across the cavern was age-roughened and prim, not far off from some of the patrons at Crystal and Evergreen, but the creature it belonged to was anything but human.

He was bipedal, with the legs of a raptor. Wicked talons and a scaly tail scraped the ground. His torso was covered in green and white fur, and he had a rabbit-like head with tusks protruding from his lower jaw.

Echo barely kept her mouth from falling open as she drank him in. "Are you the Collector?"

He sprang over to them, crossing the cavern in a single leap, and studied them with iridescent emerald eyes. Light and dark green swirls decorated his chest and shifted with his movement, like the underside of a forest canopy blowing in the wind. "That depends. Are you still of the opinion that this is a hovel in the middle of nowhere?"

"Did I say that?" Rhienne laughed like it was a long-time joke between them. "What I meant was 'deeply impressive, mystical cave system.' Towers are so passé, aren't they? It's nice to see a fresh take."

He didn't smile, but his long ears tilted to the side, and his tail stopped twitching. "Then yes, I am the Collector. Follow me and tell me what I can do for you. Please, step exactly where I step. I would hate to lose perspective clients to carelessness."

"You mean prospective," Rhienne corrected.

"That too. Though I believe your geometrical relation is more in question than whether you will accept my services. No one ever comes to see me by accident, even if they accidentally come in the wrong door. Quickly now, before the bridge rearranges."

"Our geometric—before the bridge does *what?*"

"Just do what he says," Echo whispered, her heart already pounding. She didn't think this being was a creation of Exodus's or Oblivion's, and definitely not Reckoning's. Perhaps Harvest, given the coloring. If that were the case, they needed to tread carefully. Harvest was as variable as the seasons, sowing bounty with one hand and reaping chaff with the other. There were only so many things left for Echo to give up in a deal, minor or otherwise.

When they finished crossing the bridge, Echo swore the cavern sighed. It could've been the wind, or another piece of magic, but the sound was so *human*. She shivered but didn't turn around. Then they passed the threshold where the torches were lit, and there was no room in her mind for anything but the sight before her.

The Collector crossed a translucent floor to a large crescent-moon desk. The walls were covered in shelves that extended up and down into the gloom. Each cubby contained a vial full of glowing liquid, no two of which were the same color. Vibrant magenta to pale yellow to a blue so deep it was almost black—every shade and saturation, casting the room and the Collector in an eerie rainbow.

"Welcome to my vault. We will discuss what you wish to gain from me here. That" —he pointed with his tail at the cavern they'd come from— "is where we perform the ritual to extract your payment."

Rhienne gave the walls an unimpressed once-over. "Which is what, exactly?"

"That depends on you. Equal trade is the most basic law of magic, but I don't have to tell you that, do I?" His nose twitched as if smelling something foul. "I am nothing if not fair."

"We're looking for information," Echo said. "I need directions to a... certain library."

"Surely you could consult a map for such a thing?"

"If it were on this plane, I would." How much should she tell him? She wanted to make sure he could provide what she needed without giving too much away. "I believe it's in a pocket realm. I've been there once but haven't been able to track it down again."

"How wonderfully vague," he mused. "Is there anything else you can tell me about this library?" When Echo hesitated, he pressed, "If I don't have the information you seek on hand, I can find it. But only if you give me some-thing to go on."

The eerie light took on a mesmerizing quality, and the Collector himself softened to something less alien. Despite the persistent feeling of being watched prickling down Echo's back and the Collector's many dangerous features—claws, tusks, and a hungry glint in his slitted pupils—she *wanted* to confide in him.

"It was built into the roots of a tree," she said slowly. "At least the ceiling was made of roots, and much of the walls and floor were dirt." That was what had led her to Wildspire in the first place, but all its libraries were in the branches. "And everything was really, really old. I never saw anyone else."

"Is that all?"

"I... thought maybe..." Echo blinked, lost in the Collector's glowing green eyes. Why was she being so reticent? This creature was only trying to help. "Maybe it belonged to Horizon."

One ear twitched. "Hmm. Fascinating." He turned to Rhienne. "And you?"

Rhienne's mask slipped a little, and she shifted un-comfortably. "I'm looking for a path to the lowest cost way to perform a resurrection. Whether that's where to find Dawnglow, how to travel to the Plane of the Dead, or something else entirely."

The Collector hummed again, considering. "Yes, I can help you both. But such complex requests will require some rearranging on your part. Too much tangled up be-tween you for my magic to do its work. So I'll need you to fix my bridge."

"Fix your bridge?" Echo frowned. "What's wrong with it?"

"It appears to be sulking. Temperamental things, bridges. Vastly underappreciated, considering the amount of effort they allow us to forgo. But a good truth will draw it out of hiding, and fix your own geometrical relation. Does that sound fair?"

Rhienne's expression went blank. "And what exactly is a 'good truth'?"

"The beginning of all our dreams, lies, and hopes." He waved theatrically at their surroundings. "A good truth is the very root of all we are, buried under a mountain of unturned soil, untold potential."

"Do you ever speak plainly?" Rhienne said.

The Collector sighed. "A secret, my dear. One from each of you should do the trick." He swung his snake-like stare to Echo. "These are my terms. Do we have a deal?"

Whatever fog he'd cast over her broke. Echo's insides squirmed, afraid she'd already said too much, as she examined all the secrets stored on his shelves.

Too much tangled up between you. Did he know about Echo's lie the night before? There had to be something else she could reveal instead, some other secret that wouldn't unearth so much of both their pain. She had to think of something. Returning to Wildspire was out of the question, and they had no other leads.

Echo looked at Rhienne, who nodded once. Together, they said, "We accept."

The deal wrapped around her heart, tighter than any pact she'd formed since the one with Exodus. It stole her breath, but the Collector gave them no time to recover.

"Excellent." He clapped his paws twice. There was a tug on the thread in Echo's chest, then reality tessellated around her. When the lines of all the polygons disappeared, she found herself back in the cavern on a rocky ledge. Across a chasm too deep to see the bottom, Rhienne clung to her own patch of safety. The rest of the floor, both real and illusory, was gone.

The Collector hovered in the air between them, calmly seated on his coiled tail as if it were a stool. "I should warn you, this bridge has very little patience for falsehood. A good snack can fix its mood just as well as a truth. Tick tock." With that, he blinked out of existence.

"What the hell?" Rhienne yelled, a flush creeping up her neck. "If I ever see Aderai again, I'm going to wring their stupid neck and steal all their outfits."

"Can you teleport us out of here if things get snacky?" Echo asked, not daring to raise her voice too high. Some of the stalactites were cracked, poised to fall at any moment.

"I have to see where I'm going. I could get over to you, but we'd be stuck anyway. I could try—" she reached for her belt, but her knife was missing. Echo's mandolin was also gone.

"No cheating." The Collector's voice shook the cavern.

Echo crouched for balance, her heart in her throat. Small rocks tumbled from her ledge. If they hit the bottom, it was too far to hear. "That's fine. This is fine."

She didn't sound half as reassuring as she wanted. Under normal circumstances, this *should* be fine. Friends told each other secrets all the time, and she and Rhienne were practically sisters. But these circumstances had never been acquainted with the word 'normal.' There was too much she'd lied about or talked around, too much she'd risk by telling the truth.

Echo searched her mind for something, *anything*, other than what loomed at the forefront. "How do we know if a secret is good enough to qualify?"

Rhienne had hunkered down for the quake. She picked up a loose stone to worry between her hands and straightened warily. "Seems rather subjective, if you ask me. How many tries do you think we have?"

"I'd rather not find out the hard w—"

"Remember that windup airship Dad made for you when we were kids? I told you it went missing, but I broke it by accident and threw it away so you wouldn't be mad at me."

Echo held her breath, but nothing happened. "Why did you do that? We could've fallen to our deaths!"

"It's an unspoken truth. I'm limit testing!"

"Hardly a secret, though. You were a terrible liar back then."

Rhienne crossed her arms. "Well, you try then. Pick something you haven't told me."

There was a mountain to choose from, all of them impossible to speak. Rhienne would hate her. Or think she was a fool, which might be worse. Her friend didn't suffer fools. As she'd done with Mishara, Rhienne played with them and tossed them out when their usefulness was spent. A skill Echo had once envied.

The cavern shook again, but this time, it wasn't the Collector's voice that caused it; an inch of each of their ledges crumbled away. Rhienne yelped, and Echo pressed herself against the wall.

Tick tock, he'd said. She took it back. This sadistic creature could absolutely be one of Exodus's creations. "I think it's time-based as well," she squeaked.

"Brilliant," Rhienne said, her face pale.

Think, think, think. Her foresight didn't show her dying in this pit yet, so there had to be some way out that didn't involve her avalanche of failures. "Okay, okay, I have one. I think part of the reason Exodus was so pissed when I left was because we were sort of... together. For a bit."

Rhienne waited for the bridge to crumble, like it was a lie, or a joke. When it didn't, she went bug-eyed. "*You slept with a god?*" she squawked. "And you didn't think that was necessary information?"

"It wasn't relevant!" Echo held her breath, watching for something *good* to happen to the bridge, but apparently that secret wasn't strong enough. "It didn't mean anything anyway. I was just using him to get some magic."

"*Liar, liar,*" something low and predatory growled deep in the chasm, and another chunk of their ledges broke off.

"What?" Echo shouted at the air. Her toes brushed the edge of the void. "That was true!"

Rhienne had her eyes closed, and her legs were shaking. "Okay. No more guessing. This guy wants something deep? Here: the service I did for Oblivion last night was to unravel Jareth's dream. He was only at Crystal and Evergreen this morning because of me. It's my fault he took that arrow." She looked around expectantly, and when nothing happened, shouted, "Oh, come on, that was a good one!"

Echo thought so too. And it explained Rhienne's mood earlier. Remembering Exodus's temper and the nature of his contracts, she asked, "You said you couldn't refuse if Oblivion called on you. Is that true?"

"It's as good as." Rhienne put on that careful, blank expression again. If this was what she felt like dealing with Echo's secrecy, no wonder she hated it.

"What does that mean?"

"It doesn't matter. I've got it handled."

Even before another quake rocked the cavern and another piece of her ledge fell into the chasm, Echo could hear the lie in her friend's voice. The doubt. There was barely enough room for both her feet now. "If you're worried about not having magic, we did just fine with the enchanted items we stole when we were kids. We can always go back to that."

"Just fine?" Rhienne's nose scrunched up, and she shook her head. "Why are you okay with 'just fine'? Being responsible is one thing, but since when have you settled down and stopped fighting? What happened to you?"

She stopped short of saying 'nothing.' Her balance wasn't good enough to stand on one foot this high up. But Rhienne's accusation struck too close, and Echo blurted out, "The gods happened. Magic happened. You can try to manipulate them all you like, but they'll always find a way to exact their price."

Rhienne's eyebrows drew together. "You said Exodus cheated you."

This was horrible. They never should've come. The darkness below swam like it might reach up and grab her. Couldn't Rhienne's secret come first? Why did it have to be her?

Warm, wet air blew across her face like the breath of a hungry beast, and her foresight rose in the back of her mind. No longer a peaceful, lonely death, but a long, dark, stomach-churning fall.

She had to get a grip. Dying here in obscurity was not an option. One good truth. Just one, just enough to appease the Collector and his stupid bridge and survive. "Exodus didn't cheat me; I cheated him. Or tried to. I asked for a path to fame, and he gave me a way to see where my choices would lead me. Then I made sure I couldn't pay the price. That's why he took my singing away."

Rhienne's guard lowered but didn't drop completely. There was no quake. There was also no bridge that emerged. Rhienne's voice was a whisper, but Echo heard it loud and clear. "What was the price?"

Echo stared down into the chasm, waiting, praying, but it seemed only the root of the matter would suffice. Without intending to, she found herself mimicking Natalia's body, a more fitting shell for her wretchedness. The sorrow, guilt, and anger she'd carefully packed into this form returned, but overlaying it all was fear. Time and again since starting her journey alone, she'd learned that revealing too much, making too many waves, saying anything but exactly what someone wanted to hear meant getting pushed away.

If she lost Rhienne's friendship, her trust, was it worth saving their lives?

She fixed her gaze on the little remaining ground. "I swear, I never intended to pay the price," Echo choked out. "First thing I did was find a surgeon who would operate on a mimic so it would never happen, even by accident."

She couldn't say the rest out loud. Not with the darkness looming below. Not when Rhienne's mother had used the same bargaining chip, and the pain it caused Rhienne had led her to Oblivion, the Untold, and blood magic. So Echo lifted her shirt, revealing the ugly, twisting scar across her abdomen, which followed her in every form she took. Such a simple bargain: her fame for her firstborn. One kind of legacy for another.

"It's called a total hysterectomy. I never wanted a child anyway. I thought I was being clever. But Exodus found out, and..." It had taken two months to recover from the surgery. Two months during which she hadn't even gotten to enjoy her path before Exodus swooped in and removed another, far more vital component. "I should've told you, but I... I was afraid of what you'd think of me."

The words hung in the air like physical things, humming with electricity, or maybe magnetism, because slabs of rock slowly, silently lifted from the gloom. They formed a pathway from her ledge to the middle of the cavern. Nothing supported them; they just hung there, waiting. Echo waited too, unable to peel herself from the wall, braced for Rhienne's reaction.

Chapter 10

Rhienne

Rhienne was dizzy. Not because of the yawning pit, although that certainly didn't help. She kept seeing the shock on Jareth's face as he died, the hurt and sorrow on her mother's as she unraveled, and now, her only friend in the world, curled over in a body she hated as if she could disappear by making herself small.

"You... were afraid of me? Is this because of Mishara? I told you—"

"No. The stuff with the Untold is shitty, but I know you don't believe anything they say." Echo let her shirt fall and wrapped her arms around her torso. "After what you said about your mom—that must've hurt, to be abandoned, then to find out it was all part of some *plan.* I did the same thing, just a few steps earlier." Somehow her voice got even smaller. "And I couldn't bear it if... I don't have much more to lose, Rhi. I don't want you to hate me."

Rhienne could count on one hand the number of times in her life she'd been struck speechless. This one beat all the rest. There was a roiling storm of emotion in her chest that had her clinging to the rocky wall for stability. Though part of the bridge had formed between them, the distance seemed greater than before. She blinked against a stinging in her eyes.

"Echo, I—what happened with my mom was an accident. Not a day goes by that I don't regret it. I was angry, but I'd never, *ever* hurt you. And the fact that you thought I'd *hate* you?" That was a wound far, far deeper than anything else Echo had said.

"How could you not? If the deal I made wasn't bad enough, I also *failed*. You've always been the one with a plan. No matter the consequences, you can always find another mark to chase, another loophole to wriggle through."

"Not this time." Rhienne could feel it even now. Underneath the thread of their deal with the Collector, her other pact was a cold and constant chain. The weight of Oblivion's gaze hadn't lifted since the dream in Wildspire. A shudder ran through her. "My dreamwalking isn't the only thing I sold to Oblivion. He owns my soul. If my mother can't help me break this contract, I'm his forever. So if you want to talk about failure, you're in good company."

Echo was finally looking at her again, her expression dazed as the reasoning behind Rhienne's desperate actions fell into place, but she said nothing. At least they were even on the speechless front. They remained frozen as Rhienne's half of the bridge formed. Echo was still mimicking Natalia's form, and Rhienne felt too raw, too fragile to move, knowing that was her fault. How many times had Echo hidden her true feelings, afraid of what Rhienne would do?

The Collector popped into existence, making them both flinch. "Wonderful job. I only doubted you for a moment." With a flick of his tail, two glass bottles appeared.

Rhienne hadn't noticed before, distracted by her own thoughts, but a cloud of misty light had formed above each of them. Echo's was a brilliant cerulean. Hers was an inky black, even darker than the surrounding darkness of the cave. The mists funneled into the bottles, and the Collector hummed contentedly as he twisted the caps closed.

Emerald eyes regarded them, still motionless on their opposing walls. "You mortals get so fussy with your secrets. Can hardly expect bargains to make you comfortable, can you. Let us return to my vault for your payment."

His tail sliced through the air, creating a warping line like a wave of heat. He pushed the bottles into it, and they disappeared. Between one blink and the next, the three of them appeared back in the vault, all his collected truths glowing brighter as if to welcome the new arrivals.

"Give me just a moment." The Collector bent under the desk and stood up with a crystal orb between his paws. When he looked into it, the color of his eyes changed from green to orange to purple, then flicked between shades faster and faster until they blurred together. Light flared in erratic patterns along the walls of glowing bottles, matching his eyes.

He was searching through his collection for the information they sought.

The shifting colors froze on blinding white. Whatever the Collector saw made him wince. "That library does not belong to Horizon."

Echo's brows drew together. "Then whose is it? Another god? Someone like you?"

"Another god. But who, I cannot say. They were exiled, and their name—their very existence—was erased."

Rhienne's thoughts spun. She'd never heard of an exiled god, but she supposed that was the point of erasure. If the Collector was telling the truth, there were six gods—five still living. Another being to bargain with, and perhaps one whose domain aligned more with her needs. They must've done something pretty powerful, not to mention royally pissed off *someone*, to be wiped from history. She'd wager that put them on the same side.

Echo chewed her lip and asked, "How are we supposed to contact a god without knowing their name?"

There was a sizzling pop, and he flinched away from the orb with a hiss. "I apologize. The answers that you want are... unavailable."

"But we did what you asked!" Echo protested. "You're bound by our deal to—"

"Do not preach to me of laws that were written when you were but a speck of dust in the cosmos. It is not that I won't tell you, it is that I *can't* tell you. That distinction is significant."

Gone was the ancient, mercurial creature. The Collector sounded like a harried shopkeeper, eager for them to leave so he could move on to more important work.

Why the sudden hurry? It wasn't like he had customers lining up at the door.

Before Rhienne could question him, he became absorbed in the crystal again, searching until his irises settled into the colors of a sunrise. Her breath caught, and her suspicion evaporated. Those were the colors of Dawnglow.

"You can find what you seek by traveling to Hearthglen. In fact, you both can."

"Hearthglen?" Echo groaned.

"You've got to be kidding me," Rhienne said flatly. The constriction of the pact around her heart released. No matter how unsatisfactory the answer, their bargain was fulfilled.

His eyes returned to their usual green, and he put the orb away. "Circumstances of truths are funny enough on their own. I dare not add to the comedy. Now, is there anything else I can do for you?"

"No, I think we're—" Rhienne didn't get to finish the sentence. The Collector clapped his paws together, and she and Echo appeared at the top of the valley, blinking against golden light as the sun crept over the hills. Gods, they'd spent the entire night down in that cave. A blink later, their belongings appeared before them in a neat pile.

There was no sound other than the crackle of lightning trapped in the wildwood trees, the air heavy and still despite the briskness of the morning.

Rhienne shivered and couldn't entirely blame it on the cold. Disquiet had settled between her and Echo. "Are you going to change back?"

"Oh." Echo looked down at Natalia's body. "Right." Blue shimmered over her skin, and she became the dancer again, but without the same confidence as before.

"We should make camp. Eat. Get some rest."

Echo didn't move. "And pretend none of that happened?"

If only it were that easy. Rhienne had questions now, though, that begged and clawed for answers. Questions that reminded her of Vala dissolving into a cloud of pastel dust. "No. I want to talk... if you want to. But I desperately need some food first."

After a long, searching pause, Echo said, "All right. I'll get some firewood."

They picked a spot beneath a rocky outcropping about a mile from where the Collector had dropped them. Oblivion's gaze on Rhienne seemed to lessen the farther she moved from the cave, but she couldn't find it in herself to keep going. She really was starved, not to mention sleep deprived, and there was an ache in her that no salve or bandage could mend.

Echo stared forlornly at their pile of sticks. "You don't happen to have any matches, do you?"

"Haven't had to use a match in years." Rhienne paused before tapping into the well of power from Oblivion's bargain. "Is this important enough to use magic?" Echo rolled her eyes. Rhienne took that as a 'yes' and snapped her fingers. The wood hissed and burst into purple flames. It gave off much more warmth than light, and no smoke at all. Convenient and practical.

"Okay, that's pretty nice," Echo grumbled.

"If you're wondering whether or not it's worth my soul..." Rhienne sighed. "I used to believe it was. I don't know anymore."

Echo sat beside her and parceled out some of their stolen travel rations. They ate quietly for a moment, watching the fire, before she said, "We never should've split up."

"We had different paths to follow. You needed a place that was rich in art, and I needed a place rich in riches. But we both ended up in Wildspire; that can't have been a coincidence. Great minds, and all. Time hasn't made us *total* strangers to each other." When Echo didn't respond, the cold air leached straight into Rhienne's bones. "Has it?"

"It might have," Echo whispered. She cast a furtive glance at Rhienne. "You're sure you're not mad at me?"

She wanted to say she could never be. But after what she'd done to her mother, to Jareth... well, why *wouldn't* Echo doubt her? They'd always had each other's backs, no matter what, and gods, she wanted that safe haven again. Even if she wasn't worthy of it.

"I'm not mad," Rhienne said. "It's horrible you felt like you had to do that. The gods play with us, taking and taking until you're backed into a corner and give up everything you have, plus some things you don't. That was why I turned to blood magic with Mishara. That's the whole point of all this—to free ourselves and get what we deserve. It just breaks my heart that you didn't trust me with the truth until it was our literal lives on the line."

"I've been hiding myself for so long. I've forgotten what it's like to not need to. Can you give me time to remember?"

The ache didn't go away, but it eased a little. Rhienne crushed Echo in a hug. "Of course. And I'm so, so sorry for everything. But especially for making you feel like you needed to hide. I don't want to lose you either."

Echo made a sound of profound relief and hugged her back. She kept her face buried in Rhienne's shoulder until her tears were spent and her breath had evened. When she pulled away, wiping her eyes, she said, "You were right. In the cave. There was a point where I did give up."

"You don't have to," Rhienne said, even though she was desperately curious.

"I do. It might help us figure out what to do next. And I... I want to talk like we used to. I just need you to understand why that's more difficult now than it's ever been." Echo leaned forward, elbows on her knees, and plucked a twig from the grass. She broke it into small pieces as she talked, tossing them into the fire. "That portal to the library didn't randomly appear. It came before I made my deal with Exodus. When I couldn't see another way forward except to... *not* go forward."

"Gods, Echo," Rhienne breathed. Her friend was the steady one, the one who'd always known what she wanted in life. Echo's music had shown Rhienne there was wonder and beauty and adventure to be had, and they could take it if they wanted. The idea of Echo just *not being* anymore was incomprehensible. "You should've used the bracelet. I would've been there in an instant."

"I didn't feel important enough to bother you." Echo shook her head, blinking hard. "I thought being hated would be the worst thing I could experience, but complete and utter indifference was worse. I've had to become so many different people since then, trying to balance the right amount and right kind of attention. Wildspire was the longest I'd stayed anywhere by a long shot." She sighed and wiped her eyes. "I don't know what wanting to give up says about the exiled god's domain, or how we're supposed to contact them again if we can't get more information."

For once, Rhienne sat with Echo's words for a minute before responding. "First of all, don't you ever, ever think that. You have always been and will always be important to me." It was easy to say when they were younger and their biggest worry had been evading the consequences of pranking the town guards. This time, Rhienne felt the weight of everything they carried. She meant it down to her soul.

Echo cracked the tiniest smile.

"Secondly, my mom was looking for whoever had helped create the loophole in her bargain, but she couldn't get in contact. When I pressed her about it, she got confused. Couldn't tell me anything—not a name, or what sort of entity they were. That sounds related, doesn't it?"

"Could be," Echo mused. She abandoned her twig in favor of watching the play of the sun through the rustling pines. "Maybe that's what the Collector meant by both of us finding what we need in Hearthglen. There could be a clue there about this exiled god's name. There could even be Dawnglow for a resurrection. Or one could help us find the other."

"In a backwater swamp? I find that hard to believe... though I suppose the deal prevented him from lying. And the color of his eyes was unmistakably the same as Horizon's blood." The weight of Oblivion's attention returned with a sudden, uncomfortable squeezing in her chest. Rhienne rubbed her sternum, wondering if the exiled god's erasure extended to the minds of their siblings. Her search could be dangerous for a number of reasons, least of which being Oblivion's reaction to her trying to weasel out of their pact. "Regardless, we're certainly not repeating your method of contact."

"Then it sounds like we need to find a way home." Echo pursed her lips. "They won't be happy to see us."

She was right. They'd parted on less than pleasant terms with their hometown. Even if they went in disguise, Hearthglen was small, secluded. Outsiders were easy to spot and generally treated with distrust. But Rhienne didn't have the capacity to plan just now.

"We'll cross that bridge when we get there," she said. They shared a shudder at the mention of bridges, and then a chuckle. Though they each had burdens to carry, it felt as if the remaining tension between them cleared. Rhienne resolved not to be the cause of any more of it.

Echo heaved a sigh. "To a port, then? We'll have to scrounge up enough money for passage on a ship."

"There'll be no scrounging if I have anything to say about it." Rhienne fished in her bag for the pouch of goodies she'd nicked from the drunk patrons of Crystal and Evergreen. Rings, brooches, coins, even a couple raw gems. It felt a bit dirty to use it, but if it was her and Echo against the world, they couldn't afford to be delicate. "We're going to travel in style."

Chapter 11

Rhienne

Rhienne had lots of reasons to maintain her illusions, the main one being it made life *so much* easier. Doors flew off their hinges when a young, wealthy woman asked to open them. With Echo acting as her maidservant and jewels flashing on her fingers, they hitched a ride with a trade caravan for a couple of weeks and breezed their way into Port Saphrai. Here, they were just two travelers among the bustle and merchant ships. No questions, no angry ex-lovers. Only the distant weight of a watchful god's gaze.

The town was built up along steep hillsides overlooking a river delta, its brightly painted houses held up by rickety wooden scaffolding that seemed one storm short of toppling inward. It had looked that way fifteen years ago and it was still standing, so she wasn't too worried.

As they walked along the canal toward the harbor, Rhienne couldn't help feeling nostalgic. "Feels like a lifetime since we were here, doesn't it?"

Echo looked every part the wide-eyed tourist, taking in the city and scanning its inhabitants for new forms to take on. "Two country girls in their first big city. Why didn't we stay here longer?"

"I recall getting tired of smelling like fish and salt. Also our sleight of hand wasn't so practiced yet."

"Oh, right. You got chased out of half the bars on High Street."

"And you were banned from the other half for playing with loaded dice."

"Please." Echo scoffed. "One in five of the sorry saps in this town play with loaded dice. I got banned because, even when I lost, I somehow ended up with the pot anyway, and I wasn't good at hiding it."

Rhienne bit back a cackle. As she recalled, that 'somehow' usually involved Echo changing forms and charming her way into the winner's room for the night. In the morning, they'd wake up with an empty bed and emptier pockets.

They passed beneath the aforementioned High Street—a bridge of land far above the river that connected the city's two main hilltops. Flowering vines and vibrant greenery draped over the sides. It stayed warm enough on the coast that plants remained in bloom through the winter, though it was noticeably cooler in the bridge's shadow.

Past High Street, the houses and shops gave way to factories and warehouses until they reached the industrial center at the docks. The harbor was bustling with people and crowded with boats preparing to sail. Rhienne breathed in the fresh sea air and watched the crying gulls circle overhead. This was the first blue sky she'd seen in weeks, and it made the things that used to irk her more beautiful.

There was no denying Port Saphrai's draw, but the real prize was the two bluestone towers flanking the mouth of the river. They rose higher than the hills, cargo and passenger elevators constantly moving up and down. Anchored at the top were some of the most marvelous pieces of enchantment Rhienne had ever set eyes on.

Airships.

When they'd first arrived here from Hearthglen, she couldn't believe something so large could stay afloat, never mind cross oceans and continents at a reliable speed. They looked just like regular ships, after all, except for the arcane engines built into the stern and the golden shimmer of magic in the sails. But then she'd seen them move, disappearing into the distance twice as fast as a water-bound ship, leaving a trail of glittering magical exhaust. Watching them come and go had been one of her favorite pastimes. She still couldn't imagine what kind of deal had to be made for one. They cost a fortune in both money and magic to build, and there were *three* of them docked here.

"Rhi, stop drooling."

"I will not. At least not until we get aboard one, and maybe not then either."

Echo rolled her eyes. "Harbormaster's office is down there. I'm going to replenish our supplies. Meet you there in twenty minutes?"

Rhienne nodded and headed toward the single free-standing structure on the docks: a patchwork of treated wood from a dozen different ships, leaning slightly from constant wind. More than a few appreciative glances were thrown her way, and she slowed from a purposeful walk into a casual sashay. A true lady wouldn't preen, but she was only human.

Inside the office was a man with a receding hairline and a perennial frown. He barely looked up before returning to the massive ledger open on his desk. "How can I help you, ma'am?"

"Miss," she corrected. "My maid and I are looking for passage to Hearthglen."

A quick glance at his papers and a bored turn of a page. "No ships sailing that way for another six weeks. Winter storms haven't cleared yet."

"Do airships not fly above the storms?"

That got his attention. He set down his pen. "They do. But not out that way. That area isn't exactly a hub for trade or travel."

"I understand, but surely there's something we can do. How much would it cost to divert the ship on the closest route?"

The harbormaster studied her jewelry and fine dress (stolen from the caravan they'd ridden into town with) before looking closer at his ledger. "Nearest to Hearthglen anyone'll get is the Vermillion Enclave at the northern edge of the continent. Diverting that far would add about nine days of travel. Extending crew pay, supplies, and a deposit in case there's any damage from traveling over dangerous skies…" He scribbled down some notes. "Forty-five hundred gold."

She covered her choke of disbelief with a polite cough and spoke through the telepathy stone. *Hey, Echo. Don't suppose you've stolen anything worth nearly five thousand gold?* Out loud, she layered her voice with honey. "All that for nine days?"

You're joking, right? Echo thought back. *Does he think because you're pretty that you can't do math?*

Probable. Or he'd sniffed out she wasn't as highborn as she looked.

"Afraid so," he said gruffly, his gaze drifting to the door behind her. "Cost of everything to do with airships is on the rise. Magical sinkholes, they are. Unless you've got some incentive to lower the price."

Rhienne relayed this to Echo, drumming her fingers against her thigh.

Could we not just go to the Enclave? Echo asked. *That would at least get us on the right continent.*

Well, of course we could, *but then we wouldn't get to impress everyone by dropping down from an airship flying over the village, would we?*

"What does a young lady like yourself want out of a place like Hearthglen?" the harbormaster pressed.

That was the sort of question she'd expected from the start. In this town, the right gossip paid almost as much as trade goods, and thanks to their visit to Crystal and Evergreen, Rhienne had the perfect story. She sighed melodramatically. "I'm afraid you have me at a disadvantage, sir. It's my betrothed, you see. They're horrible, but it's an arranged marriage, and my father would be furious to learn

I've run away—never mind if he knew my heart belonged to someone in such a... remote place. Please. Haven't you ever been in love?"

"Can't say I've had the pleasure. What was your name?"

"Miravin," she whispered the Exalt's name, eyes wide. "Penelope Miravin." His fingers twitched, but that was the only sign of recognition, so she added, "I'll do anything to get out of here."

"All right, Miss Miravin. If you'll step outside for a moment, I'll make a call to the captains' lounge and see what I can do." He bent to reach into the bottom drawer of his desk. While he rummaged through, she snuck a peek at the ledger.

There was a ship heading for Devonsfort this evening. That was twenty miles from Hearthglen; it would hardly divert the route at all.

Rhienne, we've got a problem, Echo said. *A problem with a fluorescent skeleton.*

"There it is. This will only take a moment." The harbormaster straightened, a scroll and a copper ring in his hand. The paper was thin enough that she could see the outlines of a charcoal WANTED portrait, and the ring was just like the one the Untold had given Sidrin. The hair on her arms rose. 'A call to the captains' lounge.' Was that even a thing?

She put on her best teary smile. "Thank you so much. I'll be just outside." It took all her self-restraint not to run out the door.

Echo stood in the building's shadow, clutching a bag of pilfered goods. "They've got checkpoints on all the docks with those stupid blood-tracing needles. Please tell me you got us a V.I.P. pass or a private boat or something."

"I think the harbormaster recognized me. He had sketches and a Transmitter Ring in his desk, and he lied about the available passage. The Untold are really determined to track us down."

"Shit. I knew their network had grown, but I didn't think they had factions in *all* the free territories. Can you change your illusions at all?"

"No. And I can't teleport past the checkpoint unless we get close enough to see inside the tower. Can you make us invisible like you did at Sidrin's?"

"Not enough magic left. What are we going to do?"

Four figures came out of the tower closest to them, hands and faces wrapped in cloth. No red-cloaked inquisitors, at least, but she'd bet at least one of them wore a copper ring under their glove.

"Working on it," Rhienne said through her teeth. Her hand inched toward her hidden dagger, but there were too many people around to risk using blood magic. "Ok, well, you don't look like Natalia anymore, and they haven't spotted you yet. I can keep them away from the tower while you slip by, incapacitate them, then teleport to meet you."

"You're sure?"

"I'm not putting you within spitting distance of the Untold again if I can help it. The ship on dock six should be almost ready to leave."

"Be careful," Echo said as she peeled away. Before long, Rhienne lost her in the crowd of dockworkers and merchants.

She reassembled her wide-eyed innocence, just a young woman praying for the kindness of strangers. When two of the Untold approached the office, she didn't have to fake her worry. The other two were weaving through the bustle, keeping a lookout.

"Good afternoon, Miss," the one of slighter build rasped.

The way power affected the Untolds' voices—combined with how thoroughly they covered themselves—made it hard to determine gender. Rhienne named this one Twig.

"We need to ask you a few questions," Twig said.

If they weren't arresting her on sight, they either weren't sure she was the right target, or Mishara was still covering up the details of Rhienne's betrayal. She could play along with both. "Are you the airship captains? Oh dear, the harbormaster didn't mention I'd be doing an interview."

"More like security." The larger one spoke slowly, as if carefully considering each word. She named them Stump. "Captains don't want unsavory types aboard their ships, you understand."

"Oh. Of course, of course." Rhienne brushed at the dirt on her clothes with a nervous laugh. "I promise you, my current appearance is not a reflection of my typical gentility. It's been a difficult road to get here."

"Are you traveling alone?" Twig inquired.

"Certainly not. My maid is... was around here somewhere." She stood on tiptoe to scan the crowd. *How's it going? Where are you?*

Approaching the tower, Echo said. *I mimicked that oaf from your execution; with a change of clothes, he looks enough like a laborer.*

Knowing what to look for, it was easy to spot Orik's broad back carrying sacks of grain to one of the cargo elevators. Rhienne averted her eyes, frowning at the Untold. "Such a propensity to wander, that girl. I really ought to get her a leash."

Stump revealed an obsidian needle, one gloved hand wrapped around it like it was a stake to drive into her heart. The new invention had spread further than Wildspire. Troubling.

"Oh, what's that?" She squinted at the object. Like it had at Sidrin's, there was something about the glint of the dark glass that itched at her memory.

"A simple test to prove to us who you are. Your hand, please."

They're done beating around the bush. Get a move on, she told Echo, and offered her hand with a dainty tremble.

I'm on the main floor. There's a couple more of them here watching the elevators.

The larger Untold pricked her finger, and she sucked in a breath at the sting. She'd thought herself immune to the pain of such injuries after working with Mishara for so long, but this *hurt.* Blood welled, traveling up the obsidian and then soaking in.

The needle's glint became the sparkle of stars against the void.

Oh no.

Um, Echo? Remember how you asked if I recognized the magic in the Untolds' new toys?

Yes.

Well, it looks like I'm not the only one making bargains with Oblivion.

Echo cursed poetically. *Why the hell would they do that? They clearly aren't running low on their supply of magic. And why would Oblivion be helping them?*

Not sure about the first thing. As for the second... because he's the worst?

Twig lifted a hand to their mouth, bringing Rhienne back to the present. The words were soundless, but she recognized the spark of a magical message being sent. Then Stump grabbed her arms and yanked them behind her back.

"Now hold on a minute!" Rhienne struggled against their grip, mind racing. These people had no skin in her capture, especially if Mishara was keeping secrets. "That test tells you the mimic isn't far, right? Let me go, and I'll tell you where it went."

Stump and Twig glanced at each other. She took the moment to gather her power. Shadows stretched toward her from the nearby walls.

Ready, Echo said.

The Untold's grip on her didn't lessen, but they didn't start dragging her off either. "We've got a cell with your name on it if you're lying," Twig said.

"My vision isn't as good as it used to be, but I'm pretty sure I saw the mimic go..." Rhienne looked around vaguely, as if trying to remember. "Up yours, you pieces of shit."

She slammed her heel down on Stump's toes and yanked out of their grasp right as the teleportation spell finished. Darkness folded around her, but Twig grabbed on.

They grappled blindly in the void. The Untold threw a wild punch that glanced off her jaw. Rhienne elbowed where she thought their face was, felt the crunch of bone without hearing it, and felt Twig reel back and let go.

She emerged alone at the foot of the tower and barely caught her breath before racing up the stairs into the main lobby. Stacks of cargo crowded the floor, waiting to be moved by the dozen workers who were in turn waiting for the elevators that led up to each dock. The platform for number six was almost full, and Echo—disguised as Orik—stepped on, setting down the grain she carried.

Hurry, hurry, Echo said. Three Untold stood guard around the room. It was only a matter of time before they recognized Rhienne.

There was a streak of crimson at the corner of her vision. She didn't react quickly enough to dodge it. Red web splattered over her mouth. A second tendril snaked around her midsection and pulled her behind a pallet of barrels.

"Don't scream," Mishara whispered. She was dressed in civilian clothing appropriate for the coast: billowing pants, sandals, and a cropped shirt. But where the port's denizens preferred loud prints and colors, all the fabrics were dark. Better for hiding blood stains. "These fools haven't figured out where you went yet. I'd like to keep it that way."

Of all the places Rhienne and Echo could've fled to from Wildspire, how the hell had Mishara ended up here ahead of them?

Where did you go? Echo asked, panicked.

I'll give you three guesses who just showed up.

You've got to be kidding.

Nope. Don't give yourself away just yet. Seems like she's alone.

"Hmmngh," Rhienne grunted behind her gag. She pulled at the bonds, but her arms were trapped against her torso.

"Yes, I am sorry about that, but I had to make sure you'd listen. I thought about what you said, and you're right. The other high inquisitors won't forgive you, and they won't forgive me."

Rhienne blinked owlishly. What in the cosmos was she talking about?

"I can't keep modifying their memories forever, and I certainly don't want to die when they uncover the truth. If I have to start over somewhere, I don't want to do it alone. We were a good match, once. The same ambitions, the same grudges. The same beauty." Mishara brushed her thumb over Rhienne's cheek. The web over her mouth dissolved. There was no guile in the woman's wide, green eyes as she whispered, "Run away with me."

Oh, she was *good.* Just enough truth to make it believable, plus an appeal to Rhienne's vanity. If she hadn't just connected the dots between the Untold and Oblivion—and if Echo weren't a factor—Rhienne might've been persuaded. Was Mishara aware that at least two factions of her organization were bargaining with gods? She'd been so put out by the news of Rhienne's pact, but that could've been an act too. That, or the Untold had more infighting than either of them knew.

She drew back so as not to seem too eager. "You ordered my execution. You sent your men to kill me in Wildspire."

"Under duress, darling. My position was at stake. You would've done the same. I don't expect you to trust me right away, but for now, we have the same goal: get off this blasted continent."

Rhienne let her features soften, pretending to weigh Mishara's words.

I can't just stand here much longer, Echo's thoughts broke in. *Are you coming?*

Two seconds. The longer she waited, the more cracks appeared in Mishara's plastered-on smile, revealing the irritation underneath.

"We don't have much time," Mishara urged.

"Just one thing," Rhienne said. "We're a long way from home. How did you find me?"

"A woman has to have some secrets."

"Even from me?" Rhienne said, then leaned in and kissed Mishara before she could protest again. She started soft and let it grow hungrier as Mishara's lips parted in a small gasp. Her concentration broken, the magical restraints around Rhienne's arms dissipated, and she pulled the other woman against her, fingers weaving into her hair. She caressed the hollow under Mishara's ear, then along her jaw, just the way she liked. Mishara gently bit Rhienne's lower lip, and she almost forgot herself, until her fingers found the clasp of the delicate chain around the inquisitor's neck. It was tied to something under her shirt; Rhienne could feel it digging into her chest. They pulled away from each other, breathless.

Suspicion immediately flared in Mishara's eyes. "What are you playing at?"

"Oh, nothing." *Get the lift going,* she told Echo, and tapped into the well of Oblivion's magic. *I'll be right there.* "I'm just a little hurt you used the tracking spell *I* created against me." Rhienne lifted the necklace she'd adroitly removed. A vial spun at the end of the chain, containing a thread of golden hair and a measure of dark red liquid. "Gods know when you acquired the ingredients."

Mishara lunged, crimson magic rising to her fingertips.

But Rhienne was ready. She slammed a fist into Mishara's nose, and her lovely face warped in a scream of pain and outrage.

"It's been great catching up. You might not be in as much trouble over the whole divine blood thing as you think. Seems like your buddies are in favor of getting into bed with the gods." The shock on Mishara's face *had* to be genuine. "Have fun navigating that. Ta ta." Shadows detached from the stacks of cargo and gathered around her.

The inquisitor was too stunned to stop her, to say anything at all before the darkness swallowed Rhienne. She emerged next to Echo on the platform, which was already rising off the ground.

"That's them!" one of the Untold shouted.

The three guards charged forward, Mishara staggering behind with lethal intent on her face. "Give me that," she snarled, grabbing something from a recruit and throwing her hand out. Her voice sounded inside Rhienne's skull. *You've taken everything I cared about. Now you get to see how it feels.*

Rhienne caught a glint of glass, felt the blast of a conjured wind, both too fast for her to react. Echo—standing near the lever, totally exposed—stumbled.

A long, black needle protruded from her thigh.

"Wait," Rhienne said, but as the lobby disappeared from view, Echo grabbed the needle and yanked it out. She expected a gout of blood to follow. There wasn't even a drop.

Echo started to smile. It froze halfway through, then twisted into a grimace. Her whole body shuddered, the faint glimmer of her mimicry flashing over her skin once, twice, then rapid-fire, the features of a dozen people swirling together.

"Echo?" Rhienne clambered over the cargo to a patch of empty space, inches from the stone walls passing by. "What's happening? Can you hear me?"

I can't feel my legs. The thought was labored and wracked with pain.

She caught Echo mid-fall, held her while she shuddered again and again. Rhienne had never felt so helpless. "What the hell was on that needle?"

Don't worry. I'm not going to die.

"I wasn't worried about that, but I am now!"

*Untold will want me alive. Just a bit... paralyzed, I think. I—*pain seared across the rest of Echo's thought, making her eyes—one brown, one blue—go glassy. *Going to try to mimic... someone you can carry... before I get stuck.*

With excruciating slowness, Echo shrunk in her arms, taking the form she'd favored as a child—a dark mop of hair that hung in her eyes, and a face covered in freckles. Rhienne wrapped her in a cloak in case she couldn't hold the shape. Her heart beat a furious rhythm as they drew closer to the light at the top of the elevator shaft. Mishara hadn't followed them, and based on the argument filtering up from the lobby, she wasn't going to. Good riddance.

"Still with me?" Rhienne kept saying.

And Echo responded, *I'll be fine.*

It didn't allay Rhienne's panic at all; that was just what you said in these situations. "How do you know that?"

I just do. Get us on the ship.

Rhienne had spent a decent portion of her life avoiding lifting heavy objects. Pure adrenaline allowed her to scoop Echo up and cradle her against her chest. She squinted through one of the port holes as they came even with the airship and teleported them into the cargo hold. She wedged them behind the carefully packed shelves. The smells of wood, tar, and vinegar made her dizzy.

Still with me?

Mmm.

"Echo!" she hissed.

Shh. I'm fine.

A few minutes passed before calls and footsteps sounded on the loading ramp, interrupting the cadence of a crew readying to depart.

"What is the meaning of this? We've already passed inspection twice." A woman's voice rang across the deck and down the stairs into the hold.

"Indeed, Captain. But we are hunting a pair of fugitives. You would do well to get out of our way and let us conduct our search."

"I think I would've noticed two strangers boarding my ship," she argued, even as they thumped down the stairs.

The Untold took no heed, prying open trunks and barrels under the light cast from their bones, muttering about the useless inquisitor who'd let their prey escape.

Rhienne ducked down. Cowering behind the crates, she could just make out a place under the stairs to teleport. If she could get there, then onto the deck... then what? The docks were swarming with enemies who knew her face, and Echo was paralyzed. She readied her power anyway. Better to go out fighting than surrender to these monsters.

"Now that is quite enough," the captain said sternly. "This cargo is property of Falenor's Imperial Fleet. Drawing the empress's ire would be twice as bad for you as it would be for me. Let me take the lead."

They acquiesced. Splintering wood became turning keys, thunks, and the sliding of heavy containers. Rhienne waited, holding her breath and straining to judge how close they were.

Still with you, Echo said weakly.

Just a little longer. When the captain and the Untold were only a few feet away, she reached for the shadows under the stairs.

Her magic fell short. Rhienne choked back a gasp as the captain shifted the crates they were hiding behind. She met the startled eyes of a middle-aged woman in sharp military dress, hugged Echo tighter against her, and mouthed, "Please."

The captain scanned them both and straightened, her expression turning saccharine. She blocked their hiding place with her long navy coat as she faced the Untold. "As you can see, there is nothing out of the ordinary. Your quarry must have escaped."

Rhienne couldn't see around the cargo, but she recognized the shift of magic in the air, the strange undercurrent to the captain's tone.

"They... escaped. Yes, of course."

"I hate to be rude, but we have a lot to do before we depart. I trust you won't need help finding your way out?"

"No, ma'am. Excuse us."

The Untold shuffled away. An agonizing minute passed where no one moved. Then the captain said, "You have ten seconds to come out, tell me who you are, and what you're doing on my ship."

Rhienne tried and failed again to jump to a different shadow. Her magic had never run out so quickly before. Had she really been using it that much?

She'd gone stiff from holding herself still in the cramped space. "A little help," she muttered, uncurling with a groan as the captain pushed the crates out of the way.

The woman glowered at her. She stood at roughly Rhienne's height, all tan, wiry muscle beneath a heavily embellished coat—silver buttons, medals on the left breast. Tarnished, though. Now that she had a closer look, the hems were frayed, the tricorn hat worn. Magic, Rhienne might have expected from a military officer, but a tattered uniform?

Instead of answering any of the questions, Rhienne said, "That was a neat trick back there. How'd you learn to do that?"

"You pick up a few things, traveling the world. Such as the handful of reasons why people like that would be looking for fugitives."

"Funny. I'm a bit of a world traveler myself, and you seemed keen to get those people off your ship before you knew I was here. So why don't we each stay out of the other's business, hmm?"

The captain's jaw worked, but then she looked down at Echo and her expression softened. "What's wrong with your girl?"

Best be as... honest as possible, Echo said. *Think you may have... met your match.*

"I don't know. They were coming after us, and she got hit by something, and—" The catch in Rhienne's voice wasn't an act. "She just stopped moving."

"Put her down. Let me see." When Rhienne hesitated, she grumbled, "For gods' sake, I'm not going to harm a child, and if I wanted you out, I would've let them take you."

Rhienne flushed and eased Echo to the floor, who giggled into her mind. *Ooh, you like her.*

Shut up, you're delirious right now.

I can't move. I can still see.

Just planning how I'm going to take that hat on our way out. Now shush.

"Where was she hit?" the captain asked. "I don't see a wound."

"Here, I think." Rhienne rolled up one of Echo's pant legs and flinched. The skin had cracked and browned, like dirt after a long drought.

"Stoneskin," the captain hissed. "Those filthy reprobates."

"What is it?"

"She's paralyzed, but she'll live." After an assessing once-over that made Rhienne's skin prickle, the woman rubbed the bridge of her nose and sighed. "Come, bring your daughter to the galley. Our cook knows a thing or two about triage. We'll get you patched up and on your way."

Your daughter. Echo laughed again.

Definitely delirious. In any other circumstance, Rhienne would've swatted at her, but... well, it was a bit funny. She picked Echo up again and struggled to keep up with the other woman. "Captain? If it's all the same to you, I'd like to get as far from this town as I can. Where are you headed?"

"This is a cargo vessel, not a passenger ship. I'm doing you a big enough favor not turning you over to the authorities. I don't need a child underfoot or an extra body lying about, eating our food."

"We can work," Rhienne blurted out. "Or at least I can, and my daughter will when she recovers. We won't be in the way, I promise."

The captain stopped in a doorway, beyond which came the sound of clattering pots and muttered curses. Her lips pressed into a thin line. "This will not be a pleasure cruise. We're headed to Devonsfort, and the winds are rough this time of year. By the look of you, you've had a hard life, but not one full of much hard work. It's demanding, running a ship."

"I understand."

Another examining glance, followed by the ghost of a smile. "You're lucky you remind me of myself when I was your age. You can call me Captain Irelia, or simply Captain. Welcome aboard." Irelia leaned into the galley. "Cookie!"

she shouted, making Rhienne jump. "Clear the counter. Got an injury for you."

"Already?" The deep voice belonged to a boulder of a man who emerged from the pantry. He had dark skin and long braided hair gathered in a knot atop his head. Tinted glasses perched on his wide nose. The knife in his hand looked like a toothpick. He absolutely melted upon seeing Echo. "Oh, poor thing. Put her here. What sort of animal did this?"

We should've had you turn into a kid more often, Rhienne thought. *People give you anything!*

Maybe. It's not exactly... comfortable like this.

"The same animals who came aboard and started rifling through our cargo," the captain said. A knowing look passed between the shipmates, which Rhienne pretended not to notice. "Can you help the girl?"

"Aye. Won't be pretty, but at least she can't feel anything." He maneuvered his bulk well around the small space, boiling bandages and mixing herbs into a gelatinous substance that smelled like dead fish. "So then, who do I have the pleasure of operating on, and who thawed Irelia's icy heart?"

Rhienne expected a reprimand, but the captain only tsked and rolled her eyes. She was almost tempted to use her real name. These people seemed close enough to her shade of gray. She still had no idea how Mishara had traveled so quickly, though, tracking spell or not, and if multiple factions of the Untold were bargaining with Oblivion... "I'm Robin," she decided. "And this is my daughter, Quinn."

Quinn? Really?

What? I had to make a snap decision.

So you picked... the name of that asshole... from the guards in Hearthglen?

Oh. She'd entirely forgotten about them. *Whoops.*

"All right, Quinn. My name is Tash, or you can call me Cookie, like the captain here. I know you can't move, but you can still hear me. I'm going to make you all better, aye? Let's start by taking off the worst of it."

Don't you 'whoops' me, you—whatever insult Echo had been about to hurl Rhienne's way was lost to blinding agony. Tash had taken up his knife again and was scraping at the rock-like parts of Echo's skin.

Rhienne cringed. "I thought you said she couldn't feel anything!"

"She can't." The cook looked at her curiously. "Stone-skin deadens the nerves. That's how it paralyzes."

Someone needs to... inform the medical schools. Echo's thought was breathless and ragged.

You can tell them yourself when this is over. "Right. Sorry. Carry on." Rhienne chewed her nails so she wouldn't say anything else potentially condemning.

Once he was satisfied with his butchery, Tash washed the raw, angry wound, packed in the foul-smelling poultice, and wrapped it with bandages. "That's got to soak in and spread, same way the poison took effect."

"How long until she's unparalyzed?" Rhienne asked around her fingers.

"Depends how fast her body breaks it down. Could be a few hours. Half a day at most. Fever is the real danger, though. I'll keep an eye. I'm sure the captain's going to put you to work for the launch."

"Indeed," Irelia said. "I think we've got half an hour or so left before those cloaked fellows realize they've been charmed. Right this way, Robin."

Loath as she was to leave Echo alone, Rhienne had made a promise, and it was only to their benefit to get this boat in the air. The less time she gave Mishara to gather her wits, the better. *Don't go anywhere, and holler if you need me.*

Have you considered... a career in comedy?

Yeah, she'd be fine. Rhienne kissed Echo on the forehead in what she hoped was a motherly manner and followed Irelia to the upper deck.

She touched the vial in her pocket. As soon as they got out over the ocean, she would toss the spell anchor overboard. With Mishara's threat ringing in her head and her own magic at such an alarming low, she wasn't sure that would be enough. At least they were safe from the Untold while they were in the air.

They just had to get to Hearthglen in one piece. She prayed to no one in particular that it would remain that simple for once.

Chapter 12

Echo

Echo's body was at once mercurial and frozen solid, like she might explode if she didn't change bodies, but the ability was infuriatingly out of reach. And gods, everything hurt. Especially where Tash had peeled away the poisoned skin on her leg.

The cook kept vigil over her while he worked, sometimes humming and sometimes telling stories about the rest of the crew and the places they'd been. She caught bits and pieces. Mostly, his voice was a deep, pleasant rumble that overlaid the vibration of the ship as she slipped in and out of consciousness.

In that place of almost-sleep, memories and dreams blurred with reality, and Tash's murmurs morphed into another, far less soothing voice. One that sounded like cold, uncaring wind through a mountain pass.

"This is where most of the pilgrims who journey to me spend their time," Exodus said.

She took care never to look at him in dreams, sweeping her gaze over the palace throne room instead. Its beautiful marble arches and paneless windows evoked both a religious temple and a museum gallery. Pilgrims were scattered around, painting, weaving, writing, and sculpting in patches of sunlight. Musicians tuned their instruments, and the domed ceiling carried the sound across the room, creating a mishmash of plucked strings and brassy notes that were somehow never discordant. Cushions and low refreshment tables sat within easy reach. Maps and artwork covered the walls. It would've been a warm, lovely place, if not for the throne atop the dais, made from the tattered sails and broken masts of wrecked ships.

Still not looking at him, Echo asked, "And where do the rest go?"

"Pardon?"

"You said this is where most of them spend their time. Where do I go if I'm not 'most' people?"

There was a shift in the wind that followed Exodus, a little burst of summer heat that meant she'd genuinely amused him with the question. "You'll have to prove yourself to me first," he said. There was an almost imperceptible note of foreboding beneath the banter.

Echo studied the artists who had journeyed here and the deals they made. They all asked for inspiration, a thing that would eventually wither. She learned and shaped her own wish, but every time she thought about leaving, something made her stay. Exodus drifted through the palace, sometimes a gentle breeze, and sometimes a terrifying storm. Neither mood could deter her; she studied him too, and learned how to placate him, both with an audience and behind closed doors.

The dream ebbed and flowed, mixing disparate parts of her past with the present: Aderai made an appearance to barter with Exodus, and then Levi, and even Rhienne. But the one who turned her blood to ice was Sidrin.

Her former landlord stopped in the middle of the throne room, facing away from her. He was ragged, like he'd been traveling without rest, and twitched at every sound.

She didn't know what possessed her to call out to the man whose trust she'd betrayed. "Sidrin?"

He turned. Stared at her. And screamed.

Echo startled awake. Still unable to move, all she could do was wait for her heart to slow while her tears dripped onto the pillow Tash had placed under her head.

He bustled over and wiped them away, murmuring, "There, there, the pain will pass. It'll be alright soon."

Just a dream. It wasn't real. Sidrin was probably fine, back in Wildspire, living his life as he always had. If a touch more cautiously.

No matter how many times Echo told herself that, more questions rose: What had he seen when he looked at her? What sort of filter colored his memories of Natalia? What if he didn't look back at their time together at all? Maybe it hurt too much, or was too frightening.

The pain soon faded enough for Echo to gather her wits, but the specter of her dreams lingered. She needed a distraction.

She tapped into the telepathy stone's magic. *Can't believe I'm missing our first flight.*

Want to switch places? Rhienne thought back. *I had no idea rope was so heavy. How are you feeling? Can you move yet?*

Can't believe I'm missing you doing physical labor either. Echo wriggled her fingers and toes, then managed to twitch her nose and unlock her jaw. *Getting better. If we never see the Untold again, it'll be too soon.*

With the number of superstitious nut cases in the world, I'm pretty sure they're going to be everywhere. It might be even worse in Devonsfort, given the military presence there. A moment passed, then Rhienne groaned, *I have to go, Irelia has new orders. Let me know if anything changes.*

Things had been considerably easier between them since their conversation in the woods. Hopefully this new situation wouldn't muck it up again. Echo let out a gusty sigh—part irritation at the new mask she had to wear, and part relief that she was regaining her ability to move—which caught Tash's attention.

He turned away from chopping vegetables and said, "Good, you're awake. Figured you for the resilient type." He'd rolled up his sleeves to work. There were large, banded scars around his wrists, thick and whitened with age.

Tash followed her gaze and chuckled. "You and I have that in common. But unlike me, you had the good fortune of not being alone when the Untold jumped you."

Echo stiffened, struggling to speak. "I'm not a—"

"Don't push yourself," Tash interrupted gently. "The Untolds' poison is an altered form of Stoneskin. The only people who feel pain from it are immortals and mimics. It's all right. Irelia has an inkling already, but I won't tell anyone else. People like us have to stick together, aye?"

Mimics didn't typically play well with others. That sort of sentiment marked him as an immortal—a Child of Eternity, rather than Infinity like Echo. But as long as he thought the same blood ran through their veins, she wouldn't disabuse him of the notion.

"Thanks," she croaked. She ought to keep her mouth shut and her head down, but curiosity niggled at her. Judging by the age of those scars, he'd likely been captured by the Untold before they became an official entity. Yet he'd escaped. He had to have a fascinating life story. Maybe one to write songs about. "Is it rude to ask how old you are?"

Tash smiled, but it didn't quite reach his eyes. "You stop counting after a few centuries."

The antidote was well and truly doing its work now. With Tash's help, Echo sat up. "How long have you been on the ship?"

"A couple decades. Irelia's tough, but she has the biggest heart of anyone I know. It's safe, if that's what you're asking."

Echo nodded, blinking away dark spots. His presence and alliance with the captain explained why they'd been in such a hurry to get away from the Untold. But this was a vessel of Falenor's Imperial Fleet. Why would an immortal work for any form of government? In the military, no less. That had to put him in constant danger of being discovered. "What about Devonsfort? Is that safe?"

"I wouldn't recommend staying there, no. It's become a hotbed of Untold activity." Tash's lips thinned. "Not one of our preferred stops. We've got a special assignment taking us there. Hope to be in and out as quick as a manticore's stinger."

Echo shivered. *More* Untold than what they'd dealt with in Port Saphrai was a terrifying prospect. The 'special assignment' was strange, but she filed that away for further investigation. This room was rapidly becoming too stuffy. "Can I go up to the deck now?"

"If you're feeling strong enough. Easy does it." He helped her off the table and held her while she tested her limbs.

Garnering sympathy was one of the many tactics she used when selecting her disguises, but this time, she wasn't enjoying it quite so much. Beyond the constriction of this body, Tash was being so kind. Too kind. Nobody acted like this to a stranger, even if he'd picked her out as divine-blooded.

She relayed all this to Rhienne as she wobbled up the stairs.

An immortal and a mysterious assignment. Great, her friend responded wearily. *We'll talk more at the end of my shift.*

Echo resolved to do some sleuthing when she was fully recovered. For now, though, there was something more important to investigate.

Wind blasted her, frigid and sharp, as she broke onto the deck, but warmth emanated through the soles of her boots. Some enchantment in the wood to keep frost from forming, probably. A good thing, too; her clothing wasn't made for such altitude.

The crew gave her awkward smiles and waves. No matter what Irelia told them, they were probably not used to having a kid aboard. She did her best to wave back. Her limbs were functional in a heavy, delayed sort of way. Hopefully getting her blood moving would bring her back to normal. Echo tottered over to the railing for support.

The ocean spread like an undulating blanket far, far below, little crests of white rising and falling against the darkening blue. They'd long left the coast behind, and though she'd grown up by the ocean and crossed it once before, she'd never seen it from so high. They flew toward the setting sun, the sky full of gold and orange clouds. The emerging stars seemed close enough to touch.

Echo's lips parted, breathing in the cold and more joy than she'd felt in a long time.

This beauty and peace, this transitional moment, had been part of Horizon's domain. Echo was disappointed the realm that had saved her life didn't belong to the goddess. She wanted to know how Horizon had died, and what the goddess had been like. Surely, with something like this to rule over, she had been kind. If Echo could've made her deal with Horizon instead of Exodus, where would she be? What songs could she be singing right now?

Half-imagined lyrics stuck in her throat, and she clamped her mouth shut.

A useless line of thought. The god she was *actually* looking for had saved her once, completely unprompted and with nothing taken in return. They were likely kind too... but they'd also been wiped from history. No one in the cosmos could tell her what she was flying into.

Not the most disconcerting thought of the day, but it had to be in the top five.

"Amazing, isn't it?" A gruff, muscular woman stepped up beside her and smiled warmly, breaking Echo's reverie. She stuck out a hand, and Echo shook it. "I'm Carsha. First mate."

"Quinn. Nice to meet you. And yeah, it's..." She reoriented her word choice and speech patterns to fit her form. "Really pretty. You ever get bored seeing it all the time?"

The woman's grin stretched wider, revealing a gold tooth. "Never. Captain told me you might need a hand working off some nasty poison. I can show you around, if you like." She extended a thick, sculpted arm.

Surprised but grateful, Echo grabbed on. "Yes, please."

They walked up and down the deck, and Carsha introduced her to the crew. Their names blurred together, unless they were attached to a face Echo could see herself using later: Mordach and his rosy cheeks and bushy red beard, Nazal and their spindly limbs that reminded her of a crane, and of course, Carsha herself, broad-shouldered and self-assured.

Rhienne had been right: no one imagined a child could be a threat, and they warmed to 'Quinn' easily. But the shape was not comfortable, and between that and the poison leaving her system, her mind was slow to filter itself and find the words they'd most want to hear. The result was an appearance of shyness that didn't match her at all, which she'd now have to maintain. *Only for a handful of days*, Echo reminded herself. It was tiring, but necessary.

"Why are the sails so shiny?" she asked, turning the conversation into a lecture so she only had to make the occasional impressed noise. The first mate was more than happy to teach.

There was a staggering amount of magic built into the ship. Besides the weather protection in the wood itself, the sails were also enchanted to withstand storms. They glittered golden even as dusk fell. The arcane engines controlling the ship's altitude emitted a constant buzz that vibrated through the floor. Carsha told her to stay away from most of the equipment, 'lest you lose a finger,' but Echo had no desire to touch any of it. Wondrous and convenient as the airship was, she shuddered to think of the price of all this power.

Her mobility came back slowly, and it wasn't long before exhaustion dragged at her. She thanked Carsha for the tour and beelined for the crew's communal sleeping space, but a low hum of conversation under the stairs made Echo pause.

"—circumstances had my hackles up, you understand," Rhienne said. "I really can't thank you enough for taking us on. I've faced plenty of danger, and nothing has ever scared me so much as seeing Ech—uh, Quinn like that today."

"You two are quite close." That was Irelia. "Though I can't help noticing you don't seem blood-related."

"No. I found her... or maybe she found me. I don't know what I'd do without her. Ever since she could walk, she's known what she was meant to do in life. I wish I had her ability to dream so clearly."

There was a hint of bitterness to Rhienne's voice. As a dreamwalker, she could move through other people's dreams, but never have her own. Echo hadn't realized that bothered her.

Rhienne sighed. "Most of the time I feel like I'm stumbling around in the dark."

"Children have a uniquely powerful ability in that regard," Irelia said. "Don't worry. I worked a lot of different jobs before I became an airship captain. You have plenty of time to find your path."

Rhienne made a noncommittal noise.

Echo stomped down the stairs to save her friend from the rest of that conversational rabbit hole. She pretended not to notice how close the two of them were huddled, and pretended not to hear Irelia's gruff, "Back to work then, sailor."

Getting in with the captain was a good plan, provided Rhienne was thinking with her brain and not other body parts. Echo wondered how much of what she'd said was true, and how much was just what Irelia would find most sympathetic. *Most of the time I feel like I'm stumbling around in the dark.* That didn't sound like the Rhienne she knew.

Echo found an empty hammock and collapsed into it, troubled. Maybe the river rock was finally eroding. Rhienne's bargain with Oblivion loomed, ever ominous. It obviously took a toll on her friend, not knowing when the god would strike next, what consequences the dreamwalks would have. And now Oblivion was working with the Untold, which was even more worrying. Why would he need them, if not to specifically target Echo or her kind? He'd already claimed Rhienne's soul. Did he have some use for Echo's too?

Dread lurked in the back of her mind, just beneath her foresight, as if the vision were on the brink of change. Gods were tricky at the best of times, operating on a scale few could comprehend. Someone was bound to notice she and Rhienne were asking questions no one was meant to ask, looking for a god no one was supposed to remember. They needed to be careful, and smart, or they might meet the same fate.

Chapter 13

Echo

Echo rose in the morning refreshed and determined to be useful. She wasn't strong enough in this body to do much of the manual labor required to run a ship, so (with Carsha's permission) she became an errand runner. Passing messages up and down the deck, fetching things for members of the crew, and bringing water and food around during their breaks. It was the perfect excuse to get familiar with the ship and the people aboard.

After her lackluster performance yesterday, she had to be careful not to appear too precocious, but she and Rhienne needed to know who they'd gotten into bed with. Their list of enemies was long enough already.

The crew worked with the ease of routine mixed with impromptu problem-solving in a fascinating dance.

Mordach and Carsha were the two biggest personalities on board, endlessly bickering and making up like siblings, though the only physical trait the quartermaster and first mate shared was their brawn. She soon picked out the ones less comfortable with the steps. Nazal, the boatswain, stuck out in particular. Echo watched their unsteady hands—fine-boned, long-fingered, made for reed pens or piano keys, not hauling rope and cargo—and the way Mordach and Carsha kept an extra eye on Nazal's activities. Curious, for someone of such high rank to be new to the skyfaring life. Either they knew something important about the operations here, or she could use their greenness to her advantage. When Mordach, Nazal, and Carsha had a break together, Echo scampered over to their spot in the shade of the mast with waterskins and snacks and a beaming, innocent smile.

"Thanks, lass. See yer gettin' the run of the place already!" Mordach chuckled and ruffled her hair, and she fought a grimace. Why did adults think kids liked that? "How're ye enjoying the ship?"

Echo pondered the question with all the solemnity of a ten-year-old, looking out over the railing. Blue in all directions, nothing between them and the sun but a few puffy white clouds. The thought that she could stay here forever trickled through her head. She swatted it away, but it gave her the perfect opening to get to know these people. "It's nice. I miss home, though. Do you ever get to go home, or do you live on the ship?"

This elicited three very different reactions. Mordach grimaced. Carsha looked away. Nazal, however, perked up. "Some of us have been here longer than others, but we all live together now," they said. "Our own little family, if you will."

She furrowed her brows. "What did you do before this? You don't look much like a sailor."

Carsha snorted and threw a muscular arm around Nazal's narrow shoulders. "Who, this little bird? They were born with wind in their hair and salt in their blood."

"Actually, that's true, though not for the reason you imply," Nazal said. The gleam in their eyes stopped the other two from teasing further. "I was a scholar once."

Mordach rolled his eyes. "Aye, and I was a seamstress for the crown princess of Stormpeak."

Carsha elbowed him in the ribs. "I think they're being serious, Mord."

Echo glanced between the trio. Some family. Didn't even ask each other the simplest questions. "Really? A scholar of what?" she wondered aloud when no one else pressed further.

"Oh." Nazal blushed, taken aback by the question. She widened her eyes, every part the eager pupil, and a little spark ignited in their expression. "Well, it was a long time ago now, but I used to be a Grand Archivist of Kydorei."

"Wait, really?" Mordach asked.

"Why didn't you tell us?" Carsha added.

Nazal shrugged, shy beneath their stares. "You never asked."

Kydorei? Echo kept her face open and curious at the mention of the sanctuary isle, though her interest in the boatswain skyrocketed. It was said to be a veritable paradise. No crime, no war, sharing of art and knowledge for those who resided there—but few things left the island's shores, and even fewer were allowed in. Anyone who wanted to become part of the community underwent rigorous entrance exams and reference checks. Not something a mimic had a chance in hell of passing. What could've possibly brought Nazal *here* from a place like that?

She'd start small and work up to that question. "That sounds impressive," she said with complete honesty. "What's a Grand Archivist do?"

"They lead different areas of study on the isle. During my residency, there were thirteen of us." Nazal tapped nervously on their thigh, but seeing they had a captive audience, continued, "My specialty was the intersection of history and the arcane."

Echo's heart thumped. A scholar from Kydorei was one thing. A scholar from Kydorei who might have knowledge about the gods the rest of the world doesn't? She was not one to believe in fate, but she couldn't shake the feeling that they'd crossed paths for a reason, and this opportunity was too good to pass up.

She had to be careful not to draw suspicion or show more understanding than a child would have of the world. Luckily, the spindly ex-scholar seemed eager to share, now that the door was open. "Magic is scary," she said, rubbing the spot on her leg where the needle had paralyzed her.

All three of the crew members shared a nervous look, then Nazal crouched so they were eye to eye. "That can be true, yes. But it can also be wonderful. May I tell you a story, Quinn?"

She nodded and sat, crossing her legs on the warm deck and folding her hands in her lap expectantly.

Nazal smiled and settled down with her, and when they spoke again, their voice fell into the cadence and depth of a practiced narrator. "Before the world was born, two beings lived alone in the darkness between stars. They looked out over the vast, empty cosmos and wished to fill it. But they could not create something from nothing, and so, they broke off pieces of themselves, scattered them across the night like seeds, and waited for them to bloom." Nazal's hands swept through the air. No magic glittered at their fingertips, but Echo swore she could *see* the story playing out in the space between them. She leaned forward, enraptured.

"In time, when their wish had still not taken root, they realized what they had planted was too wild and raw to leave room for new life. So they erected a barrier between the world and their power, separating them into two planes. And they formed children who were half their magic, half beings of rock and sky, who could move between these planes. That's when they began to call themselves the Mothers, and their children the gods."

Echo's mouth was dry from hanging open. She knew there were other planes, of course, where demons, dreams, souls, or gods resided. But she'd never heard of one for pure, unbridled magic. In her wonder, she forgot the part she was meant to be playing. "Is that true? Does such a place really exist?"

Nazal steepled their fingers. "No mortal has ever crossed into it, but I have no reason to doubt. The oldest legends call it the Origin. It is the loom from which the tapestry of our lives was spun. So, you see? None of us would exist without magic. Nor would the world we call home. We all have some small thread of it within us still." They tapped their chest, right over their heart. "Beautiful, no?"

Echo touched her own chest, and for a moment, she could almost feel the thread they spoke of, winding through her blood, her soul.

"Aye, and a fat lot of good it's done us," Mordach grumbled. "The gods are selfish bas—er, blowhards. They're supposed to be the go-betweens and are keeping it all for themselves instead. What do your legends say about that?"

"Accounts are... varied," Nazal admitted sheepishly.

They had a theory, though. Echo could see it in their eyes—the reawakened part of themself they hadn't touched in a long time. "What do *you* think?" she asked.

The boatswain swiped a hand over their close-cropped hair and sipped from their waterskin. "There was a time when magic was more widely available, but a fragment of the infinite is not infinite itself. As the Mothers of Creation knew. I don't know what the breaking point was, but I believe when the stores ran low... they deemed us unworthy of receiving more. Or perhaps they had no more to give."

Echo mulled that over, but before she could puzzle out how to surreptitiously ask her next question, Carsha blurted out, "No offense, Nazal, but why the hell did you leave Kydorei? Don't tell me you weren't good enough at your job after what I just listened to."

"Ah, well." Wind buffeted the sails above them. No one else broke the silence until Nazal was ready. "It always seemed a cruelty to me, to work so hard to understand a thing we could not use. No matter how beautiful the magic you made, on the isle, divine bargains were frowned upon. Especially for one in such a visible position as mine." They twirled their fingers and a tiny flowering vine manifested between them.

Echo's stomach lurched at the casual display of Harvest's magic, and the reality of their situation came crashing back down.

Nazal dismissed the conjuring and shrugged. "I was banished, and when I went looking for work, Irelia found me." Mordach and Carsha nodded—they seemed to identify with this part of the tale. They had the look of military folk about them but didn't treat Irelia with the same familiarity as Tash. Newer to the regiment, perhaps.

Everyone's eyes drifted over to the captain, standing at the helm with Rhienne. All three tensed a little, noticing this stranger so close to the woman who—Echo was starting to gather—had saved them all, in one way or another.

Rhienne said something that made Irelia burst out laughing, a sound with as much surprise in it as joy, and the crew's shoulders relaxed. The spell of Nazal's storytelling was broken, and Echo remembered who she was supposed to be.

"Your captain seems like a nice lady when she isn't trying to be mean," Echo said.

That made everyone laugh. Carsha's gold tooth gleamed in the afternoon sun. "You've got the right of it there."

"What're you all doing?" Irelia called out across the deck. "I don't pay you to sit around looking pretty!"

"If you did, we'd all be broke!" Mordach shouted back. With a few more chuckles and good-natured barbs, they rose and returned to their duties.

Echo picked up the small bowls and waterskins they'd left behind and touched the telepathy stone. *What'd you say to Irelia just now?*

I was telling her a story about Vala. When we first started dreamwalking together, she and I found the dream of some asshole noble. He had a fear of geese, apparently, so we tormented him for a week, just moving one from the neighboring farm around his property. There was a smile in Rhienne's voice, even in her thoughts. *Irelia had shared something about her mother's passing in one of Falenor's wars, and it... seemed like a good idea to try to endear ourselves to her more.*

Of course. Echo smothered her surprise that Rhienne had been so open with this woman, even under the guise of subterfuge. *I was doing the same thing.*

Oh. Great! Did you learn anything?

They know more than your average sailors about magic and the gods, that's for sure. She shared the story Nazal had told, along with her suspicions about the crew keeping a scholar aboard. This ship was tangled up with divinity somehow, she was sure. The Origin stuck like a burr in her mind, along with the idea that the Mothers may have judged them unworthy of more magic. Not much was known about the Creators, due to the distance they kept. Could that be why? Could she really blame them for thinking the world undeserving? *Not much else yet. I didn't want to pry too much and risk my cover.*

Smart. We'll give it another couple days and see what we can find.

Echo scanned the deck, befuddled at how quickly their presence had been accepted here, but she stopped the thought from going further than that. They had a job to do. Distractions were dangerous, no matter how friendly they might seem. No matter how easy it had been to drop her mask, just for a moment, without anyone caring.

She shook her head and scurried down to the galley to lose herself in the relative safety of washing dishes.

Chapter 14

Rhienne

Rhienne had never been this exhausted. Her hands were raw from scraping against ropes and wood, her eyes hurt from squinting against the wind and sun, and her muscles screamed promises everything would hurt worse tomorrow. Two days of this, and there hadn't even been time to enjoy the splendor of being on an airship. She knew there was a good reason she'd never worked a day in her life.

By the time Irelia dismissed her, Rhienne was tripping over her own feet. The captain said her training period was over, and she'd be expected on deck at sunrise. *Sunrise.* The only people who got up that early were poets and masochists. She fell into the closest empty hammock, begging for the sweet oblivion of sleep.

She should've known better than to use that word.

The tilt into the Plane of Dreams was immediate, a heedless demand tugging on her soul. Pastels blurred over her vision, but Oblivion's presence was a magnetic pull. He'd manifested behind her. She stayed facing away so she could master her expression.

"Back so soon?" Rhienne said with a lazy grin. "I knew you were starting to like me."

"Hardly. Though I do enjoy seeing what curious circumstances you get yourself into." His voice filled the room. As her vision cleared, she found two white dots surveying her from the ceiling. Oblivion's star-filled shadow draped menacingly across the wall. He became extra creepy when he was in a bad mood, and that never boded well for her.

"Happy to be a source of amusement," she said. "Ought to add that into our contract. It has to be worth a little magic."

"And just as quickly as the pleasure came, it was gone." Oblivion sighed. "Come. Time to do your real job."

Like a parent holding their unruly child by the hand, Oblivion dragged her through the dreamscape. He moved past hundreds of bubbles containing dreams and nightmares, with an intensity that turned her stomach.

What was he going to ask her to do this time? After her dreamwalk with Jareth, she'd hoped to be off the hook for a while. Though, with her magic as low as it was, maybe this was a blessing in disguise. She'd gotten lucky with Irelia. No way would Rhienne find two helpful strangers in a row.

The scene Oblivion pushed her into was crowded. A throng of people gathered around an open pit. Unlike other dreams, where most faces were undefined, every one of them was a fully detailed person. How was she supposed to know whose dream this was?

She floated over the crowd. The pit was deep and dark except for a pinprick of light at the bottom. Silently cursing her pact, she went to investigate, and soon made out two figures illuminated by the glow.

"You've won. I don't want to fight anymore. Take this, and do with it what you will."

Rhienne couldn't see their face, but their voice was rich and full, the kind accustomed to speaking to large gatherings in vast spaces. There was no response from the other figure besides reaching out to take the light from the first. From her vantage, it looked like a marble-sized cerulean sun. The color was familiar, but she couldn't place it.

The second figure bowed and swallowed the light. Moments later, a cloud of mist rushed past Rhienne, raising gooseflesh along her arms and a prickling recognition in the back of her mind. She was tempted to follow, but soft music pulled her attention back. The crowd hushed, filling the air with anticipation.

A stone pillar rose from the pit. Spotlights flicked on, centered on the only person in the dream without a clear visage. They were humanoid-shaped fog standing atop a makeshift stage, the small blue light burning in their core.

It struck Rhienne like a physical blow; what sort of person could visualize an entire crowd but not have their own specific shape?

She didn't want to believe it, didn't want to remember that she'd seen that exact blue manifest from a truth revealed in the Collector's cave, but when the performer's first note rang out and they slid into a dangerous, sultry song, Rhienne couldn't deny how easily she recognized the voice.

This was Echo's dream.

Oblivion would expect her to get to work soon. To turn each person against the musician on stage, or plant seeds of doubt in Echo's mind about her abilities, or... oh gods, simply take Echo's voice away again and tell her there was no chance of ever fixing it. Just like with Jareth, knowing the person would make it easier to rip apart their hopes.

Just like with Jareth, the loss of the dream would destroy Echo.

The ground shook in response to Rhienne's spike of fear, making the crowd gasp and Echo's featureless figure stumble.

Calm, calm, she had to stay calm. Rhienne wrestled her emotions into submission by tearing her attention away from Echo, and the performance continued.

If Rhienne refused Oblivion, he'd stop giving her magic. She'd be stuck with whatever measly spells she could summon with her blood. One stray smack to the temple, and he'd control her soul for the rest of eternity.

Ending a dream as strong as Echo's would grant Rhienne unimaginable power. But Echo had told her what happened the last time she lost hope. Now it would be Rhienne's fault, and she had no guarantee some magical library would show up to save her friend again. There had to be a way out, through, around—godsdammit, where was a loophole when she needed one?

Amid her spiraling, one song carried into another. Beautiful didn't begin to describe the way this dream-version of her friend sang. It was ethereal. Otherworldly. The music tugged on forgotten memories and opened doors to possibilities she'd dismissed.

The crowd didn't agree. As the performance went on, people trickled away.

"Boring."

"Disappointing. That guy who was here last week was way better."

"Oh, you mean Levi?"

"Yeah, he sang stuff everyone knew. Really understood how to work a crowd. And he actually made deals with us."

"I remember this bard from a few years back; she used to do that too. Her new music is weird."

But then Rhienne blinked, and all those people were back, cheering for an encore and throwing flowers and coins at Echo's feet. Rhienne hadn't unraveled anything. Whatever was making the dream flicker to nightmare and back again, it wasn't her influence.

Oblivion chose that moment to pounce. "Have you forgotten how to perform your task? I can show you where to begin if need be. This dream is fragile. There are a hundred different ways to pull it apart."

Rhienne felt just as brittle. Magic was the highest power in this world, the only way to have any kind of control over your own life. The times she hadn't had it—the catacombs, Port Saphrai—had almost been the end of her. There could be countless other obstacles to face, never mind her mother's resurrection. Blood magic was a pittance compared to what Oblivion gave her. And he was right; if the dream wavered again, she could snuff it like a candle flame.

Jareth appeared over and over in the back of her mind: his hollow stare before an arrow punched through his throat. She couldn't do that to her best friend.

"Well?"

"I don't need your help," Rhienne growled. Perhaps she could get away with a small unraveling. One that Echo wouldn't notice but would technically fulfill her part of the bargain.

Rather than plucking at the dream's fabric around Echo and the stage, she leaned into the ears of people in the crowd. "You'll stay until the end, but it's nothing to write home about. Clap politely, be supportive, and then you don't have to think about this again. It was a nice night. A fine performance."

"A fine performance," a memory of Aderai boomed from the ether, drawn by the similarity of Rhienne's words.

Echo's song caught in her throat. Just for a moment, but long enough to give the crowd pause, and for Rhienne's words to spread and sink in.

The mood stopped shifting. The concert ended with polite applause, and people drifted away from the stage. She expected the dream to dissolve, but it didn't. Instead, Echo's misty figure leapt off the platform and hurried to catch up with the crowd.

"Wait! What did you think?"

No one answered her.

"Hello?" She stepped in front of a couple walking arm in arm and screamed, "Look at me!"

They passed right through her. *I thought being hated would be the worst thing I could experience, but complete and utter indifference was worse.* Echo's words came back to her, and Rhienne's heart stumbled.

What had she done?

In that fluid way the mind moves, the concert scene melted away. A roof and walls rose around them, with one window overlooking a garden. It didn't have the pastel edges of a dream or the desaturation of a memory. Every detail was as perfectly articulated as it would be in life, including every wrinkle and liver spot on Echo's skin. She lay in bed, staring not at the beautiful flowers in the garden, but at the open door, waiting for someone to walk through. The sun sank outside, her eyelids growing heavier with it. Still, the doorway was empty. Echo's eyes closed.

Rhienne tried to shake her awake, to say, "I'm here," but whatever this was, she couldn't affect it at all. There was a barrier between her and Echo's mind.

"How foolish to think I could leave a mark on the world that people would want to remember," Echo murmured.

Rhienne's attempt to sidestep her contract had only made things worse. She had to fix this, but how? When? Where?

The dream morphed again, to the roof of their father's house. Echo sat next to a much younger Rhienne, looking over the marsh, a bottle of wine between them. Rhienne knew exactly when this was, and from where she hung in the air, was equally powerless to change it.

"What if I never 'make it'?" Echo asked, morose and more than a bit tipsy.

Rhienne grabbed the bottle and took a long drink. "Of course you will. It only takes one important person noticing you, and I bet you'll have, like, fifty of them fighting over you."

"What if I don't, though? What if I'm not really that good? Or I am good, but I'm unlucky. What if—"

"What's the other option, huh? Stay here for the rest of our lives with these small-minded bumpkins? We deserve more. And hey, if you do need a little leg up… there's always religion."

Echo snorted. "Yeah, right. Like a god would ever give me the time of day. I've got nothing to trade with."

"Not yet. I heard people bargain with their futures all the time."

"Hmm. Would you do something like that?"

"In a heartbeat," Rhienne whispered in time with her younger self.

This was where it had all gone wrong. If she hadn't been so impatient to pursue her own goals, if she hadn't been so arrogant in her insistence that she could do everything on her own, they could've helped each other. Echo had always been the better of the two of them. She had purpose, drive, and passion; she put beauty into the world despite the world working against her.

All Rhienne ever did was break things. It was no wonder Echo had a hard time trusting her with the truth. Loathing twisted her stomach, only some of it directed at Oblivion for forcing this choice. What did it say about her, that she'd spent any time at all questioning how much she was willing to hurt her friend?

What did it say, that when she looked up at the sky where Oblivion was watching, she still had to fight to get the refusal past her lips?

"This is enough. I won't unravel anymore." The chains of her contract pulled taut, the unfulfilled bargain choking her.

Oblivion drew her out of the dream so fast, Rhienne might have left pieces of herself behind. Frigid blackness swarmed her, without even the white points of his eyes to anchor her. "You do not get to say no to me."

Strangely, his voice had lost its seething menace from earlier in the night. It still took every scrap of bravado she possessed to stand under the weight of what was coming. "That's funny. I'm pretty sure I just did."

And there was that sound she'd never wanted to hear again: Oblivion's laugh was a physical thing, worming its way through her pores and scraping against her bones. Caught within the cold and dark, the sound of real laughter slipped from her memory. Her lungs froze. Her patron's power squeezed the channel where her magic rested.

"You will be nothing," he whispered inside her skull. "Is that really what you want, Rhienne? Magic from an ending as powerful as this would make you a legend. Is one dream really worth losing everything?"

Coward that she was, she faltered. She'd have no additional power until they found the Dawnglow. Not even enough to teleport if things got dicey.

But if Rhienne was going to put her faith in anything, shouldn't it be her friend?

"Echo's dream is worth it."

Silence, like the beat before the inhale before a scream. She expected to be snapped in two and tossed out of the Plane of Dreams, for Oblivion to shatter her, break her, consume her.

Instead, he spoke with frightening calm. "I couldn't agree more. If you ever see the Collector again, thank him for tipping me off about Echo's secret, would you?"

Rhienne jolted awake. The darkness of the ship wasn't as complete as the void she'd left behind. In fact, the sky outside was turning blue. All her body parts were still in place—though, the second she moved, they protested in unison—and the core of her magic was still there, but it hung disconnected from its source. She felt like a leaky balloon as she stumbled out of her hammock. The fucking Collector had sold their truths to Oblivion.

She scrambled for the telepathy stone. *Echo? Where are you? Are you all right?*

I'm fine. Restless night. Doing a little snooping. Something's off about this ship.

'Something's off' was right. For one, this ship had far too many stairs. She was breathless by the time she reached the top deck. *Do you feel any different? Listless or... I don't know, just different.*

Rhienne, you're being weird. I'm in the cargo hold. What's going on?

Cargo hold. Godsdamnit. She started back the way she'd come but thought better of it. Drawing attention to a snooping Echo was a bad idea. Did the woman not remember she'd been paralyzed two days ago? *I just had a visit from Oblivion.*

Already? Is that normal?

No, it's not. It would've been easy to obfuscate, or lie, while she didn't have to look Echo in the eye. But Rhienne dug her nails into her palms, reminding herself of their conversation in the forest, and how much it had hurt to be left in the dark. *And we... went into your dream.*

Chapter 15

Echo

Echo froze in the middle of opening a trunk. She'd come down to the cargo hold after tossing and turning most of the night, wondering if the Untold had missed anything during their search. They had, in fact. But the firearms stacked beneath layers of ore and gems were far less worrying than what Rhienne had just said.

My dream?

You fixed your voice, and you were singing to this enormous crowd. It kept flickering between going well and not.

Ah, no wonder she'd been restless. *Yeah, that's a recurring one.* She remembered Jareth's face the morning after Rhienne had dreamwalked with him. Like he'd lost both his inner compass and the wind in his sails. Echo scratched a tiny X into the side of the trunk and eased it shut. *I don't feel any different, though.*

Okay. That's good. Great, actually. Doesn't explain what he wanted, but at least I didn't mess anything up.

The hair on the back of Echo's neck rose. Telepathy was one thing, but sifting through someone's innermost thoughts? She straightened and quietly hurried toward the stairs. *Rhi. What happened?*

I started to end your dream. As little as I could get away with. And then I saw you in the future, and what you wanted, and gods, Echo, you never told me why this was all so important to you. If I had known, I never would've started. But once I did, I couldn't keep going.

Passing by the galley, the sound of shifting crates and someone muttering under their breath overlapped with Rhienne's nervous explanation. No one should be in there at this hour. Certainly not with the door locked.

What do you mean you saw me in the future? Echo pressed her ear to the door. That was definitely Tash's voice, but he sounded strange.

I don't know. It wasn't a dream, exactly. You were old, but I knew it was you. In a house, all alone.

She fumbled with her lockpicks. *You saw that?*

Yeah. And I just... Oblivion talked to the Collector, who apparently told him most, if not all, of what we said. Oblivion seemed very interested in your dream in particular.

This was too much to focus on at once. Echo held her question. The lock clicked open, and she peered through the crack in the door. The prep table that took up the center of the galley had been pushed to the side, revealing an open hatch. Tash's voice drifted from below in a language she didn't recognize, a chant that wove around itself so it almost sounded like two people speaking.

Vividly aware she'd been paralyzed two days ago, Echo crept across the floorboards. Just a tiny peek to see what the hell they'd gotten themselves into.

Tash was hunched over a trunk of firearms similar to the ones in the cargo hold, but these had runic script etched into the metal. Fresh iron shavings littered the floor. He put down his carving tool and opened his other hand.

The light of a sunrise lay condensed in his palm.

Echo's breath caught, a horrible feeling twisting her stomach. *Rhi, you remember how the Collector said we'd find Dawnglow on our journey to Hearthglen?*

What? Why are you bringing that up now? I'm trying to tell you—

I found it. It's here. On the ship. The glow funneled from Tash's hand into the runes decorating the guns. Firearms were illegal for anything outside of official government use. Enchanted firearms were outlawed by international agreements. Not even pirates dared to be caught with them. And Tash was *making* them.

When the Dawnglow's power was spent, no light remained in the crystal. It looked utterly unmagical, just a piece of clear, jagged rock about the length of Tash's thumb. He put it inside a small lead container that held more of that brilliant sunrise.

Looks like they have an entire box of it.

Holy shit, Rhienne said. *Where did they find... actually, I don't want to know.*

With that much Dawnglow, they could fix Echo's voice, resurrect Rhienne's mother, and have enough left over to live like queens. Now that she knew where it was, it would be easy enough to retrieve. Echo couldn't believe her luck.

The little girl she was pretending to be wasn't so thrilled, though. She'd begun to like Tash. And that little girl wasn't so careful where she stepped as she backed away from the hatch. A floorboard creaked beneath her.

The cook said, "Irelia, is that you?" The ladder groaned under his steps.

She fled from the galley, rounded the corner, and took the stairs two at a time to the main deck. At the top, she ran straight into Rhienne.

Her friend looked like she'd been on a week-long bender with multiple bar fights. It was different from her last dreamwalk, which changed her air but not her appearance. Now, even though the glamor was still there, Echo could see every sleepless night, every cold, hungry winter.

"You got out of there all right?" Rhienne whispered.

It dawned on her then what her friend had been trying to say about the dream. "You didn't."

Rhienne smiled shakily. "Good news is, Oblivion won't be putting you in the path of any flaming arrows."

"You broke your pact... for me?"

"Call it even."

"But what about your magic?"

Rhienne shrugged. "I've got a little left."

"What about..."

"My soul?" The facade slipped, revealing something bitter that Echo didn't fully understand. "He'll have to fight me for it."

Echo had wondered how far Rhienne would be willing to go. It brought tears to her eyes to know *she* was the line in the sand. "I don't know what to say besides thank—"

"Don't," Rhienne said harshly. "Don't you dare thank me."

Footsteps on the stairs stopped Echo's response. Tash appeared, glancing between the two of them with concern. "Everything all right up here?"

"Yes," they both said too quickly.

He raised an eyebrow and seemed on the verge of pressing further, but his gaze moved past them. "What in the cosmos is that?"

Echo turned and peered into the distance. There was a dark spot in the brightening sky, rapidly growing larger.

Thunder shattered the quiet calm of the morning. A blast of wind rocked the ship and sent all three of them into a tangled heap. The howling didn't end when the gale died down; it became a multitude of horrifying screeches and screams that chilled Echo to the core.

"Storm on the horizon!" the lookout called from the crow's nest. "All hands to stations!"

"That's not a regular storm. What the hell is it?" Echo repeated Tash's question. She grabbed Rhienne's hand, and they staggered to their feet. The dark mass had clarified into gray-green clouds crackling with lightning. Deeper shadows twisted within.

The blood drained from Rhienne's face. *That, I believe, is my retribution.*

Chapter 16

Rhienne

"Bastard couldn't give me one moment of peace?" Rhienne swore.

The storm rolled toward them with hungry malice. Of course, Oblivion wouldn't let her infraction slide. Her soul belonged to him, and he wasn't going to wait to collect it.

She grabbed Echo and raced for the stairs, fighting the wind with each step.

Irelia called out from the helm, "Robin! We need to stow the sails before the storm takes them."

Rhienne pretended not to hear Irelia over the screaming maelstrom. She just needed to get into the hold and hide in a nice, safe barrel. The ship lurched as the captain spun the wheel to steer them around the clouds, but the storm mirrored their movements, cutting off their escape.

"That's an order!" Irelia shouted. "Quinn, tie yourself to the main mast and make sure the rest of the tethers are tight. No one's going overboard on my watch."

Echo yanked Rhienne's arm, pulling them both to a stop. Her eyes were bright with fear, but she said, "If we help them, maybe they'll help us. They can't need *all* of that Dawnglow."

The storm was closing in fast. Rhienne cursed again, her heart pounding. "I really hate it when you're right."

They crawled to the mast, where several other crew members were tying ropes around their waists and scrambling to their stations. Echo did as she was told, checking and rechecking lifelines once she'd fastened her own. Rhienne kept one eye on her and took up a position at the halyard. She hadn't even known what a halyard was two days ago, and now she not only had to release one, but also protect a ship full of strangers from her patron's wrath. Wrath *she'd* caused.

"We're not outrunning this," Carsha, the first mate, shouted. There was a strange, not at all confidence-inspiring resignation about the muscular woman. Quieter, she said to Mordach, "She came early."

"Maybe our favor's run out," he grunted. "Couldn't expect it to last forever." The quartermaster produced a wooden charm from beneath his beard and started muttering prayers.

Wait, what? What did *they* think was going on? She remembered Echo's suspicions about their divine involvement. Hauling on the rope, it took a moment for Rhienne to gather enough breath to yell, "Favor with who?"

Mordach and Carsha clammed up. If Rhienne wasn't so busy fearing for her life, she would've pushed the issue, but the clouds loomed ever closer. Self-preservation won out, and she focused on her job.

No sooner had the sails been safely stowed than Irelia called, "We're going through! Everyone hold on!"

Clouds blotted out the sun. The temperature dropped and hail pelted the deck. Wind buffeted the ship like a toy; it was a miracle Irelia held it upright.

"There's something out there!" Carsha's voice trembled.

Rhienne ran for the railing, straining to see. Frost formed between her numb fingers, but she clung on. Not in a million years would she give Oblivion the satisfaction of such a meaningless death.

Amid the swirling clouds were flashes of ragged wings, gnashing teeth, and grasping tentacles more tangible than shadow. They were nightmares conjured from the void, wreathed in... was that maroon? Darker than crimson blood magic, but brighter than Oblivion's black.

He wasn't working alone.

He wasn't targeting her either. Rhienne couldn't dream; she was immune to the aura of doom encroaching on the ship. The shapes in the clouds weren't her deepest fears made real. These nightmares were for the crew.

Oblivion was going to use her reliance on these people to destroy her.

Rhienne looked around wildly for inspiration. She didn't have enough magic to get herself and Echo out of the sky, never mind survive the frigid ocean. But somewhere in the belly of the ship was something with enough power to do both, and more.

Echo, where are they keeping the Dawnglow? We're not escaping without it.

Her friend didn't respond. She was clinging to the mast, trapped in Oblivion's spell.

One by one, fear seized the rest of the crew. They stopped performing their duties, some finding whatever meager cover they could while others simply hunched over, shivering in the middle of the deck. Voices twisted across the ship, and Rhienne couldn't tell if they were the crew's or conjurations.

"We're going to die."

"Better it happens in the air, before we plunge into the sea."

"There's nothing we can do. The gods have decided."

Rhienne shrugged them off, but the whispers fed the crew's terror, and the nightmares grew. One massive shadow fell across the deck and took the shape of a kraken. Its huge, red-purple eye fixed on Irelia.

The captain's grip on the wheel went slack, and the airship began to list. Loose cargo and equipment tumbled across the slanted deck.

The beast opened its mouth, revealing concentric circles of jagged teeth. It crunched down on the sliding crates. Its cry pierced the air, and Rhienne gagged as a wave of foul breath hit her. This one was no illusion.

Two tentacles reached toward the mast. Toward Echo.

If this wasn't an emergency, nothing was. Rhienne drew her dagger, slashed it along her calf with a murmured bargain, and sent a volley of blood missiles into the abomination. It shrieked and spasmed, but only slowed for a moment.

"Echo!" Rhienne's scream fell on deaf ears. She let go of the rail, sliding and falling and throwing a shield of her own blood up in front of her friend. It cracked as the tentacles slammed into it, but held.

The beast reared back for another strike.

Rhienne crashed shoulder-first into Echo and Carsha. The impact jarred them from their trance, the shadowy glaze of Oblivion's spell clearing from their eyes.

"Help me!" Rhienne yelled to the first mate.

Carsha drew her blade with a shaking hand and stepped in front of Echo.

Rhienne's dagger and Carsha's cutlass slashed the tentacles, leaving wounds that leaked black mist—so small compared to the monster's size. Rhienne wove blood into her strikes as best she could, willing it into poison or fire or anything that might help fell this nightmare.

Then Carsha lost her footing on the sloped, icy deck. Rhienne grabbed the woman's arm, but her hands were slick, her muscles weak. She formed her blood into a web, tying them together, but the airship pitched, and her concentration frayed.

The red cords snapped. The list became a dangerous lean. Carsha's feet dangled in the air.

Sensing weakness, the shadow-kraken screeched and lunged for them.

An incomprehensible calm settled over the first mate's face. "Protect your girl. I'll balance the scales." In one smooth motion, she sliced her lifeline and wrenched free of Rhienne's grip.

Carsha collided with one of the tentacles as she fell, jabbing her blade into its flesh. Gravity pulled her down in a torrent of black mist.

Maroon magic flared, joined by a woman's spine-chilling laughter, as the beast's mouth closed around Carsha. It disappeared with her into the clouds.

Rhienne stared in disbelief, but the crisis wasn't over. The storm was still roiling. The ship was on the verge of capsizing. Echo trembled on the ground next to her. Rhienne heaved her upright and shook her by the shoulders. *Where's the Dawnglow?*

It's under the galley, but... Echo's gaze grew distant, and Rhienne feared she'd have to do something drastic to break the fear aura again. *There are a bunch of nightmare creatures down there already, and facing them would not end well for us.*

The whirling chaos made Rhienne slow to understand. *Wait, are you saying... I didn't think mortals could see the future.*

Shame flushed Echo's cheeks. *They can if it's a very, very specific moment.*

Oh. *Oh.* Was that what she'd seen in Echo's mind? Echo could see her own death? "Holy shit, that would've been great to know earlier! We could've avoided this fucking mess!"

"That's not how it works! I'm sorry, I—"

Rhienne shook her head. She was doing it again. Hurting the one person she cared about. "Never mind. It's fine. Any other ideas?"

Echo brushed her soaked hair out of her eyes. "This is going to sound stupid, but I need you to sing."

"What?"

"We have to dispel the aura in the storm. Make a deal with me, and we'll bring the rest of the crew in as we wake them up." Echo unslung the mandolin from her back. "The words are the important part. I'll be second fiddle if you sing something that can break this spell."

The magnitude of magic they could conjure would never make up for the resignation and jealousy on Echo's face. But, knowing what she was conceding, it might just be enough power to save their lives. There wasn't time to consider further.

"Deal." The contract formed between them and pulled taut. "Did you have a song in mind?"

Her friend strummed the opening bars of *Tavern at the End of the World.* Rhienne pushed everything else aside for now, sucked in a deep breath, and sang as loud as she could.

In a tavern dark and dusty, adventurers gather 'round
With tankards full of ale and tales from realms un-
bound
We raise our voices high where the fire's all a-glow
As we sing of quests and battles in hope our legends
grow

She moved as she sang, grappling her way around the mast to the cluster of crewmates frozen on the other side. Echo clambered along behind her. They struggled to be heard over the raging wind and hail. Her voice had none of Echo's practiced beauty, but once she grabbed someone and shook them a bit, her singing pierced the veil of Oblivion's nightmares. All four crewmates broke from their stupor and clutched at the mast for safety.

"Sing with us," Rhienne urged. When no one joined in, she pointed to the other crew members still slipping toward the railing, caught in the spell and unable to save themselves. "Those lifelines won't hold forever."

Tentatively, they started to sing. Motes of blue and gold gathered in the air as the crew's apathy and terror faded, and they agreed to join the pact. Each branching tether was like a tiny fishhook tugging at her heart. It was dizzying, being magically bound to so many people.

They formed a protective huddle, struggling not to fall across the deck. They reached three more of the crew, and three more voices joined her. Echo had chosen well. Everyone knew the tune; it was one of those songs that inspired visions of a life greater than the one you led. A song to push back the dark.

From forests deep and haunted, to mountains tall and grand

We've roamed through darkest dungeons and crossed prismatic sands

We've slain great beasts and stolen treasures too many to name

Now we'll stake our place in history and forever share our claim

Some were harder to break free from the spell's influence than others. By the time Rhienne reached Nazal, the airship was at a forty-five-degree angle, everyone's lifelines straining. She shook the boatswain awake before easing them back from the railing.

That left Irelia.

The helm was obscured in darkness too deep to make out the captain.

With the clinking of our tankards and laughter in the air

The closer the crew got to the helm, the more the shadows clung to them, trying to drag and tear them away from each other. The howling wind swallowed their voices.

"Come on!" Rhienne shouted. Just one more link in the chain to break the spell, and then they might have a hope of sailing away.

If we all band together, the gods better beware

But the captain wasn't at the helm. Her lifeline was wrapped around the base of the wheel, the other end frayed where it had snapped.

The crew's song faltered. Tendrils of night swarmed, eager to reclaim them.

Rhienne's throat was raw, every muscle exhausted. But she couldn't stop now. Nascent magic hung in the air like a lightning strike, waiting for the end of the verse—the final spark. She didn't so much sing as scream the last two lines.

With blade and pen and bravery what stories we have spun

We may have reached this ending but our journey's just begun

A shockwave emanated from Echo's mandolin, pushing clouds, hail, and nightmares off the ship. In the resulting bubble of ringing silence and clarity, Rhienne spotted Irelia's limp body draped over the railing.

One of the captain's arms was bent at a horrible angle, and she had a bloody gash on her head. She was unconscious.

And about to tip over the railing.

With no one close enough to catch her.

Rhienne must have made a distressed noise, because Echo winced, accompanied by a blue flash—the start of her changing forms. "Get Irelia. I'll right the ship."

The rope holding Echo to the mast broke with a swipe of shale-like claws, and she scrambled to the wheel on all fours.

Rhienne didn't wait to see what the rest of the mimicry looked like, or if anyone else noticed Echo's transformation. She didn't have enough magic to teleport, but the memory of Irelia at the wheel yesterday, illuminated by the sun and laughing at a story Rhienne had never told anyone before, overrode her caution. No one else would die because of her.

Illusions didn't take much power to maintain. But they took enough that if she let them go, she could manage one more spell.

Rhienne launched herself at the captain. The deck blurred below her, the crew's shouts lost to the wind. There was no wonder to the feeling of flight, only blood thundering in her ears and Mishara's voice whispering *count your heartbeats, darling.*

She'd clung to her illusions through so many dangers. In the end, it was embarrassingly easy to dispel them. Her body shimmered, and the magic drained back into her core. She collided with Irelia, and they both rolled off the side of the ship.

The weight of Oblivion's gaze pressed the air from her lungs, but his malice was a quiet thing. It was the cold female voice that said, "Come, brother. We got what we came for."

Rhienne grasped for the shadows, for one last teleport, right before the storm swallowed them.

She and Irelia reappeared beneath the mast.

The airship shuddered and jerked, wood and metal groaning as Echo fought with the wheel. The world tilted again, slowly, so slowly, back to equilibrium.

Rhienne held Irelia against her, a sleeve pressed to the wound on the captain's head, taking ragged breaths and trying not to panic over the empty hole where her power had been.

The void dispersed, and the wind and hail calmed to a fine mist. The clouds disappeared as if they'd never been there. Oblivion hadn't wanted to kill her. Not yet. He just wanted to leave her vulnerable.

The rest of the crew began to gather, though not too close.

Irelia woke with a wince as the sun washed over her. There was a moment of nonrecognition that Rhienne would pretend for a little while longer was due to Irelia's injuries.

"My ship?" the captain asked as she struggled to sit up.

"Might need a few repairs, but it's in one piece."

"My crew?"

Rhienne glanced around the deck. Tash emerged from below, limping, with a long gash across his chest and medical supplies in hand. Everyone was accounted for except... "We lost Carsha. I tried to protect her, but she said something about balancing the scales."

Irelia whispered, "It was too soon. Damn the gods, it was too *fucking* soon."

Some of the crew were staring at Echo, whose hands were tinged gray and tipped with dark, overlong nails. Rhienne didn't want them asking questions, so she said, "You have a divine pact?"

The captain took in Rhienne's new appearance. "It seems we're not the only ones."

"We ought to toss 'em over," Mordach said with a voice like crunching gravel. His eyes were red, and she couldn't tell if it was melted hail or tears wetting his beard. "We were supposed to be safe until we delivered. These two've brought us nothing but trouble."

"I'll hear no such talk."

"But Captain, Carsha—"

"Knew the risks. Robin and Quinn saved our lives, at no small cost to themselves. We'll not tarnish that, nor Carsha's memory. Your quarrel is with the gods, not them." Even weakened as she was, Irelia's tone brooked no argument. "However, to ensure no further loss, I believe it's time we had an honest chat."

Can you schmooze? Rhienne slumped against the mast. *I don't have the energy right now.*

I think the time for schmoozing is over, Echo responded.

Just talk then, whatever. I've given enough away today. Rhienne regretted the thought as soon as it left her mind, but she couldn't take it back.

Hurt flashed across Echo's face, but she pushed through the circle of crew members and said, "Oblivion and Reckoning. Those were the gods in the storm, weren't they? That's why Carsha said what she said. You made a deal with the Balancer of Scales."

Irelia nodded. "And you with the Guardian of the Void."

"Yes." She glanced at Rhienne, then away. "A deal that's now broken."

"I don't think he'll be coming for us again, at least for a while," Rhienne mustered the will to say. "When we went overboard, Reckoning said they got what they came for. Oblivion wanted me to use the last of my magic. She took Carsha's life."

Even if Rhienne hadn't known about the weapons and the Dawnglow, the awkward glances that passed between the crew told her there was more to their deal.

"Why would they be working together?" The captain directed the question to Tash, who came forward with bandages and salves.

Tash knelt, paused, and at Irelia's nod, pushed her dislocated shoulder back into place. She hissed through her teeth and took a few steadying breaths.

"I don't know," Tash said, forming a sling for her arm as he talked, ignoring his own wounds. "Infinity and Eternity are called Mothers for a reason. The gods are their children in name and function. They squabble, forming ties and fractures as all families do."

"What are the chances Reckoning comes back?" Nazal whispered.

Solemnly, Tash met their eyes. "Something's been brewing between the gods since long before this storm. I doubt this is the last we'll see of them."

"Then we have to decide what to do before we arrive at Devonsfort. Whatever Reckoning's motives today, our bargain remains." Irelia swept her gaze over the crew.

"Tonight, we will celebrate Carsha. We'll reach land in three" —she paused, examining the damaged ship— "four days. Then we'll vote on how to move forward. Dismissed."

Tash helped a wobbling Irelia to her feet, and they limped into her cabin together. Mordach stormed away. Most of the others gave respectful nods or murmured thanks, then scattered to their duties.

Nazal clapped Rhienne on the back, patting Echo more gently. "It really was amazing, what you two did. Carsha was the closest thing Mordach had to family. Give him time. He'll come around."

They ambled away, leaving Rhienne and Echo alone at the mast.

"I'm sorry," Rhienne whispered. "That was a shitty thing to say, earlier. I can't blame you for my own stupidity."

"It was shitty. It was also true. You were very, very brave today, Rhienne."

She didn't feel brave. She felt like a harvest festival pumpkin with all its seeds scooped out, but with no pretty carvings on the outside to make up for it.

As if reading her mind, Echo said, "You know, I like the gray on you. You're like somebody's hot grandma."

"Oh, shut up. I'm not that old." But a smile tugged at her lips. "You were brave too. Couldn't have done all that without you. I'm just... not really sure what to do now." Or what she even *was* now, if she were being honest. Without her main source of power, how could she hope to face what was coming? "This goes beyond me trying to break my pact. Oblivion's sticking his nose in everything—first the Untold, now uniting with other gods against us. What-ever he wants from your dream, it can't be good."

"Certainly not." Echo shivered. "And I don't like our fate being in someone else's hands. They could change their minds and throw us overboard any moment."

Rhienne scanned the deck, her gaze lingering on the captain's door. The captain who had lost her mother to the horrors of war, who had pulled Rhienne's past from her lips without coercion.

During the storm, the thought of another person joining the list of those she'd hurt had been unbearable. But with more time to sit with it, there was a specificity of *who* she didn't want getting hurt that terrified her. She blurted out, "Then we need to get some leverage. If there's a true sailor's send-off for Carsha, everyone will be nice and drunk tonight. That'll be the perfect opportunity."

She pretended not to notice the unease on Echo's face, or the twinge of it in her own stomach. This was survival. People always cut you loose eventually; limited as Rhienne's resources were, it was better to be the one to do it first.

Chapter 17

Echo

The mood on the ship that night was strange. Echo's experience with mourning was limited to the somber funerals in Hearthglen, which had been for people she had nothing in common with except a mutual dislike. She'd heard stories from her time in Exodus's palace about the ways of sailors, but seeing it was something else. No tears were shed. They traded stories about Carsha. They made toasts and cursed the gods. Tash prepared a feast of savory pie and spiced vegetables for dinner, and Irelia, rested and bandaged, broke out a cask of port. It took some persuading—and permission from 'her mother'—for her to get a drink, which Rhienne thought was hilarious, but Echo refused to be the only one sober.

And then, strangest of all, they asked her to perform for them, and for Rhienne to sing.

Echo's throat tightened. It was stupid to be jealous, but she couldn't help it.

Rhienne took one look at her and said through the telepathy stone, *Next time I sing, we'll raise our voices together. The floor is yours.* "I'm far too tired, but I'm sure Quinn would be happy to oblige."

Thank you. She strummed her mandolin and let her fingers decide the song, no deals made, no magic demanded. Caught up in the music, the tension of the day faded to the background. She put her own flair on well-known songs, and no one shot her down. The airship's jovial atmosphere became doubly infectious because she was encouraging it.

Mordach asked Rhienne to dance, prompting a chorus of whistles and hoots from the crew. Honestly, Rhienne was gorgeous even without her illusions; more tired and weathered, sure, but Echo couldn't fathom why she'd been so worried about letting them go.

Echo played until her fingers ached, smiling all the while. This was the kind of performance she'd wanted to give at Crystal and Evergreen, the kind of reception she'd always dreamed of. If only this moment could last forever.

Sitting on top of a stack of crates as the evening cooled, belly full and mind softly buzzing, she'd almost forgotten what she had to do.

Rhienne spun away from the makeshift dance floor, breathless with laughter, and grinned tipsily up at Echo. "I didn't think I could have this much fun." *Are you ready? Seems like they're properly sauced now.*

"Don't speak too soon." She nodded toward Irelia, who was approaching with a look in her eye that made Echo suddenly very interested in tuning her mandolin.

The captain adjusted her coat with her uninjured arm and sidled up oh-so-casually to Rhienne. "Enjoying the night?"

"I am. I'll be honest, I'm a little surprised we're being included in the festivities."

"They're a rough bunch at times, but they're good people." Irelia smiled fondly at the cavorting sailors, dancing despite the lull in the music. "And you did save my life today. You're as much a part of the crew as anyone."

"Well, you saved us back in Port Saphrai, so I suppose we're even."

"Not yet. I know what it means to give up the power of a pact. Though I can't help but wonder what other secrets you're keeping." She paused and gave Rhienne a sideways glance. "For what it's worth, I like this version of you better."

Echo bit her tongue to keep from smiling. *Hot. Grandma.*

Shut. Up. She's just doing this for information. "You... really?" Rhienne said to Irelia.

I wouldn't be so sure.

"Really." Irelia leaned in closer. "It's been a long day. I'm going to have a glass of wine in my cabin, if you'd like to join me."

"Don't you have a concussion?" Rhienne sounded flustered, which was very unlike her in situations such as these.

What's wrong? Echo teased. *Never been with someone your actual age before?*

Of course I have. It's just... we have a job to do.

Blissfully unaware of the secondary conversation, Irelia murmured, "So says Tash. Which means I need someone to help me stay awake."

The things people said when they thought no one around them understood subtext. *Oh my gods, Rhi, you obviously like her. If you don't go right now, I'm going to mimic you and go in your place.*

You're so embarrassing.

You're welcome.

This is for distraction purposes only. Rhienne cleared her throat, her cheeks beet red. "Oh. Well, I—I suppose if it's medical, I can't say no, can I?" She followed Irelia away from the party and disappeared behind the double doors of the captain's cabin.

Satisfaction warmed Echo's chest.

Watching the party from the fringes, she wondered just how much they'd misunderstood this crew. Tonight was as much to mourn Carsha's death as to celebrate that they were still alive. Their anger at being lied to had barely any roots at all. She was growing to like these people; she didn't *think* they'd hurt her or Rhienne. But if the crew returned any affection, it was for a false version of her. A lie that asking for the Dawnglow would expose, and she knew all too well what happened when people found out what she really was.

That left a choice between stealing the Dawnglow or submitting herself to a lonely, unremarkable life, and submitting Rhienne's soul to Oblivion's mercy. That was hardly a choice.

No one paid Echo any mind as she slipped away, grabbing a lantern on the way down to the galley.

The door was unlocked, but the table was too heavy for her to move quietly. If she could mimic that brute from the Untold, it'd be easy, but traces of the paralytic lingered in her system. It had taken ages just for her claws to change back into fingernails. Getting stuck between a massive, muscular man and a little girl would be far more noticeable.

She waited, anxiety rising with every passing minute, until a cheer went up on the deck above, and she heaved. The table scraped against the floor, and Echo pressed herself into a hiding spot between the spice cabinet and a barrel of pickles until she was sure no one had heard.

It was the work of a moment to pick the lock on the hatch and climb down into the secret room. There were six sealed crates against the left wall—the ones with finished enchantments. Against the right wall were three more, open and awaiting their illegal magic. She didn't see the strongbox anywhere.

Echo worried the inside of her cheek and rifled through the rifles (if she didn't laugh at her own jokes, who would). The guns were the length of her leg and heavier than she'd imagined. Carefully maneuvering them and putting them back strained her already worn-out muscles. By the time she got to the last crate, her arms were shaking.

But there, under the first row of weapons and a handful of straw, was the lead strongbox.

It had no keyhole. Not even a seam where it would open.

She'd seen devices like this before. Either there was a specific phrase to open it, or it required some form of identification from the owner. On a hunch, Echo picked up one of the carving tools and sliced it along her finger. Blood welled, and she smeared it across the side of the box. It soaked into the lead and spread into a thin line that bisected the top and bottom. Rhienne would be proud.

Another offering of blood popped it open with a hiss. Her and Tash's nature may have come from different sources, but diluted as theirs was, divine blood was divine blood.

Dawnglow, on the other hand, was as pure as it got. The light nearly blinded her when she opened the box, and her eyes wouldn't—or couldn't—adjust. She ran her fingers over the crystals within, their energy buzzing up her arm. There were eight shards. Enough power to rule a queendom with. She snatched one of the non-depleted crystals, wrapped it in several layers of cloth, and pocketed it before she could change her mind.

Echo returned everything to its proper place and was halfway up the ladder when Tash said, "Thought it might have been you."

Her heart lurched. The cook loomed over the hatch. How the hell had he snuck up on her? The creaky floorboards should've given him away. She tried to look as wide-eyed and innocent as possible.

"Why don't you come out of there so we can talk properly."

Echo gripped the lantern tight in case she had to use it as a weapon and climbed the last few steps. She hesitated at the top, primed for anger, betrayal, but the flickering light only revealed the deep lines of resignation etched into Tash's face.

"It was you I heard this morning, wasn't it?" he asked.

Confirming his suspicions was the absolute last thing she should've done, but Echo found herself nodding. This disguise was ruining her.

Tash settled onto a stool and gestured for her to sit as well. "What did you see down there?"

"Guns," she said. He waited, so she amended. "Lots of guns."

"Come now. I thought we agreed that people like us had to look out for each other. I already covered up your claw marks on the deck."

Her heart dropped. She kept her mind fixed on her foresight as she said, "Robin knows what I am. We haven't hidden any more from you than you've hidden from us."

He laughed without humor. "You're not wrong."

Tash didn't press her further. What did he want? He knew she was a mimic, knew she'd discovered part of his secret, but there was no hatred or fear on his face. Just timeless, weary patience.

The Dawnglow in her pocket weighed a thousand pounds. But perhaps knowing what the crew had made a deal for would make her feel less awful about disrupting it. "You're not really part of Falenor's military, are you?"

"Not anymore. Hence the pact with Reckoning. The empire doesn't take kindly to deserters."

"So the weapons... the goddess asked you to make them?"

"Yes." Tash leaned forward, elbows on his knees. For the first time, she saw the immortal instead of the man—something ancient and exhausted behind his eyes that only came from living too long and seeing too much.

Reckoning was the Balancer of Scales, the Settler of Accounts, but she rarely traded in money.

The ball of guilt tightened in Echo's stomach. "Do you know why she wants them?"

"No," Tash whispered. "And I have a feeling I don't want to. We make our delivery to the prescribed location, and we get to stay hidden from the empire. At least, that's how it used to work. Now Irelia's talking like we might not hold up our end of the deal. So what I *would* like to know is how you and your mother plan to come out ahead of this business with Oblivion."

Echo looked down at her hands. Only the faintest tinge of gray remained. She had the sudden urge to change forms in front of him, just to see what he would do. Not into her original body—she wouldn't wish that sight on anyone—but one closer to what she liked. He'd been so honest with her, so helpful and fearless, it almost felt safe enough.

Just as quickly, the urge was gone, and she couldn't believe she'd ever thought it.

"Horizon was alive in your lifetime," Echo said quietly. "Is there anything you can tell me about the world before she died?" She'd been developing a theory about the sudden 'disappearance' of free magic. It didn't line up precisely with Horizon's death, but between that and the exiled god, *something* had to have happened among the gods to change their behavior. "Or perhaps shortly after?"

Confusion furrowed Tash's brow. "What are you getting at?"

"Do you remember the sixth god?" she asked, surprised at the desperation that leaked into her voice.

His expression turned wary. "I don't know what—"

"Please, Tash." She couldn't do this. She wanted so badly to trust these people, but more importantly, for them to trust her. Echo took the wrapped shard of Dawnglow out of her pocket and put it on the table between them. "We know one of them was exiled. I have reason to believe they're different from the others. Kinder. Their realm opened to save me, once. A library within the roots of a great tree. If we can find it again, the knowledge there could help us circumvent our deals."

He barely glanced at the Dawnglow. "You saw the library?" he breathed. "I had forgotten... no, I had been *made* to forget. I haven't been there since..." He rubbed the scars on his wrists. "I thought that realm would be erased along with them."

The exiled god must have saved Tash from the Untold. "Did you see them? Do you know their name?"

Tash was quiet for a long time. By the look on his face, he was walking back through memory. White flashed over his eyes, and he winced. Exactly like the Collector. "No. Their name has been erased. If I ever saw them, that's gone too."

Her shoulders drooped.

"But if that is what—*who*—you're searching for, I can tell you this: I meant what I said, about the gods forming factions. Some miss Horizon more than others. Not all of them were happy when their sibling was exiled either."

If they could reach out to the exile's allies, that might give them another lead. But Oblivion and Reckoning were clearly on the opposite side. That left two living gods. With a sinking feeling, Echo asked, "Which ones?"

"Horizon and the exile were the closest. Your next best bet would be Exodus."

She closed her eyes. "It's been a long time. You're sure you're remembering correctly?"

"I am."

What a cruel joke the Collector had played. The god-kin hadn't lied about where to find Dawnglow and the library, but he had given them *just* enough information. If Exodus was the only one left who might be able to contact the exile, traveling *to* Hearthglen wasn't going to cut it. To reach the God of Journeys, the journey had to be meaningful. She and Rhienne would have to go some-where important in town and do something impactful.

Whether or not Exodus would help her was another matter. The very idea of seeing him again made Echo's insides shrivel.

Tash must have understood some of the impact his news had, because he covered her hand with his. "This changes everything. We have another choice, besides sub-mitting to or defying Reckoning. I'll speak to Irelia and the rest of the crew. But just in case... I'll be right back." He took the Dawnglow she'd almost stolen and went down into the secret room. A couple minutes later, he returned with a shard half the size of the one she'd taken. "This is all we can spare. If we end up separating, I hope it's enough."

Stunned, Echo took it, its power tingling in her palm. "*If* we separate? You mean you're... going to convince the crew to work with us? Even knowing what I am, and that I was going to rob you?"

Tash shrugged. "I'm going to try. The crew might need some time to adjust to a mimic, but they got used to me just fine. And if what you say is true, we'll be doing more than freeing ourselves of our pact. Finding the exile would restore some much needed balance to the world."

This was more than she ever could've hoped for. Now she really was speechless.

"We've got a few more days until we reach the coast. Get some rest, and promise me you'll keep those sticky fingers out of my kitchen."

"Yessir." Echo tucked the Dawnglow away and wandered to bed in a daze.

Rest was a fantasy that night. Her head was full of marble, mist, and song, and a creeping dread about what would happen if Exodus saw her again. But all of it was overlaid by Tash's impossible acceptance.

She hooked her leg through the netting of her hammock, afraid she might float away. Echo felt lighter than air, and more than a bit vindicated. For once in her life, honesty had helped her. Smiling, Echo held the crystal in her pocket. Rhienne was going to have a heart attack.

Chapter 18

Echo

The day after the storm was a blur of activity. With the repairs made, Irelia pushed the crew hard—less to make up for lost time, and more because no one wanted to wait around to see if the sky would remain clear. Echo kept watch in the crow's nest for any further divine shenanigans, using the lookout's borrowed goggles to enhance her vision and block the wind. So far, the only disruption had been a malfunction with one of the arcane engines. The back of the airship still smelled oddly like lemons from the small magical explosion.

Nice as it was to be away from the bustle with a gorgeous view of the sea and sky, she was getting cold. And impatient.

Rhi, are you coming?

There was a long pause before her friend answered. *I don't want to climb up there. I told you, I don't have anything else to say.*

Echo peered down at the deck. She'd thought acquiring the Dawnglow would cheer Rhienne up, but revealing her conversation with Tash had had the opposite effect. Rhienne had been moving around the ship like a ghost all day, avoiding everyone. Including her. *I'd rather we talk about it face to face. I don't understand why you're being like this.*

Just because Tash likes you doesn't mean the whole crew will risk more of Reckoning's wrath to team up with us. And who says we even want their help?

That was deliberately obtuse, even for Rhienne. *Did something happen with Irelia?* The lack of response told her enough, so Echo changed tack. *Whatever we decide, and whatever the crew decides, you should take the Dawnglow.*

Footsteps sounded on the ladder. Rhienne's head poked through the opening at the bottom of the crow's nest. Her cheeks were sunburnt, but underneath she looked pale and tired, and her eyes were narrowed. "Why?"

"Because there's only enough for one of us." Echo scooted over and patted the space next to her, then took the cloth-covered shard from her pocket.

"I know that." Rhienne pulled herself up the rest of the way and sat across from her. A salty breeze kicked up and blew her hair into her face. Grumbling, she wrangled the graying strands into a braid. "I mean, why me instead of you? You shouldn't have to face Exodus again."

"We know for sure Dawnglow is a component in your resurrection ritual. We *don't* know how to use it to fix my voice or find the exiled god." Echo crossed her arms. She'd been mulling this over all day. The God of Journeys owed her. Destroying her life was *not* an equal trade for trying to shirk her payment. "Besides, I'm not going to let you waltz off on your own to barter with that asshole, so if I have to see him anyway, I might as well be the one making a deal. I've been to his realm before, I know what it takes to get there, and I know *him.*"

Rhienne took the Dawnglow and worried it between her hands. "If you come poking around about his dead and vanished siblings, don't you think he'll get a bit prickly?"

"He'll be a veritable cactus no matter who asks the questions." Echo thought of the dreams she'd had while healing from the Untold's poison, the strange mixture of terror and joy she'd felt traversing Exodus's halls, and hid a shudder. "But I don't like the idea of him toying with you."

Shame flickered across Rhienne's face. "So that *is* it. You don't trust me."

"What? Of course I do! You just said yesterday that you've lost enough already. I'm *agreeing* with you."

"You're trying to prevent me from making any other stupid bargains."

Echo threw her hands up. "Oh, yes, I'm so terrible for valuing my best friend's life. How could I do such a thing?" Rhienne remained quiet, curled in on herself. Echo released a breath and said more gently, "What's going on? Talk to me."

"I'm just feeling... trapped here. That's all." She took a knife from her belt and carved tiny patterns into the wooden floor. "This boat is too small. There's no getting away from anyone. And now they're thinking about tagging along? I don't like it. This was *our* mission. The more people we bring, the more we'll have to divide the spoils. The more we risk. Eventually, they're going to find out we lied to them."

"Valid points," Echo conceded. "But we need help, Rhienne. Our list of enemies is too long, and we still don't know what Oblivion is planning. If it's not these people, then who?"

"Someone else. Anyone else."

"You're going to destroy the ship if you keep at it like that." Echo reached over and stilled Rhienne's hand before asking again, "Did something happen with Irelia?"

For the amount of doom and despair in Rhienne's expression, Echo half expected to find another storm brewing on the horizon.

Rhienne glanced at the ladder like she was assessing her escape routes, then let out a long sigh. "You were right. Irelia didn't want information. She wanted company. *My* company. We talked the whole night. Well, not the *whole* night, but when we weren't... busy."

"And she said something that made you doubt she'd help us?"

"Not exactly." Rhienne fidgeted with her dagger. "It's just... Irelia's done so much with her life, and she's got all these ideals and ambitions and stories. And I..." Rhienne spread her fingers as if to cast a spell, but no magic came forth.

Ah. Between this and Rhienne's bitterness about her lack of dreams, Echo was beginning to see why the illusions had mattered so much. Partly for vanity, but mostly because they had let Rhienne pretend she had more time to find her path, with fewer debts holding her down.

"You've got all that too," Echo said. "We wouldn't be here if you hadn't summoned me to the catacombs, and you wouldn't have been there if you weren't trying to bring your mom back."

Rhienne shook her head. "It's not the same."

"So I was right." Echo couldn't help but smile. "You do like her."

"That's not what I said!"

"No, but you want her to like you. The real you. And you're scared that if she finds out who that is, she'll turn you away." She held up a hand to cut off the inevitable protest. "You can't lie. I am extremely well acquainted with the feeling."

"I don't even think I know *how* to be real. The longest-running relationship I've ever had was with Mishara, and that was a con." Rhienne's lip curled in disgust, but then her shoulders drooped. "It's not a matter of *if* I screw it up but *when.*"

And if they stayed with the crew, there was no running away. From that, or any other mistakes they made, danger they attracted, or people they hurt. "We have left quite a wake of destruction, haven't we?" Echo murmured.

"My mother, Sidrin, Jareth, Aderai, Carsha." Rhienne ticked them off on her fingers.

"Yeah." Echo sighed, letting the heaviness rest in her stomach and staring out over the ocean. She understood exactly what Rhienne was feeling. They were in uncharted territory. But looking back at the path that led them here, something had to change, and Echo couldn't shake the feeling that this ship, this crew, was their best chance to succeed without taking any more losses.

Nothing could move Rhienne once she put her foot down, but if she wanted something and didn't know how to get it, Echo could work with that. "Look, nothing is set in stone yet. Hang onto the Dawnglow, and for the next couple days, pretend we *are* going to stay with them. See how it feels. If you don't like it, we send them off to Devonsfort and go to Exodus alone."

On the deck below, there was a loud bang, followed by Mordach's distinctive litany of curses.

Rhienne almost cracked a smile. "Okay. Pretend. I can do that."

As soon as Echo's watch was over, she found Irelia at the helm.

The captain was as relaxed as anyone in her position could be, hair coming loose from her bun, her coat absent and shirt sleeves rolled up past her elbows. Her eyes were lost in the sky, but her expression became guarded as Echo approached. "Evening, Quinn. What can I do for you?"

Quinn. They would have to do something about that if they stayed. "I was wondering if you'd talked to Tash today."

"Ah. Nazal, take the wheel!" Irelia called out to the boatswain, then ushered Echo to a more private corner of the deck. She leaned her good shoulder against a crate of oranges. "Yes, I've spoken to Tash. We all have."

Echo's skin prickled under Irelia's gaze. Suddenly, she feared Rhienne had been right. "And...?"

"And we have some stragglers, but we're leaning into the idea. Carsha's loss has most of us itching for a way out of our pact, if not a fight." The captain bent closer. "You two have done more to anger the gods than anyone I've ever met, and you're still standing. I think we both have things to offer each other."

"I think so too." Echo bit her lip, only partially relieved. "My mom isn't so sure though. I'd wondered if you... might be able to convince her."

Irelia's brows went up. "My opinion can't be worth more than yours. Whether or not you're really parent and child, you certainly seem like family." When Echo paled, the captain added, "Don't worry, your secret is safe until you wish to tell it."

Even Tash hadn't sussed out that her age was part of the mask. Denial rose to her lips, but it withered under Irelia's scrutiny. Echo plucked an orange from the crate and pretended to focus on peeling it while her thoughts churned. She'd said to Rhienne, *If not these people, then who?* But it was always easier to encourage someone else than to take one's own advice.

When she could speak past the tightness in her chest, she asked, "What gave me away?"

"Robin, for one." Irelia chuckled. "The way she talks about you sometimes, it's almost as if *you* were the parent. You're also not the first of your kind I've encountered."

"Really? I've never met another person like me... at least that I know of."

"He worked for Falenor's spymaster. Called himself Q, short for Quicksilver. I think he enjoyed the joke." Irelia looked at her sidelong. "He said the same thing, about not knowing if he'd ever met someone like him. He seemed very lonely. You've got the same air about you—you and Tash, actually, despite my best efforts."

"I can tell Tash cares for you a great deal," Echo said, because that was the only part of Irelia's story she knew how to respond to. "You and the crew."

"Oh, I don't doubt that. But he knows one day we'll be gone, and he'll remain. There will always be distance because of it. When you are constantly reminded of the ways you're different, it's hard to carry yourself as if you're the same." She smiled sadly. "I don't hold that against him. Or you. Having to hide who you are isn't quite the same as outliving everyone you love, but I can't imagine it's any easier. Anyway, that's how I knew. It's in the eyes."

There was a feeling in Echo's heart that she couldn't name, something tight and squirming, but also... the opposite. Something approaching possibility. It felt like music, the *real* kind, like she'd played during Carsha's funeral.

Better not to ponder it too long. She popped an orange slice into her mouth, savoring the burst of juice. "So, about Robin."

"Yes." Irelia straightened, abruptly business-like again. "How can I help?"

Echo didn't want to give away her friend's feelings. Rhienne would have to talk through them in her own time. "I told her what I think. Now she needs room to become comfortable here. Keep it breezy, if you can. She doesn't like being pressured into things."

"Understandable. I'll see what I can do. Or not do, I suppose." Someone shouted for Irelia, and she said, "I ought to get back, unless there was anything else."

What do you think the crew would do if I switched bodies? The question begged to be asked, but when she opened her mouth, it didn't come out. Echo waved for the captain to leave.

She returned to her regular post helping Tash in the galley. The cook didn't press her about their interaction the previous night, and for that she was glad, but now that Irelia had pointed it out, she couldn't unsee it. *He seemed very lonely. It's in the eyes.*

It came with a pang of self-recognition. She didn't want to be that way, always keeping distance. Echo had ardently hoped fixing her voice would bridge that gap, but that hope was beginning to feel very unsteady indeed. Everything just *had* to lead back to Exodus.

If her vegetable chopping was more aggressive than normal, Tash didn't press her about that either.

Chapter 19

Rhienne

Rhienne spent the next few days pretending, and for the first time in her life, she settled into a pattern. During the day, she worked and found herself unwittingly getting to know the crew. They'd come from every region and walk of life. Some knew Irelia from her days in the military and had fled Falenor's wars with her, some had just wanted to get away and explore the sky. And they asked *her* questions in return. It was unnerving, bizarre, but also... nice. She spent her breaks playing dice with Mordach and Nazal, and told more stories about Vala, the pranks they'd pulled, and the places they'd traveled in dreams. Reliving that chaotic, beautiful freedom simultaneously made her ache and loosened the knot of grief. Rhienne would get that autonomy back. She would get her *mother* back.

At night, Irelia filled the hollow in Rhienne's chest where her magic had once been. And tonight—the last night before they made landfall—the hole was threatening to become a vacuum and swallow her from the inside. By the time the double doors of Irelia's cabin closed behind her, Rhienne was halfway out of her shirt. So she was more than a little peeved to find Irelia fully dressed, sitting at her desk with a book in her hands.

"Am I early?" Rhienne asked, knowing she wasn't.

"I thought we'd try something different tonight." Irelia slipped a scrap of paper between the pages, closed the book, and gestured to the edge of her bed. "Sit."

A nervous chuckle escaped her. "Am I in trouble?"

"Not yet." There was a knock at the door. The captain answered it with a whispered, "Thank you," and came back with two mugs that smelled of cloves and cinnamon. She gave one to Rhienne and sat on the bed beside her, their legs pressed together.

The ceramic warmed her hands. Mulled wine. A drink for long nights by the fire, wrapped up in blankets and stories. Rhienne's voice came out strained. "Please, Irelia, I don't want to talk right now." She didn't want to pretend tonight. She wanted to forget. Lose and erase herself, like the exiled god.

"Who said anything about talking?" Irelia sipped from her mug. "We've done things your way. While I still have the chance, I'd like to show you mine."

While I still have the chance. Rhienne hid a shiver. "What does that mean?"

Irelia leaned in and kissed her. Rhienne put her drink on the nightstand and pulled at the captain's clothes, but

Irelia grabbed her hands and whispered, "Slowly," against her lips.

"Why?" Rhienne whined.

"When was the last time you lingered in anything?" Irelia left a trail of kisses up her jaw, behind her ear. "When you truly enjoyed yourself?" She slipped a hand under Rhienne's shirt. "Or enjoyed someone else?"

The touch left her skin tingling, but something in her rebelled against the gentleness. "I don't w—"

Irelia silenced her with another kiss. "I will tie you to this bed if I have to."

Rhienne might have preferred that to Irelia's unhurried pace, easing off their clothes when Rhienne wanted to tear them free, delicately tracing fingers between her legs when she wanted everything harder, faster. She couldn't shut her brain off; she needed *sensation* to block out the racing thoughts of Oblivion, her mother, Exodus, Echo—to fill the emptiness inside her, even for a moment, as Irelia had the past several nights.

Perversely, her thoughts strayed to Mishara. How similar these women were. Useful for the power they held, commanding and beautiful. But Mishara's allure was a trap that ended in bruises, claw marks, and poison. This was... different. Irelia actually seemed to care.

Only then did it occur to Rhienne that she'd never asked Irelia what *she* wanted from this.

The captain was right. Rhienne couldn't think of a time she'd lingered in this particular brand of pleasure instead of using it to gain something.

She took a deep breath and tried to relax. Irelia took that as a signal, gently pushing Rhienne onto her back and sliding down between her legs. Rhienne caught a hint of a smile before Irelia's mouth became much more occupied.

This too was a slow, purposeful thing. Rhienne closed her eyes and wove her fingers into Irelia's hair, trying to anchor herself and empty her mind. She let her other senses take over, focusing on the creaking of the ship, the rustle of sails, the vibration of the engines, the lingering taste of wine, until her worries faded.

Then there was only Irelia, touching her with slow, methodical, dizzying affection. Rhienne wondered if this was how gods felt when they were worshiped. Soon she thought nothing at all. And when she begged for release, and Irelia murmured, "Not yet," against her thigh, Rhienne didn't begrudge her. It made the moment—not long after, because her body was ablaze—all the sweeter.

She did her best to take revenge on Irelia in kind, and some small part of her shuddered at all the time she'd wasted doing this any other way. But mostly, she lost herself in the sounds of Irelia's pleasure, the way her back arched and her legs tensed around Rhienne's neck until, breathless, she moaned, "Robin."

That broke through the fugue of the moment just enough to get her mind working again. She pulled herself up and nestled into Irelia's chest, and waited for the woman's heart to calm. In the warmth and dark, the terrors of the world outside seemed far away, and she realized, even if she was destined to screw it up, she wanted to see where this would go.

"Rhienne," she whispered. "My real name is Rhienne."

Chapter 20

Echo

Echo woke in the morning to the call of, "Land ho!" She dressed in clothes that were too large for her current form and stumbled up to the deck. The day was clear and brisk; the crew were already gathered around the mast, and from the redness of their cheeks, they'd been in the cold a while. Tash and Irelia stood at the center of the group. Voices overlapped, indistinguishable. She spotted Rhienne emerging from the captain's cabin, her grogginess abruptly replaced by anxiety as she took in the scene.

Rhienne caught her gaze and gave the tiniest nod before her eyes locked back on Irelia.

A little thrill ran through Echo, part joy and part terror. Her plan for Rhienne to come around to joining the crew had worked. That meant it was time for step two. She met

Tash's eye, who waved at her over the crowd. Everyone fell silent.

Echo had to clear her throat twice to find her voice. "Before you vote, there's something I need to tell you all."

"We've already voted, actually," Tash interrupted with a look that said, *you don't have to do this.* "The decision was unanimous. We'd like to come with you."

"If you'll have us," Irelia added, glancing at Rhienne. "We have two days before our deadline—before Reckoning will realize we've decided to break our deal. We'll do everything we can to prepare for the fallout and help you in the meantime."

Despite the chill, sweat beaded on Echo's back. She gripped her telepathy stone. *What do you think?*

You were right. I don't want to hear any gloating about it.

Oh, there will be gloating, but not right now.

With the entire crew watching, Rhienne rolled her eyes and crossed the deck to stand beside Echo. *What are you going to do?*

I can't stay like this forever. Her body was entirely too small and helpless for who they were going to face. Not to mention she looked ridiculous in her oversized shirt and pants. *Better they find out now, rather than in the middle of something important.*

Rhienne squared up to the rest of the crew, ready for a fight. *What does your foresight say?*

Still dying old and alone.

Great. Rhienne didn't change her stance.

"We would greatly appreciate your help," Echo said. "If *you'll* still have *us* after some... reintroductions." She closed her eyes, wondering if she was about to make the second biggest mistake of her life. She winced a little when the crew gasped at the flash of blue magic over her skin. Bone and muscle stretched, curves filled out her clothing, and hair no longer hung in her face. She was back in the dancer's body, but without its typical confidence and relief. Echo wrapped her arms around her torso and peeked through her lashes, only opening her eyes fully when she realized no weapons were drawn.

Shock. A few traces of fear. The inevitable questions: *How didn't I realize* and *Who else could she have mimicked?* All of this swirled across the crew's faces. Even Tash blinked hard, lips parted in surprise at the difference in her forms.

Then Nazal came forward and stuck out their hand. "And who do we have the pleasure of formally inviting to our crew?"

Echo's fingers trembled a little, but Nazal's grip was firm, warm, and welcoming. She'd expected Irelia to cross this bridge first, but the captain had been waiting for someone else to do it. This was an honest offer of peace, rather than an order. Echo was suddenly glad for Nazal's history lesson in a way that had nothing to do with the information she'd gleaned.

She managed to smile. "You can call me Echo. And this is Rhienne."

The boatswain shook both their hands before turning back to the crew. "What do you think, Captain?"

Irelia didn't hesitate. "This changes nothing, and if anyone believes otherwise, I am more than happy to drop you off at the nearest port." Though there were a few wary glances, no one protested. "Excellent. Then it seems we're in need of a new heading."

The twisting, bubbly feeling in Echo's chest was back, and now she realized what it was. Someone besides Rhienne had seen her, and terrifyingly, wonderfully, *understood* her.

Irelia beckoned them over to the navigation table and rolled out a thick sheet of carefully inked parchment, weighing the corners down with stones. Echo took a moment to gather her thoughts while admiring the jagged lines of continents and rivers, the small annotations and illustrations of landmarks. There was something both grounding and exhilarating about seeing the whole world spread out in miniature, vast distances reduced to the width of her hand.

"If we're going to enter Exodus's realm, simply arriving at a destination isn't enough," Echo explained. "It's the healing—or, in rarer cases, destruction—that happens at the end of a journey that opens the way." She'd stepped out of the exiled god's library with new hope, after going into it with none. The way to Exodus appeared shortly after.

This time, with Hearthglen as their destination, there were plenty of burned bridges to rebuild. One in particular, she hoped, would be easier than the rest. "We grew up here." Hearthglen was too small to appear on the map, so Echo pointed to the town's approximate location on the coast. "We're going to see our father."

Chapter 21

Rhienne

As the dark smear on the horizon solidified into a land-mass, Rhienne busied herself among the rest of the crew, making defensive preparations. She paired up with Mordach, deconstructing whatever containers they could spare to reinforce the ship's hull and protect the engines and sails. Once they passed the weapons' delivery date, the odds of Reckoning launching another attack were high. They needed to be ready.

Rhienne might have preferred another bout with the gods to seeing her father again. The last time they'd spoken, he was very clear that she and Echo were no longer welcome in Hearthglen. That had been over a decade ago, but she did not share Echo's optimism that he'd softened. Adopting Echo had been one of the few times he'd shown his gentler side, and his reward had been for his two children to ruin his life.

Wrapped in these thoughts, Rhienne misjudged the swing of her hammer. It slammed down on her thumb. "Fuuuucking shit!" she hissed, holding her throbbing hand to her chest and curling over it, eyes watering.

Mordach winced on her behalf. "Happens to the best of us. Here, let me see."

She glared at him, but only for a moment, and extended her hand. Her finger was already turning stiff and red. Mordach examined it, muttered something about her not being strong enough to break anything, then made an undulating gesture in the air. Cool, silvery liquid manifested from nowhere and seeped into her skin. Her pain lessened at once.

When she could speak again without cursing, Rhienne breathed, "Thank you."

"Aye, don't mention it." He paused, giving her a sideways glance while holding the healing magic in place. "Somethin' on yer mind?"

A week ago, she would've brushed him off, but with all they had survived together and forgiven each other for... well, the words didn't come *easy*, but they did come. "I never thought I'd have to show my face at home again. I'm not looking forward to it."

Mordach made a deep, contemplative noise. "Burned some bridges on yer way out, did ye?" He raised a bushy eyebrow, and she nodded. "I'm familiar. Never had the chance to go back and repair 'em, though. Be a shame to waste the opportunity."

She thought of the bridge in the Collector's cavern; repairing it had been a two-person job. "What if they won't meet me halfway?"

"Ye've a talent for persuasion. If that fails, ye'll need to go a mite further than halfway." Mordach's spell dispersed as the healing finished, leaving only a faint bruise to show her error. "Whatever it is ye did, are ye sorry for it?"

Rhienne opened her mouth and closed it without responding.

"Hmm. I'd start there, then."

Nazal called for a break, and Mordach gave her a little salute before heading down to the galley.

Rhienne sat in a patch of shade to drink from her waterskin and palmed the telepathy stone, turning over the prickly man's advice. *You know, I always imagined swooping back into town with triumphant I-told-you-so's.*

With fireworks and music in the background? Echo thought back from her position in the crow's nest. She'd volunteered to keep her distance while the crew adjusted to the idea of having a mimic on board.

Obviously. But we don't really have anything to lord over them yet. And the fanfare is the reason everyone hated us.

Well, that and the fact that we brought trouble wherever we went, Echo said. *And the town guards took their hatred of us out on everyone else. And we always talked about how we couldn't wait to leave because we were better than them.*

Rhienne chuckled. *I mean, we* are *better than most of them, but maybe we didn't have to say it so loud. I was thinking, if we want to heal wounds, maybe we shouldn't draw so much attention at first. Keep the ship out of sight, go in with only a few of us. I think you, me, Tash, and Irelia will be enough of a shock to their system.*

Oh. That's a good idea.

Don't sound so surprised. A tiny pebble sailed down from the crow's nest and smacked into her chest. "Ow! Where the hell did you even get that?"

"It was in my pocket." Echo grinned down at her and ducked back to safety. *And you know I didn't mean it like that. I'm just glad to see you thinking ahead. I'm having a bit of difficulty with that myself… beyond a certain point.*

Rhienne rose to update Irelia about the plan. The captain muttered something about not wanting to get involved in family matters, but Rhienne waved off the concern. Irelia needed to stay close so they could enter Exodus's realm together. The more people there were to petition for the god's aid, the more likely he was to give it. And honestly, the more people there were around her father, the kinder he'd be.

To Echo, she said, *Say the word, and I* will *punch Exodus for you.*

Her friend's laugh was dry and humorless. *Only if he won't help us.*

Nah, I'll do it even if he does help. He deserves it.

There was a long pause, and then, so soft Rhienne almost missed it, Echo said, *We'll see.*

The airship stopped a few miles outside Hearthglen, out of sight of anyone who might be looking. The marsh was deceptively serene from above, the lush ground shot through with dozens of branching streams. One little dirt road connected the town to civilization. The terrain would be a bitch and a half to walk across, parts of it flooded, all of it stinking and humid and filled with insects. Rhienne gulped down as much of the fresh, cold breeze as she could before the ship descended.

Irelia took Rhienne's hand and placed a heavy coin purse in it. "In case we need to ease our way in anywhere," the captain said, "here's your pay for the work you've done. I've got a flare charge to signal the ship. Anything we should be wary of when we disembark?"

Everything and everyone. Rhienne bit her tongue. This woman had experienced true hardship in Falenor's army. Complaining about small minds in small towns seemed... well, small. So she shrugged and said, "Just stay close to us. They don't like strangers."

Irelia turned to address the crew. "Be safe. Be smart. We'll be back as soon as we can. Mordach is in charge until we return."

The man's cheeks went almost as red as his beard as he stood to attention. "Aye, Captain. Fair winds and clear skies." The others echoed his farewell.

As new and unfamiliar as this entire situation was, Rhienne couldn't deny the warmth that swept through her at the idea of strolling through town with Irelia by her side. "Let's go. The bugs get *really* nasty as the sun goes down."

Mordach and Nazal waved them off, wishing them luck. She, Echo, Tash, and Irelia walked down the lowered cargo ramp, which hovered a few feet off the ground to avoid the muck.

Rhienne jumped onto home soil for the first time in over a decade. Her boots immediately sunk two inches into the soggy ground. "Welcome to Hearthglen," she muttered as Tash and Irelia joined her.

"Ugh." Echo grimaced at the squelching noise her steps made. "I might be a little too flamboyant for this place. Should I look like someone else?"

"You're perfect." Though the question was a sharp reminder that Rhienne no longer had illusions to hide behind. She'd been avoiding mirrors for the past week. "Do *I* look okay?"

Irelia answered, "Gorgeously windblown and sun-tanned."

Rhienne blushed. *Blushed.* Like a schoolgirl. Sharing a bed was one thing. Advice and compliments and taking her to meet her father? By Irelia's grin, she knew exactly what Rhienne was thinking. She rolled her eyes, smoothing her hair and pulling her boots out of the mud.

Gods, she missed magic. A levitation spell would've made life so much easier, and she almost reached for her dagger. But she'd promised Echo, and she didn't want Irelia to see her use the forbidden power. Heading into town with a bunch of bleeding wounds was probably the second worst thing she could do, behind heading into town at all.

The thought must have been plain on her face, because Echo said, "You could sit the discussion out, you know."

Tempting. So very tempting. It would be easier for everyone involved. But no. "If we're not separating for Exodus, we're definitely not separating for Dad." Rhienne heaved a sigh. "I could use a spell anchor for the resurrection anyway. It's not necessary for the ritual, but having something of Mom's would mean I don't have to use as much of my own blood."

Tash swatted a mosquito on his neck. "Let's make sure we have enough blood to use by the time we get there. Where to?"

"Follow me." Echo squared her shoulders and took Rhienne's hand, and they set off across the swamp to summon a god.

After so long away, Rhienne expected Hearthglen to have changed. For the town to have either built itself up or worn itself down. But as they entered the village proper, the whole place seemed frozen in time. Harlan's fence still leaned, Liliana's garden was still overrun by weeds, the paint still peeled off Cyrus's front door. At least they were far enough from the water to avoid the low-tide-dead-fish miasma.

Then there were the guards, dutifully protecting the hamlet from evildoers at a card table outside the only bar, empty mugs scattered around them. None of them called out to her, but she felt like a fugitive returning to the scene of a crime.

"Maybe we should've waited until nightfall," Echo said as people stopped what they were doing to watch them pass by.

"Word would've gotten out anyway that I came back, especially with *three* strangers." She looked pointedly at

Echo's new form. If you thought something too loudly in this town, it'd be the subject of gossip in less than a day.

Rhienne gave tight nods and polite smiles to her old neighbors. Even when they moved to the other side of the street to avoid her.

One small blessing was the lack of Untold lurking about. This was probably not the kind of place they assumed mimics liked to be, and with good reason. There was nowhere to hide.

Finally, they made it to the familiar workshop door. A hammer and anvil were lovingly carved into the wooden sign overhead. Smoke rose from the furnaces in the back, and the rhythmic thunk of metal hitting metal rang out into the street.

This was not the way Rhienne had wanted to feel young again.

"Should we stay outside?" Tash asked.

"There's a little waiting area in the shop," Rhienne said. "If you don't mind, just in case—"

"We're here wherever you need us," Irelia assured her.

There was that surge of warmth again, bringing a little bit of strength with it. For all the doubts that had plagued her mind, Rhienne was glad to have them along.

Echo went in first. *Keep your telepathy stone close. We have to tread carefully here.*

A bell tinkled above, announcing their arrival.

"I'll be right there," her father called. His voice had gotten huskier. Or the accent sounded more provincial after so much time in cities. "Feel free to take a seat." Clank. Clank. Clank.

Rhienne swallowed but couldn't find her voice.

"Silas... Dad," Echo called out. "Rhienne and I are here to see you. With friends."

There was a pregnant pause, then the hiss of molten metal being quenched. She could picture precisely the way he moved around the forge, setting everything in a safe place, removing his gloves and apron before he opened the door to the storefront. It took longer than it used to.

The man who walked through was both her father and not. Where Hearthglen was untouched by time, he'd aged double. His profession had always kept him fit, and the bulk of muscle was still there, but there was also a hunch to his back and a paunch to his belly. New wrinkles lined his face, and his hair had gone completely gray. Silas stopped several feet away, taking them in as if they were ghosts. There was only a counter covered in tools, hardware, and horseshoes between them, but the space yawned, cavernous.

"Thought you two were never coming back," he said gruffly. "What're you doing here?"

"Like Echo said, we wanted to see you," Rhienne managed. "A lot's happened."

His gaze flicked to Tash and Irelia, taking in the tattered military garb. "I don't want any part of whatever trouble you've gotten yourselves into. This town has nothing left to give you."

Under thirty seconds. That had to be a record. She knew they were supposed to be mending fences, but Rhienne couldn't help herself. "Dad, how many times do we have to say this? Captain Quinn was stealing from people—you were paying triple in taxes so he could skim off the top."

"Which you didn't know until after you stole from him and vandalized his office."

"If we had known *before*, would that have made it okay? He got what he deserved."

"And then the rest of us paid for it for years after you were gone!" Her father rarely raised his voice, but time had obviously not healed this wound. "You don't think before you act, either of you. Never have. Or if you do, it's only to think about yourselves. Take after your mother that way."

The last was said under his breath, but it took all the hot air out of Rhienne's sails.

Echo stepped between them, hands up in a gesture of peace. *This is our in.* Out loud, she said, "Vala is actually why we're here. We just want to ask a few questions about her, and then we'll leave."

Like it always had, Echo's presence softened him. Rhienne understood why (she reminded him too much of her mother), but the difference in the way he treated them still hurt.

Silas closed his eyes and sighed. "Come into the back, then. I need to finish this order by the end of the day. Your friends can stay here, unless they want to help."

"It won't take long," Rhienne protested.

"Don't tell me you've forgotten how to work the forge." He crossed his arms, and once he did that, there was no arguing with him.

Rhienne barely kept herself from groaning like a child. She waved for Irelia and Tash to sit down—there was no reason to subject them to any further awkwardness—and followed Silas into the workshop. She'd never liked smithing and he damn well knew it, but it'd be easier for him to talk if his hands were busy.

Two swords hung on the wall, filigreed hilts and folded steel blades still gleaming with the sparks of magic their completion had created. They would rust and dull more slowly than a regular sword. Far finer work than any guards who were assigned to this backwater deserved.

"This one's almost done, but I need two more to finish the set." Her father removed a third blade from the quenching oil and set to work reheating it, giving no more instruction than a vague gesture toward the sketches and pieces of steel waiting on the other side of the workbench.

Rhienne grimaced as she suited up in a heavy apron and gloves, already sweating from the heat. The designs were simple and clean, and she was pretty sure she remembered the basics.

"So then. What's this about your mother?"

She chose her words as gingerly as she picked up the tongs and held the steel in the forge. "When was the last time you saw her?"

"Not since you were small, you know that." Another hiss of oil, then back to the heat to work out the brittleness. "Has she come to see you?"

"Yes. She was teaching me to control the dreamwalks, but she... went missing. We're trying to find her. I wanted to know if she said anything strange to you before she left."

"Whatever it is you're getting at, Rhienne, you'd better just ask. You know I never liked this dance you do."

Lucky for him, her steel was turning yellow, and she was too busy bringing it to the anvil to snap at him again.

"Let me do the next bit," Echo offered, hammer in hand.

"I'm not in danger of whacking anyone. Yet," Rhienne muttered.

"I know, but you could never get the taper even on both sides."

She relinquished the metal with a half-hearted eye roll and turned to watch her father's reaction. "Did she ever mention a deal, Dad? A deal that involved me?"

He froze for the barest second before shuffling over to the whetstone. "If you're looking for answers about her past, I'm the wrong person to ask. All she ever told me about herself had to do with you and the way you would turn out."

"What's that supposed to mean?"

"About your nature. What you inherited from her. 'Dreams are the most robust and brittle things that mortals have,' she liked to say. And because you couldn't have any of your own, you'd constantly be chasing something you'd never catch."

Rhienne bit her tongue, caught between offense and guilt, but she wouldn't rise to either. He was avoiding her question. "She told me about the deal the last time I saw her, and that she'd left to protect me."

The whetstone scraped against metal for a long minute, punctuated by Echo's hammer. At last, he said, "Then you know as much as I do."

"She never mentioned what she made the deal for? Or who she made it with?"

He shook his head. "Only that she couldn't say."

Not wouldn't. Couldn't. That supported the theory that her mother had been consorting with the exiled god, but Rhienne couldn't help being disappointed. She'd let go of the anger at her mother's deal a long time ago, but she wanted to know—no, *needed* to know, with a desperation that scared her—what that trade had been *for.* If it was worth it. Seemed the only place she was going to get that information was directly from the source. "Did she leave you with anything of hers? An anchor will help us find her faster."

He sharpened the blade in silence for another moment, then said, "Give me a minute," and rose from the bench.

It was the movement of an old, weary man, and it left her with a twisting knot in her stomach as he disappeared into the front room. In the not-too-distant future, Rhienne was going to look like that. Except, where Silas had been satisfied with his life before they'd barreled back into it, she had nothing to be proud of, and a lot to cause her shame.

Low voices trickled in, the rise of a question from Silas, an answer from Tash, and a longer one from Irelia. Rhienne couldn't make out the words, but she could guess: *you're really their friends, not probation officers or something?* She took a breath that did little to calm her.

Her father returned with a small lacquered box and pushed it across the table. "Dream spirits don't have possessions, but she always liked this. Asked me to engrave it before she left."

The inside was lined with dark green velvet, and a tiny porcelain dancer spun to tinkling chimes that skipped notes as gears struggled to turn. It was something a child might enjoy, and broken to boot. It didn't remind Rhienne much of the woman she'd known.

The words '*we are of gossamer, fickle and impermanent*' were carved into the lid. "What does it mean?"

"Wish I knew. The more time passes, the more I realize I didn't know your mother at all."

Rhienne ran her fingers over the engraving, but no inspiration came to her. She tucked the box away. "Well... thanks anyway."

Echo put down the tapered steel where he could easily take over. "If we do find her, would you want to see her again?"

Rhienne gave her a sharp look.

Her father didn't notice, his eyes fixed on the ground. "I... no, I wouldn't. And it was nice to see you both, but I think it's best you don't come back here either."

The dismissal rang across the room.

"Look, Dad, I'm—" Rhienne started, but even remembering Mordach's words and knowing their plan relied on it, she couldn't finish the apology. She wasn't sorry. She was *angry.* Angry that he still held this grudge so tight; angry that he wouldn't make exceptions to his code of honor for his own child; angry that he had kept what he knew about a dreamwalker's nature hidden until he could use it like ammunition; and fucking furious that only now, when she was on the precipice of giving him what he wanted, was he looking straight at her.

"You're what, Rhienne?"

The silence stretched.

Echo reached into her bag and placed their wages from the airship on the table.

What are you doing? Rhienne hissed through the telepathy stone.

"That's for any of the remaining damage we caused," Echo said. "Or you can use it if business is slow. Whatever you want. But you have no right to treat us like this anymore. Rhienne is your daughter, and I'm as good as. You gave me a home when no one else would, even though it put you in hot water with the rest of the town. Is a teenage prank really so unforgivable that you'll cast me out again? That you'll make Rhienne suffer the same fate?"

Echo, he's not going to change his mind about us based on one comment and a bag of gold ten years too late.

Sure enough, doubt crossed his face. "I don't want your money."

Without thinking, Rhienne snapped, "We didn't steal it, if that's what you're worried about. No one will come after you if you spend it."

Silas didn't move.

"We're sorry for what happened," Echo said. Her voice was ragged now, clearly holding back tears, and her body shimmered blue with the unconscious beginnings of a mimicry—freckles, shaggy hair, a child-like frame. "You're right; we didn't think about the consequences then, but we do now. We will come back. If for no other reason than to tell you we found Vala. And if it's the rest of the town you're worried about, you could come visit us instead."

"I appreciate the apology," he said quietly. "I want only good things for you both, I really do. Which is why you should go. This place was always too small for you. Take care of yourselves and your... friends. They seem like good people."

Her father turned back to the bellows, and Rhienne couldn't bear the heat of the room or the gut-punched look on Echo's face a second longer. She grabbed Echo's arm and hauled her out of the workshop, leaving the bag of coins on the table. She barely saw Irelia or Tash as she rushed outside.

The humid air was blissful in comparison to the forge, a rare wind kicking up leaves along the empty street. The sky was a dusky purple, with a sliver of the fading orange sun.

"Fuck him," Rhienne said. "We'll find another fence to mend, wound to heal, whatever. Should've known better than to try that first, but at least we got a spell anchor..." She trailed off when she noticed her friend's arms were slack at her sides, her unfocused stare directed down the road. The longer Rhienne looked, the more the street seemed stretched and unnatural. It took much longer than it should have to spot the edge of town.

Beyond it, instead of marsh, was a line of snow-dusted evergreens.

"I don't understand," Tash said, examining the impossible landscape. The pity on his face confirmed he'd heard every word. "Why did that work?"

"Destruction works just as well as mending," Echo whispered. "I really thought he'd... I guess it doesn't matter. The path is open."

Chapter 22

Echo

Could a plan fail and succeed at the same time? Echo had hoped to walk into Exodus's realm with the vigor of her adoptive father's reacceptance. Instead, she was caught in childhood memories of going door to door, trying to find a shape that would pull the heartstrings of the people inside just enough to put a roof over her head for the night. There was no time to shake the feeling. The path wouldn't stay open for long.

"Is this how Exodus's realm looked the first time?" Rhienne asked.

"Sort of. The road ended in a desert." She had no idea what the change could mean.

Judging by Tash and Irelia's astounded expressions, there was no similarity between this and the entrance to

Reckoning's realm. Strange how different the siblings were from each other. In some ways, at least.

"I don't know what kind of welcome we'll receive," Echo said. "You better brace yourselves. Follow me."

Irelia squeezed the pommels of both swords on her belt. She also had a dagger strapped to each thigh. Tash's satchel bulged with medical supplies. They'd be of little use against a god, but Echo was glad for their support, and the warm, comforting hand Tash placed on her shoulder.

Even knowing what to expect, Echo broke out in a cold sweat. The first step she took down the enchanted street made her surroundings fuzz. Another step, and their color faded away. Another, and they went two-dimensional. Her strides covered more distance than they should have, as if the dirt pushed her forward as she walked. She clung to Rhienne and kept her eyes fixed on the approaching evergreens while Hearthglen blurred and melted around her.

In the next breath, the entire process happened in reverse. Echo's ears popped. Color and clarity flooded back, but it went a few degrees too far—oversharp and oversaturated, painful to look at. Then there was a loud crack, and the road before them splintered and broke like a sheet of ice. Everyone staggered, clutching each other for balance.

Echo looked down. Inky blackness lay within the fracture. Her foresight flickered to a vision of a cold, empty death, then back to normal. "Run!" she screamed.

Clustered together, they sprinted over the uneven path, leaping over cracks full of midnight that chased them with hungry intent. This was *not* part of the usual transition, and that did not look like Exodus's power. But she was too busy surviving to puzzle out what the hell was going on. Time dragged at her. Everything disappeared but the pounding of her feet and heart. Then the ground heaved, throwing them forward in an ungraceful clump.

Echo landed shoulder-first on the damp ground. She winced and sat up, brushing off snow and pine needles. The forest stood undisturbed in all directions; nothing marked the violence of their passage. "Everyone okay?" she called.

"My back will never be the same," Irelia groaned and got to her feet.

Rhienne and Tash disentangled themselves from a patch of thorny shrubs. "Alive, at least," Rhienne said. "Where in the cosmos are we?"

The evergreen forest was utterly unfamiliar, despite how much Echo had explored this realm. The trees seemed to lean in and watch them. From the corner of her eye, the pinecones had faces that disappeared when she looked head-on. Mist rolled between the low branches, muffling sound and leaving the vague impression that everywhere she looked, someone had just walked away.

"Not where we should be," Echo said. "Something's wrong. Or Exodus is playing a sick joke on us." She wouldn't put it past him. "We need to get to the palace. That's our best chance of finding him."

Rhienne huddled close, her voice hushed. "We're being watched. I haven't felt it this strongly since we saw the Collector." She rubbed her sternum. "Is the pain normal, or is that part of the wrongness?"

Echo turned sharply toward her. "What pain?"

"Like a fucking bear trap closed around my heart."

The hair on the back of Echo's neck rose. No, that was definitely not normal. Echo was fine—physically, at least—but she didn't want to scare Rhienne. "I'm not sure. Are you okay to move forward?"

Rhienne took a series of breaths that started shallow and deepened after each measured exhale. "Yeah, I think so."

Irelia hefted a fallen branch that came up to her shoulder, testing its sturdiness against the ground before offering it to Rhienne. "To lean on, if you like."

In any other circumstance, Echo would've laughed at Rhienne's bewilderment and sheepish acceptance. For now, she was just grateful not to be here alone.

"Stay close and keep an eye out." She eased the mandolin off her back and plucked a few notes. It felt strange and foreign in her hands, as it had when she'd first begun learning to play.

Exodus was the Shepherd of Wandering Souls, the Warden of Pilgrims, but he was also the Herald of Dispersion—journeys of abandoning rather than seeking. New beginnings were not always voluntary. That was the kind of journey that had opened the realm, and the threat that there could be more destruction to follow hung in every shadow in these woods. The god was not happy she was here.

Echo may have lost the war, but she'd fought enough battles to know this was a test of her determination. She slowly worked the clumsiness out of her fingers, finding her rhythm again. The song became a buoy against the mist, one of those bright, cheerful things played at festival bonfires.

With far more confidence than she felt, Echo wove through the trees. When the first song was over, she had an idea that was either brilliant or incredibly stupid.

She strummed a few chords, and the temperature dropped. Her foresight trembled but didn't change from the lonely cottage. Keeping an eye on it in case Exodus decided to strike her down, she carried into the opening verse of *The Wanderer.* The first song they'd written together.

At Echo's urging, Rhienne hummed along, weaving in and out of the mandolin's rain-soft notes. Soon Tash added a deeper layer to the harmony.

"Hello? Is someone there?"

Echo's fingers stumbled. That voice, even with its usual warmth edged with weariness and fear, couldn't be mistaken for any of the airship crew.

There was no possible way he could be here, and no reason for him to leave Wildspire. Surely this was one of Exodus's cruel tricks. An obstacle to make her turn back.

"Hello? Lord of Journeys? Please, I've come so far. I require your aid. I—" Sidrin emerged from the mist, saw them, and froze.

Rhienne's hand slid into her pocket. *Is that...?*

My landlord, Echo replied numbly. *He doesn't recognize us.* And why would he? Rhienne's appearance had changed significantly, Echo was an entirely different person, and they had two new companions. Rhienne still stepped back a bit, using Tash as half-cover.

"Oh, what a relief," Echo made herself say. She didn't have to fake the tremble in her voice. She threw a glance at Irelia and Tash that she hoped said *just go with it.* Slinging her mandolin onto her back where he couldn't see its distinctive design, she continued, "Another traveler. You're here to see Exodus too?"

Sidrin offered a weak smile. "I am, but I'm terribly lost. I suppose it wouldn't help to ask you all for directions?"

It was an effort not to stare at him. He'd lost weight, his beard was unkempt, and his eyes never rested on one thing for too long, as if danger lurked in every curl of fog.

"I'm afraid not," Echo said. And then, stupidly, "Would you like to join us? Perhaps we'll have more luck together."

Echo, this can only go poorly, Rhienne thought to her, not without sympathy.

What else am I supposed to do? Send Sidrin on his way? Exodus loves games. This could actually help us find him.

Sidrin hesitated, and at first she feared they'd already been caught. The reality was worse. "Forgive me, I'm not entirely comfortable. It's been a while since I've been around other people."

"Well, why don't we get to know each other a bit?" Echo stuck out her hand, searching for a name that felt right to give him, and startled herself with what she found. "I'm Echo."

Bad idea, bad bad bad idea, Rhienne said.

"Sidrin." Warily, he closed the distance between them and shook her hand. "Is that a stage name?" he asked, noting the instrument on her back.

"Not yet, but I hope someday it will be. That's why I'm here."

"And your friends?" Sidrin peered around her.

Irelia and Tash introduced themselves with pleasant, if confused, smiles.

"Robin," Rhienne said. She had her shoulders curled in and her eyes downcast, and she clung to her walking stick instead of offering her hand.

"You'll have to excuse her," Echo said. "She's a bit shy. Gets stage fright with pretty much everyone she meets. That's the other reason we're here." After a beat of awkward silence, she asked, "What about you?"

"I..." He visibly struggled for words, looking for an answer that would sound nice and invite no further questions.

Echo knew these things took practice, and Sidrin had never had cause to lie before the Untold knocked on his door. Her heart twisted. "If you don't want to say, that's okay. Shall we walk for a while? I think if we find a tree tall enough, I can climb it and see over this fog."

That seemed to comfort him. "Yes, all right."

They picked their way through the woods in apparent silence, though Rhienne repeated a list of worries through the telepathy stone. *This is stupid; the longer we stick around, the more likely Sidrin is to discover who we are; I still feel like we're being watched; what's the goal here?*

Echo gave no answer, because she had none. She just... wanted Sidrin to trust her in the same way the crew did. Even if she wasn't the same person he'd known on the outside, maybe he'd still see something of Natalia in her, and... "Would you mind if I play a song?" she asked before she could finish the thought. "I find it makes this place feel less sinister."

He shrugged, and she began *The Wanderer* again. Exodus didn't react this time, which made her even more ill at ease. What was he doing? She could understand why Exodus would keep her in the fog, but not Sidrin. And why could only Rhienne feel the watchfulness?

By the time she finished her song, Sidrin had relaxed a fraction. "I've never heard that tune before," he said. "You're quite good."

"Thank you. Wrote it myself. Are you an artist of some kind? I hear lots of them come looking for Exodus."

"No. I've spent some time around musicians, though," he said darkly.

Echo fixed a grin on her face. "I promise we're not all divas."

"No, no, of course not. It's only—oh!" He lost his footing on a frost-slick rock. Echo twisted and caught his arm as he fell. Sidrin righted himself, flushed with embarrassment, and muttered, "Thanks. That would've hurt."

"No trouble at all," Echo said. Behind her, Tash cleared his throat, his dark eyes full of warning. The immortal must have gathered some of what was going on here; he knew just as well as she did the dangers of interacting with someone who'd spurned you already.

But Sidrin had been about to admit something, and she had to know why he was here before he clammed up again. Once they were out of the rocky patch, she pressed, "You were saying?"

"I meant no offense," he started. The rest came out slowly, like pulling an anchor from deep water. "My experience with this... musician... well, they were more of a liar and a thief. People started asking questions, and the neighbors didn't take kindly to the fact that I had harbored someth—one like that. They shut me out. After everything I'd done for them. And I—" his voice broke, along with the piece of Echo's heart that still *somehow* belonged to Natalia. "I couldn't stay in Wildspire, but I have nowhere else to go. I guess I'm here to either get my life back or start it over."

Echo lost her grip on her light-hearted tone. "Oh, Sidrin, I'm so sorry."

He breathed a little laugh. "You have nothing to be sorry for."

"If it means anything, I'm sure she never meant to hurt you that way."

Rhienne's voice broke into her mind, *Stop talking, Echo.*

But she couldn't. "She must've been... doing what she thought was necessary to get by."

Sidrin froze. "I don't believe I said it was a woman." The mist churned in slow motion as he turned to study not her, but the mandolin now prominently hanging across her front. The scrollwork and intricate detail were one of a kind. Recognition lit his face first. Then horror. He scrambled away from her. "Why are you following me? What do you want? Do you all know what this thing is?" He addressed Irelia and Tash, and his eyes went even wider at their lack of surprise. "Are you all monsters?"

Rhienne stepped up beside her and grabbed her arm, but Echo shook her off. There was no point denying who she was. "I'm not following you, Sidrin. I swear this was a coincidence. I really am here for Exodus's help, and I really am sorry. Please—"

"No! I will not be played for a fool again." He backed into a tree, staring at her as if she might attack him. "I have to get out of this place."

"Sidrin, wait! We can help you." Echo took one step toward him, hand outstretched.

The pure, unfiltered disgust on his face made her drop her arm. Sidrin spun and ran into the mist.

Echo watched the spot where he'd disappeared for an eternity. First her father, now Sidrin. She'd gotten lucky, desperately lucky, with the airship crew, and mistaken it for a second chance with everyone. But revealing herself wasn't enough. It couldn't be enough. Not until she was whole again, and there was something about her worth loving.

Rhienne gently took her hand. "I'm sorry."

At least she had the grace not to say, 'I told you so.'

"That wasn't right," Irelia said, her voice like flint.

Tash shrugged and said what Echo didn't have the energy to say. "No, it's not. But that's the way of the world. A few of us became spies and criminals, and the Untold spread the fear that we all carry some nefarious intent, when most of us are just trying to *live*." His words hung heavier than the mist.

"We shouldn't have come here," Echo whispered.

The wind picked up at that, and her heart sank even further. Exodus's presence brought a familiar shift to the air, wrapping around her in a strange oscillation between warm homecoming and the awe—which could so easily drop into fear—of reaching a foreign destination.

His magic tasted different for everyone. The artists she'd met here claimed it was oil pastels or musty gallery halls, the musicians argued it was rosin for their strings or lemon and honey to soothe their throats, and the travelers said it was grass and sunlight—or ozone and mud, if he was in a bad mood.

The breath she took smelled of gravedust and rot.

If Exodus hadn't orchestrated this, he'd certainly taken joy in watching it unfold.

The mist cleared to reveal a man cast in marble, sitting with his fingers steepled, one ankle propped on the opposite knee. Blackened, leafless trees bent to form the throne around him. Stone-dead eyes were fixed on the middle distance. This was not the guise of an uplifting temple statue or monument, but the cold disappointment of a tomb marker. Echo had only seen him like this once before, on the day he'd come to collect her payment.

Unlike her father or Sidrin, she could at least hate Exodus back.

Well, he doesn't look so bad, Rhienne thought.

The words didn't stay inside their heads; they rattled through the pines around the glade.

Exodus's voice came to them the same way, his lips unmoving. "Looks can be deceiving. You of all people should understand that."

Echo squeezed Rhienne hard to keep her from responding. Not even their thoughts were safe here.

"And you." A frigid wind blasted over Echo without touching a hair on her friends' heads. "I did not think you had the gall to return here, never mind bringing other oathbreakers with you. Ones still covered in my siblings' stench, no less."

"We have broken no oaths, my lord," Irelia said. Her posture was proud, but her fingers trembled around her sword hilt.

Tash added, "What would it mean to you if we had? Though history can be forgotten and rewritten, those of us who lived it know you were never fond of Reckoning."

The trees rattled with Exodus's displeasure. Echo's mouth was dry, her heart hammering so loud he could surely hear it across the glade, but she found the performer's mask she needed. "If it would ease our introductions, perhaps you could invite us inside, so we may wash away such unpleasant scents."

Echo did not blink, did not see him move, but suddenly he was right in front of her, their noses inches apart. "What makes you think I would ever allow you into my home again?"

"We made our journey. Your magic brought us here. I've never known you to turn away a traveler, no matter how distasteful you find them."

Rhienne picked her nails. "And I hate to be presumptuous, but I think you'll want to hear what we have to say."

To the untrained eye, Rhienne was totally unphased, but Echo noted a glimmer of excitement at Exodus's display of power. She wanted to warn her friend, *again*, not to get too comfortable. The god was a force of nature, twisted and ever-shifting. Always had been.

But now that he was closer, he seemed somehow... less.

He snarled something at Rhienne, but Echo had stopped listening. She couldn't focus on certain parts of him, which had nothing to do with being unable to meet his glare. Her gaze kept skipping over his shoulder, his hand, his jaw. He was more powerful than the Collector, so she couldn't simply will herself to see through it, but the traces of an illusion were the same.

With feigned pity and a prayer that he wouldn't tear her hand off, Echo reached for his shoulder. "You look different."

Exodus disappeared with another fractured teleportation. She thought he flinched before he appeared back on the throne... but she must've been mistaken. He was a god, cold and heartless as the stone form he took.

Still, there was something wrong that she couldn't put her finger on.

"Fine," he said. "Speak your piece, so I may be rid of you."

"You would really deny weary travelers rest?" The trees picked up her next thought, though she hadn't wanted to speak it. *What are you hiding?*

"What a question for *you* to ask. Spare me your platitudes. I know better than anyone what you are. A *coward.*" The foresight he'd imparted to her came forward from its tucked-away corner in her mind. "So afraid of choosing the wrong path. Why, I wonder, did it not stop you from trying to evade me? Did it not show you what would happen to your *legacy* when you made that choice?"

She'd wanted to avoid this, to jump straight to questions about the exiled god, but Exodus sounded like he'd rehearsed this conversation, eager to dig up her pain. As if he hadn't hurt her enough already.

Echo shook her head. "For all I know, you manipulated the vision so you could take something else from me. But that's not why we're—"

"Ha! Shirking responsibility, as usual. It's been a while in mortal years. Perhaps you need me to remind you what really happened."

"No," Echo breathed. She didn't want to live through that again, didn't want Tash or Irelia to see more of her scars when they'd already witnessed the wounds reopened by Silas and Sidrin.

Of course, Exodus didn't care what she wanted.

Figures from the half dozen towns she'd traveled through after losing her voice manifested in the fog. In the first, she'd tried to sing and was laughed off the stage when nothing came out. In the ones following, she'd brought out the mandolin Exodus had given her, but no one had paid her enough to stay.

On the other side of the glade, her foresight took shape. The crowd of admirers and mourners surrounding her deathbed. Other artists she'd inspired, people who hummed her songs while they worked. She watched her legacy fade as it had back then, until she'd decided to go to Wildspire and join a group, when it solidified to the lonely scene it was now.

"Funny," Exodus said, "that it didn't change until long after you cheated me."

Echo went still. "You made it so I couldn't get by on my own. It took a long time for me to accept that."

"No, no, no," he sneered. "You gave up in Wildspire. You stopped trying. You had everything you needed right in front of you and were too afraid to take it. Losing your voice just gave you the excuse to hide."

Rhienne stepped between them. "I didn't think it was possible for anyone to be more obnoxious than Oblivion, but congratulations, the trophy definitely goes to you."

"I don't believe I was speaking to you." His head cocked to one side. Rhienne sailed across the clearing and slammed into a tree.

"Rhienne!" Irelia shouted and ran after her.

Echo followed and dropped to the ground, unsure where to touch her friend in case any bones were broken. "Are you all right? Tash, can you—"

"I'm fine," Rhienne groaned when she got her breath back, waving Tash away. "Don't let him talk to you like that."

"But what if he's right?" Echo whispered, and the grove echoed back, *He's right, he's right, he's right.*

"Better to hold onto the dream than try and fail and let it shatter," Exodus said. "That way, you can pretend it's not your fault."

Doubt swirled in Echo's head, brought to life by the rustling leaves. *I failed. It's too late. Nothing I do will make a difference. I should give up. I already have.* It had been such a long journey. Wouldn't it be nice to lie down and close her eyes for a while? She could hide here. She was good at that. Maybe that was all she was good at.

"That's not true." Rhienne hissed in pain but struggled onto her hands and knees. "That can't be true."

"Yes," the God of Journeys said. "You lost your chance. Stop wasting your time on this dream. The world is never going to miss you; you're not worth a second of their attention."

A pang of recognition—the same one she'd had with Tash on the airship. As if Exodus had chosen those words because he knew from experience how deeply they cut.

What would he know about a thing like loss?

Rhienne grabbed her shoulders. "Don't listen to him. *Your* dream, *your* life, is not a waste."

"A fascinating emphasis." Exodus's laugh was as dry and brittle as the pine needles. "Are you aware that all my siblings know of you, dreamwalker? You're not the first half-breed of your kind, but you've certainly been the most entertaining to watch. Grasping so ferociously for the next handhold on the cliff face without realizing you're in the middle of a landslide. Do you even know what you would do if you reached the top of the mountain? If you succeeded in gaining all the power to break free from your cage, what then?"

"It's hard to see beyond the bars," Rhienne growled. "I can figure it out once they're gone."

His wrath was focused on Rhienne now, his voice carrying a blast of cold wind that set her trembling. "You know deep down you could have all the time in the world and never find the answer. You couldn't even apologize to your own father. Your friend had to make that journey for you. You'd never have been able to reach me without her."

"Shut up!" But the trees betrayed the fear under her defiance. *What good have I ever done with my life? What good* can *I do without a dream, without power?*

"Both of you, listen to me," Tash's features, always so warm and open, had hardened. He'd pulled back his sleeves to show the white scars against his dark skin. "This is what the gods do: strip you down to the bone so you feel better about giving up your marrow. Do not let his words get to you; remember they were not always like this."

Echo gritted her teeth. Tash was right. She had to bring them back to the reason they'd come. "*All* your siblings know of Rhienne, do they? All four of them?"

Exodus chuckled again. "Has time already so addled your brain that you've forgotten how to count?"

"You claim to know so much of what we've done. Did you never wonder what the first journey was that brought me to you?" He'd never asked, in all the time she'd spent here. Selfish bastard.

She forced herself to look Exodus in the eye. He was unreadable in this stone form. Not so for the environment around him. The mist no longer swirled, the blackened branches didn't shake. Everything was still and quiet. Whether due to curiosity or fear, she wasn't quite sure, but he hadn't been watching her back then. He didn't know. "I found a way forward when I thought there wasn't one. With the help of a library that belongs to someone dear to you."

Frost snapped in the air. "That's impossible."

"Is it?" Echo said as she helped Rhienne stand. "Give us a real audience at the palace, and I can tell you more."

"Why won't you *give up?*" Exodus was on his feet again, threateningly frozen mid-stride. "I left you with your foresight; you know this dream takes you nowhere. It is too late to get what you want. Cast this foolishness aside.

Go back to playing necromancer if you must, but if you continue to try my patience, you will find me even less welcoming."

Rhienne opened her mouth, but Echo motioned for her to wait. He was only saying things she had thought a hundred times. They stung, yes, but a theory was brewing in the back of her mind. Exodus never turned down an opportunity to lord his magnificence over mortals. The passage to arrive here had been tampered with. And they'd been here long enough that he should've turned into his mist form at least once. By nature, he couldn't remain in one state for long. His evasiveness was due to more than their history.

Echo closed the door on the last of her fear. Not only did he remember his exiled sibling, he was upset enough to lash out. They had him in a corner. This was her chance to learn how to find the library again. "You can't shift forms, can you?"

"I never should've let you stay," the trees hissed. "You've brought me nothing but trouble and grief."

Grief? She hadn't thought him capable of such an emotion. And yet, Echo couldn't find a trace of a lie behind his words. This encounter was more than a tantrum, more than a performance to turn her away.

"You've lost your magic?" Rhienne butted in.

"Gods do not *lose* their magic," Exodus snarled.

Tash said, "It can be depleted or diverted, though, if they don't have enough pacts to sustain them."

The mist went flat. Exodus would've looked cagey if he wasn't a marble statue. With more visibility in the glade, there were more places Echo's gaze skipped over. More illusions. Something was very, very wrong.

One such spot was only a few paces from where Rhienne had been thrown—a low cluster of branches on an evergreen. Echo closed the distance, hand outstretched.

"Stop." Exodus appeared in front of her with a blast of icy air. She pushed down the roiling in her stomach and touched the glamored spot on his jaw.

Beneath her fingers, there were cracks in the marble.

Part of her was glad and wanted to taunt him. Part of her cracked in response. She didn't know which masks those parts belonged to. "What happened?"

"You happened," Exodus said with such venom that she stepped back. "You and your friend."

Rhienne crossed her arms. "Hold on, what did I do? I just got here."

"*You* brought Oblivion's attention to *her.*" The trees bent accusingly around them. "And your little visit to the Collector led him back to me."

Rhienne paled, hand going to the pain-point on her chest. "Oblivion was here? I mean, you got rid of him, obviously. You're more powerful than he is."

Exodus turned his flat stare to her. "That is a poor jest, coming from someone who once held a pact with him."

"But he was a first draft." Irelia frowned. "His domain is so small. A mistake that the Mothers corrected with the rest of the gods."

"And that has made him bitter." All the mist spiraled inward, with Exodus at the center. The glimmer of illusions peeled away with it. "But it has certainly not made him weak."

The glade looked to have been shattered and poorly pieced back together. Chunks were missing, and the spackled seams showed pure darkness beyond. Some of the shadow still oozed through the cracks. Exodus's entire left side was a spiderweb of fractures, and instead of blank marble, his left eye was star-speckled void. Everything was healing, knitting back together, but slowly, painfully.

"Why?" Echo asked. "Why did he do this?"

"Your song. The dream within it. Swinging between the possibility of beginning and ending, it has built up energy like a pendulum." His mismatched gaze was razor-sharp. "These things are not unique by themselves, but add in a drop of Infinity's blood and our broken deal, and your voice holds the most intoxicating amount of magic I have ever come across."

A ringing started in her ears that spread across her entire body, like she was a mandolin string, plucked once in an otherwise silent room. "My song?" she breathed. "All this time, you *kept* it?" She had thought it gone forever, destroyed in his fit of rage, but this... "And then you let Oblivion take it?"

The ground and trees and sky shuddered, like a tiny aftershock of the battle that had taken place here. "There was no *letting* involved."

"The storm wasn't just to make me use the last of my magic," Rhienne realized. "It was to delay us. So Oblivion could get here first."

Echo's throat constricted, the loss of her voice fresh all over again. She let the trees speak her thoughts. *Where did he go? What is he going to do with it?*

"He will go to the Origin and consume it."

The Origin. Like Nazal's story. "The Origin is real?"

"Real as the ground beneath your feet. It is where the rules of this world were put down, and Oblivion aims to bend those rules in his favor. Your voice will give him power equal to one of the Mothers themselves. So if you will do away with your selfish tendencies for once in your life and *let your dream die*, we can avoid this" —the trees shivered, the cracks in the glade growing deeper for a moment— "spreading across your world."

Echo's gaze swept over the destruction. She imagined it consuming Wildspire, Hearthglen, every corner of every continent until not even an unregistered airship was safe. That was not the kind of mark she wanted to leave. But she didn't want a world without her music either. She might as well not have lived if she left no legacy at all.

"There has to be another way to stop him."

"Ah, yes, since standing against one of us worked so well before, I'm sure you could face Oblivion, Harvest, and Reckoning with your hands behind your back. Not to mention the mortals he's rallied to his side."

"Is there a deal I can make to get you to shut up for two seconds so I can think?"

"What is there to think about? The solution is simple."

"That is no solution, and you know it," Echo snapped. "You're one to talk about being selfish. I want to track down your exiled sibling, I want to get their help, but you're still so pissed I almost beat you that you won't look at any possibility that doesn't screw me over."

"You did not almost beat me, you *left*." Relieved of the need to hold the glamors in place, Exodus dissolved from marble to mist—also shot through with streaks of midnight—and back again, shuddering between the two. The darkness in him seemed to contain a fathomless roar just beyond her hearing. "You hid when I opened the world for you. You ran when you could have stayed."

"Funny thing about journeys. When they're done, people have to go home."

The god's form shuddered again, rage building. But then he sagged back onto his throne, all the menace gone in a puff of wind. "You always had a talent for getting to the core of a matter."

She wanted to yell, to throw something horrible back at him, but a look from Tash quelled her wrath. *It's in the eyes.* He saw it too. Much as she wanted to, Echo couldn't deny it any longer.

Like her, like Tash, Exodus was *lonely*. The two siblings he'd been closest to were gone; mortals visited him for his power and left. She'd stayed in his realm for a few years, and that set the record by a mile. They'd had good times together, but it had needed to stay a means to an end. Remaining with him meant giving up her dream. And when part of her had started to enjoy the performance of their companionship, to wonder if it could be real, she'd made her deal and fled.

The ache in her heart told her that on some level, it *had* been real. Masks be damned.

They'd taken too much from each other to cross that gulf again. Still, she needed his help.

Echo took a minute to find her way through the tangle of grief and aggravation born from those two disparate ideas. "I don't expect you to forgive me. But if Oblivion becoming more powerful is as dangerous as you say, then we're on the same side here."

"Everything I said was true," Exodus said stiffly. "It's a dangerous undertaking, tampering with the Mothers' laws. And he's recruiting all the help he can find. Reckoning has ever been his confidant, and Harvest... likes to pick the winning team."

She sat down, digging her fingers into the damp soil. This had suddenly become so much bigger. They weren't just circumventing one god—or even two—with a grudge. And if they failed, it was no longer only her future and Rhienne's soul at stake. It was the crew's fate. The fate of the world. How could they hope to face the forces Oblivion had amassed?

Having only Rhienne's mother and the exiled god on their side wouldn't be enough. She saw the despair on Irelia's face, the fear on Tash's; Reckoning had already taken one of their friends. There could be so much worse to come.

Echo had to fight to get the next words out of her mouth, praying Rhienne wouldn't call her a hypocrite. "I'd like to make a deal."

She watched the glade, expecting another surge of vitriol. It remained heavy and still.

"Is that so?" Exodus whispered.

"We will share everything we learn about your exiled sibling. We will work together to find them. Then you will join them, and us, in this fight against Oblivion and get my singing voice back."

"I fail to see how these are equal contributions."

"In return, we'll find a way to break their exile."

Silence for a long moment. "How?"

Echo turned to Rhienne, whose eyes were wide, but they couldn't argue in front of Exodus. This was a huge gamble. "We happen to know someone with a penchant for loopholes. I won't make promises for her while she isn't here, but if you'll allow us to 'play necromancer,' as you put it so poetically, we can see what she has to say."

"She'll help," Rhienne said. "I know she will."

"And if she does not agree to the terms, or is not as helpful as you believe she'll be, what then?" Exodus asked. "You have only one thing left to trade."

The vision. Recent revelations notwithstanding, Echo wasn't sure if he'd meant it as a curse or a gift, but it had become a lighthouse, a north star. If she got her voice back and set out to spread her music, how would she know if she was doing the right thing without its guidance?

No, she wouldn't return the vision to him, not when he was so eager to see her fail.

There was only one other thing Exodus could want, the thing you were never supposed to offer: free rein to choose his payment. If they succeeded, it would never come to that.

So they just had to succeed.

"Echo," Rhienne hissed a low warning.

Her thoughts must've been clear on her face, because the god's eyes lit up like prayer candles within the mist before she said, "Then I'll owe you a favor."

He took a step forward, eagerly, but stopped himself. "And why should I believe you'll make good on *this* bargain when you shirked our prior agreement?"

Echo gritted her teeth, but before she could argue, Tash said, "It seems to me, with your realm as fractured as it is, you need all the pacts you can get. What if the two of us sweeten the pot?" He gestured to himself and Irelia. "We'll each agree to owe a favor. But it's all three of us, or nothing."

"Tash, wait, you don't have to—"

"It's alright." His smile was full of comfort she did not deserve. "We came prepared for something like this."

Exodus's voice thundered around the glade. "Deal."

The bond wrapped around Echo's heart, and she thought for a moment that it stopped beating. Thorns filled her chest and something bitter and cold burned the back of her throat. It could not have been more different than the first deal they'd made. Even when the initial impact faded, her breath came shorter, and a chill lingered in her bones.

How did it feel to him?

She shoved the question away and said instead, "Take us to the palace, so we may begin our ritual."

"If I must," Exodus intoned.

Chapter 23

Rhienne

Still with that unsettling glimmer in his eyes, Exodus conjured a massive spiraling gust. The wind picked them up and carried them over the trees, then past a hodgepodge of other biomes—deserts smashed up against snowy plains, forests of giant mushrooms, and red rock cliffs—but Rhienne scarcely had room in her mind to marvel. She was too busy boggling at Echo's dynamic with this deity and smarting from the switchblade words he'd used in the glade. Never mind that her friend had offered an open-ended favor to a god who hated her. Never-*never* mind how Irelia and Tash had become entangled in their mess. The list went on, and it compounded the dizziness of their travel until she felt sick.

One concern rose above the others, though. Despite Exodus focusing entirely on Echo, the pain in Rhienne's chest was sharper than ever. He wasn't the cause of it. Either Oblivion had left something nasty for her in this realm, or he was waiting to claim her soul at last. She needed her mother. She had to unravel this contract *now*.

Exodus deposited them unceremoniously among a fractured ruin. It looked like the epicenter of an earthquake that had hiccupped without gravity kicking in. Sculptures, fragments of columns, and pieces of the building itself hung disconnected from each other, floating and slowly rotating in place. The floor was cracked and blackened. Blast marks peppered what was left of the white marble walls. Rhienne had been hopeful for a bit of luxury at the mention of a palace, but this must have been where the fight took place. Every patch of darkness felt heavy and watchful.

Exodus rematerialized on the dais, which was currently missing a throne, and perched on a broken column. That could not be comfortable, even with an ass you could literally bounce a coin off of.

The wind that kicked up was a light summer breeze compared to his earlier winter storm. It made her bones itch, how suddenly he moved from one pose or mood to the next. A different kind of creepy than Oblivion's hovering malice.

"Whenever you are ready, the space is at your disposal." His voice emanated from the fragmented stone, making it sound as if dozens of Exoduses were all speaking just off-beat from each other.

Rhienne shifted uneasily. "Are you going to watch?"

"I'd like to make sure you're keeping up your end of the bargain, yes."

"It's all right." Echo put a hand on her shoulder. "Just focus on what you need to do." *Can he still hear us?* she added through the telepathy stone, and this time the thought stayed between the two of them. *Forget what he said in the glade. You've brought plenty of good to my life. You saved Irelia and the crew. And now you're going to save your mom.*

And then you're going to tell me all the torrid details of your time here, because now that I've seen him, I have some logistical questions. Rhienne chuckled when Echo swatted at her. "Okay, okay. Really, though. Thanks."

She drew her knife and took a deep breath. Irelia hadn't run away screaming yet, despite seeing some of the worst parts of her and Echo's past in the last few hours. But blood magic was a category of its own, especially with a spell this powerful.

"You might want to look away," Rhienne warned.

The captain shook her head. It was clear she had thoughts—and those thoughts probably had many accompanying words—about Rhienne's history, but she only said, "I can guarantee you I've seen worse."

Not from me. But Irelia remained immovable, so Rhienne got to work. There was one clear spot on the floor large enough to sketch the series of interlocking runes she'd memorized from Mishara's spellbook. Rhienne sliced open her forearm, the pain a welcome distraction from the fire burning under her sternum. She traced the pattern—one central rune, and four smaller ones in each cardinal direction—placing the Dawnglow in the middle and the music box at the northern point.

Exodus leaned forward, not toward Horizon's crystallized blood, but her mother's trinket. "What is that?" he asked.

"A spell anchor."

He appeared in an instant beside the circle, bent over the box.

"Hey! Don't touch—"

"I won't disrupt your spell," he said, missing the point. Exodus reached for the music box with a curl of mist, but when he touched the lacquer, there was a blaze of white light. He reared back with a hiss and became marble again. Thunder rumbled in the distance, low and contemplative.

"I told you not to touch it." Not that Rhienne had known it would do that. Had Vala put some kind of protection spell on the box? It hadn't affected her or her father at all.

"Are you aware of the complications you're about to face, dreamwalker?"

He'd mentioned 'her kind' earlier, but the way he said it this time made her shiver. "I'm aware it's incredibly powerful and *delicate* magic to resurrect someone, so I'd appreciate it if you didn't interrupt."

"Get to your point, Exodus," Echo said.

"The aura of that music box belongs to a dream spirit."

"Correct."

"They do not have bodies for a physical tether. There is nothing to use to pull her back. We will need to reach into the Plane of the Dead and catch the soul ourselves, and we won't have much time to do it. Living souls don't react well to that place."

Rhienne bristled. "We?"

"What does that mean?" Echo asked.

"It means you will eventually deteriorate, pulled apart by the natural forces of being somewhere you're not supposed to be. And yes, *we*. This endeavor requires more than my distant observation. I'm going with you."

"No," Rhienne growled at the same time Echo said, "Why?"

"Because if you fail, our entire deal falls apart before it's begun."

I don't like this, Rhienne thought to Echo. It was never good when a god had a 'sudden' change of heart. *He got all that from touching the music box?*

I don't like it either, trust me. But I think he got all that from not being able *to touch it. Whatever that flash was, it convinced him your mom can hold up her end of the deal. He wouldn't risk himself otherwise.*

"Fine," Rhienne said. "But if you're coming, someone has to stay behind to call us back."

"We'll do it," Irelia said. "Tell us what you need."

Fear and gratitude took turns tightening Rhienne's throat. "Hold thoughts of us in your mind." Hurriedly, she added, "They don't have to be good ones, as long as there's some connection there."

"I think we can manage that." Irelia's smile and the crinkling corners of her gray eyes settled some of Rhienne's nerves. Tash nodded in agreement.

"Ok then. Echo, stand at the east rune. Exodus, the west." Rhienne squeezed a final dribble of blood onto the Dawnglow and took the southern point. The spell circle hummed—a deep, resonant sound that vibrated through the broken floor. She breathed in the power, wrapped it around herself and wove it into the potential of her spilled blood. The painted runes began to glow. Everything else had to be put aside; this was the moment she'd been waiting for.

"Vala, spirit of dreams. Mentor, muse, and mother. Removed from the world too soon" —the words stuck in her throat, tangled up in magic and regret— "by the actions of a foolish daughter. One who has crossed continents, oceans, and planes to bring you back. One who needs you more than ever. If you can hear me, please, answer my call. Let me return you to where you belong. Life for life, blood for blood."

The bright sheen of sunrise funneled out of the Dawnglow, concentrating on the northern and southern runes: Rhienne and the music box. It surrounded her and soaked into her skin. It washed away her grief and pain with intoxicating euphoria, and she wondered, briefly, if this was what the Untold were chasing when they siphoned magic from mimics and immortals. She could almost understand. She felt like she could separate from her body and float away.

Only when the light faded did she realize that was exactly what had happened.

They were no longer in the palace. They floated over an infinite field of gray grass and white flowers. The sky was the deep blue of the minutes before dawn, but the sun never rose. All in all, it was a little anticlimactic for something called the Plane of the Dead. At least the warmth of Irelia's hand on hers remained, despite being a realm away.

Rhienne scanned the endless, flat expanse without spotting any variation. "Shouldn't there be people? Or souls, or whatever?"

Echo hovered beside her, also searching the distance. They were both translucent versions of themselves. Exodus was made of marble again, except it rippled like fabric blowing in the wind, and a gold veil covered his face. He motioned toward the field—a fluid movement, despite his form—and said, "Look closer."

Rhienne swooped down, giddy with the lingering euphoria of the spell. It had been a long time since she'd moved through another plane of her own free will. But the feeling faded as soon as she understood what Exodus meant.

Each flower left her with the sense that she'd brushed against a person's mind, their emotions and memories leaving a trace of who they were, which dissipated as she moved past.

Every blossom contained a soul.

Something tugged at her, and she feared it was those 'forces' Exodus had mentioned already coming to claim her until he said, "Do you hear that?"

She followed his veiled gaze. He was looking in the same direction Rhienne had felt the pull, but the field was quiet. "No. What is it?"

"She is answering your call."

"Why can you hear it and I can't?"

He shrugged. "Perhaps that will become clear as we get closer."

How had Echo spent three years with him without losing her mind?

Rhienne decided to pretend he wasn't there and set off over the plain. A handful of flowers shivered, their white petals turning to regard her. Some gave her the impression of hope, which quickly faded as she flew by. Some were *hungry*, and those gazes lingered on her long after she had passed. Between the stems and blades of grass, all she could make out was darkness. Were there stars in it, or was she being paranoid? Her chest ached, but that could've been from the ritual, or Oblivion's broken contract, or the fact that this *had* to work and it was already more trouble than she'd anticipated.

She needed something to fill the silence, to block out the prickling along her soul.

"Mom?" she tried. "It's Rhienne. I need your help. I didn't mean what I said; I *do* want to see you again. Please come back." None of the souls in the flowers felt like her mother, so she kept going, faster and faster, following the trajectory of the tug. She clung to thoughts of Irelia, too, in case they needed a swift escape, and because they were a small comfort in this barren place.

Distantly, Echo said, "Where are you going? It's coming from over here."

But she was wrong. Surely it was *there*, just there. Rhienne *did* hear something. "I understand now. You made a bad deal. So have I. It's not your fault. I—"

Something wrapped around her ankle, yanking her to a stop. One of the flowers had reached up and grabbed her. Rhienne yelped and tried to shake it off, but thorns dug into her leg.

Her mind filled with a voice too warped to recognize. "I'll come back, it's okay, no apologies necessary if you free me. Bad deal. I should've known it was a bad deal."

A cascade of memories came with the touch. A caravan passed a familiar coastal town, its wagons filled to the brim with enchanted knickknacks for sale. The hamlet was not the kind of place they liked to stop; its residents were too poor for good business. But a pair of young girls approached them on the outskirts. One chatted them up, and they lost track of the other, and by the time they realized their most valuable merchandise was missing, the girls and the town were long gone. They didn't make enough profit that year to fulfill their contract, and Reckoning had come for them.

When Rhienne finally managed to break free from the vision and the thorny stem, it left ragged puncture wounds in her leg. Instead of blood, they leaked black mist.

After that, it didn't matter how high she flew. The dead had her scent, and they reached up for the warmth of the living. She was certain there were stars in the void below now, and they followed her too. Of course, Oblivion would have some influence in the Plane of the Dead. But she'd come too far to stop.

She lost track of Echo and Exodus. She lost track of the pull from her spell, and any thoughts of home or who waited for her return. Over and over, she begged her mother to come back. Over and over, she got an answer, but never the right one. So many souls seemed to know her, but she had no idea who they were. People she had scammed and forgotten, not caring for the greater context of their lives. And then—

"You." A voice she did know, even stripped of its pomp. *Jareth.* "You're the reason I'm here, aren't you? I thought I was unlucky, but I recognize the shape of you, and the hole you left in your wake."

The petals of his flower were midnight black. Rhienne tried to move away, but a cluster of roots and vines launched at her, constricting and tearing.

"Oblivion made me do it!" she protested, struggling against the weight of the souls pulling her down. "I didn't know why he was manipulating things so close to me."

"Excuses, excuses. My, you have so many."

"It's the truth!" Mist poured out of her from a dozen wounds. It became harder to focus, to remember why she was here. "How was I supposed to know the Untold would show up?"

"No, the truth is you thought my dream was meaningless, and you did not care to consider the consequences, as long as you got what you wanted. The truth is you killed me before the Untold did."

"I didn't know that's what it did to people," she argued, but it was weak. She had known, because she'd seen it happen to her mother, and hadn't wanted it to happen to Echo. She hadn't cared about Jareth, or anyone else who got in her way. "Please, I'm trying to stop Oblivion from hurting anyone else."

"Why should I trust you?"

"I don't dreamwalk for him anymore. I have other people helping me. I'm trying to do better. Be better."

What will you do, when you break free of your chains? The question floated through her mind in a hundred different voices. She still didn't have an answer. Rhienne was listless, unraveling, a shadow of what it must have felt like for all the people whose dreams she ended. Except she didn't have a dream. She never could.

The soul-flowers dragged her down. Ice cold grass brushed her back. Maybe Exodus had only come here to watch her die. She ought to fight against that, shouldn't she? It wouldn't be right to let the gods win. There was something that would happen if she did, some-one-thing she was trying to avoid... but the ground sapped the will from her. Thorns and leaves and petals blotted out the sky.

"Where did she go? Rhienne! Where are you?"

Vaguely, she knew that voice too. Never with that much panic, though—a variation of the unraveling happening to her. How was she still hurting people that way?

She didn't want to do that, so she opened her mouth to say *I'm here.*

Instead, a scream came out as something inside her sheared. It sliced across her chest, then out through her spine. She looked down.

There was a hole where her heart had been, clear through her to the ground below, where two white eyes danced with glee.

Consider this a gift, Rhienne, Oblivion said. *I've taken a piece, instead of the whole. Your old friend Mishara will make good use of it. She came to me, you know, begging for a pact to get her revenge. I can only imagine what you did to her, but her passion makes her much more creative than I could ever be. I'm sure I'll receive the rest soon enough.*

He vanished, but the flowers continued to smother her.

The last vestige of warmth in her hand flared hot enough to burn, sending a beacon of golden light into the sky. Rhienne saw herself through someone else's eyes: lost and afraid and trying to pretend otherwise. Directionless desperation hung about her like a cloud. The source of the heat understood that feeling, and how much it would mean for someone to *stay*. The undeniable attraction was a nice bonus. Rhienne blinked, and the vision was gone, but the light and emotion remained.

Summoned by the beacon, a beautiful woman and a stoic, chiseled man appeared above her. The man was doing something odd with his hands, like he was holding a large, invisible box. Rhienne felt she ought to recognize them. She struggled against the exhaustion and emptiness that threatened to drag her down.

The woman made a choked noise that would've been a sob if ghosts could produce tears. "Why didn't you follow us?" She turned to the veiled man. "What do we do?"

No one spoke, but *something* happened because there was a sudden burst of moonlight that had all the flowers shrinking away, and then the lovely woman was reaching for her.

Rhienne touched her hand, and everything flooded back. "Echo," she gasped in pain.

"Get us out *now*," her friend said, pulling her up to meet Exodus.

Rhienne couldn't think straight, could barely see through the agony of the gaping hole in her chest, but she managed to say, "I'm not leaving without my mother."

"She's right here." Echo gestured at the empty space between Exodus's hands. "Are you okay?"

What a stupid question. Couldn't Echo see Rhienne was missing a piece? "Oblivion—" she started.

"We can have this discussion later," Exodus said through clenched teeth. His arms shook, marble flaking off him and falling into the field below. Where the flakes touched down, the flowers briefly turned gold. "You still have your connection to Irelia and Tash, yes?"

"Yes, but I—"

"Pull us back, now!"

"Do what he says, Rhi."

She released the spell's energy and grasped for the warmth that had saved her. Reality hooked its talons into her and dragged her back. When she slammed into her body, she could still *feel* the hole, though thankfully it wasn't physical.

Irelia hovered over her, concern etched into the lines of her face. "You're alright?"

"Thanks to you, I think," Rhienne said, pushing herself to her hands and knees. "How... why...?"

"I wouldn't go to all this trouble to keep you alive just to let you go that easy." The captain's tone was light, but the look in her eyes and the protective curl of her body was anything but. With her help, Rhienne straightened, but her legs were too wobbly to stand.

Echo was there. Exodus was there. The ritual circle and the Dawnglow had dissolved to ash. "Where is my mother?" Rhienne asked.

Echo was looking at empty air. "What's wrong? Why can't she see you?"

If the silence hadn't torn at the last of Rhienne's sanity, the way the air changed around Exodus would have.

"When a dream dies, it can be brought back, but it will never be the same as it once was," he said. "The process is often... scarring. What happened on the day she died?"

No. No, this couldn't be happening. Rhienne shook her head, blinking hard against tears, and collapsed back onto the ground. *I never want to see you again.*

"I said... It was a figure of speech. Why would it—No." The dam broke, because that was pity in Exodus's aura, and Echo was crawling over and embracing her, and Rhienne had no idea if her mother was comforting her or how much of the woman she knew was there at all. "Oh gods, Mom, I'm so sorry." She buried her face in Echo's shoulder and sobbed.

Chapter 24

Echo

Even as Echo cradled Rhienne against her, she couldn't stop staring. Vala was radiant. When they'd crossed back into Exodus's realm, Vala's soul had bloomed from the center of the flower and taken its own shape. The woman was like a watercolor before the paint dried, all blues and purples and splashes of orange and pink that bled together as she moved. Other than her coloring, she looked so similar to Rhienne.

Her heartbroken expression matched her daughter's, but she attempted to smile at Echo. "I've heard much about you; it appears Rhienne did not exaggerate the quality of her friend. Thank you for bringing us together again. Can I get a better look at her?"

Echo leaned back and murmured, "She wants to see you."

Rhienne ducked her head, eyes squeezed shut. "How much has she changed? Does she remember what happened? Is she... angry?"

Vala floated closer to them and cupped Rhienne's face in her hands. "My beautiful girl. I could die a hundred times and never forget you."

"She's not angry. Open your eyes."

There was a tiny spark of hope on Rhienne's face, as if she had reset the damage by not looking for a moment, and when she opened her eyes, her mother would appear. The hope died immediately. She looked past Vala, who tried to brush away her tears to no effect.

"A touching reunion," Exodus said with forced blandness. "But I believe we have a bargain to fulfill."

Vala whirled, the calm pastels covering her body turning to hot reds and oranges. "What gratitude I have for my rescue does not leave much room for patience with your kind. They are right to call you Children, the way you squabble and think only of yourselves. Give me more than a moment."

Shame locked Rhienne's gaze on the broken floor. Tension crackled between Vala and Exodus. Irelia and Tash were here for moral support, but today had been such a whirlwind, they'd hardly had time to fill in the gaps of everything going on.

Echo would have to do all the charming, then, which was usually Rhienne's job. She took as deep a breath as she could with the barbs of the contract constricting her. "Everyone sit down. There's a lot to explain."

Echo gave Vala the details about Oblivion, the forces he was gathering, and what he hoped to do with her voice. Irelia settled close enough to Rhienne that the two could touch if they wanted, but Rhienne didn't move. All the while, Echo's gaze kept drifting to Exodus. The god was disconcertingly still. Primed, perhaps, for their deal to fall through. She shuddered to think what favor he might ask of her friends, never mind her.

"If we have any hope of stopping Oblivion, we need allies. Exodus agreed to work with us, if you had useful information," Echo finished and focused on Rhienne's mother. "Is there anything you can tell us about the exiled god?"

Rhienne broke from her stupor to whisper, "What did you gain from your bargain with them?"

The colors swirling over Vala's skin calmed. Mostly. The occasional streak of red came through, but she broke her glaring match with Exodus and settled in front of Echo again. "Will you tell her everything I say?"

"Of course."

She did her best to relay Vala's story word for word. "I'm so sorry, Rhienne, that I could not tell you the full terms of my deal before. I was afraid that it might break something in the contract, or draw attention to you, or encourage you to seek out a deal of your own, which was the last thing I wanted." Rhienne flinched, and Echo put a hand over hers. "Not because I thought you would make a poor choice, but because I realized there *were no good choices.* My fears were not unfounded, but they shouldn't have stopped me either."

With a furtive glance at Exodus, Vala addressed Echo. "You are sure he is on our side?"

No. Yes. The answer seemed to change with every sentence out of Vala's mouth. "He wants to stop Oblivion just as much as we do."

Vala grimaced. "The enemy of your enemy will turn on you the moment your common foe is dealt with."

Exodus shifted, stone and mist and back again, silent, waiting. He maintained the marble form much more than he used to. The illusions were dispelled and the cracks in his body had almost healed, so that couldn't be the reason why. Had Echo done that to him when she'd left?

She didn't like the weight of certainty that settled over her. Couldn't one thing she'd blamed on someone else not actually be her fault? The guilt was getting too heavy to bear.

"He's brought us this far," Echo said carefully. Exodus had the excuse of their new deal as a first impetus, but he'd risked himself in the Plane of the Dead. He'd followed Vala's call and saved Rhienne. She thought of her father and Sidrin, and almost lost her nerve, but she forced the words out. If they weren't true yet, she wanted them to be. "I trust him."

Exodus shimmered ever so slightly.

"Very well," Vala said, then Echo continued relaying her story.

"I promised my firstborn for the ability to have my own dreams. It was decades before any of them took hold, but once they did, I started pining for someone to share them with. That's when I found your father. He and I wanted the same thing, in a way. I wanted a way to make the world better. Easier, kinder, full of magic and wonder. For your father, that was you. And for me, you gave my dream deeper meaning."

"You created a child, knowing you'd have to give it up?" Rhienne asked.

"No, no, my dear. The god I bargained with chose that phrasing because spirits do not *bear* children. I was given a gift, not a deal. Or so I'd hoped. But the Mothers were angry at the imbalance. They were looking for any excuse to get rid of me, and you. When you were young, I left to renegotiate my pact, to keep you safe, but the method I'd used to contact the exiled god before didn't work. I didn't find out until later that they'd been banished."

This news only made Rhienne curl further in on herself.

"It was you." Exodus's voice rattled between the fractured stones of the palace. "Yours was the wasteful deal the Mothers spoke of. 'A trade that could never be fulfilled,' that would have us leaking more magic than the deal that killed Horizon. You're the reason my sibling was *erased*." The last word boomed in time with the step he took toward the five of them, huddled on the floor.

"Now, hold on." Echo was on her feet in an instant. An insane and inane thing to do. Lightning flashed and wind howled through the broken ceiling, and Exodus took another step. But Tash stood with her, his size and presence a comfort. "She's going to help us fix this."

"It wouldn't need fixing without her!"

"Please." Vala scoffed. "Your sibling would've given a similar gift to the next person in line if they hadn't been exiled. They were better than all the rest of you combined."

"Don't you think I know that?" Exodus shouted. "And look where it got them. Look where it got Horizon." Thunder rumbled, but despite the storm, all the floating stones inside had stopped moving. The same stillness from the glade.

This time, Echo recognized it for the heartbreak it was. Their deal couldn't fail, not now. She grasped for a way to calm him.

"That man in the woods," she whispered. "He gave me a roof over my head, a job, a friend when I had none. In return, I stole from him and left him to the Untold. I took away his home, his community." It was only saying it out loud, with the horror of the interaction fresh in her mind, that she felt the full extent of her grief. Too much, far too much, for it to only belong to Natalia. It had been easier to spread the pain among other personas, but that wouldn't serve her here. She had to meet Exodus as an equal. To show him every tally on her list of losses.

"An Exalt in Wildspire offered me an opportunity to perform," Echo continued. "And I brushed it off for being beneath me, because I didn't want to keep up the facade I'd put on there. And today, I found out I *so completely* ruined the life of the one person who gave me sanctuary, that I may never find it again. Everywhere I've been, I've always convinced myself it didn't hurt to leave and become someone else." Exodus shuddered. She kept going, even though she felt the same. "Every time, I'd be damned if it didn't rip out a piece of me. But at least I have their names to hold onto, and the happy things they gave me.

"What the Mothers did to your sibling, what Oblivion did to *you*, wasn't fair... and neither was what I did." Echo hesitated, waiting for his permission, then put her hands on his shoulders. One of his eyes was still dark, but the tiny stars within gleamed. "We can make some of it right, but only if we work together."

The marble under her fingers dissolved. Like a long sigh, the rest of him became mist, and held that way. He nodded once.

"That goes for you too," she said to Vala, who had the grace to look ashamed. Echo breathed the tension from her shoulders. Mediation was not high on her list of talents. The fact that she was doing it on Exodus's behalf, and had very nearly apologized for breaking their deal, was a knot to untangle later. "Do you remember anything at all about how you contacted the exiled god that might give us a hint about their domain?"

Vala's brows drew together, her skin taking on deeper, pensive tones. "Specifics are difficult. The Mothers' erasure was thorough. I used my dreamwalking to do it, but..." Vala winced and rubbed her temple. White flashed over her eyes.

Tash nodded in sympathy. "The same thing happens to me when I try to think back."

"Wait a minute. It also happened when we asked the Collector about the library." Echo hurried over to the music box, forgotten on the ground. "And when Exodus tried to touch your spell anchor."

This, finally, woke Rhienne up. Something to do, a puzzle to solve. A temporary distraction, but it would do for now. "Yeah, you're right. Is there a protection spell on it?"

"Not that I cast." Vala floated over, almost entranced, and cautiously reached for the object. "I can't believe Silas kept it all this time." She opened the box and ran her fingers over the inscription. "We are of gossamer, fickle and impermanent."

"Why didn't the Mothers want me to see that?" Exodus murmured.

Echo held her breath, waiting for something to happen, but there was no flash of light, no spark of epiphany. The tiny dancer spun, skipping notes as broken, rusty gears turned inside.

Vala smiled sadly. "She may not remember, and it's rather distorted now, but I used to hum this song to Rhienne when she was little. It came to me in one of my dreams, and it helped her sleep. Isn't that funny?"

Funny was not the word Echo would've chosen. Gods were specific in their deals. There had to be a reason for that dream, *this* song, *these* words in the engraving, left behind for Rhienne.

Vala sang along, her voice rising and falling in a simple, wordless lullaby, filling in the parts the music box skipped.

Rhienne drifted over and touched the trinket, right next to her mother's hand. To her eyes, it would be floating in the air. "All right, this is a little spooky. What's going on?"

"It's a lullaby that Vala sang to you," Echo explained. "Do you recognize it?"

She frowned. "It hardly sounds like a song at all."

Echo opened her mouth to pick up the tune. Stupid, stupid habit that she thought she'd kicked. It must be because she was back in this place. She knew in her bones how important this was, and she couldn't do the simplest thing to help. Dejected, she reached for the mandolin.

Exodus stopped her with a gentle touch. Then he began to hum. Sonorous notes wove together with Vala and the music box, filling the throne room.

"Oh." Rhienne's eyes went wide. "I... I do remember."

"Sing with them," Echo urged. "I think the exiled god left her a clue, and she left it for you. It must be keyed to you both."

"I promised you I wouldn't—"

"It's fine. Do it!"

Rhienne's voice joined the chorus. And if there was another jealous pang in Echo's chest, it was quickly eclipsed by the new line of golden letters that appeared beneath the first engraving.

Everyone stopped. Though Rhienne couldn't know, she and her mother read together: "*So whenever we can, we must be bastions for hope and light.*"

Exodus made a small, breathless sound. The storm outside halted mid-peal of thunder.

"What is it?" Echo asked.

"Your dreamwalks, Vala," the god said. "When they helped you contact my sibling before, was it because you were traveling rapidly between dreams?" The question was punctuated by a flare of white and a pained gasp from each of them—a warning that they should not, could not, push further, and clearer confirmation than if Vala had nodded.

The dust on the floor swirled around Exodus in a cyclone of mounting excitement. "*Fickle and impermanent.* Your method of contact did not stop working because of his exile. He always hated his name, my little brother. Most of the implications of Gossamer are unpleasant. When the Mothers erased him, it was the perfect opportunity to change his identity."

"Not me of course," Rhienne cut in, "but for those of us a little slower on the draw, what the hell are you on about?"

Irelia was the first one to put it together. "He picked a new name. And with it, a new domain, a new way to call to him."

"No wonder they didn't want me to see." Exodus laughed, a sound like the joyous ringing of bells. The last bit of void cleared from his face. "Bastion. His new name is Bastion."

"Thank you for that, brother." The words seeped from the still-healing spaces between the stone walls.

A chill went up Echo's spine. The blood drained from Rhienne's face, and Exodus's form solidified into marble.

Oblivion had never left.

"I'll be sure to let the rest of our siblings know that his infractions have continued. If 'Bastion' hasn't withered away like our dear sister, he must be getting magic from somewhere, hmm? Skimming off the top of the rest of our deals. Naughty."

Echo whirled, searching the darkened cracks for the god who held her voice. He was nowhere and everywhere. Her power was nothing compared to his. Still, she swung the mandolin off her back to try *something*.

Oblivion said, "Before I go, should I tell Mishara where you are, or let her finish up in Hearthglen first?"

Vala and Rhienne erupted into profanities, and Echo's fingers froze on the strings. "Exodus, can't you—"

"I'm not strong enough," he whispered.

The shadows chuckled. "Either way, she'll find you soon. Count your heartbeats, oathbreakers." Starless void surged across the palace walls.

Exodus screamed—a sound that would haunt Echo's nightmares for whatever was left of her life—as the weakened boundaries of his realm shattered.

Chapter 25

Rhienne

Rhienne's head rang. The side of her neck was wet and sticky. Sound was muffled and her eyes were bleary, but she smelled smoke clear enough. Thick black clouds of it rose into the sky from the south. Screams carried on the wind.

Hearthglen. Oblivion. *Mishara.*

Every instinct of self-preservation told her to pick up and run, or walk, or crawl as far from that smoke as she could.

She staggered to her feet, and the world turned over. Rhienne fell, her hands sank into the soggy ground, and she spit up bile. Oblivion had never stopped watching her. She'd handed him everything he needed to gain power, lost a piece of her soul, and they were no closer to getting Echo's voice back. Now Mishara wanted to play with her like a rabid dog with a toy before sending her to the afterlife, which apparently meant burning the homes of innocent people.

Vala had said Rhienne was created to make the world better. What a fucking joke.

"Rhienne?" Echo said from somewhere in the marsh grasses to her left.

Odd that she could hear from that side just fine. She raised a hand toward her right ear, then thought better of it. "Here. I'm coming."

Crawling through the muck was both disgusting and agonizing. Her knee twinged with every shuffle forward. She found Echo cradling the body of a small gray and white bird with angular wings. It looked like one of the migrating terns she'd seen in an ice-fisher's dream, except its eyes were flat golden disks. Its chest rose and fell with rapid, shallow breaths.

"Is that... Exodus?"

Echo nodded, and when she spoke, her voice was thick. "He changed forms right before the realm broke apart. I don't know what's wrong. He won't respond."

The grass rustled and Irelia appeared, straining to drag an unconscious Tash behind her. "We need to get back to the ship and get out of here," she panted. "Rhienne, are you all right? I think there were some bandages somewhere..."

Oh, right. Gods, she was rattled. "Don't worry about it." Rhienne reached for the magic in her blood and wove it back into her body, stitching and patching up as best she could. Healing was not her forte. It would probably leave a horrendous scar. "Can everyone else move? Is my mother here?"

"I-I think so," Echo said shakily. "And yes."

Rhienne's throat itched, her muscles were jelly, and she had one knife against who knew how many Untold and a god's fury. But the urge to run away became the urge to run *toward.* The Untold would destroy the town, either looking for her, or because Mishara thought it was fun, or because Oblivion had told them to, and they weren't likely to take prisoners.

"We can't leave yet," Rhienne rasped. "We have to do something."

Echo shook her head. "You can't go back there. Mishara will kill you."

Rhienne rubbed at the aching spot in her chest. "She'll have less of a chance of doing that if my soul is no longer tied to Oblivion's. What does my mother say about breaking my contract?"

Silence fell. She couldn't tell if Vala was thinking or speaking. This was what it had all been for, yet the longer the question hung in the air, the more Rhienne wished she hadn't asked it. Everything else had gone so spectacularly wrong. Why would this be any different?

Echo's lips pressed into a thin line before speaking Vala's words. "A soul oath is not a deal the cosmos takes lightly. It will require a powerful ending to balance out the bargain, one way or another. If not yours... it must be his."

Great. All she had to do to save her soul was *kill a god.* "So it's impossible," Rhienne whispered. No one responded, which was answer enough.

She closed her eyes and took a deep breath through her nose. The smell of smoke brought her back to reality. Echo was right. Running into Hearthglen would be suicide, and there was no escaping what waited for Rhienne on the other side of death. But she couldn't sit idly by and watch the destruction in her wake any longer.

"Mishara is here because of me. You didn't see what I saw in the Plane of the Dead. All the people I..." Rhienne couldn't say *sent there*. "I'm tired of being fickle, selfish, impulsive, and what's that thing you like to say? A stone in the river? Well *you're* the river, Echo. You need to keep going. I've never met anyone with a current as strong as yours."

It had pushed Echo through her whole life, and it would carry her forward now. One moment of weakness, and a god had offered his aid. Two now, actually. Where was the divine intervention for all of Rhienne's mistakes? Was she not good enough without a dream?

She would've laughed at the question if she hadn't felt like crying. Given a single second of thought, the answer seemed pretty obvious.

Insanity solidified into necessity, certainty. Maybe this once, she could do something good without messing it up.

Chapter 26

Echo

Echo hated the look on her friend's face. Resurrecting Vala should have helped Rhienne find a path forward, but she was more lost than ever.

"Find Bastion," Rhienne said. "Get your voice back. I can draw the Untold away, and once Mishara has me, she'll have no reason to keep working with Oblivion. Whoever follows her will leave with her. That takes out some of their numbers and gives you room to get anyone out of town who hasn't already fled."

Ever since Exodus had brought Echo's vision to life in the glade, something had been niggling at the back of her mind. It wasn't because anything in it had changed, or because the god was right about needing to let her dream go. When she imagined those two ever-oscillating versions of her death, they *both* felt empty now, even when her deathbed was surrounded by fans. For the first time, she looked hard at each of the faces of the crowd.

Most of them, she didn't recognize. Tash and Nazal were present. Rhienne had been such a fixture in her life that Echo had just assumed her friend would be there. She hadn't wanted to spend any more time examining this piece of her future than absolutely necessary.

But Rhienne was not one of them.

Whether her absence was due to some rift that would form between them later in life or the choice Rhienne was about to make, Echo couldn't know, but she would not risk it. Not if there was any other way.

Exodus's rapid heartbeat slowed, and his wings relaxed. The worst of it was over, but he wouldn't be able to answer her questions for the time being. She looked to Vala, who was visibly torn between the very different kinds of destruction happening in Hearthglen and within her daughter. Somehow, Echo was the soundest of mind here. She had to do something. A ghost of a smile crossed her face as an idea came to her.

"Exodus was trying to get me to end my dream to stop Oblivion. If I die, the dream dies with me, right?"

"Correct," Vala said.

"I'm not letting you sacrifice yourself—" Rhienne started.

ed.

Echo held up a hand. "So if I get caught, they'll want to put me somewhere for safekeeping until Oblivion is ready. I'm in better shape than you to draw them away. Irelia, would you and the crew be willing to take on a rescue mission?"

The captain looked up from tending to Tash's wounds. "I can signal the ship. I'm not sure how low we can stay in the sky with that smoke, but we'll bring as many of the townsfolk as we can aboard."

"Thank you. I'll buy you as much time as I can to get them out and for Exodus to wake up." It felt so strange to hold a god in the palms of her hands. She carefully slid the bird's delicate body into Rhienne's lap. "Then I'll give you directions on how to find me through the telepathy stone."

"But I—you—" Rhienne stammered. "How are you going to draw them away? Mishara doesn't care about you anymore."

"Same way I did at your execution." Echo adopted her friend's swagger along with her form. The change was comfortable, a shape she'd taken once before, and one she knew better than her own, even with the added scars. "It worked long enough the first time."

Rhienne swallowed hard. "What does your foresight say about this plan?"

She really didn't want to look again. If there was still a gaping hole where Rhienne should be, or if Mishara shot her on sight... Echo frowned at the blank gray cloud in her head. "I can't see."

"Don't lie to me."

"I'm not! The space where the vision should be is still there, but it's filled up with fog."

"There are some places even divine sight cannot touch," Vala said. She was staring unerringly toward Hearthglen now. "Whatever your decision, make it quickly. We're running out of time."

Echo's stomach flipped over, but her voice was firm. "Listen to me. Or if you won't listen to me, pretend I'm actually you. You're going to take this." Echo shoved the mandolin into Rhienne's hands. The encounter with Sidrin had shown her it was too recognizable to keep. "Then you're going to figure out what service will summon Bastion and kick Oblivion's ass, because you are not a river stone, you are a godsdamned mountain, do you hear?" She put on one of her friend's signature smiles. "This will work. Trust me."

"It's a little freaky how good you are at that." Rhienne still looked unsure, but she took the mandolin and said, "Make sure to call her Mish; she'll hate that. The second they start getting stabby, you mimic the dancer again. Promise?"

"Promise. Take care of each other." Before anyone could change their minds, Echo took off toward the smoking town.

Ducking through reeds and avoiding the boggiest patches of ground, it took Echo precious minutes to reach Hearthglen's edge, and precious more to wind through the buildings and alleys without being spotted by patrolling Untold.

There was a rip in reality in the middle of the main square. It opened into the inky blackness of space, distorting the air around it as if it would eat away at the sky until no color or light remained. Mishara stepped out of the void and surveyed the carnage with a smile. She wore full crimson leather armor, a red cloak sweeping out behind her, a ruby-hilted dagger at her belt to match her circlet.

"No sign of her yet, High Inquisitor," one of the underlings said to Mishara.

"Keep looking. I've just been informed that our quarry is close at hand." She observed the burning buildings with a moue of distaste. "Tear the place apart if you have to. I doubt anyone will notice its absence."

Echo crept around the town square's perimeter to get a closer look at the Untold. None of them had glowing bones, or any clothing that would obscure them. Mishara had stuck to *one* of her principles. That meant no paralytic needles, hopefully. She'd take that small win.

A handful of Untold pulled people from their homes or grabbed those still fleeing in the streets. They hustled the townsfolk into the square and forced them onto their knees. Hostages. And Mishara looked ready to turn them into corpses, sparks of Oblivion's magic coalescing around her.

Echo's adoptive father wasn't among them yet. "Let him be safe," she whispered, before stepping out from her hiding place, hands raised in surrender. "All right, Mish, that's enough fucking around. You can let them go."

"Aha. She has a heart after all." With a threatening leer at a man in the hostage line, Mishara extinguished the black-red flame at her fingertips.

The townsfolk looked astounded to see Rhienne here at all, never mind martyring herself for them.

"Hmm." The inquisitor narrowed her eyes. "I see you've shed your fake skin at last. Life on the run hasn't agreed with you." The lower ranking recruits surrounded Mishara, weapons raised. No magic glittered among them; they hadn't shared in her bargain with Oblivion.

Echo affected nonchalance and shrugged. "More than it's agreed with you. You had to stoop to making a divine pact to get to me, huh? Pathetic."

Silas appeared in an alley across the square, bloodied, burned, and limping, but still standing. Echo didn't dare meet his eye. The Untold hadn't spotted him yet. She had to make sure it stayed that way.

They're gathering people in the square, she thought to Rhienne. *How close are you?*

Edge of town, over the docks. I'll come back to lead them to the ship.

Good. I'll lure the Untold away from there. Echo leaned in conspiratorially. "I can't help but notice there aren't any other high inquisitors here. Did they finally uncover your lies and kick you out?"

"There are no other high inquisitors of Wildspire anymore," Mishara sneered. "Oblivion helped me take care of them. Strip her down and tie her up. I'm sick of her running her mouth."

"What about the other one?" one of the officers asked. He held a greatsword in a white-knuckled grip, teeth bared, eyes darting around like they'd be attacked at any moment.

"Don't worry about that creature. It'll be taken care of presently. I said, *tie her up.*"

A chill washed over Echo. *Be careful, Rhi. They might have reinforcements.*

As ordered, the Untold came forward with enchanted chains. Though there were six of them and one of her, they moved slowly, wary.

Echo shifted into a running stance. "Oh, Mish. Were you under the impression I was going to come quietly? Pathetic *and* stupid." She took off through the familiar streets, away from the docks, the hostages, and Rhienne. Mishara's goons had left nothing untouched. If a building hadn't caught fire, its windows were smashed in, or its doors were broken off their hinges. Blood smeared across porches and walkways. The air was thick and choking, hot enough to vaporize her sweat. Smoke and magic turned the sky red.

Crossbow bolts tore through the wood and stone around her. The Untold were hot on her trail. She ducked and wove through rubble-strewn alleys, but one shot grazed her arm, forceful as a hammer blow. Another hit her ankle, and Echo screamed. Agony spiked up her leg with every step, but she didn't stop moving. Her friends just needed a little more time.

"Enough!" Mishara roared. With a concussive *whoomph*, all the fires went out.

Echo glanced over her shoulder. Red sparks from the lingering smoke gathered in a cloud over the town. A bargain, no matter how great, could not have made Mishara so powerful. She must have absorbed the Dawnglow Rhienne had tried to steal. That combined with Oblivion's aid... no mortal should have that much divine power.

Echo shivered, glad Rhienne was gone. The blank cloud of her foresight was growing more ominous by the moment.

Then the sparks fell. She raised an arm to shield her eyes and kept staggering on. Burns peppered her shoulders and scalp, and where the sparks touched her, flares of crimson shot up into the sky to mark her location. They left an unwavering trail. Her breath shortened from pain and exertion. She ran anyway, stumbling onto a road where the marsh finally became visible between two buildings.

Mishara appeared in front of her in a puff of red smoke. Her eyes were filmed over with black. Before Echo could turn around, the ground at her feet erupted. A massive spectral hand closed over her with a crushing grip.

The high inquisitor cackled. "Do you know what this is?" With a flick of her wrist, a bottle floated from her robes into the air between them. A small black sphere that seemed to suck in light rested at the bottom. It was frighteningly reminiscent of the way her voice had looked when Exodus siphoned it from her.

"A marble?" Echo wheezed, struggling against the spell holding her.

"A gift. From Oblivion." Mishara's smile went feral. "I'll admit, I was surprised you even had a soul to take a portion from. There can't be much left." She spun the bottle in the air before returning it to her pocket. "In case you hadn't put the pieces together, this means you're not getting away from me again. You're *mine*. And I'm going to enjoy watching every moment of your suffering." The spectral hand squeezed.

Mishara had part of Rhienne's soul? Was that what had happened in the Plane of the Dead? Why hadn't Rhienne said anything?

Echo waited until spots danced over her vision and the fog in her foresight started to part. She had never mimicked so fast in her life. Her ribs cracked under the combined strain of the change and Mishara's magic. The spectral hand vanished. Blood lined Echo's teeth, sharp and metallic. Between gasps for air, she spat on the ground near Mishara's feet, hoping to hear her shriek at being foiled again.

But the inquisitor *smiled.* She waved for her cronies to come forward, and they filtered into the street cautiously. Echo had no strength left to fight as they tied her up.

"Are you sure, High Inquisitor?" That was Orik, the man whose form Echo had borrowed twice before. There was a javelin in his hand, aimed at Echo's heart.

"Quite sure," Mishara said. "All we have to do now is wait for our luminescent friends from Devonsfort to do their work. It'll be an even trade. They may even give me a reward."

Fear thundered through her. The reinforcements weren't members of Mishara's faction. They'd have no qualms about siphoning. *Rhienne, the Untold from Devonsfort are here, you have to r—*

"Ah, that's where that awful buzzing is coming from." Mishara grabbed the cord around Echo's neck and yanked the telepathy stone free. She held it up and spoke her message aloud: "If you want to see your pet again before you both die, return to the ashes of your home. Or don't. We'll find you either way." Black tendrils wrapped around the stone and crushed it to dust. Mishara brushed off her hands and looked down at Echo with disgust. "Take this *thing* to the forge."

Chapter 27

Rhienne

The mandolin sat heavily on Rhienne's back. She wasn't leaving Echo behind, just following orders for a plan that was marginally less harebrained than the one Rhienne had come up with. She wasn't a river stone, she was a gods-damned mountain.

The words didn't feel quite as invigorating as when Echo had said them. A mountain was just a really big rock, after all.

Exodus was still unconscious in his bird form, tucked into her shirt while she, Irelia, and presumably Vala carried Tash around the boggy outskirts of Hearthglen. After one close call with an Untold patrol, they didn't dare speak. Rhienne barely breathed until they reached the docks. Fishing boats and dingy sloops bobbed on the waves, not on fire but hardly seaworthy. The airship hovered over the water and flew in to meet them when Irelia waved them down. For such a large vessel, it was eerily quiet compared to the snap of flames and the wash of the tide.

They're gathering people in the square. How close are you? Echo's voice made her jump.

Edge of town, over the docks. Rhienne made a split second decision. *I'll come back to lead them to the ship.*

Good. I'll lure the Untold away from there.

The crew lowered the cargo ramp and hurried down to take Tash off their hands. Irelia and Rhienne sagged in exhausted relief.

Right before Echo unleashed hell in the town.

Under the crashing, shattering, and shouting, Rhienne grabbed Irelia by the shoulders and kissed her firmly. "I'll find everyone and send them here. If I don't come back—"

"Come back," Irelia commanded. "Vala says she can remain hidden and go with you."

Rhienne wasted a precious moment drinking her in, mud and blood, soot and wrinkles, ferocity and strength. "Aye, Captain." She dashed back across the quay, heading at an angle for the square, where smoke and the shadows of half-standing buildings swallowed her.

Echo's warning rang through her mind: *Be careful, Rhi. They might have reinforcements.*

The cold cruelty of Reckoning's voice swiftly followed, cracking across the sky like thunder. "You should have known better than to defy me. Behold your punishment."

The goddess was nowhere to be seen, but cries came from the beach, rasping and resonant. Figures swarmed across the rocky shore, visible even through the smoke.

Out here, the Untold did not need to hide their glowing bones, or the vile yellow whips of magic they sent at the ship, pulling it down until it crashed into the docks.

"To arms!" Irelia shouted. "Take a flamethrower to these vermin!"

Rhienne froze at the edge of her shelter, torn. There were too many for one more person to make a difference. Gunshots sounded, and the fear churning her stomach made the decision for her. She'd only get in the way.

So she did what she did best and ran.

Toward a job that was just as important, Rhienne told herself. There was a god in her pocket to protect, townspeople to save.

One block short of the main square, she turned a corner and ran right into her father. Silas was a mess, clothes torn in half a dozen places, blood soaking his right leg, eyes bloodshot from smoke, and tear tracks running through the ash on his cheeks.

"Gods and demons, what—" He froze when he got a better look at her face. A few dozen people were crowded into the alley behind him, all of whom looked frightened and confused to see her after she'd ostensibly lured the attackers away. But not her father. He understood in an instant. "You let her take your place."

"She didn't give me much choice!" Rhienne gritted her teeth. Now would've been a great time for her mother to make a dramatic entrance. "Do you want to argue, or get out of here? The docks aren't safe. We need to head into the marsh."

"Follow me," he said over his shoulder. "We can hide in the cove—"

"That's not far enough," Rhienne said. "They're going to send out search parties. For me." Her throat tightened at his expression. He wouldn't turn her over, would he? "I know a place. Echo and I played there when we were little. Everyone stay low and keep quiet."

They hurried through the smoldering ruins of the town, battle sounds fading behind them. Rhienne prayed it was because of the distance, not because her friends had already lost. She should've stayed with Irelia, should've told her to be careful, should've done something more to help Echo. This was the second time Rhienne had allowed her friend to walk into the heart of her worst enemies. Her father's gaze burned into her back, condemning her for all of it.

The path into the marsh, at least, was clear. Likely Mishara's single-minded hatred was to thank for that.

Rhienne's spine ached from hunching over in the tall grass, and it was a blessing when they reached the river. The dank water buzzed with insects, but the surrounding cypress trees gave them cover to stand. This far from town, only the faint smell of smoke lingered in the air. In silence, but for the occasional sniffle or heavy breath, Rhienne brought what was left of Hearthglen's people to the mangrove thicket she and Echo had spent countless hours climbing in. The roots wove a thick enough carpet above the water to sit and rest. She remained on the fringes while her father helped everyone make their own spaces and find what comfort they could.

Rhienne, the Untold from Devonsfort are here, you have to r—

Echo's voice cut off, and the one that took its place sent Rhienne to her knees.

If you want to see your pet again before you both die, return to the ashes of your home. Or don't. We'll find you either way.

"Fuck," Rhienne whispered. It wasn't nearly strong enough of a word, but her mind was empty of better expressions. She *was* a coward. Mishara's pact with Oblivion was Rhienne's fault. It should've been her back there. She ought to run into town and save her friend... somehow. But her legs wouldn't move.

The shadow that fell over her was undeniably her father's. "Are you going to tell me what just happened to our home? To Echo?"

Rhienne let her forehead fall against the nearest tree. The rough bark was a grounding force against the beehive of her thoughts. "Ask Mom."

Her father choked. Vala must have appeared. Rhienne raised her head enough to see his expression: blank with shock, then just blank.

"I don't want to talk to her," he said gruffly. "I want to talk to *you.*"

Of course, the one thing she'd managed to accomplish didn't matter at all. What could she say that wouldn't confirm every terrible thought he had about her?

In all the chaos, she'd forgotten about Exodus. Rhienne pulled the bird out from under her shirt. There was a golden sheen to the underside of his feathers that hadn't been there before. Whether that was a good sign or not was anyone's guess. Whatever injuries he'd sustained in Oblivion's attack, they didn't look physical.

"We've gotten... involved with a few of the gods," she said. "All of them, at this point, I guess. Dad, meet Exodus. Exodus, Dad."

Silas gaped. "This is no time for jokes, Rhienne."

"I'm not joking," she said. "We went to Exodus's realm. That's how I got Mom back. And we were going to find one of his siblings, which some of the other gods are pissed about, so they attacked us with human forces who... also happen to be pissed at us." The last of her defiance broke. Salt burned her eyes. "I had no idea they would come here, Dad. And now they have Echo." And likely Tash, Irelia, and the rest of the crew. "I ruined everything. I always do."

Cicadas whined. Leaves rustled in the faint wind. Her father stared at a spot to her left. She hoped Vala was talking, and that the dismay on his face wasn't all Rhienne's fault.

"I feared the worst," he whispered at last, and held out a hand to the empty air. "I'm glad you're alright."

Rhienne looked away. It was too hard to see half of this conversation—what should've been a happy family reunion burdened by so much grief and failure.

With a grunt, her father settled onto the mangrove roots beside her. He put a hand on her back, and it was the uncertainty of the gesture that made her face crumple and her tears finally fall. He let her cry herself out. Dehydrated as she was, it didn't take long.

"So then." Silas cleared his throat, rough with his own tears. "What are you going to do to fix it?"

Rhienne shook her head. What *could* she do? If Exodus woke up, maybe they could make a deal that wouldn't cost her a literal arm or leg, but there wasn't much left for her to bargain with. She was pretty sure blood magic wouldn't be able to heal him either.

She looked down at the god and murmured, "How about this: you give me some power—enough to fix you up, and whatever else you think is fair—and I'll take over that favor Echo owes you."

What was one more claim on her soul? Not like she was using it for anything worthwhile.

The mandolin twanged harshly. Rhienne whirled, but there was no one there. Must be her mother protesting.

It didn't matter anyway. There was no tether of a deal struck, no rush of magic.

"Vala says she can see the shape of Exodus's mind," her father said, brows drawn together. "He is trapped in it. By it," he corrected. "It's a state similar to sleep."

"She's saying... I can dreamwalk with him?"

"She thinks so."

Rhienne blinked. She'd had no idea gods could dream, or whether their dreams resided in the same plane as mortals'. But all roads seemed to lead back to this wretched ability of hers. With her pact to Oblivion broken, she had control of it again. For Echo's and the crew's sake, it was worth a try.

"Okay." She blew out a breath. "Time for a nap then."

A mangrove thicket wasn't the most comfortable place to lie down. Exhausted as she was, between all the aches in her body, the humidity and her father's watchful eye making her sweat, and some piece of root or bark jabbing into her no matter which way she turned, sleep seemed miles away.

"She's a grown woman. If she wanted my help, she'd ask for it," Silas grumbled. After a pause, he said, "Yes, fine, all right." Then, louder, "Come here, Rhienne."

She pushed herself up to find him holding out an arm, making space for her in the crook of his shoulder. Rhienne inched over, giving him plenty of time to change his mind. When he didn't, she leaned into him, and though they were both tense and awkward, there was a familiarity to the pose, the scent of iron and sweat under ash and blood.

"What did Vala say to you?" Rhienne murmured as her eyes drifted closed.

He huffed a laugh. "When we don't know what's ahead, we have to take comfort in what we have."

"Hmm." She was far too tired to try unraveling that.

Finally, pastel-hued sleep washed over her.

She hoped to see her mother here, but even in Vala's native plane, she was invisible. Rhienne shoved it down with the rest of her failures and started her search.

Exodus's mind was not hard to find. It was the singular patch of grayscale amid bubbles of color, and it screamed so loudly that she couldn't resist being dragged into it.

Rather than one coherent story, a dome of images spread around her. His dream was a collection of jagged, mismatched moments, as if someone had ripped up a hundred paintings and carelessly pieced them back together. Oblivion's magic seeped and oozed through the patchwork. Trapped by his mind indeed—it had been shattered along with his home.

The God of Journeys lay in a fetal position at the dome's center, a statue covered in cracks. Rhienne rushed over to him, surprised he hadn't broken apart from how hard he was shaking. Up close, she could see *through* his marble skin, not to bone and muscle, but to roiling storm-clouds. Rain poured from his eyes like tears.

"What do I do? How can I help?"

He said nothing; even a god couldn't see her here. Rhienne chewed her lip. She'd have to influence his dream to wake him up, but she'd never healed one before, and he was so close to breaking already.

She studied the collection of dreams. Caravans moved through mountain passes and were struck down by avalanches; travelers with bleeding feet stopped at shrines to pray and never got up again; boats crossed entire oceans only to smash upon rocky shores. Hundreds of journeys, failed and broken. Worse than nightmares because there was no waking up.

Exodus himself featured in none of them. Even in the ones set in his palace—dreams from pilgrims who had suc-ceeded in reaching him, received their boon, and left—the god was merely an ominous presence in the background.

It was hard to breathe under the burden of so much suffering. If only Echo were here. She always knew what to say to bring comfort.

"I get it," Rhienne whispered, then cringed. Was she really comparing herself to a god? "I mean, you didn't choose this, did you? You're trapped by what you are. Stuck in your little pocket realm when you ought to be able to take journeys of your own. Maybe even stop some of these disasters." Her gaze caught on one of the larger pieces of the nightmarish puzzle: a female figure, like a star con-tained in human skin, all silver and gold, and so bright she almost hurt to look at. And then it *did* hurt, as her light blazed into a supernova.

Horizon smiled as she died, and said, "It was worth it."

Rhienne wondered if the goddess would still believe that, if she knew what the world had become in her absence. "You miss her," she said to Exodus, walking over to touch the image of his sister, flaring and dying over and over again. "And Bastion. That doesn't excuse you being such an asshole, but... I guess I understand."

The sound of a small rockslide clattered behind her—Exodus painstakingly rising to his feet. He braced himself with each step he took toward her, as if the impact against the ground might shatter him, and stopped in front of Horizon's visage.

The thunderclouds in his chest rumbled, "It's not a god's place to mourn." Chips of marble fell as he stretched out his arm and touched the image. With a shudder, Exodus ripped it free of the wall. The other images grew to fill in the hole, too quickly for Rhienne to glimpse what lay beyond.

The God of Journeys bowed his head. Rain still poured down his stone face, but when he pressed the paper-thin memory to his chest, it glowed with golden light. "She scared away the darkness wherever she went. I should've stopped her. I wish she were here."

The memory dissolved. Exodus let his arms fall, and Rhienne gasped. Some of the cracks in his body had healed.

He needed to *absorb* these journeys, recognize and mourn whatever part he had or had not played in them. Feverishly, Rhienne hurried around the room, leading him to each event with her words like she was plucking at the threads of a dream. "This wasn't your fault. There was nothing you could've done. You gave them perspective. You gave them hope." She didn't always say the right thing, and sometimes when the memories dissolved, they didn't heal anything. A few even made new cracks. But Rhienne kept going. That was her specialty, wasn't it?

She tried to ignore the bitterness of that thought.

Finally, there was one image left, taking up the whole dome. One too many uncaring audiences. A long walk to the beach where the tide rose against her ankles, shins, knees. A portal opened in the air when the water reached her waist. Shelves upon shelves built into the roots of a tree, filled with books that would give her a new path forward.

"Echo," Exodus whispered, a sorrowful chord that reverberated around his mind.

Rhienne hadn't meant to leave this one for last, but as the image looped, she couldn't find words. Was this what it took to open the way to Bastion's realm? How close was Rhienne to what Echo and Tash had experienced?

Or was the better question, how far?

"There's still time to make this one right, but not much," she managed. "She's in danger. You have to wake up, Exodus. You have to help me."

"Make it right. Yes." Color flooded into the dream. The rain inside him stopped, and a single sunbeam broke through the clouds. "I can. I will."

Rhienne's eyes flashed open. The sky had darkened to a hazy purple. Fireflies bobbed between mangrove trunks, and nocturnal birds called to each other across the river.

Her father had fallen asleep against a tree, his arm draped over her. She eased him off and sat up.

Exodus regarded her, ruffling his feathers and testing the stretch of his wings. As before, he didn't speak, but she got the impression of his words from the sounds of the marsh. "I couldn't understand Echo's attachment to you. I think now, I'm beginning to see."

"You're welcome." Rhienne's tone was sour, but without much bite. "Can I ask... why did you keep Echo's voice? What were you going to do with it if Oblivion hadn't shown up?"

"I wasn't going to *do* anything with it." Exodus ducked his head, ashamed. "I considered it a trophy, I suppose. All that built up magical potential, wasting away on a shelf. It felt like justice. It does not feel that way anymore."

Rhienne nodded slowly. "That means you're going to help me get her back, right?"

"My power is limited in the lower realms, but I will do what I can."

"Not good enough. Swear that we're going to rescue her. I promise we'll find Bastion after. Maybe during, if we're lucky," she added, considering the danger they were in. The specifics of Bastion's domain remained a mystery, but the name meant *protector.* They could all certainly use some protection right now.

Rhienne stuck her hand out to shake before remembering Exodus was a bird.

He hopped up onto her arm, digging sharp talons into her skin. "I swear it."

If the tether of a deal formed between them, Rhienne could not feel it. After what she'd seen in his mind, she believed him anyway. "Then go do some scouting. We need to know what we're up against." She shook him off.

Exodus flapped his wings with an indignant squawk but took off toward Hearthglen.

Any amusement she felt for successfully telling a god what to do was short-lived. Rhienne was so tired of having to scrape and scrabble for every millimeter of success. What had Exodus said? 'Too busy grasping for the next handhold to realize she was in the middle of a landslide.' That had never felt truer than it did right now. She would save Echo and the crew because she had to. But after that... after that, the way was shrouded in fog.

"Mom, are you here?"

A gentle pluck of a mandolin string.

"You have my back, don't you?"

Another note rang out and faded into the night. A hollow *yes*, but hollow was all Rhienne had.

Chapter 28

Echo

Echo tried for the hundredth time to maneuver her body into a more comfortable position. She'd been gagged and bound for hours now, while Mishara paced the length of Silas's workshop. Whether the inquisitor knew the significance of the building or had chosen it because it was one of the few left standing, Echo didn't know.

The low-ranking Untold huddled against the walls to stay out of Mishara's way. It was cramped, with tools, scrap metal, and weapons littering the floor, along with shattered storage crates and benches. All of it was covered in a layer of ash. Compared to the Untolds' original numbers, not many had come on this crusade. That partly answered why they'd laid a trap for Rhienne instead of searching for her. Mishara had said the other high inquisitors were gone. She must have executed them before they could do the same to her. How many others were 'dealt with' at the same time? How many who remained did so out of fear?

From the way some of them flinched when Mishara drew near, Echo wagered the percentage was high. Such a group was ripe for chaos and dissension. If only she had her telepathy stone, she could help Rhienne drum up a plan. Its weight around her neck had become a constant comfort, knowing her friend was always within reach. Without it, Echo felt like a piece of driftwood, lost in the ocean.

A young woman—barely more than a girl, really—stepped in through the doorway. Her cloak was tattered and dirty, her face sallow, and she held herself with the care of someone recently injured. "High Inquisitor, the inquisitor from Devonsfort is demanding that we—"

"Have you all lost the functioning of your ears?" Mishara seethed. "I told you to tell that brute he'd receive his prize once I receive mine. And did I not tell you to bow before addressing me?"

"Yes, High Inquisitor." The girl dipped so low that Echo thought she might topple over.

"That's better. Have their search parties turned up anything?"

"N-no. They asked that, since you are not making use of the power source and refuse to give it to them, you m-might contribute to the effort."

Mishara's nostrils flared. Everyone in the room went still.

"Of course, I told them such a task is beneath you," the recruit hurried on. "And that your orders are to be treated as if they come from Oblivion himself."

Rage simmered in Mishara's expression, made darker and more alien by her magic and the late hour. Then her gaze slid over to Echo, and the rage condensed into a feral smile. "Tell the Devonsfort faction that if they require more power to accomplish such a *simple* task, they are free to feed on the immortal among the airship crew."

Tash. Echo had seen the ship downed at the docks, but she hadn't wanted to believe they'd all been caught. "Nnnnnngh," she yelled around the cloth in her mouth.

"I'll pass that on right away." The young woman made a gesture halfway between a bow and a salute. "There is one more thing, High Inquisitor."

"For gods' sake, what?"

"We didn't find the woman you described, but we did find..." She trailed off and waved over her shoulder. Another recruit entered the forge, dragging in a stumbling man with his hands bound and a cloth sack over his head. They shoved him to his knees. "He was lost in the marsh. Claims not to belong to this town, but we thought you'd like to question him."

"I also told you to leave the thinking to me," Mishara snapped. With a flick of her wrist, the cloth disappeared.

Sidrin blinked in the sudden light.

His eyes locked with Echo's. Her whole body went cold as he sucked in a breath and scrambled as far from her as he could in the tight space.

"Ah, you two know each other?" Mishara grinned. "Perhaps you *can* be of use. The rest of you, dismissed. Get whatever passes for fresh air in this revolting swamp."

No one had to be told twice. The initiates filed out, eyes on their shoes.

Echo tried to say, "don't hurt him," but the gag in her mouth garbled her words.

"Don't leave me alone with it," Sidrin blurted. His already bedraggled state had worsened from his time in the marsh, his skin dotted with bruises and dried mud. "Please, I don't know anything, but I'll do whatever you want."

Mishara crouched before him, keeping Echo in her periphery. She traced a rune on Sidrin's forehead, and he shivered. "If you are not from this town, what were you doing out in the middle of the swamp?"

"Nothing! I was trying to visit the God of Journeys. I ran into the mimic and its sympathizers there, and fled. There was a big explosion, and next thing I knew, I was here. I swear, that's the truth."

"Hmm." Mishara kept her hand on his temple. "I believe you. But you knew this beast before, didn't you?" He nodded, and there was a long pause while she read his mind, mirrored images flickering behind both their eyes. "Oh, dear. I'm so sorry this happened to you, Sidrin. But you've come to the right place. How would you like to join me in an interrogation? If you do well, I can offer you a place in the Untolds' ranks."

Echo's muffled yell of protest fell on deaf ears.

"The Untold?" Sidrin breathed. He glanced from Mishara to Echo and back again. "Are you going to...?"

"Eager, are we?" Mishara chuckled. "All in good time. Questions first. We'll hand it over for siphoning later." When Sidrin hesitated, she added, "I won't let the mimic hurt you again. You're under my protection, as long as you work with me."

Echo fought to hold back tears. She'd ruined Sidrin's life and destroyed his chance of starting over. He didn't want to hurt her, but it was clear as day that he was afraid enough of her to accept Mishara's offer.

He swallowed. "What do you need me to do?"

"I'm looking for one of those mimic sympathizers you saw." Mishara cut Sidrin's bonds and helped him stand. "Blonde, pasty, grating personality. Anything you know about her could help us extract more information from this one." She nudged Echo with her boot.

"I only know they were traveling together," he murmured. "They appeared to be close."

"Not close enough to be enticing bait," Mishara sneered. "I should've known. Why anyone would want to travel with you in the first place is beyond me."

Echo wouldn't have responded if she could.

"I suppose your kind has their uses. Skulking around, lying, stealing. Murder. And you did save Rhienne's life. Shame she won't do the same for you."

Mishara was trying to get a rise out of her, but if she hoped for some rage-fueled confession, she had another thing coming. She snapped her fingers, and Echo's gag fell away.

"I'm curious, how long after Wildspire did Rhienne lose interest in you? She put on quite the act in Port Saphrai, but I imagine your utility decreased significantly on the airship."

Echo licked her dry lips and immediately regretted it. The filthy cloth had left her mouth tasting of sweat and dirt. "Do you have any water on you, or is it only *whine*?"

Mishara stood, but not fast enough to hide the waver in her sneer. "Cheeky. Of course, you'd have to be to grab her attention, even for a short while."

"I don't think you know nearly as much about her as you believe you do." Echo said this while looking at Sidrin, hoping he would understand the double meaning, but he only clenched his jaw.

"No?" The inquisitor removed Rhienne's soul jar from her robe and placed it on the ground between them.

Echo gathered the last of her bravado. "Is that supposed to be a threat? If you knew what to do with that, Rhienne would either be here by now or be dead."

"Smart too. Good. You're right; I don't know how to use it. But you do." Black swam over Mishara's eyes until they were flat, midnight discs. "Come, Sidrin. Place your hands here."

He touched Echo's temples with trembling fingers. She tried to move away, but her back was already pressed to the anvil. Mishara put a hand on his shoulder. Shadows bled from her fingers down Sidrin's arms. Echo tried one last silent plea, but he would not meet her eyes.

Mishara said, "You dared to steal Rhienne from my headquarters. Oblivion tells me she broke her contract for you. She let go of her illusions with you. So you must know the darkest corners of her soul. Why don't you *share them with us?*"

Talons dug into Echo's mind. Because of the inquisitor's taunting, her thoughts were already full of Rhienne—was she safe, where had she gone, had she managed to heal Exodus—and Mishara grabbed those worries with the intent to follow them to deeper secrets.

She writhed, resisting, but Sidrin's voice punctuated the lancing pain. *Let me in, Natalia. After all you've done, don't I deserve that much?*

Something deep in her chest cracked open, and her mind opened with it.

All of her senses shut off. No sight, sound, smell, touch. Her perception fractured and spun, trying to conjure something in the utter nothingness of the void. It clawed at her, like she was alone-but-not in the worst possible way.

Then a line of people appeared in the dark. Though they took many shapes, they all held some essence of Echo, and she saw into their hearts. One was a version of her who had grown old in Hearthglen. Another had traveled the world with Rhienne instead of splitting up. One had made a fortune; another lost it. She received fame and accolades. She was thrown in jail until the Untold found her. She never went to Exodus's palace. Never *left* Exodus's palace.

These were the possibilities that had ended with every choice she'd ever made. They left her breathless, sobbing, weak, and raw, her emotions tacked around her like a dissection display.

Stop, Echo begged.

"What's the matter?" The void carved Mishara's words into her mind. "Life flashing before your eyes? Or should I say *lives*? You've been so many people. All these lost opportunities. All these mistakes. If you give in, I can make them go away."

I have nothing to give you.

"Oh, that's not true. You know all the best ways to destroy Rhienne."

As the onslaught continued, Echo tried to fill her mind with song. Every brave, heroic lyric she could think of. But even in her head, her voice shook. Cracks formed in her resolve. She would never give Mishara the tools to hurt her friend, but something else was going to break under the strain. It was only a matter of time.

"What is this?" Sidrin asked, breathless with fear.

"A monster's terrible choices." Mishara laughed cruelly. "This mimic should've stuck to the shadows with the rest of its kind." She pulled forth another lost possibility: Echo stepping into the ocean, except no portal opened to stop her.

That didn't make sense. She hadn't *chosen* for Bastion's library to appear. Had she?

Sidrin faltered. The spell's stranglehold weakened, and a small fissure of light appeared in the void. Echo seized it. But it didn't lead her to freedom.

It led to a space marginally less dark than this one, lit by a single lantern, with walls of bone dotted with fungus: Wildspire's catacombs. Mishara sat across from Rhienne, spell components, parchment, and small bowls filled with fresh blood strewn across the floor.

Echo had turned the inquisitor's magic back on her.

Mishara crumpled a piece of paper and threw it against the wall, where it joined a pile of other discarded notes. "This is hopeless. Maybe there's a reason true sight is reserved for the gods."

"Don't worry, love." Rhienne leaned forward and kissed her. "You're as brilliant as you are beautiful. You'll crack it eventually."

This possibility had a sour, greenish cast to it, the edges curled and burned. The idea of this future had once brought Mishara joy, but no more. Rhienne's affection had been fake the whole time; she'd been stealing Mishara's work and planning to run away with it from the moment they'd started sleeping together.

With an animalistic growl, Mishara ripped all three of them from the spell.

Echo collapsed onto solid ground, her muscles too weak to hold her. Tears streamed down her face. The inquisitor didn't look much better, all her snideness gone, gripping a table leg like her life depended on it. Sidrin remained standing, shaking and uncertain. Was he realizing who the true monster in the room was? Or had those visions put them both in that category?

Echo bit her tongue against the question. It didn't matter right now. Mishara was the threat, and this was the first time she had appeared vulnerable. Human. A woman who had believed that if all else failed, she had one person in her life to hold her up, and that person had not only let her fall, but torn everything else down around her.

"I'm sorry she did that to you," Echo said. "You want Rhienne's deep, dark truth? She's sorry too."

Mishara stood, using the table for support. "Both of you are going to burn." She whispered it, more like a prayer than with any sort of venom. "You," she turned to Sidrin, "get out of my sight." Without another word, she strode out of the workshop.

Sidrin didn't move. Echo sat up and watched his hands, which had once so confidently kneaded dough and taught her signing, curl into fists. "Why did you choose me?" he asked, his voice thick. "What did I have that someone like you could've possibly wanted?"

There was really only one answer, and she poured as much feeling and honesty into it as she could. "A home."

He nodded slightly, a muscle jumping in his jaw. Then he knelt and placed something cold and metal in her bound hands. "If you see an opportunity."

The key to her shackles. She squeezed it tight. "Take the west road out of town. Turn north when you get to the fork. It's a couple days' walk to Devonsfort from there. Go, before Mishara comes back."

Sidrin stopped on the cusp of saying something, nodded again, and slunk out the door.

Chapter 29

Rhienne

Rhienne slipped away from the refugee camp without saying goodbye. There was no sense in disturbing their rest. None of them were in any shape to aid her, even if she'd wanted help, and she had no desire to explain her lack of a plan. She could picture the way her father would shake his head well enough.

Exodus had given his scant report—two factions of the Untold had set up headquarters within the town, but he couldn't get close enough to divine why they were separated or what they were doing. Her only option was to go see for herself.

She crept back through the marsh with Exodus flying overhead, using gentle gusts of wind to steer her away from the Untold patrols. Their bones glowed yellow in the night, bright with recently siphoned power. Sickening. The sight pushed her forward past her exhaustion. How had she ever justified getting close to these monsters? She'd already left Echo with them for too long.

The town was exactly as the God of Journeys had described, but seeing the burnt shells of buildings and smoking ashes herself was an unexpected punch to the gut. It would be too difficult to get materials out here to rebuild from scratch. Hearthglen was gone. And it was her fault. The absolute least she could do was rescue the friends she had dragged into this catastrophe.

Rhienne snuck into the ruins, holding a cloth over her mouth and nose to block the worst of the smoke. The airship had been moved in front of the town hall. The Untold were scavenging everything they could from the cargo, including the enchanted weapons. Not ideal. And there were no red-cloaked inquisitors in sight, which was strange. Mishara wouldn't give up her chance at revenge so easily, not when she had Echo to gloat over.

Exodus landed on a piece of broken wood next to her, silent as an owl. "Note the barrier," he whispered. "Something is going on in that building that my sight cannot pierce."

She squinted. In the dark, it was hard to pick out, but there was a faint trace of purplish haze around the town hall. She moved closer, keeping low against building foundations and rubble, only to find the town hall's windows were obscured. As the Untold who were unloading the ship passed through the spell, they disappeared. Rhienne cursed under her breath. How was she going to get in if she couldn't see what she was walking into?

She could think of one way. It might be stupid enough to be brave, or simply stupid, but time was not on her side here. "Exodus, is my mother with us?"

"Indeed."

"Take her to the airship. See if you two can cause some chaos. If you can get it up and running, even better."

The bird cocked his head. "Vala doesn't like where this is going."

"You said you had my back," Rhienne hissed. "I'm just going to get a peek. Besides, neither of you can really stop me, can you?"

A sharp piece of wood floated up and jabbed her, leaving an ash mark on her thigh.

"Yeah, that's what I thought." Rhienne scurried off before there were any further protests. She dipped into neighboring streets and wove around to the far side of the town hall unseen. There was a short set of stairs and a door at the rear of the building that appeared unguarded. She approached the purple haze unaccosted, took a deep breath, and stepped through.

The air became stuffy and gave her an uncomfortable prickle on the back of her neck. She climbed the stairs and waited to hear sounds of commotion from the ship, but none came. Either this spell blocked noise as well as sight, or Exodus and her mother were refusing to carry out their part of the plan. Rhienne prayed it was the former, counted to thirty for good measure, and eased the door open a crack.

Humid air blew against her face and stuck to her lungs. The hall was one large, open space, used for meetings, weddings, and the like. The benches had all been pushed aside to make room for supply crates and dozens of milling Untold, but they were not the brightest glowing things inside. Purple fungus ran in patchy, undulating stripes across the ceiling and down the walls. As Rhienne watched, the glow changed to pink, then yellow, then turquoise, and back to purple. Living and breathing, making the room seem to do so too. Why could they never make their lairs into normal, beautiful places? Some crystals, or cushions, or even a *lamp* for gods' sake.

In the far corner, Irelia and the crew were contained in cages made from glittering magic. Rhienne couldn't see Echo among them, nor were there signs of Mishara and her recruits. As much as Rhienne wanted to help them, she had to find Echo first.

But a cluster of Untold standing in a circle caught her attention. They murmured an incantation and took a synchronized breath. The luminescent fungus on the walls flared, then they exhaled a cloud of multicolored mist that grew until it enveloped them. The bones of everyone who breathed it in glowed such a brilliant yellow that she had to look away.

When the spots cleared from her vision, the cloud had dispersed, and so had the Untold, revealing a figure spread-eagle on the floor.

Rhienne's heart dropped. *Yellow for immortals. Blue for mimics.* She'd forgotten.

Tash lay convulsing, staring unseeing at the ceiling. His chest was bare and slick with sweat. Runes were carved into the chains around his wrists and ankles. There were matching ones on the floor painted with his blood.

All the fear and horror, all the instincts of flight kept at bay by adrenaline, slammed into her at once. Bastion should've been here. This was the same scenario that had brought Tash to the library before. If the literal God of Protection didn't want to get involved, what could she possibly do?

"My friends, it appears we have a guest." The voice came from right behind her. Someone grabbed the back of her collar and hoisted her into the air.

Rhienne's legs flailed with an alarming similarity to when she'd been at the end of a noose. She threw her elbow back, but instead of crunching into bone, she hit metal. Agony vibrated down her arm.

The figure tossed her into the room like she weighed nothing. She skidded across the floor, her left side scraping against the stone hard enough to bleed.

Most of the Untold were sallow, gaunt creatures, but the man in the doorway was a hulking seven feet tall. Harsh yellow bones illuminated corded muscles. Instead of a circlet, an iron mask covered his face, carved to look like a demon with ruby-tipped horns.

"No," Irelia breathed into the silent chamber.

Rhienne met the captain's eyes as she struggled onto her hands and knees, trembling. Under Irelia's gaze, her breath eased, and her heart slowed into absurd calm. This must have been what Carsha felt in the battle with Reckoning.

She knew, suddenly, what she had to do. It didn't matter why Bastion hadn't come. This, more than her half-intention to save Hearthglen, was her chance to do something meaningful. Echo would understand why Rhienne had to break her promise. This was, after all, the most crucial kind of emergency. Echo would be fine. Echo had always been fine.

"Sorry to drop in unannounced," Rhienne wheezed. "Don't believe we've been introduced. I'm—" She stuck out a hand to shake, and there were suddenly a dozen rune-laced guns pointed at her. She retracted the offer immediately.

"We know who you are," the giant rasped. He didn't tell anyone to lower their weapons. "You're the one Oblivion and that traitorous bitch are looking for. You must be mad to have come here."

At least she'd gotten him talking. And he didn't like Mishara; that explained the separate camps. They were probably only tolerating her because Oblivion told them to. Rhienne smiled her best 'I've never done anything wrong in my whole life' smile. "I could be mad. Depends who you ask. Your sources might be biased. But since you haven't shot me yet, perhaps you're open to parlay?"

"What could *you* possibly have to trade with?"

"Oh, you know..." With her injured palm pressed into the ground, Rhienne pulled the blood oozing from her scrapes into the shadows cast by her body. Where it pooled, she hardened it, sharpened it, but instead of throwing her new weapon, she turned it against her own skin. "Secrets about the Wildspire faction. Mishara's weaknesses. I'm sure you've noticed they're not the most pleasant of allies. Already starting to work against you, I bet." As she talked, she painstakingly sliced open her fingers, up her wrist and forearm, all the way to her shoulder.

Furtive glances around the room let her mark each of her targets. Not the Untold themselves, but the guns they carried. Thirty powder chambers waiting for a spark, plus the leftover stockpile, which was close enough to the wall that a medium-sized explosion would disrupt the barrier spell. That ought to leave enough room for the crew to escape and find her mother and Exodus, and together, they could rescue Echo.

"And why should we believe anything you say? We know your history."

Her eyes watered and her teeth hurt from clenching, but she kept her breath even and did not shake. She could do this one good thing. Call it a purpose, even. One that no one had demanded of her, that she had complete control of. Rhienne willed the blood from her wounds to run down her arm and collect in her hand, fighting dizziness.

"Well, if you know my history, you know Mish and I have a score to settle. And that I don't mind telling you she created the only successful resurrection ritual I've ever seen that doesn't require a deal."

The inquisitor laughed. "That's not possible."

"It is. I've done it myself. It's not even complicated. I could give you the runes and incantation, if you'll allow me."

The rest of the Untold waited while their high inquisitor stroked his chin.

Just a little more time, and a little more blood. Come on.

"Don't give it to them, Rhienne!" Irelia shouted from the cage. "They'll only use it to torture Tash longer."

Even in her half-delirious state, Rhienne could hear the note of falseness, like an unskilled actor reading a script. Was Irelia trying to sabotage her?

"Don't do this," the captain begged.

No, not sabotage. Stall. But no one else was coming; there was no other way out.

"I'm only doing what needs to be done," Rhienne said to Irelia, to the Untold, to herself. That was all she'd ever done: grabbed at power to move one foot in front of the other, never seeing any further ahead than that.

"High Inquisitor, what about Mishara's demand?" someone piped up.

Another long, considering pause. "I will handle her." The Untold leader waved his hand, and the weapons pointed at Rhienne lowered.

The blood under Rhienne's palm was sluggish. It took every bit of her concentration to shape and move it while appearing normal. Thirty paper-thin darts, invisible in the strange light, zipped across the cavern in all directions. One more for the powder keg. And one for each of the siphoning runes on Tash's chains.

"I'm sorry, Irelia," she whispered. But part of her was relieved to not have to wonder what the next step should be.

My life for theirs. With her last ounce of strength, Rhienne snapped her fingers, and the world ignited.

Chapter 30

Echo

Echo didn't realize she'd passed out until the shuddering ground jolted her awake. Leaping to her feet was impossible with her chains, but she made a go of it anyway, and managed an awkward standing crouch, clutching the key Sidrin had given her in one fist. Confused shouts came from outside the workshop. She picked out Mishara's voice among them, yelling commands to gather their weapons and move on the town hall before she stormed into the forge, holding the bottle with Rhienne's soul. The little orb inside had gone from black to gray, and was fading by the moment.

"What has she done?" the inquisitor spat.

No. Please, no. Echo shook her head, afraid that saying it out loud would make it true, but deep down, she knew.

Rhienne had been gunning for this since they'd resurrected Vala. *You said I wouldn't be alone. I'm not ready.* You're *not ready, I know you're not.*

But her soul hadn't disappeared yet. Maybe there was time.

"Orik, Cidan, Anesi, get in here and bring the prisoner with us!" Mishara ordered. "We cannot let them take our quarry. I don't care what Oblivion says; Devonsfort is not on our side."

The sounds of footsteps and whispered prayers seemed amplified in the night. People swarmed around Echo, and she let herself be carried in their current.

She never should've left Rhienne on her own. She should've known better, given the way her friend was thinking and with her own foresight obscured. Surely Exodus and Vala wouldn't have let Rhienne do something so foolish.

Hearthglen's main square was full of smoke and screams. The source was easy to pick out: the blasted-open doorway of the town hall. Mishara and her miniscule army surged forward, and in the chaos of rushing across the threshold, Echo was knocked aside.

She rolled to avoid being trampled and tried to get her bearings through the haze in the hall. There were bodies everywhere, not all of them whole, and the iron tang of blood mixed with the smell of sulfur and burnt metal. The screams came from both the injured and those fighting. She spotted members of the airship crew among them. The focal point was to her left, near an incinerated hole in the wall and ceiling.

"Kill the traitors!" a pained, power-laced shout rang out. No one seemed to know who 'the traitors' were, as the Untold factions clashed with each other as well as the crew.

Somewhere in the madness, a sea bird called, and there was a flash of pastel blue. Exodus and Vala *were* here, but Echo couldn't focus on them. She fumbled with the key, her pulse pounding so hard she could feel it in her fingers, and at last, she managed to unlock her manacles. Echo crawled across the floor, heedless of blades and bullets, looking for a familiar face and terrified of finding it.

She spotted long blonde hair. Rhienne's braids crusted in blood.

Echo choked on a sob and dragged her friend to a corner of the hall, away from the worst of the fray. Rhienne's shirt was soaked through in a spiraling pattern. There were deep, careless lacerations all over her left side. Echo put an ear against Rhienne's chest and held her breath to hear anything over the din.

A faint, struggling heartbeat, growing fainter.

"Vala!" The scream ripped from her throat. "Exodus!" Her mandolin was nowhere in sight. She put pressure on what parts of the wounds she could. It all felt useless. "Irelia, somebody!" Then, quieter but just as broken, she said, "You are not going to Oblivion. Not today. Not ever."

The next breath that rattled from Rhienne sounded like, "Echo?"

"Yes, yes, it's me. You're all right, it's going to be fine—"

"I wanted... to bring Bastion. Here. For you. And Tash." Each word was a gasp, separated by pain.

"Well it didn't work, so you're going to have to try again, okay? Stay with me." Vala and Exodus appeared together, the bird's golden eyes not meeting hers. There'd be time for blame later. "*Fix her.*"

"I c—"

"Make a deal with me. I'll give you anything you want, just do it."

"There's no need for that." Irelia broke into their huddle. Her coat was torn and bloodied, and soot streaked her face. The ferocity of battle bled out of her when she looked down at Rhienne. "I told her to stop. She wouldn't listen."

"Can you heal her?" Echo choked.

"I still have some of Reckoning's magic saved for a rainy day. I'd say this qualifies." As she spoke, she removed her coat and shredded it with her knife, tying strips around Rhienne's wounds.

"No." Her friend coughed. "I had. Purpose. I'm. The rock. You're. River."

"*Fuck* purpose. Where has that ever gotten me, huh? Look at me, stay with me." Echo cradled Rhienne's lolling head. "Knowing what I want hasn't made it any easier to get. In fact, I think it's royally screwed me over. I saw what would've been if we'd stayed in Hearthglen, or if we'd stayed together, and it would've been small, but it would've been beautiful. Because both our lives are better with the other in them."

"Tired," Rhienne said as her eyelids fluttered closed. "If that's true... why isn't... Bastion here?"

Echo had no good answer for that. If this didn't qualify as needing protection, she didn't know what would. "I don't know, but we'll figure it out together, okay? I need you to stay awake."

Vala swooped up to defend them when any of the Untold got too close, wielding weapons she picked up from the dead.

Irelia's eyes never left Rhienne. The captain moved with an efficiency that said she'd done this before. "We need to replace the blood she's lost."

"Don't," Rhienne wheezed. "Too many. Mistakes to fix."

"Take mine," Echo said.

"I don't think your blood would play well with hers." Irelia looked around at the mimic, the dream spirit, and the god trapped in a bird's body. "It'll have to be me, with you as the channel. Take this." And then she was handing over weapons and giving instructions that Echo barely heard, but her body automatically followed. She put one hand near a wound in Irelia's side, the other over Rhienne's heart, and murmured the words to Irelia's spell along with her. A buzz started in her fingertips, shivering up one arm and down the other. It left a trail of cool refreshment where it passed. Green sparks jumped out of her fingers and spread over Rhienne's chest.

Irelia slumped, gray and strained. "She should be stable. That's all I can do."

They waited. The battle in the background seemed impossibly far away.

"You don't corner the market on mistakes," Echo whispered. "For gods' sake, none of this would've happened if I hadn't broken my deal with Exodus. Before that, I couldn't even give up properly. I thought I had nothing, and I was still afraid of losing it."

The realization struck like lightning. Bastion hadn't come for her or Tash because of the danger they were in. It had nothing to do with danger at all. It hadn't been a conscious choice at the time, not like the others she'd seen in the void, but she had wanted help. She just thought she didn't have any. Bastion had answered because he was the only one who could. And Rhienne, in these moments, may have needed protection, but she didn't want it. Not really.

Echo could beg and plead with the cosmos until her voice was raw, and Bastion wouldn't hear.

Chapter 31

Rhienne

Rhienne expected darkness—one moment where she could sit with her victory in contentment, before Oblivion took the rest of her soul. Irelia and the crew were safe from the Untold. They would save Echo and help continue her journey. Rhienne's part was done. She could rest.

What she didn't expect was the rowboat, moving resolutely forward through the black without the aid of oars or currents. A cool, light wind blew her hair away from her face. The darkness was thick as ink beyond the prow, growing deeper as the light behind her faded.

Echo's voice reverberated around her. Rhienne had heard everything her friend said, and heard it still as she drifted away.

"You don't corner the market on mistakes. For gods' sake, none of this would've happened if I hadn't broken my deal with Exodus. Before that, I couldn't even give up properly. I thought I had nothing, and I was still afraid of losing it."

You thought *you had nothing.* The words didn't make it to her lips. Speaking was too much of an effort. Her friend had always had something worth moving toward, and she always would. That was the difference.

The breeze and the darkness promised quiet, calm, release. A doorway appeared ahead, a simple arched cutout amid the rest of the emptiness, its shadows full of distant, unfeeling stars.

Irelia's voice broke in, heavy with old grief and new. "This is not peace; it is desolation. They may feel the same for a while, but in the long run, for all its difficulty to find, peace is worth so much more once you have it. I promise you."

Rhienne shook her head at that. Of course they weren't the same, but this was the best she was ever going to get. Her time with Irelia had been wonderful, brief as it was. She'd gotten a taste of real love. And even that hadn't been enough to change her in any meaningful way.

The doorway grew, alive and hungry. Rhienne was not afraid. She wasn't anything at all, and in this abyss, how could that be a bad thing?

Echo again, fading now, said, "We were supposed to sing together. You're the only person who knows me—all of me. What's the point if you're not here?"

The boat stopped before the doorway to the void. Rhienne would miss her friend dearly. She wouldn't hear the first note Echo sang when her voice returned, wouldn't get to watch her shine in all her glory, wouldn't get to drink or laugh or make up names for the constellations with her, like when they were kids. Of course that made Rhienne sad, just as it did to know her absence would hurt Echo, probably for a long time. Maybe forever. But Echo would find someone else, something else. She had too much to share with the world not to.

"Are you really going to give yourself up to Oblivion? How can that be better?"

Rhienne turned around. The light Echo's voice came from was a tiny speck, yet somehow she could still see into it, right to Echo's and Irelia's tear-streaked faces.

"It has to come from you," Echo sobbed. "You don't have to want to fight, but you have to want *something*."

Rhienne looked. She really, really tried. Echo, Irelia, and somewhere unseen, her mother. They were all bright and beautiful in their own ways. It would hurt Rhienne too, not to be with them anymore. That had never been the question. It was everything *else*. Failure, mistakes, pain she'd inflicted and pain she'd endured. Beyond that, the future remained a blank and formless thing, impossible to hold or shape no matter how much power she hammered it with, no matter how many wonderful people stood beside her and cared for her. She'd been given so much, and managed never to reinvest any of it, too concerned with taking more. Even resurrecting Vala had primarily been about assuaging her guilt and breaking her contract—having her mother returned was a side benefit. What kind of wretched person thought that way?

"I love you all," she whispered. "But I can't live just for you. I don't see anything else for me there. I'm sorry. I wish I did. I wish I could."

"Well, that's as good a start as any."

The voice did not belong to one of her friends. Rhienne turned, slowly, back to the darkness. She was no longer alone in the boat.

The thing on the bench across from her looked like a human-shaped pile of garbage. Amid the torso and limbs, Rhienne picked out bits of bent, rusted metal, paper with charred edges and blurred ink, foggy pieces of glass, gears missing teeth, cracked gems, random coins, and a sock. A tiny lizard climbed out of the junk pile at the figure's approximation of a shoulder, scurrying into a conch shell at the rough location of an ear. The face was a mask of minute mechanical pieces, all in the same banged up state as the rest of the body.

Despite its ramshackle construction, the mask was quite expressive, regarding her with polite concern—like a school teacher, save for the deep, deep sorrow in the empty eye sockets.

"Hello, Rhienne," Bastion said. "I am so glad to finally meet you."

She swallowed. "You're a little late. And in the wrong place."

"I am exactly where and when I am called to be. Though I admit, your timing is fortuitous. Harvest and Reckoning were breaking down my door. They'll never expect me here, so close to the enemy." He smiled gently. "Would you like to sit?"

Rhienne stared at the maw of the void.

"I would not blame you if you left right now. I would not blame you if you got up at any point during our conversation and walked away. And I would not blame you if, when we are finished, you still decide to go. I have seen, and I understand."

"Then why are you here?" she asked.

"To listen. To witness. To make things easier, if I can. Life is not the only thing I protect. Moments, memories, even objects. Anything that would either be lost or forgotten."

Gods, she'd never been so tired. But it was no small amount of relief to know he wouldn't stop her. "You've seen everything?"

He nodded. And she saw in that odd contraption of a face that he *did* understand, and he wouldn't make her explain herself. There was a greater relief in that. Much greater. She sat.

"Wonderful. We can stay here as long as you like. Tea?" Bastion reached into a pouch at his waist. It was only big enough to hold a few trinkets, yet he produced two cups and a steaming teapot, all with mismatched floral patterns and chips or cracks in the ceramic. He winked and poured for both of them. "I've had all the essentials packed for days."

"Do you have anything a bit stronger?"

"I think you'll find this exactly to your taste."

Numbly, begrudgingly, she took the tea and sipped. Butter and sugar and cinnamon—the cookies her father would make for the winter solstice, paired with warm berry cider. It carved a path of warmth through her chest, as if she'd just come in from playing in the snow.

Rhienne pulled away from the cup. "I'm not going back."

"I never said you were."

She grimaced. "I know what this is. Make me look at all the good things from my past to counteract the bad ones and convince me they're worth fighting for. It's not going to work."

"I am not here to convince you of anything. As I said, I am only here to listen and present the facts as I see them." Bastion drank his tea. How exactly he swallowed or digested, Rhienne had no idea, but he sighed in momentary bliss. "Nothing like some good conversation and my favorite beverage before the world goes topsy-turvy."

"If you know what Oblivion is doing, you're wasting your time here." She gestured back at the light. "Echo needs your help. She and Exodus and Vala are the reason I summoned you."

"Summoned me, did you?" He chuckled. "Like some demon from the Lower Plane? I seem to be missing a pentagram."

"You know what I mean."

"I do. But I don't think *you* know what you mean." Bastion set his cup down on empty air, where it rested as if on a shelf. He steepled his hands. Each finger was made from a different object—spoons, pens, springs, and other things she couldn't identify—some that bent like joints and some that didn't. "Mortals travel to the gods, not the other way around. Yet my older brother came to you. As have I. Even I am not sure why that is, but I do know one thing, my dear: gods cannot be called on behalf of others. I am here because you asked for help that no one, including yourself, could give you."

"I don't want to go back." Rhienne looked down at her cup, filled with a taste of her childhood. Her father would pinch pennies for weeks to save enough for the ingredients to make those cookies. She'd been so terrible to him. To so many people who'd tried to love her. And for what? "It's too hard," she whispered.

"I know," Bastion said, and she believed him. "But you wanted to want to live, even if you can't see how. That was what brought me here, not your antics with blood magic, or the trouble your friends were in. *You* made the wish."

Her throat was dry, so she took another wary sip of tea. It tasted the same, almost, except for an added staleness. She'd bought the same cookies from a shop in Port Saphrai when she'd first arrived, and the baker had laughed that out of all the delicacies available, she'd chosen a peasant's treat. She never bought them again.

"I can't see a way forward. I know Echo's dream has brought her pain too, but it seems like her life is so much *clearer*. She always has a guiding star to turn to if she gets lost." Rhienne gestured at the void. It wanted her; she could feel it in the way her body leaned, in the way the breeze beckoned. "I just have that."

"I have seen many great souls drive themselves to madness with comparison."

"All right, but even if we're not comparing, I'm not *made* to have a purpose. My mother had the same problem; that's why she made that deal with you. An avenue that closed after your exile, so there's nothing left I can do."

A hum came from deep in his chest, like an off-key harmonica. "It is true that I could not make that deal again. But Vala was not searching for purpose when she came to me. She was searching for a way to contemplate things she had no name for, because they didn't yet exist. It is hard—so, so hard—to imagine things *better* when you've only known the way they are. Giving her the ability to dream was my solution, but it is not the only way."

"I'm not signing any more contracts."

"I would never ask you to. Wretched things." Bastion picked up his cup and didn't say anything else. There was no expectation in the silence; he seemed content to sit and drink tea.

Rhienne shook her head. "You're not at all what I expected."

"How boring life would be if it went exactly how we thought it would."

"It would've been nice for it to go as expected *once* in a while."

The shadowed eyes of the mask shouldn't have been able to hold so much pain. "On that, we can both agree."

She drank again, and this time, the flavor was entirely different. Earthy and green. 'Graveyard tea,' Mishara had called it, and Rhienne had never figured out if she was joking. Another person she'd used and tossed away.

It wasn't quite curiosity sneaking up on Rhienne, but she wanted to know why Bastion claimed to understand her so well. "What flavor is your tea?"

"Ah." The harmonica sounded again, lower this time. "Sunrises."

"What does a sunrise taste like?"

"Depends on the day." Bastion's smile was sad, his gaze far away. "Sometimes like a promise. Sometimes like rain. Sometimes like oranges, which I've never quite understood. I've tried to find peace in the change—it was part of my sister's domain after all—and sometimes I do. Not always. Not even mostly. But it keeps her close."

He was talking about Horizon. "Were you there when it happened?"

"I should have been. We came up with the plan to put loopholes in our pacts together, you see. It made mortals happy; they came to us more than our other siblings. But without proper exchanges, our magic eventually ran low. Then came a deal that asked for a great expenditure of power from both of us. The details were erased along with my previous name, but" —Bastion cleared the roughness from his voice with a sound like marbles falling down stairs— "I do remember that when the time came, I was afraid. Fickle, you might say. I didn't fulfill my part. Horizon had to carry the burden alone. And rather than renegotiate, she used every last drop of magic—of life—she had." He drank his tea and frowned. "Well, that's new."

"What?"

"I'm not entirely sure. Mountains... no. Earthquakes? That's not it either. Odd."

Rhienne found herself leaning toward the god now, instead of the door. It still hovered there, ready for her to leave at any time. Somehow, she found that encouraging. "How did you keep going afterwards?"

"For a long time, I didn't. A luxury of immortality, that. Then your mother showed up with ideas she couldn't articulate and frustrations that I shared. I did not choose to be what I was, nor to operate within the confines of tit-for-tat and gossamer impermanence. She did not choose to exist solely within other people's dreams. There had to be something *more* than the cards the Mothers dealt us. So we looked. And there wasn't. Not within this deck."

Again, he paused, this time waiting for her to ask stay the next obvious question.

She didn't want to, not yet. But she still *wanted to* want to. "How, then?"

"Making new cards, of course. I started with my name—a new domain, Protector of the Small and Lost. And now Oblivion has paved the way for more change. As we speak, he is heading to the Origin to absorb your friend's voice. My brother aims to bend the rules so that he may shackle all of humanity in pacts they can never hope to end. But together, perhaps we can *rewrite* those rules, and make a world my sister would be proud of."

Something so small as to be unidentifiable shivered through Rhienne. It followed the same path as her first sip of tea and disappeared just as quickly, but it left a crack in her chest. "How do you know that will work?"

"I don't."

"What if you change things, and it's worse than before?"

Bastion drained his cup, and his mechanical eyebrows rose. "Plate tectonics!"

"Pardon?"

"The flavor of my tea! The movement of the earth far beneath us. It is what makes mountains, and breaks continents, and vents lava to the surface to create new land. It is possible that I may make things worse, but it is important, vitally important, that I try. Even if I cannot see what moves beneath me, or above me, or right in front of me, the one thing I know for certain is that I cannot stay where I am." He glanced over his shoulder at the speck of light and stood. An assortment of screws and baubles fell off him and clattered along the bottom of the boat. With a flick of his wrist, they rolled back and disappeared into his form.

"It's time, I think." As Bastion returned the tea set to the unfathomable pouch, he asked, "So, Rhienne, what is it you want?"

To go back and face her mistakes all over again? No.

To blindly forge ahead, grasping for power as if it were a handhold? Definitely not.

She looked to the void, still beckoning, still tempting. Bastion would let her go, if that's what she wanted. He would carry out his plan with or without her. Life would go on, with all its twisting paths, whether obscured or laid brick by brick before the feet of those who walked them. He wasn't asking her to look back, or to keep going on as she had before. He was asking if she had the courage to face the uncertain, knowing it might be uncertain forever.

"I don't know if I can do it," Rhienne whispered.

Bastion held out his hand, made of lost, forgotten, and broken things. "Do you want to try?"

Chapter 32

Echo

They were going to lose. Echo had known it since Irelia stumbled away to hold off Mishara, and she heard it in the fading defiance of the crew's shouts. The smell of blood was thick in the room, and the acrid tang of magic and gunpowder burned the back of her throat, but all of that was distant. Her mind was empty of words. There was only Rhienne and her weak, too-fast pulse, her shallow breath.

Echo didn't look up when a shadow fell across them. Didn't move when Mishara said, "Hand her over, mimic. She's mine."

"Do you really hate her so much that you'll let Oblivion take control of our world, just for a chance at revenge?" Still cradling Rhienne against her chest, watching every fleeting sign of life, Echo felt rather than saw the inquisitor sneer. The shadow on the ground was larger than Mishara, with many more arms wavering in the glow of the fungus on the walls.

"You saw what she did to me." Mishara stepped closer. "Strung me along, stole my work, dragged my name through the mud, and forced me to destroy everything I'd helped build. It makes no difference to me what Oblivion does with her soul or with this plane as long as she is *erased* from it."

Rhienne's breath hitched. Everything else went utterly quiet. Echo waited for the next one.

And waited.

And waited.

For the first time in Echo's life, being songless, speechless—*soundless*—was the only thing she wanted to be. All she could do was stare. She felt frozen in time. If the clock just moved one second forward, surely Rhienne would breathe. Surely, if she hoped hard enough, her friend would come back.

Echo tried to raise her head, only to tell Mishara that she'd never get her revenge, that Rhienne had taken that from her too, but her muscles were locked in place. As the quiet stretched on, Echo realized it was not from a ringing in her ears or warped perception. The battle had gone still. Her thoughts moved, but that was all.

Beyond her line of sight, someone hummed softly to themself, accompanied by indistinct clattering.

"Apologies, dear Echo, but this spell is an all or nothing affair. I'd have left you out of it if I could. Just a few more of these bothersome individuals to tie up, and I'll restart the clock."

Who was that?

Mishara's monstrous shadow disappeared without a sound. The yellow light that fell over Rhienne made her look sickly in her stillness. Echo wanted to close her friend's eyes, but she still couldn't move. What the hell was going on?

"That's a new shape for you, brother," the same voice said. "I quite like it, though I'm most curious to know where you got the idea." A loud thunk, and then, "There we are. Now if everyone will just calm down, we can have a civilized conversation. Doesn't that sound nice?"

Someone snapped their fingers, and the world resumed. Echo had been making such an effort to move that she pitched forward, jarring her elbows on the ground.

Across the hall, the airship crew—Tash and Nazal included—were staring agog at the scene. The Devonsfort Untold were decimated. Those who remained of the Wildspire faction were bound and gagged with glowing spiderwebs, Mishara at the forefront. The inquisitor struggled against her bindings, her screams muffled and meaningless.

"There's no need to be so rude. You'll have your turn, I promise." A figure made of hundreds of broken objects patted Mishara on the head. "There are more important things to be said first."

Rain-scented wind blew into the building through the hole in the wall. It brought with it the feeling of spring and new, hesitant beginnings as it became Exodus's voice. "Brother? Is that you?"

"Bastion?" Echo breathed.

The strange mishmash of shapes did in fact resemble a face, and it grinned. "Am I so unrecognizable?"

Exodus took off from his perch and landed on the other god's shoulder, kicking up a small tornado around them that kept their conversation private. He pressed his head against Bastion's cheek, and the golden sheen on Exodus's feathers grew brighter, like he was lit up by a rising sun.

Echo watched the reunion, stunned. If Bastion had made it here...

Still curled over her friend's body, she felt for a pulse.

It was there. It was *stronger.*

"Ow," Rhienne said. "You're squishing me."

"Sorry." The response was automatic as Echo reared back. Rhienne's eyes fluttered open, and she looked like... well, she looked like death. "Wait, no I'm not sorry. You—you—" There was too much to say, scream, yell, cry. Echo scooped her up and squeezed her tight. "I thought you were gone."

Rhienne sat awkwardly for a moment before returning the embrace. There was no strength to her touch, but Echo didn't let go.

Eventually, Rhienne whispered, "I was."

Echo pulled back enough to look at her friend's face again. She was haggard, missing her Rhienne-like spark, and her gaze kept drifting to the middle distance.

"I can still see the door," Rhienne said.

"Door? What door?"

Vala floated over, elation and heartbreak fighting in her expression. Wisps of her spirit leaked from slashes and bullet holes, but she didn't seem to care. "Dreams may be particularly susceptible to it, but no one returns unchanged from a thing like death."

Echo swallowed. "Did Bastion save you?"

Rhienne looked around the room, still in that fugue state, lingering on Tash, Irelia, then Mishara, before landing back on Echo. "He asked if I wanted to face the uncertain again. And I'm still not sure what that entails. But..." A ghost of sharpness returned, an ember ignited. "I want to be able to."

Echo wouldn't pretend to completely understand. The current emotional cocktail had a few too many opposing flavors anyway, so she gave Rhienne another hug, and waved for Vala to join them. "For whatever it's worth, I'm really, really, really glad you're here." This time, Rhienne squeezed back, and they stayed like that until a little of the cold around her melted.

Irelia coughed politely. "On your feet, sailors." She was barely standing herself, wounds hastily bandaged and shoulders slumped with exhaustion, but she held out a hand to pull them up. The captain kept a firm grip on Rhienne's forearm. "Some days, the door will be all you can see. But any day you can ignore it is a victory. It will shrink, and grow, and shrink again with time."

Rhienne made a small noise of surprise. "You can see it too?"

"What, you thought you knew everything about me?" Irelia kissed her cheek. "Not the same door, I think, but I've had my share of hopelessness. I can help you fight it, if you'll let me."

"I'm sorry," Rhienne whispered.

"I know." The captain pulled her aside, murmuring things too low for anyone but the two of them to hear.

Echo stood on wobbling legs and brushed herself off, fully taking in the exiled god. Looks could be deceiving, but it was still a shock that all this effort and pain had been for... some sort of animated scrap pile. Should she be offended that Bastion had counted *her* within his domain to save, or did it make a twisted kind of sense?

Tash shouldered his way out of the crew's protective circle. "It's you." He half knelt, half collapsed in front of Bastion. "That's twice now you've saved my life and the lives of the people I care about. What have we done to deserve such favor?"

"Oh, dear fellow, there's no need for that." Bastion took the large man by the shoulders and effortlessly lifted him up. "You haven't done anything at all, nor should you need to."

Rhienne sniffled and stepped away from Irelia. "He doesn't like deals," she explained.

"A preference that my other siblings are quite unhappy with," Bastion agreed. "In fact, I'm surprised they didn't pounce the second I entered this plane." He frowned. "I hope they're not burning down my library."

Mishara laughed behind her gag.

Echo gritted her teeth. She had seen Mishara's heart at the forge, if only for a moment. The woman was trapped by her hatred, and the only path she could see was revenge. Echo wanted to give her an alternative, but by the gods, she was making it difficult. "Perhaps Mishara can tell us what's so funny. She clearly has some idea of what to expect next."

"An excellent suggestion." Bastion knelt in front of the inquisitor so they were eye to eye. Whatever Mishara saw in his face made her stop laughing. "Now, before I remove your bonds, I'd like to make one thing clear. We know Oblivion is heading to the Origin. I can assume that is where Harvest and Reckoning have gone, where the rest of the Untold have gathered, and where he ordered you to convene. I don't particularly need you... though I am most interested in how my brother planned to ensure your survival there. But if you continue to be recalcitrant, I'm sure at least one person here has some frustrations to take out." He said all this in a tone one might use to describe a picnic on a sunny afternoon.

It shouldn't have been a surprise that Bastion's kindness had another face. All the gods were mercurial by nature, Bastion's previous incarnation especially so. Echo was unsettled, despite this logic, and found herself watching Exodus instead. Hard to read a bird's expression, but he seemed troubled too.

"Alternatively, you can be helpful and provide any extra information I may have missed. Understood?"

The web over Mishara's mouth dissolved. "You're bluffing. Oblivion said you don't have enough magic of your own, so you've been stealing it from the others. That's the only reason he's worried about you interrupting the ritual."

"Is that what he told you?" Bastion said pleasantly. "I suppose that would explain why I was able to stop time long enough to subdue you and your little retinue here, and why the spell you're trying to cast behind your back won't work."

Mishara froze. "How—"

"One of the few benefits of my exile: time and energy to collect and tinker. I've become rather good at it, if I do say so. *I* may be low on magic, but there are plenty of powerful artifacts from the early days of this world that simply needed parts replaced. They're one-use items, for the most part, but I have *plenty.* I'd love an excuse to test out more. So I'll ask again." Bastion reached into a pouch at his waist, and his arm disappeared up to the elbow. It reemerged with a glowing red pearl. "And if I'm not happy with the answer, we get to find out what this does."

Echo hid a shiver. Where did Bastion draw the line between something lost and broken, and something not worth saving?

The god beckoned Rhienne forward and said to Mishara, "Is there anything else you wish to tell us about what Oblivion is planning?"

Chapter 33

Rhienne

The door loomed in Rhienne's periphery. Its whispers filled Mishara's silence, promising relief from the trouble of dealing with this woman again, avoidance of any more pain. She tried to ignore it. "Answer him, Mish."

"Or what? I know *you* don't have it in you to carry out threats. You're a lonely coward who finally lost the misplaced vanity that held you up for so long. You and your mimic are perfect for each other: fit only to scrabble in muck until the world grinds you beneath its boot."

Mishara's head whipped to the side, a red handprint blossoming on her cheek. That had to be Vala's doing. Rhienne would've thanked her mother if she hadn't been reeling herself. Oblivion's power cast a dark aura around Mishara, accentuating the manic light in her eyes. Had

Rhienne ever looked this way to Echo? The thought made her nauseous.

"You know, I think you're right on just about all accounts," Rhienne murmured. "I'm... sorry. I drove you to this, but there's still a chance for both of us to set things right."

"Don't bother," the inquisitor snarled. "I'm done falling for your pretty, empty words."

Bastion stepped forward and placed the pearl in Rhienne's hand. She rolled it around her palm. For the first time since she'd awoken from the darkness, heat filled her chest. The longer she stared at Mishara, the hotter it became, surprising in its violence. She'd never *hated* the woman like this. Scorned, yes. Been repulsed by, a few times. But this rage was entirely unexpected after the numbness of the void.

Mishara had burned Crystal and Evergreen. Destroyed Hearthglen and many of its people. Almost killed Rhienne twice and Echo once. It would be such a relief to take care of one problem. The only one with an obvious solution. With Mishara gone, she wouldn't have to watch her back anymore or be constantly reminded of her mistakes.

The pearl was blazing now, heat and maroon light leaking between her fingers.

"Bastion," Echo said warily, "what is that thing?"

"I thought it was simply a hellish pocket dimension," the god said. He leaned in to examine it. "But it appears to be drawing on Rhienne's deepest emotions and manifesting them as monsters inside. What a fascinating piece of magic!"

Rhienne hissed and dropped the pearl. These were old thoughts, old methods. This was not how she wanted to start over. As soon as it left contact with her skin, the heat and fury drained out of her. The hollowness wasn't *better* exactly, but certainly less murder-y.

"Perhaps we should be careful with the old magic we fix, brother," Exodus said. "And more careful still with how we parse it out."

Bastion picked up the pearl and tucked it away. Rhienne swore he was pouting.

Nazal stepped away from tending the wounded and offered a different tactic. "If Oblivion wanted Mishara to meet him in the Origin, he must have given her some way to get there. Have we tried searching her for spell components?"

"We ought to gag her again, for good measure," Rhienne added.

"Hmmngh!" Mishara protested as web splattered over her mouth.

"First things first." Echo reached for a pocket within Mishara's cloak and pulled out a bottle of something gray and shapeless. She handed it to Rhienne. "I believe this belongs to you."

Rhienne stared, stomach turning. The thing inside the glass tugged at her chest, begging to be reunited with the rest of her soul. But how could it belong there? It looked lifeless, slimy, disgusting. Not something she'd touch with a ten foot pole, much less absorb into her body. "What happened to it?"

"I think when you... died, it..." Echo gestured helplessly.

Rhienne pocketed the bottle for now. She had no idea how to put the piece back where it belonged, or if she even wanted to, but she said, "Thanks."

"Of course." Echo squeezed her hand, and they watched Bastion finish searching Mishara. "He's not what I expected."

"I said the same thing. He may have taken it upon himself to be a protector, but he's as twisted up as the rest of us. Exodus too." Rhienne glanced at the door to the void. It had gotten a bit smaller. "There's comfort in that, somewhere. I think."

"Hmm. We'll keep an eye on him. Both of them." Echo looked over at her. "You'll be careful too, won't you?"

Her friend had either kept eye contact or physical contact since Rhienne had returned. Like she was afraid Rhienne would disappear again. It strengthened her to have that connection, but the lack of trust hurt. "I'm trying my best."

"Here we are!" Bastion declared before either of them could say more. From Mishara's belongings, he produced a tuning fork. It was made of an undulating, white material, shot through with streaks of green and blue. "Ah, clever, clever. He's not going to the Origin after all. He's bringing the Origin to us."

"What does that mean?" Rhienne asked.

"It means, for a brief time, the two planes will overlap. Good news for you, as it will be marginally less dangerous than a mortal traveling to a metaphysical space. However, things here are going to get very... strange."

"Specifics, if you would." Irelia had seen to her crew's welfare, and now stepped up to the two gods, all business. Some of her color had returned, and new bandages wrapped her wounds. The slightest twitch of her hand toward her sword was the only hint of fear. "If we're going to fight your siblings, we need to talk strategy."

"It's too dangerous," Rhienne started. "Half of you can barely walk—"

"We don't need to walk. We'll give you air support." Irelia gestured to the airship, waiting on the street where the Untold had been scavenging it. "Besides, Reckoning is due for a taste of her own medicine."

Bastion leaned toward Rhienne conspiratorially. "I like her."

"Battle tactics," Irelia reminded him.

"Yes, quite. Though I wouldn't say the Origin is a place for rigid plans. It is, simply put, chaos incarnate. The essence of all life resides there. The best analogy I can make is a tapestry whose threads the gods can pull and weave to our whims."

Exodus ruffled his feathers. "It's been a long time since you've seen it, brother. There is no magic left to weave; it has all been spoken for. Every strand is the heart of *something* in this world, from the smallest pebble to the tallest mountain. I'm not sure how it will manifest when drawn here. We'll need to see it for ourselves to decide how to move forward."

Everyone went quiet at that. Even the gods were wary of what came next.

"We should let the recruits leave," Echo said. "They're not any happier about this situation than we are. But I'm not sure if it's better to release Mishara or bring her with us."

Rhienne glanced askance at her friend. "Why the hell would we bring her with us?"

"If we don't, we'll have to leave someone to guard her and make sure she doesn't cause more trouble. If she comes with us... I don't know. There's a human in there somewhere."

"I must have missed one doozy of a conversation between you two."

"That's one way to put it. I just can't shake the feeling that we could reach her if she actually sees what she's helping Oblivion do."

Rhienne closed the distance to Mishara. The magnitude of her earlier rage felt ridiculous. She didn't see the human that Echo claimed was there; Mishara was an animal, with the walls of her cage closing in.

And didn't that sound familiar.

"Keep her restrained on the ship, for now," Rhienne said. "She may still find it in herself to be useful."

"Those sound like marching orders to me." Irelia looked relieved to have something to do besides talk to the gods. "Crew! We have a ship to get into the air. Gather yourselves and any salvageable weapons. Anything that looks useful and isn't nailed down is ours." She held a rune-engraved pistol out to Rhienne. "You can take this one in return for saving Tash's life, as long as you promise never to do anything like that again."

"Aye, Captain." Rhienne took the gun, looked down the sights, and traced the grooves where magic thrummed inside the metal. "I've never used one of these before."

"It should do a lot of the aiming for you. It's got six shots in it, so make them count. You blew up most of the spare ammo."

The town hall was soon bustling with a flurry of activity: crates were dug through, pockets searched, low-ranking Untold stripped of their weapons and sent on their way—most of whom didn't give Mishara a second glance as they fled. With a start, Rhienne remembered that not all the important belongings in here were firearms.

"Echo, your mandolin should be here somewhere." They searched the bodies and scattered bits of furniture, but it was Tash who approached with a bundle of cloth that he laid out on the ground.

"It must've been damaged in the fight," he said, pulling back the fabric to reveal jagged, broken wood. The strings were the only thing holding it together. "If we had time, I might be able to fix it."

Exodus fluttered over. "I could attempt to craft another—"

"No, it's okay," Echo interrupted, blinking hard. "If all goes well, I won't need it." She covered the broken instrument and quickly changed the subject. "The Untold didn't take too much out of you, I hope."

Tash gave her a long look but didn't press the matter. "Not enough to stop me picking up a sword. Or a gun, I suppose. Thanks to your friend."

The lines of the cook's face were deeper, and he hadn't quite recovered his previous vivacity, but there was a fierceness in him that gave Rhienne a small flare of pride. She *had* done something good.

Echo nodded toward the crew, who had finished recovering their supplies and were hauling them onto the ship. "Looks like we're almost ready. Shall we?" She held an arm out, clearly itching to get out of this blood-stained reminder of how the world treated her kind.

Rhienne whispered, "Go ahead, I'll be right there." Echo hesitated, so Rhienne added, "I promise."

She waited until the Untold were gone, Mishara was on the ship, and there were only a few boxes and crew members left. Maybe her mother was still here. She hoped so.

Rhienne walked the length of the room and back, taking inventory of the carnage she'd caused, all the souls that had become white flowers in a gray field with hateful memories of her. The Untold were monsters, and it had been necessary, but it didn't make her glad. If the first step on this new, unseeable path was to have mercy on Mishara, maybe the next one was to stop leaping for the thing that felt necessary. Maybe she had to leave that determination to the people who could see further than her and get comfortable following blind.

Easier said than done. But Bastion hadn't promised this would be easy.

At the end of her circuit, the entrance to the void remained.

"Do you see it too, Mom?" she whispered. "Or is it the human half of me that keeps it here?"

The dust and debris on the floor swirled, forming uneven letters. *"I see it reflected in your eyes. My fault. I'm so sorry."*

"No, it's not. I... I hope someday I can explain. It's sort of a lot right now. But I talked with Bastion about you, and about everything, and I..." Gods, she was making this far more complicated than it needed to be. "I forgave you a long time ago, and I hope you can forgive me."

"*Nothing to forgive*," Vala wrote. "*I love you.*"

"I love you too. Let's go, before we make anyone worry." Rhienne wiped her eyes and glanced one last time at the door. "See you around."

She left the ruined building and climbed the ramp to the airship deck, where an inconceivable number of her friends and family waited to go to war against the gods.

Chapter 34

Echo

Echo stood with Rhienne, Vala, and Bastion, with Exodus perched on his shoulder, at the airship's prow, high above the ruins of Hearthglen. They'd tied Mishara to the mast after Bastion dusted her with some sort of 'sleeping powder' from his pouch. Echo had made sure the inquisitor still had a pulse—she didn't think Bastion was malicious enough to kill Mishara on purpose, but he was certainly negligent enough to do it by accident.

The fact that he was the one binding two planes of existence together set her teeth on edge.

Beneath the wind and creaking sails, Bastion muttered words in a grating language. He held the tuning fork they'd confiscated from Mishara in front of him, and as he spoke, hit it three times against the airship's railing. It made no sound, but sent out visible shockwaves that parted the clouds in front of them. With a final grinding syllable, the tuning fork turned to ash. Bastion blew the white and blue-green dust from his palm, and it swirled into the sky.

Echo lost it among the clouds, and when nothing happened, worried the spell had failed.

As if reading her thoughts, Exodus whispered in a gentle breeze through her hair, "Patience. You can trust him."

"If you say so." Bizarrely, his words were comforting.

"All hands, take defensive positions," Irelia shouted from the helm. The wind abruptly died, so even her following whisper carried across the deck. "And pray to whoever you still have faith in."

Then there was a horrible screeching, rending sound, and Echo threw her arm up to block a flash of blinding white.

"Keep your eyes closed," Exodus warned them. "It will get worse for a moment."

The ship hadn't moved, and though her feet remained rooted to the deck, her stomach rose like she was falling. She sucked in air that tasted of midnight and music, and she heard sunlight and smelled gravity and then everything

slowed

down.

Meteoric gunshots forced her eyes open onto a coruscating aurora. Streams of green, blue, and pink light moved around the ship in waves, extending in all directions against a starless night. But it was the landscape below that captured her gaze. *Every strand is the heart of something in this world,* Exodus had said. There was no way to truly understand without seeing it.

The ocean, the sand, every blade of grass and scrubby tree, every rock and creature had gone semi-transparent, revealing threads of colored light that trailed down and disappeared into the earth. A glowing tapestry, woven from the heart of all things. The gunshots had come from somewhere down there, hidden in the brightness.

Her body was not nearly as impressed as her mind. Echo pressed one hand to her rioting stomach, the other to her heart, beating far too fast.

The majority of the crew staggered and were sick over the railing. The only one keeping it together was Nazal; the former scholar had abandoned their duties, including the notebook they'd prepared for observation notes, and was staring at everything with unfiltered joy.

"It's real," they whispered. "And we're really here. By the Mothers."

Rhienne hyperventilated beside her. Even the gods were affected. Exodus sighed in relief as the bird form melted into mist that stretched into his typical shape. Bastion had become unrecognizable. Gone was the clockwork face and the body of paraphernalia. What remained was a humanoid shape of incandescent web, its face featureless, its limbs ending in drifting bits of spider silk. An aura of deep displeasure hung about him.

Echo thought she'd gotten past the worst of it until her skin shuddered. A familiar precursor for something she had *not* asked her body to do, and certainly not to the shape it was demanding she take. She moved away from Rhienne and dug her fingernails into the railing, fighting with every breath not to let her bones elongate or her skin turn gray.

"What's wrong?" Rhienne asked, brows drawn together.

Echo wasn't sure she could speak without her canines sharpening. Looking between Exodus and Bastion—Gossamer, his name had once been—it started to make sense. They'd brought the Origin here. The birthplace of the world and its magic would reveal things as they truly were.

"It's affecting you too, I see," Bastion mused. "How very interesting. Identities are sticky things. Perhaps changing into *something* will keep it at bay."

Echo mimicked Rhienne. The shivering left her long enough to heave a full breath and relax her muscles. The sourceless command to change still lurked at the edge of her mind. She'd have to deal with it when it came back.

There was another round of scattered gunshots. Echo tried to trace the sound. "Why does that sound like it's coming from out over the water?"

Rhienne peered over the railing. "Because it is. Over there." She pointed east. There was a patch atop the sea that was brighter than the rest, where threads ranging from indigo to turquoise were gathering. Little wisps of yellow danced like sickly candle flames around it. "There are people down there. The other Untold, it looks like. How are they standing on the water?"

"We need to get closer," Exodus shouted to Irelia.

The captain took the ship down. The crew aimed their guns through portholes and between barricades, ready to fire.

An enchanted bullet whizzed by and detonated a few feet above Echo's head. Sparks and shrapnel rained down. Echo grabbed Rhienne and ducked behind the bulwark.

"Ah, I am beginning to understand. The water is not precisely liquid," Bastion explained, unperturbed by the warzone. "Don't stand in one place too long, and you should be able to walk on the surface."

"Sounds like the swamp," Rhienne said with a grimace.

"Yes, except if you *do* stand still too long, you risk being pulled under. I would highly recommend against that. The closer you get to the core of the world, the more threads of the tapestry there will be to process. Sink too far, and the assault on your senses will tear you apart."

Rhienne paled. "Lovely."

Another shot blasted a hole in the hull. Echo squinted through it. Individual figures were impossible to make out, but there was a dark spot against the ocean's light: a black circle, veined with maroon and green.

"What is that?"

"Oh dear," Bastion said. "Oblivion needs to go to the core to properly absorb your voice and expand his domain. They've already started the ritual to assimilate him with the Origin. We need to get down there before it's finished, or we'll never be able to reach them."

"There must be dozens of Untold," Echo breathed. Not to mention Oblivion, Reckoning, and Harvest at their center. Somewhere among them was her singing voice. "How are we going to get through them all?"

"Ready. Aim. Fire!" Irelia shouted. A round of retorts came from the airship.

Tash had a gun the size of a small cannon strapped to his hip. Where his bullets landed, plumes of smoke went up. Anything that hit the darkness of Oblivion's ritual ricocheted away.

"That'll help," Rhienne said wryly. "We can take some out from up here, but they'll have to stop shooting once we go down."

Echo chewed her nails, which were beginning to blacken and curve into claws. She mimicked the first person she saw: Nazal, who did a double take upon seeing a perfect mirror of themself.

Which gave her an idea.

"Those Untold come from all over the world. They'll be speaking different languages, using magic differently. Getting them all to coordinate would be a nightmare."

Rhienne nodded. "One I bet Oblivion wouldn't bother with."

"Once we whittle down their numbers enough, you three can attack from one side, and I'll slip in from the other, disguised like them, and give conflicting orders. All that chaos should make it possible for the ship to come down so the crew can join us, and buy us more time to interrupt the ritual."

"I don't like you going off on your own," Rhienne said. "They've got that paralytic, never mind enchanted bullets."

"She won't be alone." Exodus had changed as well, into the same rippling marble form he'd taken in the Plane of the Dead. Instead of the veil, golden armor wove over his chest and arms in a pattern of branching rivers.

"Are you sure?" Echo asked, though her heart lifted. "You're not exactly inconspicuous."

"Better to lend credence to your orders," he said. "Besides, I have a score to settle with these leeches. Vala should go with Bastion and Rhienne in my stead."

Out of habit more than desire, Echo checked her foresight. Gift, curse, guiding star—it was impossible to tell now. She saw only fog and gray, and with a pang of fear, she understood a bit more of how Rhienne felt all the time.

The dark patch below had solidified into a protective dome, and the strange material that made up the ocean had started to grow up the sides. Echo didn't know exactly what that meant, other than time wasn't on their side.

"All right," Echo said. "If it gets bad, send up a signal flare for Irelia to come get you out. Promise?"

Rhienne shook her head with a sad smile. "No more running. That's not a death wish speaking; there's nowhere left to go. We get your voice back or we don't."

"Quite right," Bastion said as he extracted a battered rug from his bottomless pouch. "The world will not be nearly so habitable for mortals if Oblivion succeeds."

Right. World-shattering stakes. She hadn't had time to comprehend the idea that her voice held the potential to give Oblivion such catastrophic power. It was mind-boggling. Horrifying. It wasn't fair that one mimic with a broken divine pact and an oscillating dream could destroy everything. It made her want to disappear.

Looking at her friend—not for the last time, she wouldn't allow it—Echo was hit with an overwhelming surge of feeling. After the way the Origin had scrambled her senses, she couldn't name the emotion. It was an earthquake in her bones, an avalanche, a wildfire. When she hugged Rhienne, polarity shifted. Echo mimicked Carsha, the dead first officer, to avoid being pulled under with it.

"Be careful," they both whispered.

Bastion chuckled. "Plate tectonics." He knelt on the rolled out carpet and patted the spot beside him. "Come along, then."

Rhienne raised an eyebrow. "Seems like a poor time for a picnic."

"If you have another way to fly down into the fray, I'm open to suggestions."

The tension in Echo's heart eased a little as Rhienne's eyes lit up. Another step away from the darkness.

"Did you say fly?"

Chapter 35

Rhienne

In a vacuum, the concept of a flying carpet was incredible. Speeding through the air on an old rug with bullets zipping past and Bastion throwing random (and sometimes explosive) objects from his pouch was considerably less so. Rhienne gripped the edge of the carpet with white knuckles. Somewhere on the other side of the battle, Exodus's near-invisible mist cloud was bringing Echo down to the surface.

Rhienne was close enough now to see the faces of the Untold, their hoods thrown back, arms and chests bare, bones blazing with magic and the glory of not needing to hide it. Six bullets, she reminded herself. Not that she could shoot with Bastion flinging the carpet around to avoid getting hit. He was enjoying himself far too much.

There were brief pauses in the battle as the Untold reloaded their guns. "Next time we hear a break, get me on the ground," she said.

"On my mark. Remember to keep moving," Bastion crowed, and swung them down in a dizzying arc. "Mark!"

Rhienne tucked her head and rolled. She meant to spring to her feet and hit the ground running, but the Origin had turned the ocean's uneven surface hard as rock, and her joints screamed in protest. It was more of a sad flop into a staggering limp, but hey, she'd been mostly dead an hour ago.

Was it a good or bad sign that she could force some humor about that?

"It's the oathbreaker!" an Untold shouted.

"Kill her! It's the other one we need."

There were many more Untold between her and Oblivion than there had been in the town hall. Blue threads had climbed a quarter of the way up the ritual dome. Bastion had explained that the gods needed to incorporate parts of the Origin into themselves before they could sink into the core and manipulate it, but he didn't know how long the ritual took, or how difficult it would be to disrupt once they reached it.

One problem at a time.

Rhienne brandished her daggers. Blood magic was a last resort. The void was hungry and waiting, and she didn't yet trust herself not to slip into it.

Bastion harried the Untold from above. Rhienne was pretty sure a literal kitchen sink hurtled by. Then she was too busy to watch anything but the swarm of glowing figures around her. She wielded her knives like a woman possessed. Or perhaps utterly unpossessed, untethered, looking for something to lose but not having it yet. She parried, dodged, and slashed, getting in too close for the Untold to bring up their rifles.

Don't stop moving, she told herself over and over.

The Untolds' magic made time pass in fits and starts. Each stroke she landed on their bare skin dragged too long and didn't cut deep enough, but all she had to do was distract them so the rest of the crew could join the fight.

She rolled sideways to dodge a blow and caught a glint of steel behind her. The blade's arc was perfect, and it was too late to change trajectory. Rhienne braced herself for the impact.

Another blade clanged against it. It had materialized from nowhere, appearing to Rhienne to be floating in the air. With a graceful twist, the man was disarmed and stabbed neatly through the throat. Vala had come to her rescue.

"Thanks, Mom," Rhienne gasped. After that, any time one of the Untold got behind her, an invisible force pushed them back or felled them altogether. She wished desperately that she could see Vala, if only to witness the source of the new fear on the Untolds' faces. She had never been more grateful to have her mother by her side.

Echo had been right. Languages clashed as the battle went on—her friend's voice among them, she was sure—struggling to be heard. The disparate groups got in each other's way as much as hers. The airship had started a cautious descent.

But Rhienne hadn't gotten close enough to Oblivion's ritual. The dome was now halfway covered in a film of the ocean's blue threads. Her strength was flagging too. Magic could only heal so much; her body had been robbed of the rest it truly needed.

There was a moment when she thought about reaching for her blood again, when the edge of her dagger called out. *You wasted your beginning,* it seemed to say. *The only power left to you is in a worthy end.*

In that second of contemplation, the semicircle of Untold backed away. "Mom?" Rhienne dared a glance behind her. A silly impulse that saved her life—a bolt of darkened crimson shot past her ear.

"Leave her be." Mishara's snarl was laced with an otherworldly voice. "This one's mine."

The inquisitor's body hung in the middle of a massive suit of shadowy armor that mirrored her movements. Tattered webs still stuck to her limbs from where she'd torn free. She wobbled under the dregs of Bastion's sleeping powder, but she'd gotten off the ship—a column of fire and smoke blazed where the mast had been—and she was pissed at one person and one person only.

Rhienne pulled out her pistol. It felt terribly, terribly small.

Chapter 36

Echo

Exodus was a storm unleashed. Whatever had contained him in the mortal plane was gone, and on top of fighting the invasive desire to mimic another body, Echo had to stop herself from staring in awe—and disbelief at her past self. How had she ever thought she could best the wind?

A tornado whirled around him, blocking bullets as he carved a path of destruction through the Untold. Exodus left no wounds, no blood. He wrapped them in marble, trapped them in memories of journeys failed and untaken, so they fell to their knees and sank into the Origin.

Let the magic they stole be returned to the world, he'd said during their descent. *Let them know how it felt for those they stole it from.*

And Echo helped him do it, gladly. She started by mimicking a soldier on the front lines, bumbling her attacks and throwing off formations. It didn't take long to pick out the various leaders of each faction. They were the ones with the most bare skin, the brightest bones, and the loudest, most resonant voices. She worked her way inward and got as good a look at each of them as she dared before mimicking one.

"No, no! Left flank, fall back!" she called after the order was given for them to rush. Echo moved, lost herself in the press of bodies before they could place her direction, and changed into the next leader. There was a group channeling magic into their guns, and she shouted, "Fire!" early so the volley didn't hit all at once.

Even with these small sabotages, the fight was taking its toll on Exodus. His realm was shattered. That left him with the magic given to him at his creation and whatever he had squirreled away from deals. With every bullet and spell he deflected, the tornado lost a bit of its fervor. With every bubble of distorted time he popped, he moved a little slower. She had to do this fast.

Carefully maneuvering, Echo reached the center of the fray, where Oblivion's ritual was more than halfway complete. The three gods stood in a circle within the dome, eyes closed, hands loose and open at their sides. Oblivion was exactly as she'd imagined: a black hole forced into the shape of a man. Reckoning's body was made of interlocking pieces of maroon carapace, with wicked, gold-tipped spines along her shoulders, arms, and legs. Harvest's limbs were constructed from woven vines and branches, blooming and withering as she cycled through seasons in minutes.

They faced a mote of cerulean light. Light she could hear, light that made her heart spasm. Her song. It was real, undamaged, and it called to her. Almost close enough to touch.

Far enough to steal her breath when Exodus cried out in pain.

Echo whirled. She'd only looked away for a moment, but his shield had faltered. By some strange flow of the battle's currents, the path between them was open, giving her a perfect view. One arm hung limp at his side. The golden armor that flowed across his body had frozen. Paralyzed.

A squadron of Untold circled him like vultures. Beneath their glow, they had the snow-white skin of Stormpeak's people. She tried to redirect their attack, but they ignored her order. They either didn't understand her attempt at their language, or they'd caught on to her meddling.

The collective assault blew Exodus off his feet. The Untold surged toward him with triumphant cries.

She was so close to the dome. Her voice was *right there.*

So was the need to change forms. Scratching like a beast at a door—*let it out. Show them what you are.* The Untold would come after her if she did.

Exodus flung out his still-functioning arm, and a wall of marble blocked some of the advance, but there were too many for him to handle alone.

"This better count as my favor." Echo gritted her teeth and let the monster take her.

Ironically, it wasn't a dramatic shift from an Untold's magic-ravaged body to her original one. Too-long limbs covered in dark gray skin, nails like chips of shale, a mouth full of sharp black teeth, and silver, pupilless eyes. Taller than the forms she preferred to take, it felt like there was extra space between her soul and her body. Everything about it was wrong.

There had only been one time in her life when this form had fit: when the breaking of her voice had left her hollow, and she could understand why so many mimics became what they became. How strange, to use it to protect the very person who'd made her feel that way in the first place.

Echo fought to keep her shoulders back and her chin high. "Hey, fuckers!" she yelled. "Looking for me?"

A swath of Untold turned from the god at her call. Siphoning him would be a prize, but she was the one Oblivion had demanded. Exodus's eyes bore into her too. Was he surprised? Disgusted? She didn't look long enough to figure it out. Echo cast one last glance at her voice in the dome—three-quarters covered in blue—before she ran for her life.

Chapter 37

Rhienne

"Go make sure everyone on the ship is okay! I'll hold Mishara off," Rhienne yelled to Bastion, who zipped away on his flying carpet.

Her first bullet tore through the shadow armor's bicep without slowing Mishara's pace at all. Apparently an enchantment could only help her aim so much.

The inquisitor's face was twisted in rage, and she flung a boiling bolt of crimson in response.

"Can't you see there are bigger things going on?" Rhienne shouted across the rapidly closing distance. "How is killing me worth Oblivion reshaping the world to his whims? You've met the guy, right? It's not going to be a happy place!"

Mishara laughed, high and hysterical. "Always so condescending. I can't believe I ever loved you."

"I said I was sorry! And I meant it this time!"

Black tentacles erupted from the ground. Rhienne tried to leap out of the way, but one grabbed her ankle, another her arm. Her second shot went wide.

"You think an apology is going to fix everything?" Mishara seethed. "You used me. Pretended to love me, pretended to believe what I believe, whispered falsehoods into my ear so I would spill my truths, and then you destroyed everything I built, down to the foundations. The high inquisitors doubted me when you breached my vault. They turned on me when you escaped Port Saphrai. And now the rest of my followers have abandoned me because of *you* and your little friend, and to *top it all off,* you knocked me out and tied me to your fucking boat! And I'm supposed to forgive you?"

Rhienne's third bullet obliterated the tentacles grappling her. She stumbled away from them, and from Mishara, as a crown of stars formed around the inquisitor's head.

This wasn't power. This was madness, radiating off the woman in waves that sent even the threads of the Origin skittering away.

The rage Rhienne had felt holding the pearl suddenly made sense. The two of them weren't all that different. If she had made some slightly worse choices, if she had been desperate enough, if she hadn't had someone like Echo to pull her out... Rhienne could see herself in that void armor, subject to Oblivion's will, not caring as long as she got what she wanted.

"You're right," Rhienne admitted. "I used you."

One of the stars streaked toward her, blinding her before it hit. She dodged enough to avoid the killing blow, but the impact against her shoulder knocked her to the ground, gasping in pain.

"Believe it or not, Mish," she grunted, "I understand why you're doing this. It's the same reason I made a pact with Oblivion. I mistook magic for control over my life. You feel like it's the only path left to you."

Mishara didn't stop her advance. Rhienne's fourth bullet collided with three more rapid-fire stars. The air between them filled with fire and radiance. The massive, shadowy figure sliced through the cloud. Rhienne was running out of space, backing toward the Untold—who scrambled out of Mishara's way—and the gods' ritual dome.

Rhienne squared her shoulders and held the pistol with both hands, aiming at Mishara's heart.

Two bullets left. If one last plea didn't work, Rhienne just had to squeeze the trigger. "I promise you, this isn't going to get you what you want." The words tasted bitter and hypocritical.

It still stung when Mishara laughed again. "Your little friend said I didn't understand you. Perhaps it is *you* who never understood *me*, if you think I will ever join your side." She and the shadow armor stepped forward as one.

Something lay beneath Mishara's fury. Rhienne might not have recognized it if she hadn't felt it herself: *Where else am I supposed to go from here?*

And she hesitated. Echo had never given up on her, even at the end of the line. If Rhienne didn't try to believe there was a chance for everyone, why had she come back?

Mishara's eyes blazed, and fire gathered in the shadow's maw.

Rhienne lowered the pistol a few inches and pulled the trigger.

Her aim was true. The bullet went right through Mishara's foot. She yowled and lost control of her spell. The darkness holding her faded, and the momentum of her step sent her toppling onto the ocean's surface. Her foot was a mangled mess. Blood pooled around her as she lay there, screaming.

It hadn't struck Rhienne before how young Mishara was. The beauty Rhienne had envied and emulated looked almost childish now.

"You don't have to help me," Rhienne said as she approached. One bullet left. At this range, she couldn't miss.

But the inquisitor had been still for too long; she was sinking.

Rhienne holstered the gun and offered a hand to help Mishara up. "You also don't have to do what Oblivion says. If we win, Bastion wants to change things. No more unfair deals. No more exchanging more than what you have."

Flat on the ground, jaw clenched as she willed the blood back into her gaping wounds, Mishara stared her down.

Then she grabbed her hand.

"I would rather we both lose than let you win," she said, and pulled Rhienne below.

Chapter 38

Echo

When Echo had imagined being chased by a mob, she'd pictured more people asking for autographs. She skirted the dome and the Untold who remained to guard it. There was a curious lack of fighting on the other side. Most of their enemies lay dead or had retreated. A beat later, she registered why. They'd fled from Mishara's hulking shadow armor.

So this was where mercy and honesty got her.

She heard Rhienne's gunshot and saw Mishara fall, but she had to focus on running. This body was so awkward to move, and the Untold snapped at her heels. Bastion was nowhere to be seen, and Exodus grappled with the other half of the Untold's forces.

Of course this was her payment. How could it not be, when showing her truest self to the world meant *this*. A thing that people loathed, or feared, or hoped was a story to cause paranoia. A thing forced to keep to the shadows lest it be drained to a husk. Masks and walls were not protection, they were mandatory for survival. She'd spent her life fighting against an inexorable tide, and now a tsunami loomed. The Untold behind her had put their guns away, replacing them with paralyzing needles. Her music could never be good enough to convince anyone she was more than what they saw, with or without her voice. If Sidrin had seen her like this, he would've signed his soul over to the Untold.

What a fool she'd been.

What a way to waste her life.

Concentrating on the movement of her unfamiliar limbs over the strange surface, Echo did not see Rhienne slip under. But she heard Vala's wordless scream, abruptly cut off when she dove after Rhienne. And when Echo risked a glance and fell, she screamed too.

A nightmarish mass of colored tendrils rose from the deep—part of the Origin's tapestry, reaching hungrily for her friend.

Chapter 39

Rhienne

A thousand sights, smells, and sounds assaulted Rhienne. It felt like she was in the center of a large city for the first time, surrounded by all its overwhelming cacophony, but also inside a volcano, and walking through a breezy meadow, and a bakery and a hospital and a temple and a waterfall, and the calm darkness of the surface was fading as she sank into a hundred thousand colors. Each sensation tore at her attention and threatened to break her apart. Mishara was right up against her, ropes of hardened blood tying them together, but the inquisitor could've been miles away for all that she mattered compared to the vastness consuming them.

Rhienne chuckled humorlessly. One attempt to step forward and forge a new path, and fifteen steps back. Bastion could've saved her the trip. She did not regret returning, though, and that was something to cling to in the madness.

And then she looked down.

What had seemed like random streaks of color from above had clarified into a living, writhing tapestry. The strings moved in patterns too large to decipher, sometimes disappearing further into the mass, sometimes lashing out. But there was a section rising, shaped like a colossal, tooth-filled maw, pulling the rest of the weave up with it. Everything grew louder and brighter the closer it came.

Bastion had undersold what would happen if they sank. The Origin was going to swallow her and Mishara whole.

Rhienne's mind rattled, but she had just enough sense of self left among the chaos to speak. "Was this how you pictured going out? A grand exit, I must say." The abundance of sound ripped her words away, but their intent got through.

The inquisitor's wild fury crumbled, revealing the naked fear beneath. "At least I'm not going out alone."

The bindings around Rhienne tightened, but she was absorbed in the enormity of the weave. It would tear her apart before it devoured her. But it also felt like, if she could get past that point... she didn't know what exactly, but there was something *else* there that was tangible, shapeable. If she could sort through the madness.

A disturbance above tugged on her mind, only noticeable due to its proximity and familiarity. Its passage was invisible, but it reverberated through the tapestry, a pastel sunrise of grief and outrage and *look, Rhienne, remember.*

What was her mother doing here? No, no, no. A delicate dream would be crushed in a place like this. Rhienne struggled against Mishara's spell, managed to wriggle one arm free, and flung her hand into the ether, reaching for magic she didn't have anymore.

Vala didn't reach back, but something else did.

One strand of the tapestry had unraveled, stretching further than the rest. Her mother had pulled that string—Rhienne didn't know how she knew that, or how Vala could do so. This thread was several colors striped together, encased in a layer like glass.

When she touched it, the essence of what the strand represented flooded into her.

Mountains. From the first dreamwalk her mother had ever taken her on. Far to the southwest of Hearthglen, at a height most mortals couldn't reach because the air was so thin, lay the Prismatic Mountains. Their peaks changed color with the light, absorbing and reflecting it into great rainbow striations, glittering with snow. It had been the most beautiful thing she'd ever seen. Looking at them now, in this place, feeling the cold and hearing the stone's breath, Rhienne saw all the way down to the roots of the earth, and knew that someday those mountains would shatter and fall. A tragedy, yes. But in their breaking, they would leave something new behind.

Her awareness expanded outward to the entirety of the Origin. Bastion might call the feeling that overtook her *plate tectonics*. To Rhienne, it was power, potential, all the things she had once craved and that had threatened to drown her, held in the palms of her hands.

This place contained too much concentrated *life* to ever fully comprehend the push and pull of its pattern. Maybe her nature would always prevent her from seeing the big picture, even in the Material Plane. But this one, small piece, right where she stood, she could influence. Rhienne grabbed the string and pulled with all her might.

"Sorry, Mish," the mountains roared for her. "I'm not ready to let go quite yet."

Rhienne cracked the light-string like a whip and looped it around Mishara's injured ankle. The woman screamed—small, that noise, so small—as the vastness of those mountains hit her all at once. Rhienne released her grip on the thread before it could overwhelm her too, its sudden absence leaving her scraped hollow.

Blood vessels burst in Mishara's eyes as she grappled with Rhienne. "You. Will. Not. Escape. Unscathed." Her face lit up with triumph as she tore the bottle with Rhienne's soul from her coat pocket.

The blood binding them together evaporated. Rhienne reached for Mishara, but the inquisitor was falling away now, face twisted in agony.

Mishara broke open the bottle, grabbed the piece of Rhienne's soul before it floated away, and *ripped.* It was the last thing she did before her body locked in tension, and the thread spooled back into the weave, taking her with it.

Pain didn't register among all the other sensations, but blood drifted away from Rhienne's face, neck, and chest, and the vision in her left eye went fuzzy. Mishara had scarred her—to make the lie Rhienne had told all the way back in the catacomb cell true. Once, such an imperfection in her appearance would've been intolerable.

Now, it felt like a record of what she'd survived.

Who needed their *entire* soul anyway?

The monster in the tapestry was still coming for her. She needed to move. Rhienne half swam, half flew to the surface, and she could almost feel Vala beside her, pushing her on, holding her up. That was, after all, what both dreams and mothers were for.

"Do you see the door, Mom?" Rhienne whispered, tears in her eyes.

Gentle as an evening breeze, the Origin carried Vala's voice to her. *Do you?*

Rhienne did. But it was no bigger than she was, and if it murmured sweet nothings, the sound was lost to the symphony below.

Chapter 40

Echo

Echo was surrounded. Greedy hands reached for her. She slashed at them with tooth and claw. Let them see the monster in full. She mimicked each person she saw, cackled as they recoiled from attacking themselves or their friends, and changed back into her true self when they found their bravery again. The sounds that came from her throat were the furthest thing from music, while her heart screamed *Rhienne, Rhienne, Rhienne.* In the press of Untold, she'd lost sight of her friend, of Vala, and the leviathan-like amalgam below.

Agony sheared across her back—a blade, laced with that infernal paralytic toxin. It seeped into her spine and her muscles froze, with none of the preamble of the last time. She was already in the form they were trying to force her to take.

Echo collapsed. Glowing faces leered in triumph. They rolled her over and dragged her toward the dome. There was only a small portion at the top that wasn't covered in blue.

A hundred feet from the dome, something broke through the surface of the ocean, rocketed up, and fell in a graceful arc, emitting a string of expletives that could've only come from one person. She couldn't move her head toward Rhienne, and part of Echo was glad. She wouldn't have to witness her friend's first reaction to seeing her like this.

Several Untold peeled off to handle Rhienne and Vala. Of the dozens who had been here at the start, there were maybe twenty left that she could see. So much progress, but not enough.

What had happened to Exodus?

The Untold threw her down at the edge of the dome and closed ranks around her. "Don't let it sink," one barked. "We deserve the recharge when this is done."

It. Echo wished they'd forget to move her so she could disappear below. The cerulean light of her voice hung an arm's length away. Here, at the end, shouldn't she let it go? Nothing she'd done had mattered. She'd tried, oh she had *tried*, to be someone people wanted to listen to. To see. She'd even been lucky enough to meet a few who did. But there was always going to be the rest of the world. There was always going to be this *thing* at the root of her that made her dream impossible. Why would anyone want to see the truth, when the truth looked like this?

Kill her dream, and her voice would lose its power. Exodus had begged her to do it. Giving it up had seemed tantamount to suicide. But there had to be another dream out there for her, right? She still had some good years left, assuming they got out of this alive. She'd make a terrible assassin. Too much skulking. A politician, maybe. At least with that, she'd get to be around people, do some traveling.

The light of her song flickered.

Oblivion's eyes flashed open, two stars against the void. But it wasn't his voice that reverberated off non-existent marble walls and summoned a howling gale that blew the Untold off their feet.

"NO!" Exodus's roar shook the marrow in her bones. He appeared in the space the Untold had vacated, one arm limp at his side, the other slashing out with a great golden scythe that lay waste to everyone in its path.

"That's mine," Harvest cried.

"Leave him, sister," Oblivion said. "He will join the chaff soon enough."

A shimmer passed over the dome. The ritual was complete.

The First God of Endings, Harbinger of Nothingness and Guardian of the Void, smiled at Echo and bowed his head. "Thank you for the gift." He and his sisters dropped like stones into the sea.

Echo was stuck as an observer as the fighting dissipated. Above her, the airship leaked smoke and arcane energy in a blue-black column, listing heavily to one side. It didn't look long for the sky.

Bastion descended with the crew crowded onto his flying carpet. They finished off the Untold swarming Rhienne at the same time Exodus cleared the way around Echo. He planted the golden scythe in the ground, careless of its slow sinking, and knelt before her.

She strained to speak, but the poison had frozen her vocal cords too.

He scooped her up with his one good arm and murmured a spell to hear her thoughts.

Why did you stop me? Echo asked.

Exodus's voice was a prayer whispered to a candle flame. *You held on for this long, only to give up now?*

I was prolonging the inevitable. You were right. I should've let it go a long time ago.

You *were right.* I *was bitter.*

Tears spilled down her cheeks, and she was powerless to wipe them away. *I could've stopped all this.*

Yes. But at what cost?

One worthless dream against the future of the world? How could he even question that?

They were alone now, Mishara and the Untold dead, Oblivion and his sisters assimilated into the Origin's core. The rest of their allies were making their way back to shore, where it was less perilous to stand. They stopped when the ocean's blue light transitioned to the browns and greens of rocks and plants. All that was left of the docks were some scattered sections of charred and broken wood, and a few lone posts sticking out of the water. It hurt Echo's heart. So much damage and pain, for nothing.

Exodus followed the others, holding her against his chest. *Do not lose hope. Not yet.*

"I am sorry," Bastion said as they approached. "We were too slow."

Rhienne shook her head. "No. No! There has to be something we can do. When I was down there, I saw—I felt—I *everything'd everything*. It's dangerous, yes, but it's also—" She made a frustrated, all-encompassing gesture that cut off when Exodus joined the circle. There was a question in her fever-bright eyes, a hitch in her breath that made Echo's chest cave in.

"Brother," Exodus murmured, "do you have anything in that pouch of yours to counter poisons?"

"Oh dear. Let me see."

Don't bother, Echo wanted to say. Rhienne's gaze hadn't left her, and gods, she couldn't stand it. What if this was why Rhienne didn't appear by her deathbed? That flash of understanding on her face was going to twist into disgust. "All this time," she'd say. "This was what the lie had been to cover. No wonder."

Exodus turned her away before her fears could come true, and a soothing warmth pressed into her back. The rigidity of her muscles thawed, faster than the first time she'd been paralyzed, but not fast enough for how she ached to get out of this body.

"Rhienne," Bastion said. "You cannot go down there again. It's a miracle you survived the first time."

"But—" Rhienne started.

"Even if you were to reach my siblings, you could not hope to outmatch them in their own territory. They can manipulate any thread of the weave now. You and Vala barely managed to *hold* them."

"Could we... avoid the threads somehow?" Rhienne asked. "Make ourselves so small that the Origin doesn't notice us?"

"And once we get to Oblivion, what then?" Bastion's tone was gentle, sorrowful.

"Don't look at me like that. Let me think."

Echo worked her jaw and waited for feeling to tingle back into her fingers and toes before mimicking her favored form.

Or trying to.

There was the beginning shudder, but nothing further. She'd never had to think about the change before, but she did now, picturing the details of the shape she wanted and how it would feel to mimic them. Her body refused to leave this form behind.

Panic squeezed her chest. "Something's wrong," she rasped, too quiet for anyone but Exodus to hear.

He put her down and looked her over. *What is it?*

She couldn't get enough air. Echo raked her claws over her skin, as if she could peel it away to find something better underneath. *I'm stuck.*

The Origin wanted you in your original body. It's likely loath to let you go, now that you've been in it so long.

Will I be able to change back once the planes return to normal?

Exodus's pause was a beat too long. *I believe so.* Echo almost sank into the earth right then and there, but the God of Journeys took her gently by the shoulders. *Just as I believe your friend is onto something.*

Rhienne paced from the shore to the edge of town, kicking through piles of ashy sand and passing back and forth through the weak, muted auroras that made up Hearthglen. No living creatures had survived the fire, yet the Origin's light shone, drifting through the remains of buildings and streets. She stopped in the middle of a gray-green light strand, brows furrowed, and moved her hand through it like she was directing a river's current.

"Hold on," Rhienne murmured, clearly speaking her thoughts as they formed. "I have a history of not being able to see things everyone else can, so this could be a me problem. But has anyone else noticed that none of the threads in the Origin feel like people?"

Irelia stepped up and examined the light with her. "You're right. Creatures, objects, nature... but I don't see you or me." The captain looked to her crew. "None of you, except Tash."

Indeed, the cook had a faint sunny glow about him. "Echo has one as well," he said. "And the gods."

Everything had been so bright and overwhelming before, and Echo had been so focused on her body, she hadn't noticed the small blue thread running through her. Bastion's and Exodus's were a stronger white-gold.

"But none of us without divine blood," Rhienne said with a wry twist of her lips. "Why not? And more importantly, can we use that to our advantage?"

"It's quite strange," Bastion mused. "By my memory, you ought to have a connection to the Origin. You were made from it, after all. Brother?"

"By my memory as well." Exodus shook his head, deep in thought.

Excitement brightened Rhienne's face. "If we could reconnect ourselves, assimilate like your siblings did, would we be able to manipulate the Origin? To stop Oblivion?"

"Perhaps," Bastion said. "The Origin has a heart and mind of its own; we'll need to persuade it that you are a missing part of the whole."

"How do we do that?" Rhienne asked.

Echo had been listening with half an ear, not truly expecting the conversation to go anywhere, but Bastion's words snagged in her mind. Humans didn't have a tether to the Origin, but she knew what they *did* have tethers to. She thought of the bonds made in her performances, the feel of them squeezing her heart. "We form our own tapestry," she whispered.

Louder, Exodus urged.

"We form our own tapestry," she said. "Our own web of deals."

The spidersilk of Bastion's face shimmered, and for a moment, he was made of clockwork and debris again, his expression grim.

"I know you don't like it, Brother, but it could work. Look." Exodus moved away from Echo, and his sudden absence left her feeling horribly exposed. But in that space, the favor she still owed him was an infinitesimal blue and gold aurora. It branched away to connect with Tash and Irelia, tying them all together. "You'll need to make a *lot* of them. And you'll still need a link between you and the Origin. Something that can merge the two tapestries. Something that contains a thread from both."

"A little divine blood?" Tash said heavily. He rubbed his wrists. His face was still sallow from his stint with the Untold, and the battle hadn't helped.

"Yes," Rhienne answered. "But not from you. When I was down there, underneath the immenseness of it all, it felt like there was a pattern. A *rhythm.* Like a concert put on by the whole world. If we want to add our voices, we need someone who can move with the melody."

The weight of a dozen stares fell on Echo. She couldn't meet any of them. Bile rose in her throat. This wasn't happening, not like this. Not now.

"Hey." Rhienne stepped forward and reached for her.

Echo flinched away. "Don't. I can't."

"Of course you can. I've been in your head, remember? What you were capable of in your dreams was enough to draw Oblivion's attention. You can get the Origin to listen too."

She shook her head, fixated on the ground and the enormous tapestry far, far below. Hadn't she done enough? Been through enough?

All of the usual pre-performance fears rose up—no one would listen, or they'd listen and wouldn't care, or they'd laugh—but above all that, "How am I supposed to make beautiful music when I'm like this?"

"Echo, look at me." When she didn't, Rhienne gently lifted her chin.

Shadows haunted her friend's face. The angry red slash that Mishara had left was a reminder of all that had brought them here. Grief and exhaustion deepened the lines that Rhienne's illusions had hidden for so long. But there was fire there too, more than an ember now. Echo searched and searched for disgust, distrust, doubt, and found none.

"You said I'm the only one who knows all of you," Rhienne said. "What I see right now doesn't change that. You may be the only one who *can* do this. It doesn't have to be beautiful, it just has to be yours."

Echo couldn't hold her friend's gaze. She waited for someone to say it was a terrible idea, that there were a thousand-and-one reasons it wouldn't work, none of which had to do with her.

Mist churned around Exodus, a blatant display of his worry. "If you're going to survive, you'll have to make some modifications. Dull the effectiveness of your senses, so you won't be overwhelmed when you go below."

"So it's impossible." The rawness in Echo's voice betrayed her relief. "Even if I could mimic, I've never come across a person with a body like that."

"Someone has to have an idea," Rhienne pleaded.

The silence stretched, and Echo dared to hope she wouldn't have to risk failing them.

Then the mist around Exodus went still. "Our innate abilities aren't that different, though I was made to be even more fluid. I could give that to you."

He was so quiet, so calm, so matter-of-fact that Echo didn't register what he'd said. "I'm sorry, you could give me *what*?"

"My fluidity." Exodus shifted into a cloud of fog, back to marble, and then into pieces of both before solidifying again. "You wouldn't have to copy an entire form; you could mimic individual parts as you need."

"But then... wouldn't you be stuck?"

He nodded, solemn, but not sad. "I will not force anything upon you that you do not wish. The final choice is yours."

She glanced around at Bastion, Rhienne, and the airship crew. Of the dozen they'd started this misadventure with, only seven remained. Some of them stayed a cautious distance away, but Tash and Nazal came forward to stand beside Rhienne.

"Anyone can sing any old tavern song," the big man said. "But you picked the one that saved us. You gave it enough light and life to fight off a god's nightmares. I, for one, would love to see what you could do with the Origin as your stage."

Nazal's smile was shy, but their voice was as strong and sure as it had been reciting stories on the airship. "It took you two days to bring our crew closer together than we'd been in years. I wouldn't trust anyone else to connect us with the heart of all things."

"I know great art can't be rushed, but unfortunately time *is* a factor," Bastion added.

Echo felt like an unspooling thread, dizzy and tangled. All of these people believed she could control the pattern of the Origin itself. Exodus was willing to give away a vital piece of himself for her. There were so many *ifs* and *mights,* beliefs and assumptions in this plan. Was there ever going to be any certainty? That was the only thing she'd wanted when this started: some assurance that her time, effort, and tears would be worth something.

But she had to make the attempt. She'd be the world's biggest hypocrite if she didn't, and that was not the kind of example she wanted to set when Rhienne had just gained some sense of purpose.

As long as she didn't think about the enormity of the task, maybe it would work. Keep her focus on Oblivion. Whatever she felt about her voice, her dream, he did not deserve to win.

"I'll try," Echo said.

Chapter 41

Rhienne

Rhienne explained as best she could what her friend should expect once she touched the magic below. Then they embraced. If they had any hope of catching Oblivion before he finished absorbing Echo's voice, they had to form their little deal network and connect with the Origin simultaneously, and pray they could meet in the middle. There was no time for Rhienne to reassure Echo that she was beautiful no matter what she looked like, that she had never been and could never be the frightening creature in the stories, that Rhienne understood how frustrating and hopeless it felt to have her choices ripped from her.

But as Echo stepped away, Rhienne wished they'd made time. Whatever had been holding Echo up since taking on her original form, it was starting to collapse. All the scaffolding in the world wouldn't support her if her foundation crumbled.

"It's just a container," Rhienne blurted out. "It's not all you are."

Echo gave her the barest of smiles, close-lipped so as not to show her fangs, then dove into the ground.

The longer the words hung in the air, the more it felt like she'd said the wrong thing. There had been a moment of shock seeing Echo's original body, but then it was normal. Just another part of her friend, the final piece of the puzzle. Rhienne had to make sure she got the chance to set the record straight.

Tash broke the silence. "She can do this."

"Aye," Irelia agreed. "We better be ready for our cue. Any particular kinds of deals we ought to make? A threshold for the prices we're paying?"

Rhienne tore her gaze away from Echo's descent, trying not to think about how small her friend was against the light. "Perhaps... deals that aren't concerned with the amount of magic they'll make." She looked around at the crew, saving Irelia for last. Her cheeks warmed when their eyes met. "We're doing it for the connection, this time."

"Well, I've got one to start." Irelia stuck her hand out to Tash. "I promise that if we survive this, I'm going to take you to a remote island where you can lay on a beach and drink spiked punch, and no one will bother you for as long as you like."

Tash gave her a lopsided grin. "And my payment?"

"You cook us the best meal we've ever had when you come back."

"Easiest deal I've ever made." He laughed and shook her hand.

Rhienne's breath caught as the gold light that spun out of Tash met Irelia's magenta.

The captain gasped too. "This feels... different. Not quite so sharp." She noticed everyone watching and commanded, "Get a move on then! We don't have all day."

Their little corner of the ash-filled ruins suddenly came alive as the crew shook hands and made bargains they could easily, even *gladly,* fulfill. Nazal's deals manifested in vibrant tangerine, Mordach's in lavender—which he stopped pretending to be cross about after the second handshake—and soon they could hardly see the ground beneath them for the tapestry of light they'd created.

Part of Rhienne had been worried she wouldn't know what to offer, or what to give away. But she'd come to know these people. Nazal liked to play cards to spend time with their companions rather than to win, Mordach needed time off to visit his ailing father, and Tash wanted nothing more than to be able to sail through the skies, free from the demands of gods and men. Without knowing where her life would take her next, she tried to promise the things she had now: her time, her protection, her faith. Her deals spun out in faded gray. Better than black, she supposed, but not nearly as beautiful as anyone else's.

The gods stood apart. Exodus was unreadable, while Bastion had the look of a parent watching their children grow up. When she gestured for them to join, both shook their heads. A golden thread was very slowly twining together between them.

Whether by choice or something subconscious between them, she and Irelia saved each other for last. The captain approached, words ready on her lips.

"Wait," Rhienne whispered. "Let me go first." She took Irelia's hands between both of hers, her voice suddenly shaky. It seemed absurd to be doing this *here*, among the smell of charcoal and low tide, in the ashes of the place that had once been her home. "I can't promise to be everything you need me to be. And I'm probably going to mess up *a lot*. But if you're willing to give me the space to do that, and the grace to forgive me, I want to learn to be myself with you."

Irelia leaned in and stopped just short of a kiss. "I have one addendum to your proposal. See, I don't think the sides are quite even."

Rhienne's heart dropped. Had she asked for too much? "No?"

"No. You are giving me far more than I am giving you. So, in addition to your terms, I promise to help you shrink that door as small as it gets, to drown out the call of the void when I must, and to show *you* all the corners of myself you haven't seen yet. There's a lot more to discover." Irelia's wicked grin set a fire in Rhienne's chest.

"What in the cosmos did I do to deserve you?"

"I believe you used my airship to hide from your multitude of crimes and enemies."

"Oh, right." Rhienne was smiling now, tears of joy pricking her eyes.

Before she could kiss the infuriating, amazing woman in front of her, another voice rose through the ground and surrounded them in a cloud of icy darkness. "How sweet,"

Oblivion said. "And how naive to think that such paltry promises could make up for all you have done."

Irelia drew her sword, but there was nothing to swing at. The god had become one with the earth and sky. "Stay together!" she called. The memory of their first battle on the ship was plain on her face.

The crew huddled closer, and still, half of them were obscured by shadow. The light of their bargains, so strong a moment ago, dulled and flickered.

Oblivion said, "I see Mishara failed to bring a satisfying end to your soul. No matter. I am the expert, after all."

Mordach brandished his axe and shouted at the darkness, "Ye'll have to go through us!"

"Your loyalty is fascinating. Before you throw your lives away, don't you all want to know what sort of person you're shackling yourselves to?"

Shadows warped, twisted, and dissolved. When they cleared, Hearthglen was gone. Familiar dripping walls, iron bars, and the stink of death surrounded her and the crew.

Fear lanced through Rhienne, frigid and paralyzing. Oblivion had pulled them into a memory from the catacombs. He was going to show the crew the true blackness of her soul.

A specter approached the cell. It wore Mishara's face and her crimson ceremonial armor, but its eyes were Oblivion's—white and full of depthless hatred.

"A fitting place for the beginning of the end," he said.

Chapter 42

Echo

Echo thought she'd braced herself for the cacophony, but what she'd experienced as the planes merged was a fragment of the reality below. This was a war on her senses, stimuli pulling her attention in so many directions that it was an effort to save any space for her own body or mind.

The mass of glowing, colorful threads hadn't noticed her yet. She was too small, too quiet, with just enough magic in her veins to appear like she belonged. Down, down, down she went, slipping through the empty space, afraid of starting too early, or with the wrong note, or with the right note only for it to fall on deaf ears.

Exodus's power was like a pool of cool water around her heart. Inconceivable, for him to have given it away. The strangeness of it fought with her own ability and with the Origin's desire to keep her as she was. She tried again to fully change, this time into Irelia, who had endured so much and still managed to stand tall. When that didn't take, she tried Vala, a woman whose courage to defy the cosmos had persisted through death. Even Rhienne, whose form she knew better than her own, who had been brave enough to try again with no path in sight, eluded her. She was still just Echo. Just a mimic with no masks left to hide the ugly truth, without even her singing to carry any beauty.

It had to be a partial mimicry, then. Only small changes allowed; no new identities accepted today. She directed Exodus's magic to specific places in her body, shivering as it moved through her veins.

Echo changed her eyes into those of a blind fruit seller from Wildspire to dampen the Origin's light. That was easy, but everything in the weave had a texture and taste and smell to it as well. Those would be harder to eliminate.

She flipped through her memories of the people she'd collected over her travels. There was a baker in Port Saphrai who had to have her daughter taste test all her creations. That could be a taste or smell problem, so she adopted the baker's nose and mouth.

Some sense of touch would have to remain to feel for the vibrations of this 'instrument.' Sidrin had often complained of numbness in his hands and legs. Taking on parts of his shape seemed too friendly, too familiar for where they'd left things, but there was no one else Echo knew enough about who also matched her need.

She must've looked even more monstrous with her collage of body parts, like some unfinished abstract sculpture.

When the wall of sound became impenetrable, Echo stopped her descent and listened. Rustling branches, animal growls, clanging tools, burbling streams, creaking doors, birdsong, and a million more noises clamored to be heard.

There was no more excuse to delay, other than the absurdity of making herself noticeable to a stage and an audience that had no reason to listen and plenty of grounds to destroy her.

Echo sucked in a shaking breath. She just needed to make a space big enough to fit her friends into the weave.

The first thread she tried to push aside was raindrops. They fell on roads and metal roofs and slid between leaves to hit the forest floor, growing from a slow drip to a steady patter. Rain had always brought her peace. It made tavern audiences swell as people sought refuge from the outdoors; it had a life and music of its own that inspired a multitude of moods and songs. It should've been easy to move, but the thread did not obey her.

She reached for another: the scratch of a match being lit, and the crackle as the spark grew into a fire. It reminded her of home, a long day at the forge or running around town with Rhienne, which sometimes ended with scolding but always with a hot, comforting meal. This too refused to budge. Other sounds swarmed in, as if called by her memories. The clang of a hammer against an anvil, the shrill whistle that the town guards blew, breaking pottery, and the clucking of chickens disturbed in their coop.

These were all familiar sounds, yet they did not *belong* to her. They were from an old life, a mask that no longer fit. They had no reason to cooperate.

The main mass of the weave thrummed below. It was growing louder, rising closer, catching up to the small threads she'd tried to pull, ready to chew her up and spit her out. That was how her entire musical career had gone. Why had Rhienne thought it would be any different now?

It doesn't have to be beautiful, it just has to be yours.

The Origin had wanted her in this body. It had demanded the unvarnished truth. Perhaps she could only open a path if she opened herself. *Dangerous,* her instincts argued. The Untold were gone, but their biases were not. Rhienne had accepted her, and so had Tash, Irelia, and Nazal; Sidrin had at least laid aside his fear. But with her foresight blocked, there was no way to be sure it was safe.

Something moved in the deep, sending vibrations across the weave and rattling through her brain. It must have been *immense* to touch so many threads.

Echo struggled to control her breathing. She tapped into the sounds of rain, of home, as an anchor. Time was running short. She had to get a hold of herself—and the pieces of the Origin that would respond to her.

She reached for missed notes. The clink of a single coin in an empty cup. Wind on a lonely road as she traveled to another new place, and another, looking for somewhere that would take her in. A song of pain, embarrassment, and failure.

A song that made the Origin *shift.* Enough to hear the sliver of silence amid the noise, but just a fraction of what she needed. What else could she draw from? It already felt like she'd ripped out her heart and served it on a silver platter.

"Oh." Oblivion's voice shivered down her spine, multi-layered and... melodic. "I can think of plenty. Quite the history you have bottled within this dream, and I've only seen part of it. Here, let me give you a hand."

A few threads lashed at her—jeering crowds, scattered, pitying applause, landlords demanding rent she couldn't pay. The first human sounds she'd heard down here, all with that same wordless melody woven beneath them. *Her song*, she realized.

These were her memories, twisted into the Origin by Oblivion's budding connection to her. Echo's stomach lurched. She tried to pull away, to continue her work, but the noises only grew louder, burrowing like needles into her brain.

Why was it so impossible to ignore what a bunch of strangers thought? She had Rhienne, the crew, even Exodus. People who believed in her. More than she'd ever had before. Yet they were drowned out by derision, and hate, and the deafening silence of being passed over time and again.

Oblivion's laughter wove through it all, and Echo knew she had to stop him. That this torture was only to delay her. Sobs wracked her body as she reached for the Origin, and—

A tidal wave of sound slammed into her: Levi chastising her for daring to play something outside the 'preferred' list; Sidrin wondering why someone like her had wormed her way into his life; Aderai suggesting she take a position far below her means; and everywhere, *everywhere*, the Untolds' dead, hungry eyes, their rattling voices calling her *it* and threatening to drain her life and magic away, and if that was the only way she could bring joy to people, maybe she should've let them take her, and all of it was too much, far too much to hold in this cage of a body that was, at its core, the symbol for her deepest, ugliest truth.

I will never be enough.

Chapter 43

Rhienne

Using the Origin's threads, Oblivion spelled out every mistake of Rhienne's life. The memories were real enough to touch, to make the crew feel as she had felt. The cell, the catacombs, her unwillingness to part with the last scrap of her magic for some imagined dignity. Her long, dark march to the gallows and the door to the void, which had begun long before she'd ever met the God of Endings. And with it, he showed her all the things she should've done differently, all the paths she'd been too blind to see, the dreams she'd destroyed both by his command and on her own.

It was one thing to recognize these things for herself, but seeing the sudden reticence of the people she considered her friends was more than she could bear. What were they thinking? Would they keep their bargains, knowing what kind of person she'd been before they met?

The shadows warped again, coalescing into the yawning void at the entrance to Oblivion's realm. "Come home," it seemed to say. "This is where you belong."

How much can a person change, really? Rhienne wasn't sure if the thought came from her or Oblivion, but her soul quailed regardless. Promises and hopes could be such empty things. She didn't want to go through the door, but she didn't know how to fight. How to make the things she *did* want real. That had always been her problem—not the lack of desire, but the futility of wanting.

From what felt like very far away, a deep, forest-green tendril pierced the darkness.

"Rhienne, I had no idea."

Oh gods. Her father couldn't be here, witnessing this. She'd been satisfied enough with where they'd left things. Now his opinion of her would deteriorate all over again.

"Rhienne, I'm so sorry," he said.

What?

"I was hurting. And in my hurt, I refused to see that you were too. If I could... I'd like to make a deal with you. We all would."

Oblivion hissed as more colors joined her father's. Purples and yellows, reds and blues, some familiar from her childhood and others she knew only from passing by today: the people of Hearthglen.

"If you can forgive me, forgive *us*, we can forgive you. We'd like to start over." Silas stepped out of the darkness, arms outstretched. "This is how you fight. With friends and family at your side."

Rhienne ran to her father. He enveloped her in an embrace, solid and real and warm. His tears fell into her hair. Her throat was too tight to say anything except, "Deal."

The pact formed between them, expanding the web. And for the first time, dread that wasn't hers curled through the void.

Oblivion was afraid.

The shadows retreated in a sudden rush, returning Rhienne and her disoriented army to the edge of Hearthglen. She would've fallen if her father hadn't been holding her.

"Thank you, Dad," Rhienne whispered. "How did you know to come? Did Mom send for you?"

"I am capable of acting without her advice, you know. Though I can see why you'd think otherwise." Silas chuckled dryly. "We all felt a... commotion. And none of us wanted to say we didn't do everything we could to protect what's ours."

There were nearly twenty of them now, all connected in the network of light, with Rhienne, absurdly, as the focal point. She bit her lip, looking askance at the crew, but their bargains hadn't wavered. If anything, the thread between her and Irelia was stronger.

Bastion and Exodus stood at the edge of the group, ragged and shaken, leaning on each other for support. She wondered what memories they'd seen in the void but thought better of asking.

The important question was, where had Oblivion gone?

Outside of their small tapestry, Hearthglen was dimmer, missing the ghostly lights that had added a semblance of beauty to the carnage. As if Oblivion had pulled them with him.

As if he wanted to use them on someone else.

Rhienne looked down and swore. The gentle swirls of color below had become sharp, tearing claws. Echo was a tiny gray dot among them, curled over, unmoving.

The music had synchronized, but not to create an opening. It rose up, whispering in a thousand voices, Echo's among them, *You-she-I will never be enough.*

Rhienne whirled to the two gods. Exodus was fixated on the scene below, his marble body newly frozen with the loss of his ability. Bastion watched the sky, for some ineffable reason. What was wrong with them? Couldn't they see? "What's going on with Echo?"

"History repeating itself," Exodus said mournfully.

With all the energy buzzing in her body, he was lucky she didn't smack him. "And we're going to sit here and watch?"

"There is little I can do to protect anyone while I'm in this place." Bastion gestured to his spidersilk body.

Exodus shook his head. "What else can we do?"

Gods, Rhienne was an idiot. She'd seen Echo's dream, and still she let her friend go down there to face an uncaring world and Oblivion's barbs, alone. No amount of mimicry, partial or otherwise, was going to overcome that. Old habits told her to go down there *right now*; she had to do something to help, no matter how stupid or short-sighted.

But the way the tangled mass of light moved gave Rhienne pause. She had that same tip-of-the-tongue feeling as when she'd gone below, so close to understanding the pattern. Oblivion's game was familiar, replaying history over and over, lingering in failures and endings. He could not use the totality of the Origin's potential; that was why he wanted the power in Echo's voice.

Oh. She almost laughed at the realization. Like Rhienne, Oblivion could not see the paths ahead.

He'd waited until her bargain with Irelia to interrupt their strategy. He'd retreated only after her father's deal.

Both had been promises of new beginnings.

"I know how to beat him," Rhienne gasped. "I need something from all of you."

And they would need something from her too, if they hoped to reach Echo in one piece. One last deal, with the only tool she had left at her disposal. Giving it away would leave her bare, defenseless. But with everyone around her, that didn't feel so terrifying anymore.

With a murmur of explanation to Irelia, Rhienne sliced a dagger along her palm. "I forfeit my blood magic, to shield us from the worst of the Origin's chaos." Crimson dripped from her clenched fist and soaked into the ground. A shiver passed through her as the deal took hold, a hollowing deep in her mind and soul as the knowledge of Mishara's rituals and Rhienne's connection to her last source of power faded. The emptiness it left wasn't a black hole like the end of her pact had been; it simply *was.* She wobbled, unsure if she was going to fall or float away.

Irelia caught her. "Are you all right?"

Rhienne waited for the dizziness to pass before answering. "I'm on my way to it."

As she laid out the rest of her terms to the crew, the people of Hearthglen, and the gods, auroras spun out from her body. These were not gray, but the beautiful pastels of the Plane of Dreams.

Rhienne smiled at the thread that reached for her mother's invisible form. "Follow me."

Chapter 44

Echo

Echo had become quicksilver: malleable, impressionable, fluid, yet heavier than stone. There was so much noise that it blended into one massive, endless note, until the vibrations of several disturbances hit her at once, followed by a scream that wrenched her heart.

Had Rhienne not moved forward enough to resist jumping into the void? Perhaps that had been wishful thinking on Echo's part. In one way or another, they were all stuck the way they were made.

I'm sorry. The Origin snatched away her words. *You believed in me, and I couldn't do it.*

Gentle hands landed on her. Echo tried to move—her mind shrieked, *Don't touch me when I'm like this*—but there was nowhere to go.

Each touch resolved into a pattern of breath and heartbeat, or a marked lack thereof, that she knew: Bastion, Exodus, Vala, the airship crew (even the ones who were afraid of her), and Rhienne. Always Rhienne. All of them were here, hurting worse than she was as the weave grabbed and tore at their senses.

Why had they come? They'd wanted to see what she could do, what she truly was. Well, it was all out on the table. A monster at worst, a copy at best, with nothing to say that hadn't already been said, nothing worth noticing. They must be here to rescue her, then, and put an end to this failure.

Rhienne embraced her, shaking and shuddering.

The Origin receded a fraction, like the noises were behind a door instead of within Echo's bones, far enough away for her to find her breath again. "We have to leave, before you're all destroyed."

Only Exodus moved, piercing the wall of sound with his body, not up and away but *down* farther, to pull on a strand of crashing waves and seabird calls.

Dull your hearing and bring back sight, he urged.

If it would make them flee, fine. Echo changed her ears to those of a deaf child who'd lived down the street from Sidrin, and her eyes back to their original form.

She stood on a beach.

No, not *a* beach, *the* beach, where Bastion's realm had opened. The sand was cool on her bare feet, the sun just breaching the horizon. Waves lapped at her toes. "Why are you showing me this?" Echo choked, unable to hear her own words. She did not want to live through this again.

Her body moved of its own accord. But then the memory tilted, altered. Other people materialized on the sand beside her. They all walked forward when she did.

Echo had stared at the water that day, marking the rising line where the tide reached and wondering which wave would pull her under. On the first step, her attention was there.

Before the next footfall, she was looking through someone else's eyes, fixed not on the waves but on the sand caught in a battering cycle beneath them. Without looking at her body, Echo knew who these thoughts belonged to. *Rhienne.*

Another shift, toward large rocks further out to sea. They were far smaller than they had once been, but they remained standing against wind, water, and time. *Tash.*

Up to the sky with its dappled clouds. The desire to return was strong, but it had been so long since being on the ground had brought anything other than meaningless death; now that there was something worth fighting for, perhaps staying a little longer wouldn't be so bad. *Irelia.*

Out to the rising sun. A new day, whatever that might bring. *Bastion.*

To the sea's endless expanse. The world was so impossibly large compared to the ways anyone could change it. *Vala.*

To the driftwood caught in the tide, waiting to come to rest on the shore, unsure if it could make it, but fighting to stay afloat all the same. Was that... *Silas.*

To a bird flying high over it all, an observer, a witness, and never anything more. *Exodus.*

Echo backed out of the water and looked down at herself.

She was an amalgamation of all of them. Patchworked across her gray mimic skin were feathers, scars, clockwork mechanics, sun tans, and pastels. She had seen through all of them, *been* them, however briefly. As Rhienne had so aptly put, she'd 'everything'd everything' without losing the original pull that had called to her.

Echo flipped between all the perspectives again. With each change, a thread of tinted light formed between her and someone else standing on the beach. She recognized the tug of a dozen deals, even though she hadn't made any, and an odd weightlessness bubbled in her chest.

"Look at all the people you've touched, Echo," said the birds and waves and sand.

And that was true, and wonderful, but so were all the people whose lives had touched hers. She had been using her ability wrong all this time.

These were not masks. They were *lenses.*

It was precisely this body that had never belonged to her that let her see the world this way. There would always be those who didn't understand her or didn't care to try. There would, even with the Untold gone, always be people who called her a monster. No amount of fame or fortune would change that, and no, it was not fair. But it was also unfair for her to hold up a mirror and call the reflection unworthy of love, just because there were pieces of so many people in it.

More than unfair, it was plain wrong. Looking at Rhienne, there were parts of Vala, Irelia, Oblivion, Bastion, Mishara, and even herself—not physically, but in the impact their presences had. She saw all of Rhienne's mistakes and hardships. And yet, she was still just Rhienne.

Everyone here was a collage of who they'd met and where they'd been. That didn't make them monsters, or frauds, or anything other than who they were.

And standing here at the center of this web, Echo finally understood what she had to do. She could be all the people she'd ever collected and still be herself, as long as she didn't hide behind them. The Origin didn't need a conductor or a link to accept them as part of the tapestry.

It needed a conduit.

She integrated pieces of all her friends—her family—into a new body. Tash's steadfastness, Nazal's curiosity, Mordach's rough shell and hidden softness, Vala's hope, Irelia's vigilant care, Rhienne's determination. She even kept her claws, but she made them gold like Exodus's armor. The rest she left open, free to channel or reflect whatever called to her, and reawakened her deadened senses.

This time, when the full weight of the weave crashed into her, Echo made no demands and searched for no individual threads. She simply let it in.

Her body became a kaleidoscope of sound and color, and now she could make out the darkness and silence between each thread. Spaces shaped like the people around her, all reaching out to help.

Tears ran sparkling down her cheeks. For so long, it had been just her and Rhienne, unwilling to show themselves to anyone else. Not anymore, and never again.

"This is me," she said, pulling the airship crew closer to her. And again, when the way forward remained closed, "This is me!"

She took Exodus's hand and shouted again when sneers pierced through the music and Oblivion's wrathful roar reached her from miles away. She would shout it over and over, as long as she had air to breathe, because doing anything else but telling her story would be a waste, no matter how many people laughed or tried to stop her. Slowly, slowly, the shadows in the weave began to fill in with light.

Blood dripped from Echo's ears. Her body sheared under the stress of so many disparate parts.

Oblivion's distant scream of rage rose to meet them.

Then there was the unmistakable release of a completed deal across their web, and Rhienne sighed in relief. Whatever motes of magic she'd made were invisible within the Origin's blaze. But the tethers between them all remained.

"What did you do?" Echo asked.

Rhienne's grin was exhausted but triumphant. "I asked everyone if they'd show themselves to you, and in return, they'd get to see the real you."

"How'd you know that would work?"

"Because you're the most *you* when you're helping other people see themselves." Rhienne cleared her throat. "Also I didn't *know* it would work, but I really hoped it would."

Warmth bloomed within her, and finally, wonderfully, the new tapestry she and Rhienne had woven pulled taut. It was real, and it was *theirs*, and when the rest of the

Origin swallowed them, it wasn't to consume them, but to integrate their piece of the world into the whole.

Echo gasped at the sudden lack of sensation. It was like she'd been dunked underwater, but instead of blurred and disjointed, everything became clear. She could parse the Origin's light, smells, sounds, and textures, the creatures and objects at the heart of each thread. There were little tugs on her heart where the connections to Rhienne and the crew and the people of Hearthglen still clung.

All of them gaped at their surroundings. They hung in the middle of a sea of multi-colored light, nothing solid around them except each other. Great washes of scintillating heat and power drifted by like wet paint across a canvas. They'd made it to the Origin's core.

Exodus squeezed her hand. "You are incandescent."

Echo started to laugh, but he wasn't being metaphoric; she was lit up from the inside, still holding dozens of different forms at once, refracting rainbows all around them.

"And also in deep trouble," Bastion chirped. He pointed further into the aurora, at the three gods hurtling toward them in a cloud of fury. Oblivion led the way, with a cerulean light half-absorbed into his chest that sent streaks of blue and purple stardust through his previously shadowed form. The spines of Reckoning's red carapace were longer, sharper. Harvest's vines and branches had stopped cycling through the seasons. She was fixed in winter, leafless and jagged.

"We're not finished," Rhienne said. "There was one more part of our deal, Echo. I would totally understand if you said no, but I think it's the simplest solution by far, and—"

"Time for qualifying your thoughts later," Irelia interrupted.

"Fresh starts. Clean slates. That's how we unravel a God of Endings. No more being buried beneath the past. Or fearing the future. I gave up my blood magic so we could reach you. And you still have..."

"My foresight." Echo reeled under the implications of what Rhienne had said, and what she was asking for.

Rhienne had no magic left. But she didn't look afraid.

Echo could draw strength from that, until she found her own. She turned to Exodus and whispered, "Take back the vision. I have a plan for the power, though."

The God of Journeys arched a brow. "And what's that?"

"We're going to show Oblivion something *truly* new. Can you and Bastion keep your sisters distracted?"

Bastion was already pulling magical artifacts from his pouch. "With pleasure. We'll hold everyone off until you're ready." He gestured to the crew and the survivors of Hearthglen, handing out weapons, baubles, and trinkets as they formed a defensive line. "When in doubt, just throw things and see what happens!"

A wall of mist and wind kicked up, blocking her view of Bastion's charge and his collision with the other three gods.

"Are you sure you're ready to give this up?" Exodus's murmur was gentle. As was the touch of his cool marble fingers against her cheek.

"No," Echo breathed. "But I think that's why I must."

His fingers warmed against her skin. Like sunlight evaporating morning dew, the corner of her mind that had been focused on the future for so long vanished. A small jolt of fear went through her at first, but when she took a breath, it came freer than it had in years. She hadn't realized what a suffocating weight the vision of her death had been. The space was warmer, lighter, ready for something new to fill it.

Exodus chuckled quietly as he saw the shape of her idea. "Yes, that should do." From wind and marble and filigree, a mandolin formed. He gave it to her reverently.

Speechless, she ran her fingers over the strings. The instrument was more beautiful than she could've imagined, lighter than the first one he'd given her, with acoustics like she stood in the center of a temple. Echo strummed a few chords, letting the sound fill her up. Pure magic.

There was still so much to untangle between them, but for now, all she could say was, "Thank you."

"No, thank *you*, for reminding me that I sheltered artists in my realm so I could experience all the things I could not see myself." He dispelled the barrier protecting them.

The world outside was chaos. Figures darted through clouds of smoke-like magic in a glowing rainbow of color. People shouted and artifacts exploded, and Oblivion sang, using her stolen voice to manifest nightmares and darkness.

How dare he. How *dare* he twist her song into something so vile.

Echo closed her eyes against the rest of the world. She would show him what the true power of her voice was. Just her and her music, making a new beginning for her dearest friend.

Chapter 45

Rhienne

Rhienne fought at the tip of their spear formation, with nothing but a dagger and a prayer to aid her. This was possibly the stupidest thing she'd ever done, and yet, with Bastion beside her, and her friends and family charging into battle behind her, she was not afraid.

"For Horizon!" Bastion called.

And Rhienne bellowed, "For Hearthglen!"

"For my fucking ship!" Irelia shouted, and led her crew to face the goddess, Reckoning, whose red carapace-like armor was growing and splitting into extra appendages with gold-tipped talons.

Harvest sent roots and vines rippling outward to restrain them. Bastion produced a scroll so ancient it almost crumbled apart before he read the spell, but his words spread decay over the plants. They shriveled and died in moments. The Goddess of Seasons let out an ear-splitting screech that sent half of the refugees and crew members tumbling through the air, hands over their ears.

Rhienne pressed on, hacking and slashing her way through the gods' attacks. She was here for one thing, and one thing only.

Oblivion, the infuriating coward, hung back from his sisters. He sent power out around them, much like he had on the airship, except this time, the void creatures and the aura of fear held streaks of blue, red, and orange among their glittering stars. They all emitted a low, dissonant hum that scratched at her eardrums.

Plaintive notes rang out over the battlefield. Rhienne glanced over her shoulder to find Echo holding a new mandolin, with Exodus fending off any stray roots or blasts of magic that reached her.

Echo's tune picked up speed. It was reminiscent of what she'd sung in her dream, but also of the lullaby from the music box Vala had left behind, and *also* of the way it had felt to hold a piece of the Origin, and of something else, too, that Rhienne couldn't yet identify.

Ethereal violin, cello, and piano joined in as Exodus manipulated the Origin around Echo's song. With each measure, strength filled Rhienne's limbs, and Oblivion's shadows receded, replaced by the image of a mist-shrouded road.

Look, the song seemed to say. *What do you see?*
Nothing. Like always.
Look harder.
The music changed key, bringing that unidentifiable melody to the forefront.

Rhienne's heart recognized it before her mind did. She gasped, and the fog rolled away.

Endless hills stretched beyond the path, some grassy and some jagged rock, some kissed by the sun, others shrouded by rain clouds. A black smudge far in the distance might have been the whispering door.

Oblivion stopped singing. His darkness no longer penetrated the space around her.

Rhienne stepped tentatively onto the grass. It didn't feel any different. So she stepped again, then again, and still nothing collapsed onto or fell from beneath her. The path behind her remained, a record of her struggles, failures, and few triumphs, but now...

I can go anywhere, Rhienne's heart sang in time with Echo's music. *I'm free.*

Then she was running, carried by bright flute notes that emanated from the sun itself. She whooped for joy, and felt the urge to *think bigger,* so she reached up and pulled the sky to her, no longer running but flying. She danced on top of clouds. She made the sun set and raised the moon and gave herself a cloak of stars, and all of it was as real as any dream she'd ever walked in. The music changed with her, following now instead of leading, and Rhienne found herself humming her own melody. Then smiling. Then singing.

Oh, Echo. This song could not have been written before their journey, and Rhienne was sure that if it had, it would not have felt like this. It was a gift, and one she would not waste.

Her life had been consumed with blood and destruction, mistaking power for freedom. Maybe now she could heal and create. *Where* and *how* and *why* weren't important, as long as it was her choice, as long as she spent that time giving back to the people who mattered.

The possibilities built up around her, and she condensed them into a ball of light, brighter than a star.

The scene faded just enough to bring her back to the Origin's core, face to face with Oblivion, who had not seen her approach through such infinite potential.

He blinked at her sudden appearance. Then he laughed down at her, unaware of the power in her hands. "After all your years of cowardice, of searching for loopholes, now you choose to fight me head on? The bar for you was so low, and you've managed never to surpass it. How sad."

With the tapestry of connections spread out behind her, and Echo's music soaring in her heart, Rhienne shrugged off his poisonous words. They were true, but unlike Mishara, unlike Oblivion himself, she didn't have to be doomed by the limitations of her history anymore. She didn't need a loophole. There were too many ways to move through the world to fear something as small as the end of a path. There was *hope.* And hope didn't demand a purpose from her. Only one more step.

"You can have my soul," Rhienne said. Oblivion, arrogant fool that he was, let her come within arm's reach. Echo's voice hovered in the center of his chest, the cerulean light still in its bottle, marred only by a few creeping black streaks. "One way or another, I'll walk through that door someday. But as long as I am breathing, you will not have my life. And I plan to keep breathing for a very, very long time."

"You and every mortal in this world will be wrapped in chains for the rest of your pathetic, sniveling lives. You will rue the day you—"

Rhienne rolled her eyes. With one hand, she grabbed the bottle.

With the other, she threw the ball of pent up possibility into Oblivion's midnight form.

Comical astonishment crossed his normally expressionless face. In the same moment that she tore Echo's voice free, Oblivion exploded in a cataclysm of light.

He was gone. The contract dissolved. The door to the void remained, waiting.

But not until she was ready.

Her heart sang again, *I'm free.*

Chapter 46

Rhienne

The Origin roiled. Thunder cracked. Glaciers shattered. The very earth rent open.

Plate tectonics, Rhienne thought, clutching Echo's bottled voice to her chest before every thread of screaming light turned on the collection of figures within its core and expelled them like so much waste.

She came to, flat on the soggy ground, mud and marsh grass sticking to her hair and clothes. She blinked up at the night sky. After the Origin's radiance, it seemed terribly dark. The wind was cold and sharp. Rhienne registered the moans and grunts of other people stirring and struggled onto her elbows.

"Shit!" she yelped. No more than an arm's length away, the land dropped hundreds of feet down. The steep, rocky cliffside disappeared into crashing waves. Barely visible from this height were the jagged pieces of Hearthglen's rooftops, peeking out of the water. Their battle in that in-between place had touched the real world, tearing the land in two, raising the marshes up and dropping the town into the sea. "Oh, shit," she whispered.

Her muscles cried out in protest, but Rhienne picked herself up and limped away from the cliff.

Townsfolk called out to each other. Not all of them got responses. Those who could move were walking and crawling and helping each other to congregate on the driest patches of earth they could find. Stomach in knots, Rhienne stumbled toward them.

She spotted her father in the crowd, helping Tash with triage, and Irelia, who was missing the bottom half of her coat and had long claw marks all the way down one leg. She leaned against Nazal for support. The fading glimmer of several threads twisted in the breeze, untethered deals that could never be completed. Rhienne's heart fell when she realized Mordach's was among them. She'd come to enjoy the prickly man's company. But where were the gods? And where was—

"You got it," Echo gasped from behind her.

Rhienne whirled, nearly dropping the bottle. "Hell of a time to sneak up on a person!"

"Sorry." Echo grinned. Her body was almost back to normal, the fractured rainbows dimmed to a subtle glow beneath her tan skin and white hair. She wiped at some dried blood beneath her nose, but other than that, she was probably the least injured person here. Her eyes fixed on the cerulean light peeking between Rhienne's fingers. "I can't believe it worked."

"What do you *mean?*" Rhienne gaped. "I thought we just got done accepting how singularly amazing you are."

"No, I know, it's just... it's been so long without it. And it's so *small.* A god tried to enslave our world with *that.* Makes it all feel a bit ridiculous, doesn't it?"

"I think we file that away under 'best for our health not to think too hard about it.'" Rhienne scanned the clearing again. Still no sign of the gods. "You were incredible. That song..." She shook her head, lost for words. "How did you come up with it?"

A quiet, knowing smile. "I listened to you."

There was nothing she could say to that because she was far too busy crying. Rhienne handed Echo the bottle containing her voice. Echo took it and hugged her, crying too. They held each other for a long while, the outpouring of emotion such a potent relief that Rhienne forgot everyone and everything else.

Until a snippet of conversation between her father and Lydia, their next door neighbor growing up, carried to them across the grass.

"Did you know what that child was when you adopted her?" the woman asked, horrified.

Echo tensed, and Rhienne pulled back so they could both watch—or insert themselves, if need be. Lydia made no effort to disguise her disgust or keep her voice down. A couple other survivors shot furtive glances their way.

"Not just then, but I found out quick," Silas replied.

"Our home is destroyed because of her and your daughter! I can't believe—"

"—How lucky we were to have them save us from a far worse fate," he interrupted. "I can hardly believe it myself.

We can, and will, rebuild elsewhere. And if anyone has anything else to say about it, don't." He caught Echo's eye and offered her and Rhienne a wink.

"Thank the gods," Echo muttered. "I don't have it in me to fight another battle, even one that small."

Rhienne sighed. "You and me both."

Silas gave the remaining townsfolk a *don't make me say it again* glare before hobbling over. "I won't pretend to understand what all went on in there," he said, "but you were both magnificent. We found the rest of your friends. They're not far."

"Are they all right?" Echo asked.

"Truthfully, I have no idea."

Leaning on Echo for support, Rhienne followed him a short distance away from the survivors. Tash was busy with the injured, but Irelia trailed after them, with Nazal beside her to help navigate the boggy ground with her freshly splinted leg.

Speaking of magnificent. As soon as they had everything sorted, Rhienne was going to take that woman to a cabin in the quietest, least interesting corner of the world and give her none of the rest she deserved.

The five of them stopped on the edge of a shallow crater. Harvest and Reckoning were gone, but Bastion and Exodus lay within, pressed into the mud as if they'd been thrown there. Neither moved except for a faint, pervasive shudder.

Echo made a small, distressed sound.

"Go," Rhienne whispered. "I'm right behind you."

She handed Rhienne off to her father before running over to Exodus. "He's alive. They both are, but—"

Silas helped her down into the crater. As Rhienne got closer, she saw what had stopped Echo short. The gods were fading, becoming translucent, ghostly versions of themselves.

Exodus's marble eyes flickered open, and he put a gentle hand atop Echo's. The air between them shimmered in silent conversation.

"Hello there, mortals," Bastion called out. He peeled himself out of the muck with a horrible squelch. His typical upbeat demeanor sounded forced.

"What happened?" Rhienne asked. "Where are your sisters?"

"Harvest and Reckoning are... where we will be shortly. We begged permission to set a few things right first."

"They are with our Mothers," Exodus clarified. "Infinity and Eternity are more displeased than I anticipated. It's not like them to intervene at all, never mind so swiftly. But these are not matters for you to worry over." In a blink, he was standing, absurdly pristine and statuesque amid the swamp.

Rhienne spared one thought for the former glory of her illusions. Then Irelia shuffled over and touched her cheek, below the wound Mishara had given her.

"I always wanted a girlfriend with a scar."

Rhienne cocked an eyebrow, unable to stop the flush that came to her cheeks. "Is that what I am?"

"We just fought the literal gods. Are you really going to balk at a label? I've already met your parents and everything."

A laugh burst out of Rhienne. Silas chuckled, and she hoped the little pulse of warmth around her heart meant that somewhere close, Vala did too.

"Hmm... no. No, I am not." She leaned in and gave Irelia the kiss that Oblivion had so rudely interrupted before. "My face really hurts though," Rhienne muttered out of the side of her mouth. "Can we save this for later?"

"If that means there will be a later, absolutely." Irelia pecked her on the nose for good measure.

Chapter 47

Echo

Echo was almost loath to let the bottle go, now that it was back in her grasp. Dark spots discolored her voice's cerulean light, little pieces of Oblivion that Rhienne hadn't quite managed to tear away. "Do you know what those will do? Is it dangerous for me to take it back?"

"May I?" Exodus extended a semi-transparent hand. He would disappear soon, back to the Mothers' realm and whatever punishment awaited him there.

"Don't do anything that would... hurt it." She chuckled nervously. Not from any lack of trust, but at the thought that they could've come so far only to fail now, when lyrics to the dozen songs she wanted to sing about this day were ready on her tongue.

"I won't." His voice was heavy with understanding. "I promise."

How far they'd come, that Echo willingly handed him her song.

Exodus tilted the bottle against the starlight, murmuring a spell of identification that seemed to last for hours instead of minutes. Rhienne, Silas, Nazal, and Irelia approached, followed by Bastion, and their combined anticipation whipped Echo's heartbeat into a frenzy.

Finally, Exodus said, "There is no sentience within, but those are splinters of a divine soul. Over time, they will dissolve and become part of you, and I am not sure what they will do then. But for now, they are not dangerous."

For now. Echo winced. "Can you remove them?"

"Not without risking damage to the rest."

She'd proven in the Origin that she didn't need to sing to make the music of her heart, but gods, she *wanted* to. Exodus and Bastion were more ghostly than not. If she unfocused her eyes, she could see right through them.

"We'll find a way to heal it," Rhienne said. "Add it to the list of our rebuilding efforts. We've already picked out a spot, assuming our battle didn't mess up the rest of the coast. With the Untold gone, there should be a bunch of vacant buildings in Devonsfort. It may require some redecorating, but..." She shrugged. "Seems only fair."

Echo huffed a laugh. She closed her eyes. Maybe they'd meet Sidrin there. "All right. Do it."

The bottle uncorked with a pop. An incongruous summer breeze blew around her, and she peeked through her lashes right as the cerulean light entered her chest.

Warmth filled her throat and lungs. Echo opened her mouth and abruptly shut it, hit by a sudden surge of fear that it hadn't worked, or she wouldn't sound the same, or—

Rhienne punched her gently in the arm. "Go on then."

The first song that came to her was, of all things, *The Queen's Heart.* She'd heard Levi sing it one too many times, apparently. The lyrics rose from her throat, true and glorious, if a little hoarse—from disuse, she hoped.

She burst into tears before the end of the second line. Rhienne threw an arm around her shoulders and picked up the raucous tune. Before long, Nazal and Irelia joined in, and distantly, Tash and the crew did too.

Echo reentered in the chorus, singing as loud as she could. She hadn't known her chest could ache from so much joy.

Don't let me interrupt, but we're being called, Exodus whispered into her mind. *Can you promise to do something while I'm gone?*

She turned to the God of Journeys, standing next to his long-lost brother. There was a shimmer to Exodus's marble form, and it had nothing to do with his near-invisibility. Her heart jumped a little. The terms of their deal had been to break Bastion's exile. *Did I not fulfill my end of the bargain?*

Technically, no. In fact, I believe the Mothers are going to send us all *to 'contemplate our place in the cosmos' for a while.*

What do you want me to do?

Remember me. The words were a delicate kiss of wind against her cheek, a memory of the form he'd given up for her. *And if you find yourself in need of a muse when my exile is over, perhaps you'll consider coming to visit. Tash and Irelia have promised to take care of you until then.*

Exodus shimmered again. She'd never seen him smile like that before.

I will. He disappeared.

Bastion saluted, a few screws tumbling free from his arm, then he too was gone.

The singing had died down as everyone watched the gods fade. Now they all looked to her. For a second, she swore their hearts beat together, one last whisper of the intertwining they'd experienced in the Origin. She clung to it, unsure if she'd ever be able to find the words to do it justice.

"Well," Echo said. "It sounds like we're heading to Devonsfort."

"Never thought I'd be starting over at my age," Silas mumbled, "but that does seem to be the best course."

Far out over the sea, the sun broke the horizon. Birds chirped, warily returning to the strange new landscape. There was another long, uncertain road ahead, but there was great comfort in knowing she'd walk it as *herself,* and she would not walk alone. "Don't think of it as starting over," Echo said, with a brilliant smile at Rhienne. "Think of it as the next step."

Epilogue

Exodus stood on the edge of a glass platform that fell away into nothing. Merciless black spread before him, broken by stars and clouds of red and purple dust. It would rip him apart if he touched it, but the view was preferable to the real reason he was here.

It had been centuries since he'd seen the Mothers. Hard to think of them as *his* mothers, even though that's what they were. He'd hoped never to see them again after Horizon's death and Bastion's subsequent exile. Very little could call their attention, but the death of one of their children certainly qualified as monumental enough.

He'd known this could happen, but for so long, he hadn't believed they would succeed. Oblivion had seemed unstoppable when he attacked Exodus's realm. Bastion had been unreachable. A few months ago, if anyone told him a couple of upstart mortals would change the shape of the cosmos, he wouldn't have wasted the energy to laugh before banishing them to hell. Never mind that he had *helped.*

Echo's song still warmed his soul. He clung to that as he turned to face his judgment.

Infinity and Eternity sat on an obsidian bench. Atop the transparent floor and the refracted starlight, it gave them the appearance of floating on sparkling void. The Mothers were merged into one figure, made of pieces of their children: Reckoning's red carapace along one arm, Exodus's white marble for the other, a torso of plants cycling through seasons like Harvest's, one leg made of Oblivion's shadows, the other of Horizon's light. Their head was an hourglass, each bulb sculpted into a woman's face. It was full of golden sand, pouring and pouring and never running out, dizzying to look at for too long. There were no parts evoking Gossamer, or Bastion. Even here, with the beings who'd created him, he'd been erased.

Words were too small for such infinite, eternal beings to use. They spoke in images, emotions. The weight of their disappointment nearly crushed him. If it hadn't been distributed among the rest of his siblings, it might have.

The Mothers were waiting for an explanation.

"We played no part in Oblivion's death," Reckoning said. She pointed an accusing finger at Exodus and Bastion. "It was *them.*"

"Pardon my saying so, but I hardly think that's true," Bastion quipped. "You schemed with him to enslave the mortal world beneath untenable deals."

Harvest's roots writhed like she might reach out and strangle him. "Untenable? If we had carried his plan through, we could have restored all the magic we have lost. Enough, perhaps, to one day bring our sister back. We wouldn't have to live on the fringes! We could've walked among our worshippers once more! But you put your inane sympathy for mortals ahead of your family *again.*"

"They are more like us than we give them credit for," Exodus argued. "And perhaps they could be more if we allowed them to. We all saw what they were capable of once they reforged their connection to the Origin."

The hourglass shimmered, and heat lashed across the platform. Astonishment and fury rolled into one outburst that silenced all four of them.

Your mistakes go far beyond such petty squabbles.

Exodus was thankful, just then, that he had lost his ability to change. That his face remained blank marble. He would not have been able to resist the storm that shivered through him, which would have betrayed how frightening he found those words. Oblivion's death and the reshaping of the Material Plane was a *petty squabble?* How could the Mothers think that, when they had taken such extreme measures after Horizon's passing?

His stoicism fooled everyone but Bastion, who put a hand—once again made of broken objects—on Exodus's shoulder. The promise they'd made before diving into the Origin still tethered them together: never to abandon each other again. It was a small comfort in this place.

Another waver in the hourglass sent out a ripple of thought and feeling. *You have been kept in the dark for too long. It is time you learned of the greater movements of the cosmos.*

The glass beneath him frosted over, then cleared, revealing a landscape he did not recognize. Miles and miles of undulating dunes, a single walled city nestled among them.

This world was once a lush oasis, teeming with life. But in the last thirty years, it has been sucked dry. This city is all that remains.

He saw another planet, covered in ice. Another of jagged, barren rock. Another swathed in clouds of noxious gas. And finally, a planet in pieces. Crystalline spears jutted out from its core, like roots that had outgrown their pot.

"What is this?" Bastion breathed.

This is what you and your domains were created to prevent. It is a curse that breaks worlds, one that we do not fully understand.

Harvest's leaves withered. Even Reckoning lost her aura of menace. Exodus could think only of Echo as their triumph crumbled to dust.

And in destroying your brother, we have lost our most powerful defense against it.

Glossary

Airship: a construct of great magical and engineering power, appearing like a sailboat with arcane engines at the rear and golden enchantments woven into the sails. Because of the resources required to build one, there are few in the world, and they are mostly used for trade and luxury travel between the continents. The Falenoran Empire is the exception, where they are used as instruments of war.

The Collector: a godkin who lives in a cave beneath the forest outside Wildspire, where he peddles information gained through deals.

Dawnglow: crystallized blood of the dead goddess, Horizon. An incredibly rare and powerful magical component. No one knows how much there is left in the world, only that once its divine energy is spent, it's gone for good.

Dream spirits: godkin who live within the Plane of Dreams and can move through and manipulate the dreams of beings on the Material Plane.

Exalt: a high-ranking official within the Free Territories. They often contribute to the government of their city, but they are free to walk in other spheres outside of politics; many are also prominent business owners, merchants, or community members.

Godkin: creatures created by the gods who do not have magical blood but perform some function within a gods' domain.

Immortals: descendants of Eternity, whose divine blood makes them immune to aging and illness, though they can be killed by extensive bodily harm.

Mimics: descendants of Infinity, whose divine blood allows them to innately transform into exact copies of anyone they have seen.

Telepathy Stones: a pair of small rocks that have been connected via enchantment, so that any two holders of the stones may speak mind to mind with each other.

Untold: an organization whose mission is to eradicate creatures with divine blood from the world. They believe innate magic—power not from deals—is dangerous and blasphemous, and the greatest use for mimics and immortals is as arcane batteries, so that their power might be spread to more deserving people. The Untold began as a cult, but as their numbers grew and teachings spread, along with fear of the divine-blooded, governments across the Free Territories and Havenwood sanctioned their activities, elevating them to military rank.

Acknowledgements

I can't believe I'm writing this part. This is it. The end, and only the beginning. There were lots of times I almost turned off this path, and I've only made it this far because of the kindness (and occasional, much-needed kick in the ass) of family, friends, and the writing community. I have so many people I need to thank, and I genuinely hope I have enough brain cells to remember to name them all.

My husband, Brad, who encouraged me to do the scariest thing I had ever done and take a leap of faith in myself. Maybe I would've come back to writing eventually, but it would've taken a whole lot longer without your tireless support and willingness to listen to my 2 a.m. worldbuilding rambles.

My critique partner and dear friend, Lewis. Echo and Rhienne have come a long way from Natalia and Isolde, but their voices and their bond are as strong as they are because of one silly little D&D campaign that ended too soon, and because you've shown me what it means to have, and be, a true friend.

Rebecca, I will be eternally grateful that the threads of Fate brought us together. Your advice on everything from writing to graphic design has been invaluable, our yap sessions have kept me sane (as much as I can be, anyway), but more than that, I feel like I've found a kindred spirit. I look forward to all the stories we will spin and chaos we will sow together.

Jenn, I can't believe out of all the wide world of the internet I found someone who I share so much with who is only a short drive away! It's been really hard to make friends since moving to Oregon, and getting to go to book events and run away to the woods with you has been incredibly special. Thank you for being one of my greatest hype women since the beginning.

My beta readers, Risa, Amiel, Caleb, Edward, Scott, and Allison. Your feedback, unhinged comments, and in-person writing sessions fueled me through far more drafts of this book than I care to count.

The Coven of World Weavers, I know I can always come to you for a good laugh or a piece of your infinite wisdom. I never thought I'd find a community like this, and I am beyond grateful to have all of you.

My line editor, Shay, my illustrator, Rin, and my cover artist, Kim. You took my manuscript and turned it into a real, exceptionally beautiful book (in my unbiased opinion).

Family, if you happen to read this, you've gotten a glimpse into the deepest corners of my soul. Don't make it weird next time we hang out.

If you've been part of my publishing journey at all, whether it was to give feedback on my earliest writing (sorry), or to offer emotional support along this wild ride, or to take a chance on a debut author, thank you, thank you, from the bottom of my heart. I hope we can all take the next step together.

About the Author

After realizing an engineering career would lead to the slow death of her soul and sanity, A.J. moved from Texas to Oregon to pursue her true passion: all things nerdy and magical. In her free time, if she has no choice but to be perceived, she can be found consuming copious amounts of D&D content, lurking around various bookstores and coffee shops, and hiking with her husband and her pug.

* 9 7 9 8 9 9 2 7 8 0 8 0 2 *